# Cover-Up

by

## R.L. Hayden

ANDY,
There has To be
some Thing going on!

ENJOY,

R.L. Hayden

7-14-20

R. L. Hayden

## **DEDICATION**

This is dedicated to my lovely wife who has had the patience to put up with me all these years and has been supportive of my every effort.

Elsie (L. C.) Hayden
Thank you, my love.

## ACKNOWLEDGMENTS

I would like to thank the following people for their unfailing efforts in helping me research, proofread, and edit this novel. Walter Porter and Frank Casillas who helped me locate and visit the actual debris field of the Roswell crash. Alex and Marie Wiederkehr for their assistance in locating and plotting the locations of the real cairns on the debris field. Miki Scott Cutler for proofing the manuscript. Thank you Elsie Hayden for your proofreading and editing.

A special thanks for my family's support, guidance and belief that wacky ol' dad could put it all together.

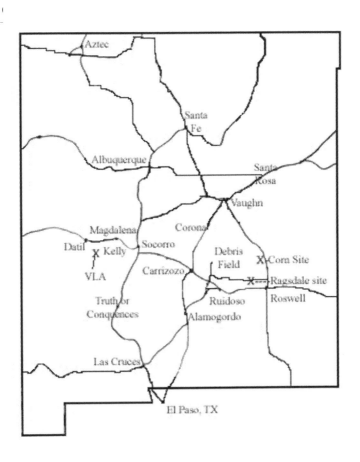

Rick's map of debris field showing cairns with X's.

Cover-Up

## *Toward Clovis*

*For more than twenty miles*
*it rode beside us up the lonely hill*
*from Roswell to Elida,*
*toward Clovis and the towns beyond.*

*A train? Not so, It rose along the tracks.*
*framed in our right hand window.*
*It's speed matched ours.*
*We'd rush ahead and it did, too.*
*We slowed; it paced us close beside.*
*Sleek--did it have winds? Who knew?*
*Just far enough away to hide behind near hills,*
*retreating, tracked us once again*
*along the empty, moonless road*

*It stayed beside us, soundless.*
*Experimental plane? We thought it likely.*
*A UFO?*
*No way. We'd watched for forty years.*

*Elida neared---*
*Piercing lights appeared;*
*and cars began ascent, descent.*
*Did they convey a signal?*
*Or scare the crew away?*

*The strange craft simply disappeared*

—

*among the shadows. . . .*

*Our family, friends? Authorities?*
*They'd likely only laugh.*
*And we? We'd always wonder.*

### Shirley Clement Fouts
Inspired by true events

# *Prologue*

With a waddling motion, the modified A-26 ground attack bomber clawed at the dry desert air in its struggle to become airborne. First Lieutenant Mike Parmenter held the control yoke well into his gut, urging the overweight aircraft off the hard white sand runway.

Rolando Herrera, pulled the landing gear handles back as soon as he felt the wheels clear the hard packed graded track laughingly referred to as runway 75.

Gaining altitude, the A-26 pirouetted on its left wing, then lumbered over the clandestine base buried in the southwestern corner of White Sands Proving Ground. The buildings, two hangers, a small barracks, mess hall, repair shop, and control tower were all painted a skuzzy faded off white in an aborted attempt to blend with the near pristine white of the wide expanse of white sand dunes to the east. The evening sun cast bluish shadows that slowly consumed the natural glare of the desert floor.

From the air, Arnold Base, named after Kenneth Arnold, the flyer who started the flying saucer frenzy, resembled nothing more than a half dozen misshapen dunes with parallel black tracks running between them.

"Hey, Rolando, don't jerk up the gear so fast next time. What would have happened if we didn't hold the air?"

"Mike, we would have lost all airlift if I hadn't cut the drag, allowing us to pick up more airspeed."

"Well, dammit, next time, don't."

"OK, OK.  What's with this evening take off shit?" Rolando asked.  "I don't like trying to locate the base after dark."

"That's why you get paid extra to be navigator."

"Extra? Extra, my ass."

A crackling sound came over their earphones. "Bravo One.  This is Arnold, over."  The control tower interrupted their conversation.

Parmenter responded.  "Go head, Arnold."

"Bravo One, switch to Kenneth, I repeat, Kenneth.  Follow flight plan Charlie.  Flight plan Charlie. Confirm."

The two looked at each other in amazement. Rolando grabbed the canvas flight pouch jammed between his seat and the rear bulkhead.  They were actually being given an air operation to conduct. Quickly, he flipped the cover and pulled out three envelopes.  Each one had a large red letter stenciled in the middle.  Tape sealed each of them.  Across the seams, 'TOP SECRET--ARNOLD' was printed in the tape.  Below the bold print was one of the first three letters of the alphabet.  Rolando grabbed the envelope with the third letter.

"Bravo, One, respond please," the Kenneth voice grumbled.

"Oh, Roger, Kenneth.  Flight plan Charlie. Roger.  Will comply," Parmenter answered.

"Good luck, Bravo One.  Arnold clear."

"Damn, that was the old man himself.  Did you

hear that?  He actually ordered us to conduct plan Charlie."  Mike wiped his brow.

"One thing for sure.  We ain't going back to that damned base anymore.  It's out of operation now.  We do this and the whole ball of wax is down the tube."

Rolando read the orders aloud, as he transcribed notes to his kneepad.  Then, the pouch and all its contents, including the envelope labeled with the large red letter C, were shoved one and two at a time into a specially built miniature oven and electronically ignited.  Within minutes, only small metal loops and rivets remained in a pile of ash.

"We're flying a heading of 42 degrees.  That's going to put us into the middle of that storm.  That's what you're telling me?"  Mike yelled, jutting his jaw toward a dark angry mass of clouds.

"That's right, Skipper, our IP is somewhere through that on the other side of that mountain range and up a valley."

"What kind of Initial Point is that, Rolando?"

"The one specified in the orders, Skip."

Flying into the thunderstorm ahead of them, they jolted their way across the mountains.  Updrafts caught the aircraft, often tossed it as much as five hundred feet higher in the air.  Seconds later, a downdraft would drop them to gut wrenching lower altitudes, threatening to pound them into a mountain side.

Relative peace surrounded them as they cleared the mountain range and moved up the valley, continuing on a northeasterly course.  The thunderstorm continued to rage, although it now lacked the ferocity of before.  The two airmen were still thrown against their restraining belts too often to become comfortable.

Their IP was a small town miles from any visage of civilization. A place where two state highways crossed. The bomber dropped two thousand feet in altitude, while Rolando looked for a collection of light against the solid blackness of the isolated terrain.

"There it is, two o'clock on our horizon." A sharp snarl of lightning induced electricity filled their earphones.

"What was that? Was there a voice in that noise?"

"Nah, you're just hearing things, Roli."

"Turn to 127 degrees as we cross," Rolando said. "Drop to two hundred feet. We're suppose to rattle their windows."

"Roger that, although I doubt if anything would be noticed down there in this mess," Parmenter said. "Put your goggles on, Roli."

"Roger goggles," Rolando replied, then counted down from five, pushing the fire button on his control yoke. Seconds later, bright strobes flashed along the wings, almost challenging the lightning in its intensity. Special mufflers kicked in, dampening the throb of the huge twin Pratt-Whitney cyclone engines.

From below, anyone looking up into the heavy sky would see a dark shadow roughly outlined by bright flashing lights. Almost no sound would be heard under normal circumstances, especially now, with the summer storm blasting its way across the valley floor. While anyone flying alongside would see a strangely lit, pregnant shaped form. The modified bombay contained a bulge that practically scraped the runway when the aircraft squatted on its tricycle landing gear, and the object filled the area between the wheel struts.

"Yahoo, we're outta here. Up, up and away," Mike called as the A-26 bomber buzzed the tiny rural community.

"Yes, we rattled their windows," Rolando said. "Next stop, middle of nowhere. We drop out of the clouds again in twenty minutes at one hundred and forty knots."

Twenty minutes later, Bravo One again dropped through the clouds.

"This is it?" Mike asked. "This is our target? Hell man, I don't see anything."

"This is it, Mike. We pickle the bombay and follow a heading of 152 degrees for two hours. Then we start repeating our call sign on frequency and wait instructions."

"OK, let's do it!" Mike counted down. "Three...two...one...bombs away."

Immediately Bravo One leaped higher into the sky as its payload fell earthward. The airplane shook through its frame as the concussion of a tremendous explosion caught up with them.

Parmenter turned the nose of his A-26 ground attack bomber southeast to a heading of 152 degrees, which hours later would take them to an unknown airfield and a new assignment.

# *1*

Beth Ringold swept the metal detector's head back and forth slowly, while clamping one earphone to her left ear with the other hand. Looking up, she saw Rick Prescott cast a fond glance at Sarina Lake.

"You never looked at me like that," she said.

With a start, Rick realized Beth had spoken. "Huh? Oh. Well, I don't know, we've worked together for so long. I guess that I never paid very much attention."

"Thanks loads, asshole." Beth shook her head. "I, too, am a woman, you know."

Rick did a quick comparison. Sarina, six years younger than him, thin, long flowing jet black hair. Beth was two years less than his thirty-four, almost his height, and slightly on the plump side of cute. Yes, he was being drawn to Sarina. "Sorry, Beth, I guess that I always considered you as my partner, never...ah."

"Story of my life, Rick." She shook her head again. "Well, Romeo, let's get back to work." Beth crammed the headset back on her head, and swung the detector's head from side to side with slightly more gusto than before. "Now, tell me how this is actually helpful."

Sweeping his arms in a circle around him, Rick gestured. "This is supposed to be the actual area where the Roswell flying saucer skidded across the ground before becoming airborne again. The site of first impact is back up toward the windmill. Then it slid five hundred feet this way, leaving a thirty-foot wide groove and saucer parts behind. Out near the end of the ridge it bounced back into the air only to crash over thirty miles away in China Draw. That's where we were yesterday."

"You mean the site they call the Corn Crash Site?"

"That's the one."

"While we were there, your psychic, Sarina, couldn't pick up any vibes of any sort, even though according to the story, four or five dead alien beings were recovered at that location, along with the mangled flying saucer."

"Yeah, that's true, but there could be many reasons for that. We don't really know that much about her, except she is suppose to be psychic to some extent. Real Saucer Magazine thought it would be a new twist to the story, so when she volunteered to help in an investigation, they naturally thought of their best investigative team."

"Bullshit. You probably took one look at her picture and begged Mac to send her with us."

"Beth, I swear, I never saw her before we picked her up at the airport in El Paso. Now, I admit, she is very cute, but I've never let anything like that get in the way of a story before."

"Oh, so that's why you never tried hitting on me, is that it?"

"Beth, stop that. I've never hit on you, and I haven't tried hitting on her either. And I won't." Rick crossed his fingers behind his back. "Here, let

—

me take a turn at that infernal machine." Rick stepped in front of Beth and grabbed the handle.

"OK, thanks, that thing gets heavy after a while. Why are we doing this? Don't you think that the army and at least one bunch of saucer nuts have swept the ground before? I mean, this event took place what, fifty years ago? Between the weather and all the people who have visited this god-forsaken area, I'd think that nothing would be left. That is, of course, if there were anything here to start with."

"Under normal conditions, you'd be correct, but the actual debris field has been misrepresented on maps and the different museums in town will tell you that they can't give out the location because the land belongs to some ranching friends of theirs."

"Then how do we know we're in the correct place?" Beth asked, kicking a stone from in front of Rick's position.

"I've carefully correlated over ten accounts of the story, cross-referenced at least that many other tidbits of information, and took Mac Brazel's first version as his most accurate." Rick stopped and set the head of the detector on the ground. "We located the old line house he was sleeping in, and the hog shed where he stored the parts before going to town. That info puts us right here."

"OK, you still haven't answered my question about the usefulness of this metal detector."

"Lawrence, a good friend of mine, re-worked the best one on the market so that it could pick up any small particle of metal down about three feet through dense soil. I'm counting on a pack rat or two having stolen some small shiny pieces of the saucer. They would take them back to their nest and drop them. Hopefully, they only burrowed down a foot into this soil, which is made up of a lot of cracks and crevasses in weak limestone."

In front of them, Sarina, head raised, arms spread, slowly moved toward a rock outcropping. Rick tapped Beth on the shoulder and motioned her to take out her camera. With a nod of his head, he followed Sarina. She stopped suddenly hugging her torso as her head dropped to her chest and a low moan escaped her lungs.

"Over here guys, over here."

"What is it, girl?" Beth reached out to touch her shoulder.

"You OK, Sarina? What's wrong?" Rick moved around to see her face.

"I've felt something, not real strong, but there is a feeling coming from somewhere around here."

Beth shielded her eyes from the sun, surveying the area in front of them. She caught her breath. "Hey, look over there. There's a big pile of rock."

Rick and Sarina followed Beth's gaze. Below and to their front, stood a rock pillar, a way to mark a specific location. It was two feet in diameter and five feet tall. For some reason in the past, at least one person felt this spot was important enough to distinguish it from the surrounding area by constructing the cairn on the crest of a low ridge. It was overlooking a long narrow valley less than a hundred feet below them.

"Why would anyone have built this?" Beth asked.

"In this part of the country, it isn't unusual for

ranchers, farmers, or miners to indicate the boundaries of their claim in this manner," Rick said.

"Must be ranchers, as I can't see anyone in their right mind trying to farm this arid land. Although we haven't covered much of it, there haven't been any signs of mining either. Besides, mining is usually associated with mountains, isn't it? The only ones around here lie about twenty miles to the south of us." Sarina said.

"So, this is what your psychic powers have found for us," Beth said chuckling.

"No, not this one, Beth, that one over there," Sarina replied in a soft almost childlike voice, a rock outcropping across the narrow valley in front of them.

Rick and Beth couldn't see anything with their naked eye. Using a pair of medium power binoculars, Rick finally located the new cairn Sarina pointed out. Beth chose a couple of landmarks on the other side.

"Hey, there's a dirt trail that will get us near Sarina's new rock pile." Beth traced a line in the air in front of her with her hand.

"Let's go. Load up all this stuff and let's head over there," Rick said.

"We'd better hurry!" Beth pointed off to the northwest where a storm was gathering. "We may only have a few hours before that hits us."

"Yes, please. There is definitely something over there drawing my attention," Sarina said.

Fifteen minutes traveling on a dusty pair of ruts brought them within a hundred feet of the cairn. Looking up, Rick figured it was almost seventy-five feet above them. Another strange rock formation just right of the rocks broke up their view.

"Oh, wow." Sarina choked. "I'm getting some really weird vibes the closer we get."

"What type of feelings?" Rick tentatively placed his hand on her shoulder.

Shrugging his hand away, Sarina said, "Death. A strong feeling of death." Tears rose at the corner of her eyes and slowly carved paths down her dust smeared cheeks.

"Ah, come on now." Beth threw her hands in the air. "Cowboy and Indians fighting to the death type of feeling?"

"No, no. Something or someone else." Tears filled Sarina's hazel eyes. "The closer we get the stronger the feeling becomes."

The three climbed the hillside almost shoulder to shoulder. Within ten feet of the pillar, they noticed four long thin slabs of rock jutting out over the ridge of a broad deep undercut. On closer inspection, they realized that the slabs pointed back toward the first cairn. As they neared the rock pile, they noticed it was almost identical to the one they just left. There was one main difference between this one and the first one. A long slender finger of stone stuck out of one side of it generally aimed back across the valley.

"Oh, my...oh..." Sarina spread her arms, palms flat facing the pile of rock. "There is something here."

"Yeah, you got that right." Beth blew out her breath. "Another goddamned pile of rock. That's what's here."

"No, not that. There is something more." Sarina abruptly turned toward the four pointing slabs and moved a couple of steps in their direction. "The strongest feelings come from down there, below the ledge."

"Girl, how can you be feeling things here?" Beth again threw her hands into the air. "Back at the crash site--confirmed crash site--mind you, you're not aware of anything. But here. Here, you've got all kinds of feelings."

"Look, Beth, I am psychic. It isn't something you can turn on or off at will. I feel as if something horrible happened around here."

"I told you." Beth wagged a finger at Rick. "I told you. This psychic stuff is crap." She moved away from the others, bringing her Nikon camera to her eye. With slow sweeps of the lens, each click captured a part of the mysterious rock formations in front of her.

Rick barely heard Sarina mumble about feelings before she cautiously climbed down the rubble mound. The swing of her hips caught his eye. Was it desire as Beth mentioned, or concern over her well being? With a shrug, he stood, monitoring her progress.

At the base of the cut, Sarina again stretched her arms outward as if inviting a lover to her bosom. With eyes closed, she began a soft, flute like chant that drifted on to cool afternoon breeze. Twisting her upper torso from left to right, she encompassed the entire breadth of rock. Almost absently, she shuffled away, further down the slope toward the valley floor.

Rick stooped, picked up a handful of pebbles, and threw one in Beth's direction, getting her attention. Gesturing, he informed her he was going to follow Sarina and for her to watch her also. Moving downhill, he tried to maintain his distance from the psychic without creating any distractions.

Rick watched as she suddenly froze. Her body stiffened. Sarina's head tilted back and a low moan escaped from her throat.

When she dropped to her knees, then pitched forward, Rick had seen enough. He broke into a sprint to reach Sarina's side. "Beth, get down here."

Beth scooted down the hillside as quickly as she could. "What happened to her Rick?"

Kneeling by Sarina's side, Rick brushed a stray hair from her face, "I don't know, she just dropped in her tracks."

Reaching into one of the large pockets of her photographer's vest, Beth withdrew a cream-colored hand towel. "Wet this and lightly mop her face. Maybe she fainted."

Cradling Sarina's head in his lap, Rick took the water bottle from her fanny pack and liberally sprinkled water on the cloth then applied it to her face.

In a couple of minutes, they were awarded a hushed groan and slight head movement. Rick sprinkled more water on the cloth and wiped her face again. Her hazel eyes fluttered open.

"What? Where?" Sarina looked directly into Rick's soul. "Hi."

"How do you feel?" Rick pulled his gaze away from hers.

"Yeah, girl. What happened?" Beth framed the two of them as she whirred off two shots in succession. "You all right?"

Rising to sit on her rump, she dusted her knees

and arms. "Yeah, I'm OK. For a minute, my senses were totally overwhelmed by a deep, cold, sadness."

"Come on. Let's get her back to the room. We've had enough excitement for one day." Beth broke down her camera and lens, storing them in separate pockets. "Besides, that storm's moving closer."

Rick looked into the distance as the dark clouds shrouded the October sun as they continued their march toward the trio. A snappy breeze brought a chill to the air. He slid his hands under Sarina's arms, becoming aware of the slight swell of her breasts as he helped her to her feet. "We better move fast, that storm isn't going to hold off much longer."

The three skirted the edge of the hillside, making their way back to Rick's restored 1980 Jeep Cherokee wood sided wagon.

Minute's later huge raindrops flooded the windshield as thunder shook the windows. Sharp flashes of lightning cast shadows across their path as Rick steered the jeep up the valley to higher ground and the well traveled track that would eventually lead back to a paved road ending in Roswell, New Mexico, U. S. A.

Ahead, Rick saw the rise, and aimed for it, hoping the tires wouldn't bog down in the soft, wet slippery sand. Cresting the slope, they could see the streambed they just vacated swell with water.

"Go, Rick, go!" Beth pounded his shoulder as she squinted out the side window. "Higher ground. Go, go."

Rick twisted the wheel to the right, leaving the rutted road, climbing toward the spine of the hill.

"Oh no." Sarina pointed out the front window. In the dim cones of light cast by the headlights, Brangus cows were hunkered down, blocking their way. Again, Rick threw the wheel over, avoiding the cows. A tall object was backlit by a glaring flash of lightening. Rick hit the brakes, bringing the jeep to a halt about five feet from the apparition.

"I think we'd better wait out the storm here." Rick sighed.

Beth rolled her window down enough to hear the angry roar of the flash flood as it scoured the streambed they escaped from only minutes ago. "I think we're above the flood."

"What is that thing in front of us?" Sarina asked.

"I'm not sure, only thing I thought was I sure didn't want to hit it," Rick said, running his hand over his face.

An hour later, as the storm abated, the three of them got a good view of the object blocking their path. Even after occasionally seeing it lit by flashes of light, they were hesitant to name the object.

"It...It's another pillar," Sarina finally said.

"You're right there, girl." Beth sighed from the back seat. "Sure glad we didn't run into that."

Rick dug through his pockets for his small notebook. Scattered among his cargo pants was a folding knife, his favorite .380 Beretta with two extra ten round clips and a pocket sized first aid kit. Flipping open the notebook, he clicked lead into the point of the silver mechanical pencil, then drew a quick map, trying to show their present location in relation to where they found the earlier cairns.

"We'll be back, soon," Rick said, turning the

key in the ignition.  "Very soon."

## *2*

Early the next morning, as the group ate breakfast in the small cafe attached to their motel, Rick was trying not to eye Sarina as she sat across from him. She looked radiant. Her jet-black hair seemed full of life as morning sunlight streamed through the window caressing her. Beth nudged him back from an improbable daydream.

"Rick, why are we doing all of this?" Beth frowned over her steaming coffee cup. "The assignment is proving or disproving another autopsy tape. What is this anyway, number three or four?"

"Three, I think." Rick set his fork down. "Real Saucer Magazine thought we could kill two birds with one stone by coming here and doing a short piece on a psychic's viewpoint of the Roswell crash. It would also help us get into the mood. You know, background material, refresh old memories, that sort of thing."

"From the looks of things, we're opening a whole new can of worms. Especially with yesterday's experience on the debris field." Beth stirred her scrambled eggs then shoveled a mouthful.

"We'll see. The magazine is forwarding a copy of the tape to our hotel as soon as they can, until then, let's see what we find."

Sarina finished her fruit plate while listening to the others talk. Finally she interrupted, "Will I still work with you two on the videotape? I know I'm mostly along for this story, but I'd really like to help out if I could."

"Damn, girl," Beth said swallowing the last of her breakfast. "You wig out on us in the middle of the desert, now you want to view some gruesome tape showing people cutting up something from outer space?" Her eyes narrowed, challenging a response.

"Why don't we wait and see?" Rick motioned the waitress for the check. "Let's enjoy the next couple of days and complete the article, then when the tape arrives, we'll re-evaluate."

The two women nodded, eyes on each other. Waiting.

"Besides, I've already called and the local Radio Shack has an inexpensive GPS.

Sarina's forehead knitted. "A what?"

"A GPS, a Ground Positioning System. It gives the longitudes and latitudes, kind of a specialty computer."

Sarina nodded and Rick continued, "Anyway, we'll get the GPS at Radio Shack, but we'll also need a topographical map of the area. For that, we'll go to Ruidoso, about seventy miles away." Rick poured a second spoonful of sugar into his coffee.

Across from him, Sarina buttered a piece of toast. "That's fine with me. I'm still a little shaky from yesterday."

Beth nipped a piece of Rick's toast, popping it into her mouth as she nodded. She looked at Rick, "You two kids go ahead; I'm going to visit the museum and check with city hall. Someplace should have records that mention those three cairns."

"You may need more information than we have if you want to locate the records." Rick wiped his mouth with a napkin as he pushed his dirty dishes to the side.

"I hope not. Those things looked to be fairly old. Lichen was growing on them. I don't think they had any fancy location equipment back then."

"Good point, Beth." Rick tore a piece of paper from his notebook and handed it to her. "Here, the debris field is just east of Vaughn Pumping station number six. That may help."

Rick paid the waitress and Beth tossed two single bills on the table as a tip.

A chill filled the morning air as Rick and Sarina headed to Ruidoso. "Can you put that thing together?" Rick indicated the package on the floor wrapped in a Radio Shack bag.

"Sure thing." Sarina removed the GPS from the box and flipped it over. "So this little thing is going to tell us our location?"

"Not only longitude and latitude, but also elevation. This way, we should be able to accurately plot the position of each cairn. Hopefully, after we see them on the topo map, they'll make some sense."

"Is there a chance they have something to do with the crash?"

"Too early to say, Sarina, but you're the one who had experiences out there. They may tie the two together." Rick leaned across the seat and ran his hand tenderly across the nape of her neck. "You tell me."

"It was weird." Sarina looked to her right. Looking north, the Capitan Mountain range blocked her view of the debris field. "As we stood there, it felt as if someone or something was tugging me. The closer I got to the base of the cliff, the stronger the feeling."

"Was it like somebody calling 'Hey you,' or a pulling?"

"More of a pulling than anything. After reaching the base, there was a jumbled sensation, like a bunch of radio stations all on the same frequency."

"What made you walk off? Were you trying to escape all that?"

"No, on the contrary." Sarina steepled her hands on her knees then rested her chin on her fingertips. "I heard this cacophony of sounds for maybe two minutes, then a silence like I never felt before. That's when I was made to follow in that direction."

"Follow?" Rick glanced her way. "What do you mean, follow? There were only the three of us out there."

"I don't know, but follow best describes what drove me. At the time, it actually felt as if I was following someone, or at least I was following in his or her footsteps."

Sarina quieted down. Rick noticed tears streaming down her cheeks and found a wide strip to pull off the busy highway. He unbuckled his seat belt and slid to the edge of his seat. Gingerly, he leaned Sarina's head on his shoulder, wrapping his arms around her, holding her tight.

* * *

Beth ran her finger down the wall map, shaking her head.

"May I be of assistance?" a docent asked, moving into view beside her.

"Oh my, you startled me," Beth gasped. "I've been looking at this map, and can't make heads or tails out of it."

"I can explain." The man pointed to the lower left corner. "This is an old area map put out by the State of New Mexico. It doesn't show much beyond county and state roads and known dwellings. Here you see those little triangular markings, those are benchmarks with elevations."

"OK, I get that, but you have the Foster Ranch and debris field located way up here." Beth pointed to a black box within ten miles of state Highway 247.

"That's right, that's where it is." He ran a finger over his salt and pepper mustache, then his hand combed through matching hair. "I wouldn't advise going out there."

"Why not?" Beth looked him over, pleased with what she saw. He was a well framed man, a little older than her, with no sign of a spare tire around the middle. He's almost attractive, she thought. "Is it dangerous?"

"Not really, only right now, we've had some pretty heavy rains that would turn all the dirt roads into quagmires. Plus the fact that few of the roads are inadequately marked and most of the land is owned by various ranchers."

"Owned by ranchers? I thought it was all BLM land that the Bureau of Land Management leased to the ranchers."

"Yes, that's true, it just seems that they own it, is all." His dark eyes challenged hers. "By the way,

I'm Layne Gunther, the head docent here at the Roswell Space Museum."

"Nice to meet you." Beth broke into a wide smile. "I'm Beth Ringold."

"It seems as if you have a more than casual interest in our crashed saucer. Most people ask about the Corn Site, the location of the crash, or just view our displays."

"To tell you the truth, I'm a photojournalist with Real Saucer Magazine and I've already been to the Corn Site, and the supposed debris field. That's why your map puzzles me."

"That explains your vest and various gadgets. OK...." He chuckled. "And you've been out there already. Well now, where were you, exactly?" Layne leaned casually into her space.

Backing away apiece, Beth pointed to a spot on the map much lower than the museum's marker. "Down here, a little over a mile east of Vaughn Pumping Station Six. You see that windmill. Well, just south of that."

Beth was puzzled by a minute change in Layne's eyes, but dismissed it. "Down there? No wonder you're perplexed. You're, let's see...." He measured the distance against a scale. "At least ten miles off."

Squinting, Beth looked up into his eyes. She spoke softly so no else would hear her. "OK, Layne. Stop bullshitting me. I've been trained in map reading and cross-country trekking. The area I pointed to is the debris field; not your fancy-assed tinted plastic thumbtack."

Layne drew back at her harsh words. "Really.

Experts came in and marked our maps for us. Exactly why do you say it's wrong?"

"Take that picture of a shack you're selling in the gift shop. According to its caption, it is where Mac Brazel and a couple of Army guys spent the night very near the debris field. Right?"

"OK." Layne arched his brows in anticipation.

"It isn't even marked on your map, but it is a quarter of a mile east of the intersection of these two dirt roads. For sure." Her eyes stared, daring Layne to correct her.

Puffing his cheeks, Layne exhaled slowly. "You're right. We purposely didn't put the line shack on the map, fearing the county would end up having to rescue stranded tourists on a regular basis."

"Also," Beth continued, "the windmill Brazel said was just north of the debris field is this one, about a mile southeast of the line shack, which means the proper locations is right about here." She jabbed her finger at the map.

"Right again." Layne shrugged. "All I can say is that most people wouldn't research as well as you evidently did, and as I just mentioned, the rescue angle."

"Give me a break Layne. I'm not stupid. This is deliberate misinformation. You or your superiors are trying to cover-up the truth. That makes people in my position just a little more than curious. We ask why. Why is this lie being perpetuated? Could it be the same reason the government claims the materials recovered were nothing more than the remains of a top-secret Mogul radar balloon?"

Layne laughed and clapped his hands. "This

is great. Tell you what, Beth. Let's move this conversation into my office and have a cup of coffee, which is my very own blend and very good if I say so myself. While there, we'll continue this conspiracy theory of yours."

"If it's all right with you, Layne, I have a couple of friends that would be interested in our talk. Why don't we meet later today, say at Denny's?"

"Hey, great. I can get out of here around five. How about five-thirty?"

"OK, I'll find them and bring them up to speed. See you then." Beth briefly shook Layne's hand. Then after another cursory glance at the map, she left.

* * *

"You did what?" Sarina laughed. "You actually told him the map was wrong?"

"Yep." Beth smiled a smile Rick couldn't remember seeing very often. "And after some humming and hawing, he told me I was right and gave some half-assed BS about protecting the public from themselves."

Rick motioned for more coffee. "When is this guy of yours supposed to show up?"

"There he is now." Beth stood motioning Layne to their table even though they couldn't be missed, as the only other customers were three elderly men taking the restaurant up on their bottomless coffee for seniors.

After introductions all around, Layne settled next to Beth. Rick tried to watch Sarina from the corner of his eye, but if she had any reaction to Layne, he missed it.

"Beth tells us you work for the UFO museum."

"Yes I do, Rick. I am actually a volunteer docent. My paying job is with the junior college in town. Not only am I one of the three history, poli-si and government instructors, I am also the department chair."

"How did you get involved with UFO's?"

"Wish I could say it was because I had seen one in my youth, but it was nothing like that. Years ago, the museum asked the college for assistance. I responded and have been with them ever since." Layne turned to Sarina. "What about you?"

"Me? I've always had some type of psychic experience, ever since I was a kid. Some of them involved flying saucers and their close presence. I finally decided to see how accurate my feelings were and volunteered to work with some journalists."

"That's interesting. How has it gone so far?"

Sarina heard a harrumph from Beth, but ignored it. "I'm not sure. Out at the Corn Site, I didn't have any feelings worth mentioning. Then, while at the debris field, I started to pick up some sort of feelings, but haven't been able to figure out what they mean."

"Could you be reacting to a historical event that may have taken place there? You know, a gunfight between some settlers and native Americans."

Sarina hung her head and responded. "I guess it is possible."

"That would make sense," Beth nodded in agreement. "I'm more conformable with that concept."

Rick watched Sarina's confidence crumble. He patted her shoulder. "I'm not so sure. Isolated, I might back Layne's comment, but with those rock pillars, I'm open to many different ideas."

"What rock pillars?" Layne's eyes switched to Rick. "I don't recall hearing about anything like that."

Glancing at Beth, Rick caught her slight negative movement. Rick realized he was releasing new information. "Sarina located a rock pillar approximately five feet tall and almost two in diameter. This was just beyond the southern end of the debris field."

Before Rick could warn her, Sarina grabbed a salt shaker. "This is the first one I found." Sweeping her hand back and forth, she set down the peppershaker. "That is the valley, and this is the second one. There is a pointer rock aimed back at that one."

"Now wait a minute. Now you have two pillars, one pointing to the other. I definitely have never heard about those." Turning to Rick, "Are you guys sure you were on the debris field?"

Beth moved the salt and pepper. "Yes, Layne. Remember I showed you where we were and you confirmed the location as the real debris field."

"Yeah, that's right." Layne placed both hands on the table palms down. "Tell you what. If you have time, why don't I drive you guys back out there and we'll take a good look around."

"That would be great." Rick said. "We're going to be in town anyway for a couple of more days." The two women nodded.

"Where are you staying? I've got two empty bedrooms at my place. Why not move in there and save money?" Layne looked Beth in the eye, then appraised her chest.

"I don't know." Rick scratched his chin and looked at the girls. "What do you two think?"

Beth looked directly at Layne. "That would be fine with me."

Sarina nodded, "We would have to pay for our food, or something."

"Great. We'll work something out. It's settled. Let me run out to my place and clean it up some. Why don't I meet you at your motel, in say two hours?"

"That will work fine. We're at the Wagon Wheel, on north Main."

Layne grabbed their bill on the way out.

Rick looked back at the two women. "I'm not so sure about this."

"You're not suppose to be having feelings, Sarina is." Beth focused on the other woman. "You have anything to say about this?" When she got no response, "Well then, let's get packing."

*3*

"What's all the equipment for?" Layne said, twisting the metal detector in different directions.

"Careful with that." Beth reached out for it, her hand briefly touching Layne's. "This as a specialty built metal detector. It can often locate most any type of metal under as much as three feet of loose soil or gravel."

""Wow, that is special." Layne shook his head. "So, you were wandering around the debris field, swishing this thing back and forth hoping to find some saucer metal."

"That's about it." Rick looked away, his mind still on the debris field.

"Now, why, after all this time do you think you could find any loose metal lying around? The Army collected it. Remember?"

"That's why we're using this metal detector. I suspect that pack rats or even the wind could have carried small pieces underground into nests or into deep crevasses."

"That's a good idea. So what have you found so far?"

Rick carried his suitcase into one of the spare bedrooms, Layne close on his heels. "So far...nothing. But I want to check out all those pillars we found."

"I still don't see the connection between them

and the crash. Why check them with the metal detector?"

Dropping his suitcase on the bed, Rick turned, almost eye to eye with Layne. "OK, you're the one who suggested ranchers or miners, right? They might have built a pile of rock to mark the corners of their claim, but to do it correctly; they needed to leave a note behind, usually in a glass container or old tin can. Inside would be their name, the date and a description of what they are laying claim to."

"Gotcha." Layne held both hands in front of him like pistols. "And we'll be SOL if they used glass."

"Yep." Rick moved back into the living room, carrying the new topo map and the GPS unit. "Let's plan for tomorrow."

The smell of eggs, bacon, and coffee drew Sarina out of a deep, unfettered sleep. Beth's soft snoring halted as Sarina rolled facing the sleeping woman. "Beth, hey Beth, time to get up."

"Oh, God, you first. Let me know when you're finished in the pot."

Ten minutes later, Sarina tried waking Beth again. She drew a tee shirt over her head. On the front, across her chest, it said, 'What are you looking at?' On the back was a winking eye and 'Thanks!'.

"Coffee is on and breakfast is probably getting cold."

"OK, girl. Go keep them busy while I get up." Beth rolled out of bed in a way-to-large pink flamingo tee. "Oh, and save me some coffee."

Rick and Layne were almost finished with their meal as Sarina entered the room. They both looked at her, then at the logo, and stared. She turned her back to them giggling. "Gotcha both."

They laughed as Sarina grabbed a plate and stocked it with food. "Is there anything to drink besides coffee?"

"Yeah, I've got both juice and milk in the frig."

Pouring a small glass of each, she asked. "What time are we going to hit the road?"

"As soon as everyone is ready and all the dishes are done. Out here on the fringe of town, unless I keep this place clean, I've got all kinds of critters crawling around."

* * *

"I'm glad we brought your jeep." Sarina shook her head. "Layne seems nice enough, but I'm still a little leery of him."

"Beth doesn't seem to be the least bit taken back with him, if I've judged her mood and the secretive glances correctly."

Sarina's laugh was low and seemed somewhat sensual to Rick. "Come on now, are we showing a wee bit of jealousy here."

"Oh, no." Rick moaned, "don't even go there. In all the years we've worked together, never have I even the slightest thought of...well, you know."

"If you say so."

"I say so."

Sarina was puzzled as she looked around at the rolling hills, scrub brush, and cactus. "Is this the same route we took? Are we sure he's taking us to the same place?"

"No and yes." Rick poked the air at the one

o'clock position off the hood. "You can barely make out the top two vanes of the windmill. We're coming in from the north side."

After climbing over three more hills and through one cattle guard, Layne's light blue Blazer swung a tight right and climbed again. Ten minutes later, Rick pulled off the well-worn rutted trail, stopping just as Beth slid out of Layne's vehicle.

Sweeping his hands back and forth and around, Layne said, "Well boys and girls, this is it. Now, lead me to those rock piles you were so excited about."

The three surveyed the slope, and then looked at each other. "This isn't quite the right spot." Beth glared at Layne.

"Sure it is." Motioning on back up the rise, his hands danced left and right. "There, if you look closely, you can barely make out the groove. It is a little over thirty feet wide and about five hundred or so long."

"This isn't it." Beth's voice had risen at least one octave.

"Here, Layne, let's spread the topographical map out." Rick shook the map open on the hood of his jeep. "There is the windmill, and this is about where we located the debris field. Here's where we are now. There is less than a quarter mile difference."

"Quarter mile doesn't count except in nuclear war." Layne grinned. "Now this is about what I expected." Turning to Beth, "I know, I know. You can read a map. I'm not saying you can't. It is just that trying to match the terrain from memory, well, it doesn't usually work."

Beth stood, her hands on her hips, lower lip sucked in her mouth and eyes aglow. "Damn you, Layne. I should'a known better. This is not the right spot."

"OK, you two." Rick pulled out his pencil and the GPS. "Let's just measure this groove and mark it on the map. Then do some thinking."

Walking along side the faint groove, Rick watched the readout on his GPS. Not only was he collecting data about the length of the depression, he was getting elevations. He noted from top to bottom the hillside dropped at a moderately steep angle.

"Look at this," Rick said. "How could the flying saucer rebound into the air when it slid down at such a steep angle? It should have just kept going down into that arroyo over there."

"Maybe it regained control long enough to take off, then it stalled and glided into China Draw," Layne said.

"Can we move to our own spot, Rick?" Sarina's eyes pleaded.

"Just a few more minutes, then we'll move over there," Rick agreed nodding his head. He slowly walked the trail left behind over fifty years ago.

An hour later, they had the groove drawn in exactly on their topographical map and were studying it. Beth, having had as much BS as she could put up with, wandered off.

"Now, let's lay down a straight line and see what we get." Layne took Rick's notebook, flipped it open and ran a light line along the edge of the marked depression. "It looks as if it is about 125 degrees southeast. Now where is that other map of yours?"

Comparing the two maps and using a back azimuth, or adding one hundred eighty degrees to the plotted azimuth, or path of movement, Layne showed them that the depression was in a direct line with the Corn crash site in China Draw.

"Now, that is interesting." Layne dropped the pencil and faced Rick and Sarina.

"Yeah, it is," Rick nodded in agreement, then after seeing Sarina's confusion, "but I still believe our location is better."

"My God, give a rest, you two. Thank God Beth isn't here, or I'd be afraid of strong verbal abuse." He threw his hands up in despair. "OK, OK. Let's go look at your spot and make a comparison."

Sarina eyed Layne. "Thank you."

* * *

Beth was a shadow on the horizon, leaping around and flapping her hands, but a shadow no less. Minutes later, Rick pulled the Jeep Wagoneer up next to her and climbed out. Layne's Blazer was right behind him.

"Look." A big smile swept across her face. "Look."

The three stood, eyeing her skeptically.

"Can't you see it?" She pointed to a shallow watering hole with a small earthen dam across the lower end. "That's where the ship impacted." She slapped one palm into the other. "It dug a hole, then slid on down the slope that way. You can see the path it made. I bet we find that cairn at the other end."

Standing near Beths' impact site, Rick was stunned. "Good grief. You may be right, Beth." He knelt down, peering across the depression. Even now, the remaining pothole was approximately three feet deep and forty or so in diameter.

Sarina squatted opposite Rick. "Look, before the dam was put in, the groove continued in that direction." Her hands flowed down slope in the general direction of the cairn.

"Yeah, you two may be right." Rick stood and brushed off his knees. Crossing to stand by Sarina, he reached for her hand. "Let's walk down a ways and see what we get." Rick moved down hill. "This is just about where we placed the debris field."

"Come on, Sarina. I need you to be feeling something. Anytime now girl. Don't let me down!" Beth huffed, practically jogging ahead of the group.

"Don't push her, Beth."

"It's OK, Rick." Sarina frowned. "I do feel something, but not like before."

"Bullshit! This is just bullshit." Layne kicked a cow paddy to illustrate.

As they neared the edge of the valley below, Rick spotted the rock outcroppings they stood next to two days ago. "Hey, this is it." He stopped and looked back up toward his Wagoneer. From this viewpoint, the depression was hardly noticeable. As his eyes swept the area, his thoughts were interrupted.

"Damn, damn, damn." Beth waved her arms frantically. "How the hell did this happen?"

Layne drew near. "What? What happened?" Looking around, he saw a small pile of rock almost two feet tall. Scattered around in a circle were stones of all sizes that at one time constituted the top of the cairn. "Is this your five-foot tall cairn?"

"Yes," Sarina said, "Two days ago it was a lot taller. I wonder what happened to it."

"I'll tell you what happened. Someone learned about our find and tried to make it disappear. That's what happened." She glared at Layne.

"Now wait a minute, Beth." Layne shook a finger at her. "Are you accusing me of something?"

"Hold on you two. Hold on. No one is accusing anyone of anything."

"Yes, I am, damn it."

Sarina reached for Beth's shoulder. "Calm down, hon, now just calm down. At least most of it is still here."

"That's right. I can still get the GPS location and that's the important thing."

"Rick, remember what you said about putting an object inside the cairn to stake a claim?" Beth dropped beside the remains, clearing small pebbles and dirt from the bottom. She pointed to a faint marking on the base rock. "Look, doesn't that resemble a rusty outline of some sort? Maybe a can."

They all craned their necks, peering inside. "Looks like some kind of reddish lichen growth to me," Layne said.

"Yeah. Right. Inside of a pile of rock. Doesn't lichen grow out in the open or to the north side of stuff. Doesn't it need light?" Beth lightly struck her forehead. "Duh."

An outline reminding Rick of the bottom of a bandage canister stained a small flat rock lying inside the base of the rock pile.

"Looks like the outline of a bandage can," Beth said.

"More like a Prince Albert Tobacco can. See how rounded the ends are." Rick traced the outline with the tip of his mechanical pencil.

"Too much imagination!" Layne stood, shaking his head. "Way too much imagination."

"Well, back to work." Rick held the GPS locator directly over the center of the rock pile and watched it acquiring information from first one then two and finally twelve separate satellites in orbit above the earth. He punched a button locking in their exact position. "OK, let's put this on the map and see what happens."

It took him ten minutes of figuring, running his finger this way then that way across the face of the map. Carefully, with the point of his pencil, he drew in a small X and the number one off to the side; he printed another one in the margin and wrote a brief description of the first pillar. As the others swept binoculars back and forth across the shallow valley, he walked back to the top of the groove and locked in its position.

After acquiring three more readings, Rick lightly penciled in the shape of the depression. He couldn't believe what he had. The depression abruptly ended almost at the pillar. Interestingly, the elevation of the rock outcropping was ten feet higher than the lower end of the groove. His only conclusion was he was looking at a natural ramp.

"Hey, guys. Let's go. We've got lots more to do today." Rick kept his idea to himself as he clapped his hands together trying to get the groups' attention. "Come on."

"Hold on, Rick. I think I've spotted another

cairn." Beth pointed to the southeast.

"Are you sure? That's not where we found the second one."

"She's right. I've spotted the second one and it is almost directly across from us." Sarina stared across the valley, almost mesmerized.

"And from what the girls said, I believe I've found the one you guys practically ran over during the thunderstorm." Layne motioned almost due west.

"OK, let's start with the new one, how can we get to it?" Rick held out his hand for Beth's binoculars.

A rutted dirt trail seemed to pass close below Beth's cairn. After comparing the map to what they were looking at, Rick decided they could get close by following a pair of dirt tracks.

"Tell you what. Why don't you go check that one, and I'll go to the one straight across from us," Layne said.

"No way." Beth spun around. "We all go together."

"Especially after what happened to this one," Sarina said.

"Are you still saying that I had something to do with that?" Layne asked.

"Calm down everyone." Rick stepped between Beth and Layne. "Since we are journalists, and this is a new development, let's stay together. This way, there are more witnesses should anything questionable happen."

Nodding approval, they packed their gear back into the vehicles. Rick and Sarina led off in his vintage Wagoneer, while Layne and Beth followed in the Blazer. Crossing the valley was a slow process due to the well-weathered ruts and lumbering cattle. Rick's Jeep must have been the same color as the rancher's truck, because it seemed as if every cow within a mile was drawn in their direction like a magnet.

Beth jumped out of the vehicle before it came to a complete stop. Rick and Sarina were not too far behind.

"Another pointing rock. Oh my God." Beth stared at the foot long projection. A flat thin slab approximately three feet long had been added to one side, purposely extending a pointer back toward the pillar now labeled X1 on their topo map.

Sarina walked around, softly murmuring to herself. Rick had seen this before as she called up her power. "Let me know what you pick up," he whispered.

Turning back to the stones, Rick held the GPS unit above it, then at its base. Watching as it locked in two sets of coordinates. Then he took the metal detector from Layne and passed it over every inch of the pile. Nothing. Not even the slightest click.

"Well, there goes that idea." Layne smiled. "Unless you want to rip it apart to see if a bottle is inside."

"Not yet." Rick waved the GPS. "We'll work with what we have."

"How about the pointer?" Beth knelt down trying to line it up with what was left of the original one. "It's not pointing at the pile, but above it."

"Oops. Almost forgot the compass." Rick passed it to Beth. "Take a reading for us, will you?"

"I hate to say it, Rick, but so far your theory leaks like a sieve."

"Shut up, Layne." Beth pointed the compass at him. "I knew we should have refused your help. You've been negative about this whole thing."

"Sorry, didn't mean to get you upset. I'm just trying to save you all some time."

"Well, try to help. Get a set of binoculars and sweep the horizon. See if there are any more rock piles around."

Rick grabbed the map and spread it on his hood again. In less than five minutes he had another X on the map. This one was labeled 2 with more information in the margin. Beth watched as he added the azimuth from the pointer. It skimmed the north edge of the watering hole.

"Look at that. It certainly looks as if this is deliberate." Rick pointed to his drawing.

"Yeah, it does, but Sarina hasn't turned up any feeling yet."

"Maybe she will. We're heading to the one where she passed out."

## *4*

"I don't believe this." Beth lowered her binoculars.

"What's that?" Rick just finished taking his GPS readings and scribbled the notes into his notebook and on the map.

"Back across the valley. If you look close by the water tank, you can see the top of a white vehicle." Beth gestured. "And unless one of the men has awfully big eyes, I'd say he's trained a humongous pair of binoculars on us."

Layne pulled the glasses from Beths' hand and brought them to his face. "I'll be damned. Sure looks as if someone is keeping an eye on us. I wonder who they are and why."

Rick raised his own binoculars and took a quick glance through the glasses. "Well, we don't want to draw anymore attention to ourselves, so let's not put on a show, just go about our boring business."

Sarina held out her arms as if embracing the pillar and slowly squatted, keeping her eyes shut. She moved a third of the way around and repeated the process, then once more to make a complete circle around the cairn.

"Oh, don't mind me, but I've picked up some sort of feelings."

"What is it? Mineral, animal or vegetable?" Beth chuckled.

Layne rolled his eyes. "Great, now the rock pile is talking."

"Rick, move in front of the pillar." Sarina whispered, motioning him to the position she wanted. He did as he was told. "OK, now, don't move. Beth, Layne, walk away. Hopefully you will draw their attention away from me."

When she was satisfied with the distractions, her hand darted into the base of the pillar and just as quickly hid an object under her blouse. "OK, everyone. Let's continue our search of the area. I'm going down into that slide area below."

"That's where you passed out the last time. Isn't it?" Layne asked.

"Yes. There was a strong feeling that drew me down there and then made me walk around."

As Rick stood near the pointing rock shooting an azimuth, he looked below. Less than a foot from the base of the cairn it looked as if someone had taken a huge shovel and gouged the edge away. A semi-circle extending twenty feet to either side that dropped almost straight down for at least another thirty feet. At the bottom was a large accumulation of detritus, the remains of the hillside.

Off to one side he watched Sarinas' lithe form gracefully maneuver along the edge of the cut. The front of her blouse, just above the waistband jiggled, reminding him of the object she pulled out of the cairn.

"Hey, Rick, earth to Rick." Beth waved a hand in front of his face. "Boy, I didn't know you had the hots for her this bad."

"What? What are you talking about?" Rick

41

reddened. "I'm looking at this cliff and wondering how it was created."

"BS. You had your eyes on something else. But, hey; seriously, what do you think these four slabs of rock mean?"

"I'm not sure, but I'm going to do an elevation, GPS and shoot an azimuth on them as soon as I'm finished recording this other information." Looking around, he frowned. "Where's Layne?"

"He is just hanging behind Sarina, sorta keeping an eye on her. I wish he'd keep an eye on me like that."

"What? You two fight like cats and dogs."

Wiggling her brows, a wicked smile crossed her face as she raised one hand like a claw. "Hiss, meow."

"Whatever you say." Rick laughed at the visual image she conjured up and finished some notes in his notebook.

Below them, Sarina was gesturing frantically.

"Great, now not only does she have our attention, but she woke up those characters watching from across the valley."

Both of them scrambled down the hillside to where Sarina and Layne were talking softly, almost as if they were afraid of being overheard.

"Some event of large proportions took place over there by the cliff, and continued in that direction." Sarina wiped away beads of sweat that formed along her hairline.

"I'm saying Indians or settlers, but she's denying it, calling it far stranger and more recent," Layne said.

Sarina moved into Rick's arms seeking protection, strength or sympathy, he wasn't sure. "We'll discuss this later, we still have one more rock pile to look at, and it's getting late."

"Two," Beth said. "There is another one up behind this one, higher and on a different ridge."

"Well, let's go. Two more cairns to visit and it's nearly three in the afternoon. This time of year, the sun sets about seven and cold breezes pick up." Rick held Sarina's hand as he began climbing.

Twenty minutes later they were backtracking down the path to the valley floor. At the first intersection, they turned up another set of ruts. Ten more minutes brought them to another pile of rock. This one had also been damaged. They could not tell if it had held any pointer rocks, although surprisingly they discovered two separate slabs that resembled other pointer rocks they had seen. Why two, they wondered.

By five, they pulled to a halt in front of the last cairn. One pointer aimed in the general direction of their first pile of rocks. Sweeping their glasses back and forth, they could barely make out the first one. With very careful scouting the small one up behind the cliff was discernable. Looking back across the valley, the voyeurs were still there, just watching.

Rick collected all the data he needed. Throwing his notes on the back seat, they headed back to Laynes' ranch house at the edge of Roswell. On the way back, he inquired about the object Sarina found.

Sarina shook her head. "Later," she

whispered.

There was no indication that they were followed off the debris field.

# 5

She pulled him into the spare bathroom, locking the door behind her. "Who's side are you on?" she whispered in his ear.

"Side? What do you mean, side?"

In a low almost husky voice, Sarina continued. "I don't really trust either one of them. Beth's always making fun of me and now with Layne along, we are suddenly being followed. Can I trust you?"

With your life, Rick thought, but said, "Yes. Yes you can, Sarina. I wouldn't say or do anything that would hurt you."

"Good." Reaching into her pants pocket, she withdrew the object from the pillar. It was an old rusty Prince Albert Tobacco tin. She held it out to him, carefully raised the lid, prying it away from her body. Inside was a folded piece of yellowed paper, surprisingly well preserved. Rick tapped it out, tenderly unfolding it. The lower half was blank, but across the top in fading but bold black ink it read:

July 4, 1947 Project Rainbow. Below that, in finer print: Second day of recovery, put into effect Project Arnold as of midnight last. Let the people at Walker play their games now. It was signed Captain Hogue.

"Wow, you know what this is? This is the smoking gun. This blows apart the whole Roswell conspiracy." Rick almost shouted. "Wait a minute. Is this real? It must be."

"Shh! Rick. We can't tell anyone about this."

"Give me time. I'll think of something." He ushered her out of the bathroom, then sat on the toilet lid looking at probably the most important document uncovered in the past twenty years.

Half an hour later, Rick palmed the tin back to Sarina. "Keep this quiet until I have all my notes caught up to date. Then I'll make an announcement and after the hullabaloo quiets down, you pull this out with a...'Oh, by the way, look at what I found.'"

After dinner, Rick helped clean the table, then laid out his topo map and started to record to rest of the cairns and pointer info. Layne brought over two cups of coffee and sat down. Over the next ten minutes, Beth and Sarina drifted over.

"I don't believe this. Look at the pointers. All of them come together at the top of the watering hole."

"Why would they do that?" Layne asked, a cloud fogged his mind.

"I think that they mark off the entire area of the debris field and crash site."

"Oh, give us a break," Beth said. "Debris field maybe, crash site. No way."

"Sure, look. At the apex, where all the pointers come together, we have the impact of the saucer creating a depression. Then the path made by the saucer skidding along." Rick's hands flew giving a visual representation of events.

"So what is this pillar for?" Layne pointed at X1.

Beth said, "Yeah, and this one?" Pointing to X3.

"Look at the elevations." Rick pointed to the numbers he had printed, and the elevation lines of the map. "Here, it's higher than the surrounding ground at this point. The Saucer was ramped back into the air, waffled across the valley and wham. Right into what we call the cliff. Disintegrating the rock on impact."

"Sounds awful spacey to me," Beth said. "This is one of the weirdest theories I've yet to hear from you."

"No, if you stop fighting it, you'll see it makes perfect sense."

"Why all the pillars then?" Layne asked.

"Oh, speaking of pillars." Sarina ran from the room.

"They were put out to delineate the area for the troops collecting pieces of flying saucer. The Army could later claim lack of knowledge, saying it was done by ranchers, miners, etc."

Bouncing back into the room, Sarina tossed the tin to Layne. "Here, I found this in the crash pillar."

Layne looked the rusty Prince Albert tin over. A questionable frown on his face.

"Open it. I found it inside the cairn. Remember when I told you guys to distract the watchers."

Beth sighed. "Open it, Layne. May as well see what's inside."

Carefully he peeled off the lid, tipped it over and watched as a small piece of paper fell out. Oh's and ah's accompanied the display, Rick leading the chorus. Layne unfolded the paper. Everyone could see words printed on it.

"Read it." Sarina clapped her hands, bouncing on her toes.

"All it has is a date, July 4, 1947 and a captain's name. Captain Hogue. Nothing else."

Rick caught the quick glance from Sarina. A faint smile crossed his face.

"I don't believe this. It appears to back up Rick's theory. The date is right. But I've never heard of a Captain Hogue being associated with the Roswell crash," Beth said.

"Me neither. That's why I still can't give this theory of yours any credit," Layne said. "I've studied the event for twenty years, and never have I seen that name before today."

Rick slowly scanned each person's face, looking for the slightest sign of surprise, annoyance or anxiety. Did one of them know more than they were letting on? Sarina, he didn't think so, often she wore her emotions on her shirt sleeve. Beth, she was deep at times, as often as not, made fun of Rick's theories, but she would support some of his more harebrained thoughts. Layne, the new guy on the block. He was still a mystery. Seeming suffering from tunnel vision. The official story was correct while any other ideas were not only wrong, but often ridiculed.

"I'd say that the entire event took place right here." Rick repeatedly tapped his finger on the topo map. "We've been there and outlined the whole area."

"Ok, Rick," Layne sighed, leaning his elbows on the table. "Since everything is in a direct line here, why is the western side longer than the eastern side?"

"Yeah." Beth leaned in for a closer look.

"Because," Sarina interrupted. "Because after the crash, two of the survivors moved off in that direction and were found hundreds of feet away from the saucer."

"Now we have little men running around." Beth rolled her eyes. "Give us a break."

"No, no, no." Tears filled Sarina's eyes. "I know. I felt them. They were badly injured and were looking for assistance. No one found them in time and by mid-afternoon the next day they died of exposure."

"Alien bodies were reported at the Corn Site. You're crosswired there, Sarina." Layne stared at her. "Or possibly you have another agenda."

With tears flooding her eyes, Sarina sobbed once than ran from the room, swishing through the swinging doors, making them flap back and forth as in the wake of a tornado.

"I'll go." Beth began to follow her.

"No," Rick rolled up his map, collected the note and tin. "I'll go. I don't think she is too happy with either of you right now."

"Leave your map, Rick. I want to examine it some more." Layne held out his hand.

Rick passed the map to Layne before pushing his way through the still vibrating wing doors. Sarina was curled up at the far end of the sofa, below a large wall painting depicting a thundering herd at night in the middle of a lightening storm. Eyes bulging in fear, and snot running from their nostrils, the cows were about to step out of the painting and over the sofa.

"Sarina, hey babe." Rick dropped to his knees, resting an arm over her shoulder. His other hand gently brushed hair from her face, cradled her chin, and turned her face toward his. Without realizing it, Rick brushed her eyes and nose with his lips. "Come on babe. Don't let them get to you like that."

"I'm...I'm sorry. That last just came out. I guess I was suppressing it. When I said it, it hurt. But I knew I was right." Sarina used a finger to wipe her tears. A frown, worked it's way into a faint smile.

"Boy, I feel dumb. I mean. The feelings were go great. It was as if I were reporting the event live instead of years later."

Rick moved beside her on the sofa, hugging her more, lowering her head against his shoulder. "Well, you know what that means, don't you?"

Sarina looked up into his eyes, and then she stole a kiss on the lips. "Tell me."

"We, you and I, will return to the crash site tomorrow morning, early before everyone is awake. We've got work to do."

## 6

Rick put his hand on Sarina's bare leg. Goose bumps from the early morning chill covered her exposed skin. "Walking shorts? In mid-October. You're going to freeze."

"Not with you to keep me warm." She covered his hand with hers. "Now, explain why the substitution of the note."

"Just like you, I don't trust them. Maybe I shouldn't trust you either." Rick glanced from the dirt road to her eyes then back. "I think the first cairn was tampered with and possibly another note taken from it."

"What did you do with the note?"

"It's here with us. Along time ago, a good friend of mine helped build a hidden compartment into the jeep. No one could find it without literally tearing the vehicle apart."

"Why a hidden compartment?"

"Lawrence is deep into all kinds of conspiracies. He feels that we need to protect ourselves. There is a small survival kit, first aid kit, more clips for my .380 Beretta and a good knife, along with duct tape and other odds and ends."

"Wow, that's a lot of stuff to be carrying around."

"Not if you believe as Lawrence does, that you have to be prepared for anything. Over the years of doing this, I've picked up on some of his paranoia, so I keep the compartment stocked."

OK." Sarina squeezed his hand. Looking around at the now familiar landscape, she took in the total desolation that presented itself to the casual viewer. "What are we going to do out here that is so secret?"

Rick told her.

## 7

Across the valley, a white Jeep Cherokee pointed its nose at them. Both doors opened, and two men hurriedly set up what resembled a video observation post.

"There they are." Sarina lowered her binoculars. "Our watch dogs."

"Right now, just keep an eye on them and check out the nearby roads."

Rick scrambled down onto the pile of rocks below the edge of the cliff. Taking a solid stance on the loose rubble, Rick swung the metal detector off his shoulder, checking all connections and flipping the switch, bringing it to life.

Thirty minutes later, he worked his way to the lower portion of the rocks. There were two or three faint blips of the LED display, but the meter never jumped in unison with the LED display. "How are we doing up there?"

"So far, so good." Sarina's soft musical voice drifted down to him.

"Hold on. I see a dust trail back to the east of us. It looks as if a vehicle is moving on the main dirt road."

"Probably only Layne and Beth, madder than blazes." Rick stepped lower and waved the base plate over new ground.

"Holy shit!" Rick almost lost his footing.

"What? Are you OK?" Sarina glanced down in his direction.

"You bet. The LED's and meter just about jumped off the casing. Come down here and help me"

"OK, but the dust cloud is getting closer."

"On second thought, stay there, and keep me posted." Rick dropped the metal detector and frantically threw rocks in every direction, trying to locate what had tripped the meter. Two broken fingernails later, he saw a faint glint of brassy metal. After exposing the piece, he kept digging. Turning up three more fragments and a foot square piece of tin.

"Oh my God," Sarina yelled. "It's another white Cherokee, headed toward us."

Rick scrambled back up next to Sarina, grabbed her hand and ran toward his jeep. As they leaped in, Rick waved the sheet of tin hoping the men in the vehicle would see it, then threw it back down the hillside.

"Oh, shit. Buckle up. Now," Rick called, climbing into the driver's seat. The engine ground and ground before starting. Sarina looked over her shoulder.

"Behind us. God. They're almost here, Rick! Drive, drive."

"I'm trying."

The starter caught. Dropping the gearshift into drive, Rick's foot rammed the gas petal to the floor. Dust and gravel showered onto the front of the white Cherokee closing the distance behind them. In the rear view mirror, Rick watched as a rock landed square in the center of the approaching windshield, starring it badly.

Rick fought the wheel as the vehicle sped up. Deeply rutted and eroded trails tried to claim control of the Wagoneer. Ahead, a gate made from heavy pipe and bailing wire blocked their way.

Sarina slammed against the passenger door as Rick whipped the jeep to the left. The Wagoneer raced cross-country parallel to the fence. Occasionally the right mirror would clatter against the wiring. Behind them, the cammo dudes careened sideways into the gate. The right rear bumper hooked the edge of the gate, ripping it from its post. Dragging the wire and metal framework behind it, the Cherokee fishtailed every time the gate slammed into a fence post.

In the rear view mirror, he saw the jeep slow to a halt as both occupants, dressed in military attire, piled out of the jeep attacking the trailing gate. Loosening it, they threw it as far away from their vehicle as possible and piled back into their vehicle. Rick drew a sigh of relief as they pulled away.

Sarina looked back. "Keep going, they're after us again."

"Keep your eyes open. We need to locate the main trail back to the Roswell road."

"Okay, just keep us out of an arroyo," Sarina shouted as they bounced across the barren desert. The Wagoneer started sliding sideways as they crested a small hill.

"Oh, my God! There is another jeep over there," Sarina cried, pointing to their left.

Rick allowed a split second to follow her

pointing finger. Sure enough, another white Jeep Cherokee was heading their way, trying to cut them off. One minute it would drop into an arroyo, the next, it was flying over the crest of a hill. The other Cherokee was still a ways behind them, but soon it would be in their tracks.

The two jeeps, engines screaming in the chase, tore down the side of the hill. Ahead of them, a large herd of Brangus cattle milled nervously. Startled cows lumbered away from the approaching vehicles.

Sarina saw terror in the eyes of one of the animals. It stood there, chewing its cud, strings of saliva and grass spilling from the corners of its mouth. The animals bulging eyes resembled tennis balls.

As they passed the animal, it jumped away, right into the path of the cammo dudes' Cherokee. Sarina heard the startled screams from the dying cow. The Cherokee shuttered as it shoved the cow aside. The driver tried to steer to his right, only to slam into another cow.

Sarina's body shook as a groan escaped her tight lips.

Rick slapped his palm on the wheel. "Yes, yes thank you. We made it."

Tears welled in Sarina's eyes. "Those poor cows. I feel so sorry for them."

"They saved our hides, Sarina. Thank them for that."

"I did, for a split second there. I felt them, their terror, and their pain. They died and I heard them." A flood of tears flooded her eyes. She buried her face in her hands, trying to calm herself.

"You what?" Rick said, "What did you feel?"

Sarina mumbled an answer he couldn't hear. As he looked in the rear view mirror, he saw the second jeep stop beside the wrecked one. A figure dressed in a camouflage uniform climbed out aiming a rifle at them. Rick reached out and shoved Sarina down in the seat. A split second later, the rear window shattered.

Rick picked up the main road off to his left. Looking behind him, he could not see his pursuers through the cloud of dust the Wagoneer kicked up.

He slowed down, the wash board road was constantly fighting him for control of the vehicle. Dust flew into the rear of the Wagoneer, through the shattered window, creating almost as effective an obscuring cloud as the one he left in his wake.

As long as they stayed to the dirt road, Rick knew they were as safe as possible. There was no way the cammo dudes could close up on them. They would have to stay about a quarter mile back. At the same time, they knew where he was.

Fifteen minutes later, Rick hit a paved road. The road to the left led to Roswell, while the road ahead passed through the small crossroads town of Capitan. He skidded left onto the Roswell road.

Sarina wiped her face. Looking up, she saw a large wooden sign. In bright yellow lettering it announced that they were now in the Smoky Bear National Park, home of the cuddly animal by the same name.

Behind them, the white Cherokee careened onto the hardtop. It slid off the opposite side crashing

57

through a speed limit sign. Rick realized that if he stayed on the road, they would call someone and block the way. He looked around. His eyes focused on a small white sign with the silhouette of a bear. An arrow pointed south. Another dirt road.

"Hang on, Sarina, we're gonna see where Smoky was found." Rick swung the wheel to the right.

She looked at him, then back at their pursuer. A moment later she giggled. "Go, go! They knocked down Smokey's sign."

They were climbing a steep jeep trail deep into the Capitan Mountains. Rick fought to drop the jeep into four wheel drive without slowing down too much. Then ahead, he saw a drop off to the right of the trail. Further up, the trail curled around to the left behind a huge boulder. The Cherokee was behind them safely out of sight, but following.

"Take the wheel, Sarina, as we go around this boulder, I'm jumping."

"No, don't leave me!"

"Sarina, it's our only chance. Do it. After I jump, drive on. Do not stop for at least a mile."

"Then what? They'll be right behind me. They'll catch me."

"Just wait. I'll be along. I promise." Rick pecked her on the cheek, opened the door and leaped out.

He fell against a large rock, the breath knocked out of him. Stunned, he slid down the rock surface. The Wagoneer slowed as Sarina shifted into the driver's seat, and then sped up. The grinding of gears shook him alert.

Rick drew his .380 Beretta semi-automatic pistol from his pocket. Chambering a round, he tried to calm himself. Drawing deep breaths he prepared himself for something he never thought he would have to do.

Not only was he preparing himself to kill a fellow human being, but supposedly a soldier from his own country. Rick's mind churned in turmoil. Thoughts cascaded through his consciousness like water over Niagara Falls. As the grill of the Cherokee cleared the rock, an image flashed into his mind. Thousands of nugget sized pieces of glass passed in front of his inner eye. They had tried to kill Sarina and him.

Calmly, standing his ground directly in front of the jeep, Rick dropped into a shooters stance. Over the sights he saw the driver. Disbelief filled the man's face as the windshield starred and a small hole appeared above the driver's eyes.

At the last minute, Rick jumped aside as the jeep veered toward the ledge. Rick stood and watched the man in the passenger seat try to push the driver's body away from the wheel as the vehicle slid over the side. Almost in slow motion, the front wheels dropped off the ledge and the rear of the vehicle tilted upward. Grinding metal announced the passage of the jeep as it slid down the embankment.

Rick, stunned with his action and its results, slowly shuffled to the ledge. Below, the Cherokee lay upside down, its wheels spinning. He estimated that the vehicle had rolled at least two hundred feet before coming to rest against a large rock outcropping.

One body hung out of the window. Rick could not see the other man. Under his breath, he mumbled the Lord's Prayer and crossed himself even though he didn't attend church regularly. Rick turned and headed up the road toward Sarina and the Wagoneer.

As he came around another bend, he saw Sarina standing behind the jeep, facing down the road. She held her arms across her chest, looking blindly down the jeep trail.

"Sarina?" Rick called. "Hey, Sarina."

Suddenly she was in motion, arms all akimbo as she rushed toward him. Tears streaked her dusty face. They fell into each others arms like long lost lovers.

Rick hugged her tight thinking it was just an emotional release, relieving tension, anxiety, and frustration. As he kissed her, he hoped not.

## 8

Dust clouded the driveway as the Jeep slid to a halt. Heavy storm clouds were settling in for the afternoon and evening, blocking out the weak afternoon sun. Despite the jeep's heater, Sarina shivered.

Since their reunion, Sarina sat teary-eyed against the passenger door. She never said a word. As they passed the boulder, Sarina did not look for the Cherokee. She didn't even ask about the cammo dudes. Rick didn't tell her about them her but he noticed her body tense and a shallow moan escaped her throat.

Back at the house, Beth and Layne were waiting at the door. As the dust settled, they stepped out to meet Rick and Sarina.

"Where have you two been?" Beth asked. "What happened to you, girl? You look like death warmed over." She helped Sarina out of the vehicle and inside the house.

Sarina automatically followed Beth. Her eyes red rimmed from crying. Low sobs acknowledged Beth's worry. As everyone settled down in the living room, all eyes turned to Rick.

"Well?" Layne finally asked.

"I need a drink, then I'll tell you the whole thing," Rick headed to the kitchen. He popped the tab on a Molson Ale, took a deep swallow, then went back to the front room and slipped into an easy chair.

"This morning I wanted to revisit the crash site with the metal detector. When we got there those cammo dudes were still on the ridge," Rick took another swallow and continued. As the story unfolded, Sarina started to breathe harder, her fists clinching and unclenching.

When he reached the point where he jumped from the jeep, Sarina flew out of her seat. With fingers spread claw-like, she threw herself on Rick.

"You bastard!" she screamed. "You left me alone."

"No, I didn't. I got out to stop those guys."

Sobbing and scratching, Sarina continued, "No, you purposely left me. Oh God. You left me."

Rick grabbed her wrists, holding her talon-like fingers away from his eyes. Beth wrapped her arms around Sarina's body, effectively pinning her arms to her side.

"Sarina, I had to get out. It was the only way, hon. I had to stop them and protect you at the same time."

Beth sat down, cradling Sarina's head in her arms. She patted Sarina on the back, whispering platitudes to calm her. Beth nodded to Rick to continue the story. Layne and Beth set quietly, absorbing the startling news.

"You mean that you wrecked one of their vehicles then ran the other one over a cliff killing the two men inside?" Layne stammered.

"No wonder Sarina's upset. I'm upset, and I didn't even go through that ordeal," Beth said.

"We're in deep shit now, Rick. Those federal

guys are going to be after us. You've put us all in jeopardy. Now we're accomplices to murder and I don't know what the hell else."

"I don't think so. Sure, they're mad, but they shot at us first. Their trying to run us down is also illegal. I thought about it all the way back here. As long as we stay in a high profile area, like in a large town where a lot of people see us coming and going, I think we'll be safe."

"Hell, I don't know, the government won't forget us. I mean we, you, killed at least two of them and trashed their jeeps."

"Do you think they're going to drag us into court on a murder charge and admit that they were trying to kill us on public land, and they wanted to recover pieces of a spaceship that our government already repeatedly swore did not exist? I don't think so," Rick said finishing the Molson and retrieving another, realizing he had said more than necessary.

"What do you mean pieces of a spaceship? What the hell do you think you found?" Layne leaned forward in his chair.

Beth continued to hold Sarina but her gaze settled on Rick, a questioning eyebrow cocked.

"Oh yeah," Rick reached into his pocket, withdrawing three of the smaller pieces of metal, leaving two larger ones hidden, and threw then on the coffee table.

Layne greedily reached for all three pieces. One at a time he held each one close to his eyes and turned it over and over catching the light. He passed the first one to Beth.

It was only about one inch square, very light

in weight like tinfoil. It was pliable as tinfoil, but untearable. There was also a slight bluish, gold tint to it.

"That one's a beaut, but this second piece is nothing more than tarnished tin, possibly from the lid of someone's k-rations." Layne tossed it to Beth.

"We, the museum, were given some metal like this back in 1996. Over a period of time, it was decided that some jewelry artist created it using a lot of heat. Now this last one, wow." Layne whistled softly. "This is a keeper. It looks as if it is from an I-beam. The coloring is a strange blackish, gray and the hieroglyphic type characters are printed in an almost silvery blue color. This closely matches an I-beam described by one of the witnesses. We also sell imitation I-beams in the gift shop."

Sarina held the first piece in her hand, fingers wrapped tightly around it. A faint smile held on her face. She nodded slightly as if there were a rhythm only she was privy to.

"Layne, you're right. This second piece is nothing but junk," Beth said.

In defense, Rick said, "Hey, the metal detector buzzed, I dug this stuff up, and then Sarina called out. I never had time to do more than shove them into my pocket."

"And, this is what all that chasing around and killing is about?" Beth snapped. "Are you sure?"

"What else could it be?' Rick retorted. "That's all that happened."

Layne shrugged, "This is totally remarkable. I never would have guessed. People killing each other over less than two ounces of strange metal."

"What are we going to do with the metal?" Beth asked.

"I'm going to put the pieces in the Prince Albert can, then hide them in my suitcase, keeping it locked until something better comes along." Rick said.

"Well, what else are we going to do?" Beth asked.

"Let's pack up. We'll leave in the morning. I have a friend in Albuquerque who will let us stay with him," Rick said. "Once we get out of the Roswell area, I think our chances of survival will improve tremendously. I need to call the magazine and have the tape forwarded whenever they get it."

"Let's get out now!" Beth exclaimed.

"We'll cut back through Capitan and Carrizozo, then north to Vaughn, switching to back roads up to Albuquerque," Layne suggested.

"Why not straight up to Vaughn, then over?" Beth asked. "It would be a lot shorter."

"You're right, but if someone were to see us leave, then it would be obvious where we are headed. This other way, there are three or four options. El Paso, Tucson, Phoenix and Albuquerque, and hopefully, we would be able to spot a tail and find a way to shake it," Rick said.

"Why wait until morning then?" Beth asked.

"Look at Sarina. Do you think she's ready to travel?" Rick asked.

"Don't talk about me as though I'm not here, you bastard. I can travel." Sarina stood shakily and slowly headed toward her room. "Is anyone else going to pack?"

Two hours later, Rick pulled into a Diamond Shamrock gas station. Beth sat beside Rick since Sarina refused to ride in the same vehicle with him. She was keeping Layne company. After gassing both vehicles, the group headed toward Capitan.

"It looks like you two are having a lovers quarrel, Rick. I know it is none of my business what two adults do, but if it interferes with our job, then I'm involved."

"Look, what happened, happened. Right now, I think Sarina is just in shock, you know sensory overload. She told me that she felt those two cows die." Rick ran his hand across his face.

"She actually said that? You're kidding, right?"

"Nope." Rick shook his head. "That's what she said." He paused. "Do you think she also received feelings from those cammo dudes?"

"I don't know, you said that she was about a half mile away. The cows on the other hand, were just outside the window," Beth said.

"But, I remember her tensing up as we passed the bodies and wreckage."

"You couldn't see it thought. Could you?"

"No, but is there any chance she could have sensed it?" Rick asked.

"Well, lover, you won't know for a while anyway. Right?"

Total darkness settled over the hilly landscape, isolating each curve from the rest of the desolate highway. An hour later, they were on the outskirts of Capitan, New Mexico, USA, according to the state license plates. The home of Smokey Bear museum. As they neared the only intersection in town, Rick saw flashing lights blocking the road. A sheriff's cruiser was turned sideways across the inbound lanes. Headlights and roof light bar warned traffic to stop.

A pickup with a large camper shell was the only car in front of them. Rick was sure the roadblock had just been established. A sheriff's deputy slowly walked past the first car, toward Rick's Wagoneer.

"Are they looking for us?" Beth asked.

"We'll see. There is not much we can do, although it looks as if they have the highway blocked on the other side also."

"Good evening folks, where you from?" The young deputy said, resting his left hand above the driver's window. The palm of his right hand rested on the butt of his pistol. He smiled as he leaned into the open window.

"Hi, we're from El Paso, spent the day visiting Roswell. Kinda cold out here. What has you working so late? An accident?" Rick asked.

"No, the military is hauling out some stuff. We'll have all this cleared up pretty quick." The deputy patted the roof, saluted them, then started to move down the line to Layne's Blazer but stopped, taking two steps back; the officer cautiously looked through the window at Rick.

"What happened to your back window?"

"Uh, oh, that." Rick frowned, then shook his head. "While we were at the Goddard museum, I was stupid enough to leave my camera lying in the open back there. When we returned to the jeep..."

"Tough break. Did you file a report?"

"Sure did," Rick turned to Beth, "Hon, it's in the glove compartment, would you get it, please?"

Dumbly, Beth opened the lid, only to see about a ton of loose papers. She grabbed a handful and began shuffling them. "Sure wish you'd figure out a better filing system, dear."

The deputy sighed, "That's all right folks. Have a safe trip home." He pounded the roof again and moved on to Layne's Blazer.

"What was that hon crap?" Beth punched his shoulder. "That whole story was weak. What would happen if he really wanted to see the police report?'

"Well, hon," Rick chuckled. "He did, but seeing the mess, realized he couldn't hold up traffic all night just out of curiosity."

"Well, don't pull that shit again. You had my heart in my throat."

"OK, hon, anything you say." Rick's comment was rewarded with another punch in the arm.

Beth grabbed Rick's elbow. "Oh, no, Rick. Look."

Rick followed her pointing finger. Creeping into the middle of the intersection was a long flatbed trailer, loaded with two wrecked Jeep Cherokees. One had a ruined front end and a smashed windshield. Even from this distance, Rick imagined that he saw the bullet hole in the windshield of the second one. Its roof was crushed down over the front end. The passenger door was sprung open and twisted.

"You and Sarina did that?" Beth exclaimed.

"No, just me," Rick whispered, the days'

events rushing back to him.

As the deputy walked back to his cruiser, Beth grabbed the CB's microphone, depressed the talk button, and called to the others.

"Sarina, Layne, do you see that? Those are the..." Rick knocked the mike out of her hand.

"Dammit. What the hell are you doing? Goddamn. The truckers probably have a CB turned to channel nineteen. If they heard you, they'll know we're nearby," Rick shouted.

"Beth, Beth what did you say. Over," Sarina's voice came through the speaker.

Rick leaned across Beth and retrieved the microphone from the floor. He keyed the mike. "Nothing. Not now." Rick's glare cut Beth short.

The flatbed halted, effectively blocking the intersection. The driver's door swung open and a head appeared from the cab of the truck. The driver was calling to someone off in the distance. From behind an ancient cottonwood tree, Rick finally noticed the front end of a white vehicle. Looking around carefully, he noticed two more.

"Shit! They heard you, Beth. That was stupid. Real stupid. Look over there and there. White Cherokees. Do you know what that means?" Rick slammed his fist against the steering wheel.

"I'm sorry, Rick. I just...I...I don't know what came over me. The sight just overwhelmed me. You know. I wanted Sarina and Layne to see that. I'm sorry."

"The damage's been done; just keep that microphone put away for a while. The officers are looking at all the cars again. Probably for CB antennas. We may be safe. Mine is hooked up to the regular radio antenna," Rick said.

Five minutes later, the trailer was gone. The Sheriff cruisers pulled out of the traffic lanes and the officers waved traffic forward. A pair of Cherokees remained parked behind a large cottonwood tree. Cammo dudes in black blended into the nights' shadows, but scrutinized each vehicle as the deputies passed them through the roadblock.

Ten miles down the road Rick found a pullout. He coasted off onto it and cut back to parking lights. Cold air tumbled through the open window as Rick motioned Layne to pull up next to them.

"Flip over to channel thirty-five. Few people use it out here. Then watch your language. We had a close call back there. Twice," Rick said, glaring at Beth.

"Do you really think they're looking for us?" Sarina asked.

"Yes, but what gets me is why that deputy just didn't arrest us on the spot. We've been under surveillance for days, everybody and their dog know what we look like and have a description of our vehicles." Rick said.

"Why would they let us go? Those white Cherokees back there surely made us at the roadblock," Beth asked.

"Maybe they want something else from us." Sarina said.

"They want our metal scraps, what else could they be after?" Layne asked.

"I don't know, but I'm sure we'll find out sooner or later. Right now let's continue our evasive actions," Rick said. "I just want to know how they're going to follow us."

"Layne agrees. He wants us to stop in Carrizozo to see if someone is tailing us," Sarina said.

"Good idea, we'll lead off. Stay about a mile behind. Don't go over fifty-five. When you get to town, turn left at the light. About three blocks down is a small greasy spoon cafe. Park around the side," Rick pulled out, rolling up his window.

The tired heater finally got a grip on the chill as the Wagoneer passed the city's golf course to their left, and rolled across the Southern Pacific overpass. A single flashing red light hung over the center of the intersection like an angry eye.

Rick pulled to a stop, checked traffic, and then turned north. A quarter mile down the on the right he spotted a gas station. Not much, just three pumps, a small shack to pay at and a mobile home out back. Rick turned around, facing the intersection.

"Didn't you tell them to turn left?"

"Yep."

"Why are we over here then?"

"We'll watch and see if they have a tail on them," Rick said.

"Want me to tell them?" Beth reached for the CB microphone.

"No, Beth. We will stay off the radio for a while. I haven't seen any cammo dudes around here yet, but let's keep on looking."

` Layne's Blazer rolled to a halt, then slowly turned left. There was little traffic at this time of night, but often eighteen wheelers would convoy through town. Long stretches of desolate New

Mexico desert and the black of night turned the countryside into a strange surreal landscape. Many drivers were not used to the feeling of loneliness that crept over a person the darker the night became. Soon, a driver would be scanning the road ahead and the rear view mirror in search of any head or taillights. Even a stranger would be a welcome addition during the lonely journey.

Rick waited. Three semi-trailers rumbled through town, the traffic light blinking caution for traffic on the main highway. He pulled out behind the last truck, following them through the intersection. Layne's Blazer was parked next to an old beat up Ford pickup, hidden from any casual searches. He pulled the Wagoneer around behind the building. Beth and Rick climbed out and stretched before entering the cafe.

The inside air was greasy. Evidently, there was no separate smoker's section as the ceiling was thick with smoke from cigarettes and a large hot griddle in the back. Beth noticed three of the six tables were occupied. An elderly couple sat sipping coffee, while a Hispanic male sat alone having a late night meal. Sarina and Layne sat in a corner where they could see anyone entering.

"You two go ahead, we've ordered already," Layne said. "What took you so long? You were ahead of us."

"What can I say? I took a wrong turn back there. Good news is there is no sign of a tail," Rick said. Beth shook her head at the waitress and slumped into her chair.

"Sarina, your job is done. You were with us

visiting the Roswell area. And after this is over, we can do an interesting piece on your feelings from the debris field. Why don't we put you on a bus home? I don't see how anyone could tail you. Besides, if they were after anyone, it would be me. I'm the one responsible for those guys dying," Rick said.

Beth and Layne silently eyed Sarina and Rick. Looking at each other, silent messages passed between them.

Sarina peered over her steaming cup of tea, her hazel eyes burning with anger. Little wrinkles formed around her eyes. Rick thought they added to her personality. They reached out and tugged at his heart. The more he saw, the more he liked. Few women interested him. This one did. Rick was drawn to her.

"Oh, no you don't. I'm in this as deep as you guys are. I'm staying. Besides, I really feel that I had some weird vibrations out there and I want to clear that up. Maybe we will find out what really happened."

"Sarina, that's the whole point. I'm the only one they're gonna be after. Beth and Layne weren't there. I'm the one who shot the driver. You were a mile away. We can get back to you when this mess is cleared up."

"I still feel that I am part of the team. I don't want to leave. Beth, Layne, what do you say?" Sarina asked.

"I don't mind, why not? We could probably use another mind on this. Like you said, maybe your instincts or whatever will help clear up a lot of questions. Otherwise, we should also send Layne home. I say they can both stay if they want," Beth said.

"I'm in. After using my house, what do you want to bet it's under surveillance? My name and picture is right below yours in the post office. Sarina should be allowed to stay also," Layne said.

"OK, OK, fine. I was just trying to protect Sarina from some of this," Rick said.

Rick pulled a small notebook from his pocket and drew a map. He wanted the team to break up and meet at a seedy motel east of the university on Central Street in Albuquerque. From there, he would get in touch with his friend who could provide a safe place to stay for a while awaiting the delivery of the videotape.

## 9

"He's a what?" Beth said. "I don't believe this." The studio walls were covered with obscene posters. Movie posters showed almost every conceivable combination of naked men and women. Movie titles that staggered their imagination shouted at them from the posters. "How can we work in these surroundings?"

"I'm not going to apologize, dear. We all do something for a living. This is my thing," Lawrence Harvey said, flipping his hand in an effeminate manner. Long silver gray hair hung loose over his shoulders. More hair stuck out from the neck and arms of his sleeveless tee shirt, only it was jet-black. A pair of extremely tight, short shorts completed his outfit.

"Do you, ugh, you know, ugh, star in that kind of movie?" Sarina asked, a rosy flush filling her face.

"No, luv," Lawrence pirouetted for her. "Do I look studdsy enough? All I do is copy those tapes for distribution."

"That's just as bad! A film pirate. Rick, how do you expect us to work in these surroundings? Where did you find this guy?" Beth said, a disgusted look on her face.

"Do you suggest we go to a video store and ask them if we can rent some of their equipment? How about visiting an Internet cafe? This is the last place anyone would look for us," Rick said. "Besides, Lawrence and I go back a long way. A lot further than you and I do. We're close friends."

"Last place, bullshit, Lawrence is probably under surveillance by the FBI for pirating. Now we show up and get added to the police department's list of undesirables," Beth said, eyeing Rick while working over his last comment.

"Excuse me. You, my dear, may be undesirable. Not me. I've got my own following," Layne pouted at Beth. "I know for a fact that no one has any idea what I am doing. Believe me, sweetie, I would know if the police were suspicious." Lawrence gave her a forced smile, "As Rick said, I wouldn't allow him to step into a situation with the police. We go back a long way and are close friends."

Beth glanced from Lawrence to Rick and back, a look of disbelief clouding her face.

"No, dearie, not that way. Rick has always been straight. Back in high school, he saved me from a serious beating. After a stupid indiscretion on my part, I was going to be the main attraction at a gay bashing party. He saved my ass. Since then, we have been friends. He is one of the few people I would do anything for."

"We need to take down those obscene posters. Now!" Beth said.

"No, you don't. You're visitors and refugees here. Be thankful you have a place to hide. Now, I'll be finished with my current project around seven this evening. You can wine me and dine me, then I'll help you get started on your little scheme." Lawrence turned and left the room with a definitely feminine sway of the hips.

Beth turned and glared at Rick. "I can't work here. We need to find a better place. I refuse to stay here."

"Beth, I'm sorry you can't work under these conditions, especially since we have been through so much." Rick patted Beth's shoulder sympathetically. "I'll tell you what. If you find us another place that offers this kind of equipment and this security let me know. Until then, you can work with us or pack up and leave."

"Calm down, you two. I find the posters offensive also, but I'm going to work around them. I'll have a talk with Lawrence and see what can be done," Sarina said.

"Here we are back to Miss Goody-Two-Shoes, again. Maybe they're not so offensive because you see yourself up there, getting boffed all the time."

"Maybe, you need to be boffed, as you put it, more often. It is none of your business if or when I get boffed," Sarina said.

"Maybe she's a dike," Layne said with a smile, nodding toward Beth.

Beth, about to lunge at Sarina, turned on Layne. She leveled a kick at his groin, missed, and struck his upper thigh instead. Layne swung at Beth's leg as she kicked, but missed. The force of the kick knocked him back into a chair.

"Dammit, Beth, you can't go around hitting people like that," Layne said gritting his teeth, "or someone will really think you are one."

"You have no right!" Beth screamed and

threw herself on him, poking, scratching, and gouging. Sarina tried to intervene, but Beth brushed her aside as easily as shooing a gnat. Rick grabbed for one of Beth's arms, and took an elbow in the face.

Layne, holding both hands over his face for protection, tried to bring his knees up, kicking at the same time. Rick finally caught one of Beth's arms and started to drag her away from Layne.

Suddenly the pair was drenched in cold water. Lawrence and Sarina stood side by side holding empty bowls. "All right children, time to stop this. If any of you fuck up my equipment while playing your silly little games, I'll fix you so you are incapable of any form of sex regardless of current or future preferences."

Beth stood sputtering, her shirt plastered to her chest, nipples trying to push their way through her tee-shirt. "If it weren't for Rick, all of you would be outta here on your collective asses."

Layne rubbed water off his face, looked at Beth and smiled. Beth, looking down at herself, crossed her arms over her breasts. Layne left the room, returning moments later with a bath towel. Trying to keep his eyes on her face, he handed Beth the towel, a leer forming on his face.

"You two, go back to the motel and change. We don't want you catching your death," Sarina said to the wet pair. Turning to Lawrence, she crooked a finger in his direction, motioning for him to follow her. Rick started to follow them when Sarina shook her head not to.

Rick wondered into Lawrence's den and was struck with the wall covering. Three compound bows hung between shelves of trophies, and pictures of successful hunts. Two of the photos showed a much younger Rick and Lawrence standing together, bows in hand sharing the honor of a large Elk. A third showed the same two young men hoisting a large trophy between then, again, the pair held large powerful bows in their other hand. Soft music came from speakers mounted high on each wall. A large wooden bookcase covered one wall and was jammed full of hard and softbound books with pamphlets scattered over every thing. He picked up a leaflet at random and sat in the only chair in the room.

What the hell, Rick thought. The booklet was entitled Anarchy and inside were drawing of bombs. All kinds of bombs. He sat quietly reading page after page, looking at the pictures.

"You still know how to use a bow, Rick?" Lawrence startled him with his quiet approach.

"Yeah, but evidently not as good as you."

"We'll work on that. That Sarina sure is some lady. She could talk a dog into meowing," Lawrence said, shaking his head.

"Oh, oh, what did she talk you into?" Rick asked. "And yeah, she certainly is some kind of woman."

"You'll have to wait and see. Right now I'm on the last four runs of a videotape. We can start on your project tomorrow. I received a call confirming overnight delivery of your autopsy tape while you were busy. Tomorrow, sometime, I want to work you with a bow."

"The bow, why? It's been a long time. Lately, I haven't had any use for a bow. A gun, yes."

"I have something to show you. You'll appreciate this," Lawrence smiled and clapped Rick on the shoulder.

Rick agreed to the practice session. The two friends moved to the kitchen and sat drinking Mexican beer and swapping stories. As Rick's story unfolded, Lawrence was surprised at the escalation of violence that took place, but not shocked. To him, the whole episode fit right into his beliefs.

"Buddy, tomorrow we will also work on preparing you. By the way, where's the space metal?"

"Where do you think, buddy," Rick smiled, "Where do you think?"

\* \* \*

The following morning found everyone out in Lawrence's backyard. Surprised, they discovered a full-sized archery range with some pop-up targets at varied distances.

"So, this is how you earned all those archery trophies," Sarina said.

Lawrence shrugged, "Well, let's say that this helps." He then proceeded to assist each of them in the proper procedure for holding and using a bow. Layne and Beth soon gave up, while Sarina kept at it until she realized that she was totally outclassed by both Lawrence and Rick.

The two men continued until the others returned to the house. Then Lawrence changed the game. He found a blindfold for Rick. Then reset all the moving targets. Lawrence put six arrows in the quiver hanging over Rick's shoulder. As he covered Rick's eyes, he explained.

"Don't move from your position. I am going to make a noise. That will be your cue to notch an arrow. When you hear the second sound, assume it is a person pointing a gun at you. Ten seconds after the sound, one of you will be dead. Remember though, the sound will be soft and low to the ground."

Lawrence then tossed a rock close to one of the pop-up targets. As soon as Rick had the bow ready, he tripped the mechanism causing the silhouette of a man to rise with an audible thunk.

Rick swung the bow, tilted his head a little then loosed the arrow. As it flew past the target, missing it by ten feet to the left, Lawrence poked him in the solar plexus. "Guess who just died."

By the fourth arrow, Rick was hitting closer to the target and his chest hurt. "Damn Lawrence, cut that out." Rick moaned.

Lawrence poked him again. "You died. Come on. You're worse than a kid, but at least you are a decent shot with a handgun. I can't keep up to you with a good pistol, but this is different." He threw another rock, dropping it directly in front of the fifth target. Rick had just finished getting the arrow settled when he heard the telltale thump. Immediately he aimed and released the tensed bowstring. Within a second he was rewarded with another solid thump as the arrow struck home.

Without giving Rick time to recover from his small victory, Lawrence dropped another rock, this time way down range in front of a stationary target. Rick hesitated, twisted his head as if it were a radar antenna then when Lawrence tripped the target, he fired. Another hit.

"Well done, my friend." Lawrence clapped him on the back, as the doorbell rang. Going through the house, the saw an Overnight Express truck standing out front.

* * *

A good dinner down in Old Town at El Sombre Restaurant got the group talking. By dessert, Lawrence had heard all four variations of their stories. He told them that he would help them out with weapons, although Beth and Layne were against the idea. Later, they returned to Lawrence's house.

* * *

After breakfast, Lawrence and Sarina went shopping. They stopped by K-mart over on Louisiana Boulevard, then a sporting goods shop on Menaul Avenue before returning home. For the next two hours the group continued their practice session with the compound bow. Then the two shopping conspirators went back to work.

"What happened here?" Beth said, looking around the studio.

"Sarina re-decorated for me," Lawrence said, waving his arm to display the black plastic sheeting hanging ceiling to floor.

"Thank you both. Now I can feel a little more comfortable working here," Beth answered.

Lawrence completed his copying job then called the other four together. With Rick's newly arrived videotape in hand, he showed them the intricacies of his workshop. Sarina and Beth made drinks for everybody as they set about the tedious task of viewing the latest in a long line of autopsy tapes.

"How do we do this?" Layne asked, carefully sitting his steaming coffee mug on a flat surface near a bank of video recorders.

"Your guess is as good as mine." Beth waved her iced tea around.

"I think we should just view the tape a couple of times to get an overall impression, then everyone should have a chance to give their impressions."

"Good idea, Sarina. That's probably the best method to start with." Lawrence said, looking at Rick for his nod of approval.

After two viewings and several heated debates, frustration set in. A little over three hours had been wasted. Lawrence suggested dinner and other activities to clear their minds. First thing next morning they would start fresh.

With a leisurely morning behind them, the group resumed their search for clues on the tape. Again, everyone was ready to throw in the towel after the second viewing.

"We can't give up on this. The magazine and affiliated radio, television stations have a lot of money riding on us." Rick poured coffee into near-empty mugs.

"I'm not sure we are accomplishing anything," Beth said.

"Same here. I feel we're wasting our time." Sarina fluttered her hands in front of her.

"I've got an idea," Lawrence said. "Let's try something different. In the film there are three doctors, a body, plus the cameraman. Let's each take one of them and follow that person only. Rick, you take the man to the right. Sarina, you do the one watching through the window. Beth, take the doctor to the left, and Layne you watch the body. I'll try to think like the cameraman. Don't lose your person as the camera changes angles."

"Two more hours wasted and I don't see anything," Beth said. "I'm sick and tired of this."

"We'll take a break and change assignments," Rick said. "Somewhere we'll find something to hang on to as a clue."

"I don't know what, though," Layne said. "I don't see anything. That damned body matches the Roswell description, unlike the other film. Three or four feet tall, four long thin fingers. Didn't see any pads on the fingertips though. Face sorta oval with egg-shaped slanted eyes."

"Yeah, to me this is a hell of a lot slower than that other autopsy," Lawrence said.

"Didn't someone say that the body in the other film was a woman who suffered from Turner 's syndrome?" Sarina asked.

"Yes, that's it. On the Internet, somebody said that film was a medical study of people with that disease. Then after making the film, the university decided not to use it and put it away. Now, some joker finds it and tries to make money off the deal," Rick said.

"Has that been proven?" Beth asked.

"No, not really, but too many doctors and special effects people say it could easily be a fake, or the Turner film," Rick said.

"But aren't there just as many people saying it's real?" Layne asked.

"True, but I understand that most people have

come to believe that it's a hoax. That's why we have been hired to check this one out before the magazine invests its money in the film," Rick said.

"There are a lot of similarities between the two films. The main differences are in the actual alien bodies. Our body actually looks like the most common description given, theirs doesn't. Our men are walking around in contamination suits that say U. S. Army on them. Theirs are just plain suits," Lawrence said.

Layne's eye narrowed in suspicion. "How do you know so much about the other tapes?"

With a shrug and a smile, Lawrence answered, "That's how I make my living, watching tapes over and over."

"Let's try something that will help clear out our minds. I know I am missing something. There's this feeling," Sarina said.

"Hey, I know, why don't we do some hiking? It's colder than a witch's teat, but that will help clear the cobwebs."

They looked at each other and shrugged. Why not? "Where would this hike be?" Beth asked.

"On the crest of the Sandia's. We'll take the world's longest tram to the top, hike up the ridge until we reach the one-mile marker, then turn back. I'll call for dinner reservations. We can sit up there and dine, watching the sunset near Mount Taylor," Lawrence said.

"Fantastic. That would be a nice way to unwind." Sarina said, smiling at Rick.

Rick smiled back dumbfounded.

\* \* \*

Early the next morning, the team got busy again. Everyone except Sarina switched assignments. Again, they viewed the autopsy over and over. Repeatedly, the surgeon or doctor cut open the body. Fluids welled in the incisions, but did not flow. Organs that resembled lumps of damp Styrofoam or honeycombed tissue were exposed.

The tape continued to roll as a discussion started up. "Does anyone know if this equipment is correct? My question is the scale they are using to weigh the organs. That looks like the same type of balance used in my science class at school," Beth said, munching on a candy bar.

"If they used that kind of scale while you were in school, then the time frame may be correct," Layne said with a grin.

Beth threw a candy wrapper at him.

"Yes, you're right. What about that clava...thing, you know, over in the corner. The thing used to sterilize instruments," Rick said.

Layne continued. "It may take a while, but I might be able to get a list of items that a regular air base surgery would have off the Internet."

"Wouldn't that vary from base to base? I would imagine that each doctor would order things they considered necessary. He might even haul some of it from base to base."

"You're probably right, Sarina, besides, we really don't have any proof of which base this is suppose to be happening at," Layne said.

"Well, there are not too many choices. Roswell Army Air Field, Kirtland near Albuquerque, Wright-Patterson field by Dayton, Ohio, or Nellis near Las Vegas, Nevada. Oh yeah, possibly Holloman near Alamogordo, New Mexico," Rick said.

"Are all of them the same size? Wouldn't a bigger field have a larger and better-equipped hospital? There are too many vagaries about the equipment or even the location," Beth said.

"We will need to specifically find items that were not in use during that time period, possibly like that balance," Layne said.

"Is someone doing a dating test on the actual film? By testing a very small piece of it, a lab would know how old it is. Chemical analysis of residual trace chemicals would show if it were processed in the correct time period." Beth asked.

"The magazine is still working on that." Rick said.

Rick was amazed by Beth's comments. He wasn't aware that she knew enough science to come up with that argument. "The magazine is still negotiating for a small piece of the leader or a clipping from one end. If they get that, and test it, then we may be out of a job."

"Do you think that will happen?" Sarina asked.

"No, not really. With the other autopsy films, people kept stalling and coming up with excuses to keep from releasing a specimen. On ours, the owner or supplier, is asking for five thousand for a couple of inches of film," Rick said.

"Can't the government step in and take charge? They should be able to do something."

"Sarina, you have to remember. The

government has been involved in the cover-up of the whole UFO enigma since it started. They will let the people screw things up. More confusion created by the people, the less work they have to do," Rick said.

"Unless they think you have something they don't want you to have, then they will send someone out to kill you," Beth said.

"Stop! Stop! Back it up about a minute," Sarina said, she was up out of her seat, moving toward the large TV screen.

Lawrence hit the remote. The screen fuzzed for a few seconds, and then the images began to move backwards. "What are we looking for, Sarina?"

"You'll see. Just look at the window of the isolation room. Don't look through it, look at it. OK? Stop, now forward slowly."

The tape fuzzed again then moved forward a frame at a time. Everyone was crowded around the monitor. Objects slightly out of focus appeared in the reflections created by the window glass. As thirty frames a second slowed down to single frames, everyone was getting nervous.

"Speed it up. This is ridiculous." Beth yawned.

"We can't, Beth. We might miss something."

"Sarina can tell us when to slow it back down, Lawrence."

"Then we will start jumping forward and back, trying to catch the correct frames. This way, we will not miss any of the frames."

"Is that backup recorder ready, Lawrence? We can copy this segment, then play it back and forth." Rick suggested.

"Got it, Rick. Ready to go. Let's see what got Sarina excited."

"Keep going Lawrence, remember, watch the images in the glass."

Minutes crawled by as one of the doctors moved frame by frame like an animated doll playing with silly putty from the brain cavity. Finally, something moved in the mirror like window. "Watch. Watch, here it comes," Sarina said excitedly.

An image appeared, moved slightly, stopped, and then moved again. Lawrence froze the film.

"It's just the reflection of one of the doctors."

"No, Beth, it isn't. Look closely."

"Wait...I'm going to back it up, then record it. We'll watch the recording. Rick, note the footage for me."

Ten seconds of film went back and forth, each showing running about a minute long. Eyes squinted at the screen. There was an image of somebody moving.

"It's not a doctor. He doesn't have a suit on."

"Sarina, you're imagining things."

"No, I'm not, Beth. Look again."

"I see an image of a person. He or she is moving around. The image is unclear because something is blocking the face." Rick said.

"It could be some sort of surgical mask. The clothing doesn't look like any form of protective suit though," Layne said.

"You're right, Layne. Maybe this guy just stepped in to see how things were progressing."

"No, Rick, that's the cameraman. No," Sarina said, "not the cameraman, but a second cameraman!"

"Sarina, come on now, aren't you assuming too much? We can't tell from this what the guy's doing," Beth said.

"OK guys. Let's see if we can find him again. I'm going to go back to normal speed. Call out if you see anything."

An hour later, they had two minutes of film showing either the same image or a similar one. They took a quick lunch break then everyone was back at the TV monitors. By now, Lawrence had quietly made copies of all the films.

"Here we go, boys and girls. The slowest, the dullest two minutes of film ever recorded. This stupendous episode of, 'see me now, see me later', is brought to you by the auspices of Mirror, Mirror, a reflective company," Lawrence announced in a deep voice.

Ten minutes later, Beth said, "We got him. Hot damn, we got him."

"That definitely looks like a camera, and not an old nineteen forty's kind either," Layne said.

"Better yet, he doesn't have any protective clothing. Folks we have a fake! Now all we need is a way to enhance those frames to get a good quality print," Beth said, clapping her hands together.

Lawrence and Rick took off at four-thirty to visit Max Glover, another of Lawrence's friends, who was a professional photographer. Layne took the two women to dinner at a mall. Everyone wanted to do some shopping.

By nine, Max Glover had printed four eight-by-five pictures of six different frames. Now they had recognizable pictures of a cameraman. Not only that, but the man's clothing was as modern as the camcorder he was using.

Layne and Sarina lost Beth right after they reached Coronado Mall. Back tracking, they found her in line at a pastry shop. Kids blocked their view. A large group were gathered around a carousel of phones, talking, laughing, joking and high fiving each other.

"Hey, sorry about that, but I can't pass up fresh lemon turnovers," Beth said.

"You had us worried. Here we were all walking along, talking, and then suddenly you were gone. Sarina thought the cammo dudes were still on our tail."

Sheepishly, Beth smiled and shrugged her shoulders, "Sorry, but the fragrance was overwhelming. It's been so long since I've had any of these turnovers. I guess you could say my nose kidnapped me."

By the time Lawrence and Rick showed up at the cafe, the group was comfortably sipping coffee or for Sarina, tea. The two men ordered pie and coffee then handed each member of the group a set of the photos. Excitement abounded. The autopsy film was definitely a fake. Beth wanted to call <u>Real</u> <u>Saucers</u> but Rick wanted to try and locate the man in the photographs. They agreed to forward a copy of the tape, the slow motion segments, and one of each still photo with a cover letter tomorrow. At the same time, they would call for permission to continue their search. Lawrence and Rick returned to his house. The others went back to the motel.

Arriving back at Lawrence's house, they

discovered the lights were on and the front door open. The inside was ransacked and their tapes were missing.

## *10*

Lawrence and Rick waded through the mess on the floor. "Well, boy, I believe those sons-a-bitches just declared war," Lawrence spat, surveying the damage to his living room.

"At least they didn't trash your equipment. That counts for something," Rick shook his head frowning.

"Yeah, that means if I discover who did this, I'll just trash their face instead of killing them."

"What I want to know, is how they knew to come here. It's just like at the debris field. Suddenly, when we find something, here they come. They shot at us, trying to kill us, then they up and evaporate." Rick hurried to his suitcase. The lock was smashed and the contents scattered about. "How did they know where the tin was? How did they know I had the suitcase here?"

"Only it wasn't the real thing, right? Didn't you say you hid the real ones in that secret compartment we installed several years ago under the passenger seat?"

"Yeah, Lawrence, that's it. That's where I keep my .380 Beretta and important irreplaceable things. No one but you and me know about it."

"Rick, I'm getting a strong suspicion that you've got a mole. Someone who is working both sides here."

"A mole? Can't be."

"Why not, Rick? Did you listen to what you just said?"

"Yeah, but, who?'

"What do you know about the others?" Lawrence asked.

"Well, Beth and I have worked together on other stories for <u>Real</u> <u>Saucer</u> six or seven times over the past couple of years. Layne is the history chair at the Roswell Community College and is the self proclaimed Roswell expert."

"You skipped Sarina," Lawrence said.

"Well, I don't know much about her except she is a psychic who is interested in UFO's"

"She's young and pretty. You have a thing for her."

"Yeah, well, I guess I do. But I don't see how she could be the one." Rick shrugged. "I really don't."

"Don't want to, you mean."

"Look, Lawrence, I can't see any of them being a spy."

"From what you told me, Rick, I would definitely keep an eye out. I'd bet you have a mole. We could check your vehicles for some sort of listening or locating device, but it's going to be one of your people. Bet on it."

"You may be right. I don't know who. I'm going to need your help in finding out. By the way, what did those assholes actually get?"

Lawrence walked over to the pile of tapes on the floor and fished around. "You don't think those bastards would be interested in watching <u>Little</u> <u>Oral</u>

_Annie_ or _Anal Lube,_ do you?" A big grin crossed his face.

"We better run over to the motel and see if anyone else had any visitors. That in itself may tell us something," Rick said.

\* \* \*

Lawrence and Rick stood at the door, looking into Sarina and Beth's motel room. Everything was in order, whoever it was only searched Lawrence's place.

"Those lousy sons-a-bitches! Every time we get close to something, those shit-heads come along and screw everything up," Beth said. "I find out who they are, I'm gonna fry their asses."

"What do you mean by that?" Layne asked. "It sounds as if this isn't the first time you've had trouble."

"That's right! A year or so ago, we were covering a really peculiar story. It was about an U.S. Navy ship having an encounter with a flying saucer." Beth crossed her arms.

"Yes, the USS Randell, a destroyer escort. I still burn when I remember that," Rick added.

"You covered the famed _Randell_ case? Wow. I remember that one." Layne waved his hands. "The Navy denied the entire incident. Did you get any good information?"

"I've never heard of that, what happened?" Sarina asked.

"Here's the condensed version. Back in 1969 during the Vietnam War, we had naval and civilian ships plying back and forth across the South China Sea supporting our military efforts. A freighter loaded with supplies bound for Vietnam was alone and was one day from port when it suddenly started sending a SOS then went off the air. The closest ship was the <u>Randell</u>." Rick walked over to the bed and sat down. "The <u>Randell</u> was ordered to intercept and aid the distressed ship, but when she came in sight of the freighter, it appeared normal except it was drifting on the currents." Rick paused for effect before continuing, "That was when the <u>Randell</u> lost all power and joined the drifting ship. The Naval Communications center in the Philippines lost contact with the ship for twenty-four hours. Then, when communications were re-established, the commander had a strange story to tell." He looked at Beth and she nodded, telling him she remembered.

"What story did he tell?" Sarina's voice rounded unusually soft.

"It seems that the freighter was cruising along minding its own business when something large fell from the sky, landing about a hundred yards of the starboard bow. The object settled on the water only briefly before sinking below the waves. Rescue was attempted, but the ship lost all electrical power, which led to the engines shutting down. The engineers couldn't find any problems with the ship's equipment.

"When the <u>Randell</u> approached, the same thing happened. For the whole day, messages were exchanged using semaphores or signal flags. Early the next morning, another large object flew across the sky, turned sharply and hovered over the two stranded ships, then dove into the water. It was saucer shaped with what looked like windows and a command bulge in the center. Shortly after the dive, a glow appeared deep in the water, causing the surface boil and steam. This continued for about an hour, then stopped abruptly. As the surface returned to normal, first one object then the other rose above the waves, hovered in sight of the two ships, then disappeared almost in the wink of an eye." Rick snapped his finger for effect.

"Beth and I got a chance to interview some of the crew, but of course, most of them either said that they didn't remember the incident, or that it never happened. Then we got a break. The two radiomen privately contacted us saying that they had 'hard' evidence of the encounter. Before we could set up an interview, one of them died suddenly while on a hiking trip, then, while just as we were getting ready to set up a meeting with the second sailor, the magazine called canceling the whole project immediately." Rick watched Beth's eyes glare with fury.

"That's not all. We still tried to contact the radioman, but were met with strong resistance. We were stopped by various police officers innumerable times, and searched supposedly for drugs. Another time, our files were confiscated from us. Once, our hotel rooms were broken into and searched, and all personal effects were stolen." Rich said, steepled his hands. "That is the most dramatic incident we've had."

"Until now," Beth said quietly.

"Why those good for nothing son-of-a-bitches." Sarina paced around in the small hotel room. Layne shook his head in disbelief.

Lawrence puffed out his cheeks. "Whoa. That's quite a story. Now we know that somebody is definitely keeping close tabs on your movements. All we have to do is figure out who."

"The government, that's who," Rick said.

"Lawrence, isn't it possible that they were after you and your stuff? I mean, here we are, and we've lost their tail and haven't seen any indications that they found us again. Then, boom, you get broken into," Layne said.

"That's what I thought at first, but they only took the labeled autopsy tapes. None of my things are gone. The house was trashed to make it look otherwise. Also, they tore Rick's suitcase apart and took the tin full of metal."

"I understand wanting the metal and the note, but why do they want the autopsy tape? They can get it from the guy trying to sell it," Beth said.

"It's more than the autopsy tape. It's our slow motion, enhanced versions they wanted. Very few people would ever see what we did. Even fewer of them would have equipment sufficient to do any serious enhancements," Lawrence said. "Remember, we watched that thing for quite a few hours just to spot the images. Then more time to narrow that down to something useful."

"All right, there isn't much more we can do tonight. Let's get some sleep then make plans after breakfast," Rick said.

All morning, they sat at Carrows making plans. Sarina believed that the military had made the film as part of a misinformation program. Beth felt it was done privately, for money. Selling the films to a large network, and arranging for royalties could be very profitable. The biggest question was how to locate the face reflected in the mirror. From the image of the handicam, they were sure the movie was shot in the last five years.

"Well, I think we need to do some serious research on this." Rick looked around.

"What do you suggest?" Beth picked up a pencil to make notes.

"First of all, somebody needs to go to Washington, D. C. to check Pentagon records for a list of surgical equipment that a base such as Roswell would have on hand back in 1947."

"I'll do that." Sarina pulled her hair back from her eyes.

Beth thumped the pencil against the table. "What about the rest of us?"

"We need to also check to see if the Army still uses their own photographers, or do they hire work out? That may narrow our search some."

"OK, Rick, why don't Beth and I do that? That leaves you here to coordinate things."

"No, I don't think I'll sit around here. Lawrence can do the coordination, I think I'll go to L. A. and look for independent camera companies there."

"Better yet, Rick, why don't you look into special effects people?" Lawrence tapped his temple.

"Special effects? What for? This guy was taking pictures." Rick looked incredulous.

"Yeah he was, but if I'd created that kind of art work, I'd want my own copy. That way, I'd have proof I did it, if nothing else."

"That sounds reasonable. Why don't you start with special effects and if we find out anything about camera people, we'll have Lawrence pass the information along to you. You'd be in the right place to look around, and by then, maybe you'll have a feel for what's happening out there," Beth suggested.

Layne and Sarina nodded in agreement.

Rick decided to visit Hollywood. Possibly the man was associated with one of the unions, probably a part time FX man. The other three would fly to Washington, D. C. Layne would try to check with the military at the Pentagon to see if they still used their own cameramen. Beth would help Layne check all the services. Sarina would visit Walter Reed Hospital trying to locate an equipment list for a standard mid 40's field hospital.

Lawrence agreed to be their contact man and keep everyone posted on each other. He would handle any mail, fax, and phone calls. That afternoon, Lawrence put everyone on flights out of Albuquerque.

# *11*

Rick had a three o'clock appointment with the president of the Special Effects Guild. Waiting in the reception area outside of Joel Linstrum's office was an education in itself.

The walls were covered with sequenced photos showing how some of Hollywood's most spectacular special effects were done. A giant dinosaur that rampaged through a town was really a two-foot tall remote controlled model. In another group of photos, a snow avalanche that wiped out an entire Colorado ski resort was only a series of very elaborate models nestled in an eight foot long valley between two foot tall mountains.

A subtle chiming interrupted Rick's train of thought. Linstrum's secretary spoke softly into an intercom, then nodded to Rick.

"Mister Prescott, you may go in now," the woman said as she stood and moved to the door. Rick noticed that although the woman was probably in her sixties, she was still trim, agile, and attractive.

Linstrum's office wasn't as large as Rick had expected. On TV or in the movies, all the CEO's or company presidents had huge offices with thick carpets and overwhelming furniture. He was surprised to see a moderate sized functional desk, a wall mounted bookcase crammed with books and a movable computer stand. Three chairs sat in front of the desk, while the rest of the room was filled with models of all sorts of monsters. Most of them faced the three chairs.

Linstrum stood, motioning Rick to a seat. "Good afternoon, Mister Prescott. Any relation to Arizona? The mining town?" He paused. "Just kidding. From what Millie said, I'm not sure how I can help you."

"I was deliberately vague with your secretary, since I'm really not sure about this myself. What I need is to have a person identified from a photograph."

"I don't do pictures. That kind, I mean. I supervise the different studios to ensure that everyone registered with the Guild is treated fairly. Sometimes, I try to help settle contract disputes."

"Mister Linstrum, let me explain," Rick said, launching into an abbreviated version of his assignment. Many details were left out, especially about the encounters with the cammo dudes. "So, you see, I am hoping that this man worked in the industry out here and someone could tell me where to find him."

"Let's see your pictures, Rick. Do you mind if I call you Rick? Call me Joel." Linstrum reached across the desk for the photos. After a close examination, he shook his head. "The man looks vaguely familiar, but that doesn't mean anything. May I have these? I know some people who know some people. Maybe they can identify your man."

"Sure, Joel, I have extra copies. How many do you need?"

"Just these, Rick. How about a phone number

where I can reach you if I learn anything?"

Rick handed him one of the cards from his hotel with his room extension scribbled on it. "I'll be in most of the evening, or leave a message." Rick stood to leave.

"Remember, Rick, I may not find anything out, or it may take a while." Joel rose and escorted Rick to the door, shaking his hand on the way out. "Let's try to keep in touch."

Rick waved at Linstrum's secretary as he passed through the reception area. For some reason, he was in a good mood. Cool, damp breezes blew over Los Angles, moving the smog away. Rick decided to visit the waterfront. There, he would play tourist, then eat a good seafood dinner.

The pier was dirtier than Rick remembered. Rotten fish, urine, and saltiness filled the air, stinging his nostrils. Choppy dark green waves topped with almost pure-white foam rolled and crashed against the sturdy pilings. Once in a while a shudder would pass upward through his feet.

As a child living here for two years with his aunt and uncle, Rick had been much more impressed with the fishing pier. He envied the other kids holding long solid fishing rods as they dangled their hooks in the foam. Dads stood with their arms around their sons, joking and giving advice. Jealousy had enveloped him, almost spoiling the visit.

Now, he knew better. Stopping in at one of the two bait shops, Rick bought a cup of coffee, Hazelnut Creme, rather exotic for an old pier, he thought to himself.

At the seaward end of the pier stood an empty

bench. Rick found that by sliding down in the seat with his feet on the lower kick rails, he could see the horizon between the wooden slats. A good time to reminisce, plan, and plain old daydream.

Already Rick missed the others. Lawrence, not really, because their relationship had always been the odd letter here and there with phone calls and all night dinners whenever they got together. Layne, Rick thought, was a strange one. One minute he seemed anxious to disprove the film, then suddenly he would be almost cold to the whole idea. Layne was mad about the stolen pieces of metal but did not appear to be willing to do anything about it.

Then there was Sarina. His growing feelings toward her had been unexpected. She was a very pretty woman, six years younger than his thirty-four. She radiated a natural sexuality that came from her whole being, not from a pleasant face or full figure, which Sarina did not possess. Instead, she was tall, slightly on the thin side with a straight-backed walk that make her stand out in a crowd. Some would call her statuesque.

Yes, Rick thought. He missed Sarina. This would be the perfect place to snuggle. He did not like the idea of her roaming around the Capital on her own.

Beth was just Beth. The two had good naturedly bickered and moaned over their assignments, but nothing serious ever happened, even after working close together over a period of years. They were just good acquaintances.

After a good dinner at The Lobster Shack and another hour of feeling sorry for himself, Rick returned to the motel. At nine, he called Lawrence back in Albuquerque.

"Hey, Lawrence. How's it going? I contacted two studios before getting a lead."

"Well good, Rick. Beth and Layne struck out. They tried the Pentagon without any luck then decided to visit a couple of recruiters."

"Recruiters? Why?"

"They wanted to see if the military had a job description that matched special effects in any way," Lawrence said. "But they struck out. They are ready to come home."

"Remind them of the Government Accounting Office. Have them check there before returning to Albuquerque."

"Good idea. By the way, so far I haven't heard anything from your lady friend. She seems to be keeping herself separate from the others. It's nothing to get worried about. Washington can get awfully slow sometimes."

"Let me know. I didn't like the idea of her going off alone, especially there," Rick said. "She's not quite alone, Beth and Layne are in the same town, but yeah, I know what you mean." He gave Lawrence his number at the motel then hung up. After setting the alarm, Rick fell into a fitful sleep.

Shrill ringing woke Rick. His hand fumbled for the phone, knocking the alarm clock to the floor. Rick noticed it said three fifteen before it tumbled off the nightstand.

"Prescott?" A silent pause, then again in a whisper, "Prescott?"

"Yeah, that's me," Rick stifled a yawn,

saddened that the call was not from Sarina or Lawrence. "What can I do for you?"

"The information you need," the voice whispered. "I have it."

"What information is that?" Rick asked disinterested.

"You know, the man in the picture."

"Mister Linstrum? Is that you?"

"No. Why are you looking for me?"

Rick thought. He only left the photos with Linstrum this evening, no wait, was it yesterday afternoon? That means that he showed them all around quickly, or he knew exactly who the man was.

"If you're not Linstrum, then you're the guy in the photo, right?'

"I already said that. You're kind of slow for a detective."

"I'm a journalist, not a detective. What's your name?"

"Look, Mister Prescott, all I want to know is why you're digging for me. I've got problems of my own without the press kicking up dust."

"OK, mister, ugh, what did you say your name was? We need to talk. Where can I meet you?"

"I didn't say my name, Prescott. As for the meeting, I'll think about it, after you tell me what I need."

"No way, I need a name, and a location, then you get your answers. Face to face," Rick slammed the phone down. Hopefully, he hadn't upset the guy too much. He went to the bathroom then slid back under the covers trying to go back to sleep. Two different ideas rolled around his mind.

After a late breakfast, Rick called Linstrum back, explaining his early morning caller. "So, I need to know who you talked to after I left your office yesterday."

"Rick, I don't know what to say. Some friends and I got together for drinks and your plight came up in conversion. After kicking the idea around, we thought that only one of the renegade studios would get involved in something of this nature. They usually have their own special effects people as well as complete film and lighting crews."

"How would I get in touch with one of them, Joel? How many are there?"

"Well, Rick that's hard to say. I mean, we're talking B grade movies, smut movies, that kind of thing."

"You mean pornography?"

"Not really porno, Rick. They have pretty well organized themselves. You don't find that many stand alones in the business. You see, they are constantly under attack by religious groups, women's groups and other goody-two-shoes outfits. They have banded together, pooling legal resources to survive. It is possible that one of them did this, but we agreed it was probably one of the B grade studios, and I use the term loosely.

"These studios have a small office in town. The man I talked to has some connections with a couple of them," Joel hesitated, then, "He asked for one of the two photos you gave me."

"Did you give him my phone number, Joel?"

"No, I don't believe I did. I thought that I would act as your contact on this, you know. Screen the information."

"Could you tell me who it was you gave the photo to? I've been harassed by other people on this story. I'd like to know if I have a new problem or if the old one has caught up with me."

"Tell you what, Rick. Give me a couple of hours on this, okay? I don't feel comfortable releasing his name, for the same reason I didn't give out your number."

"All right, Joel. A couple of hours then call me."

"You got it, Rick. Sorry if something's coming down on you. Let's keep in touch." Joel hung up, leaving Rick a dead line.

That pretty well summed up his feelings about now. Deadline. No word from Lawrence on Sarina, no cammo dudes in white Cherokees following him, only a whispered voice verging in threats. Hopefully, the mysterious voice would call back. Maybe Joel Linstrum would have a lead. Right now, Rick was in a sit and wait position. Something he wasn't really good at. His approach was more of the polite bull-in-a-china-shop. Ask permission first, then run amuck.

After calling seven more studios, Rick didn't know anymore than when he started. Feeling frustrated, he decided to go out for a while. As he drove around, he checked his mirrors to see if he could spot a tail. Although he wasn't experienced at this sort of thing, he thought he should be able to spot a white Cherokee.

Upon his return, Rick parked two blocks away from the hotel and approached it from different directions to see if he could spot a stakeout of some sort. He looked for a van with dark side windows that could conceal hidden cameras, or curtains that blocked off the driver's compartment. One or two people sitting in a car could also indicate a stake out. To the best of his knowledge, he was not being followed.

Rick felt paranoid. Every bum, every face behind closed curtains, was looking at him.

Back in the room, the message light blinked. Rick dialed the office and discovered he had two messages. One was from Joel, the other would call back at three.

Linstrum gave Rick an address and a name. John Pavolli's office was down near the waterfront, close to the fishing pier. Pavolli Productions specialized in low-grade science fiction films with lots of cheap nudity. They hired rundown out-of-work union discharged crewmembers, and Linstrum heard that the man Rick was looking for had been associated with John Pavolli in the past.

Rick checked his watch, did some quick figuring and decided he could visit Pavolli's and still be back in time for the three o'clock phone call.

Pavolli Productions was in an old waterfront warehouse that had been renovated years ago as part of a historical restoration project which was sidetracked. A wooden staircase that had seen much better days led to a second story landing hardly large enough for two people.

On the door was a sign announcing the Pavolli Productions Co. Paint peeled from the door, exposing sections of rusting metal. The window was covered in a thick layer of dirt making it slightly more opaque then a sheet of plywood.

Rick opened the door slowly, peering around its edge. A small desk stood just inside to the right. The dishwater blonde behind the gray metal desk looked up from her vintage Crown Royal typewriter in surprise. Quickly she looked across the room. A man stood silhouetted against a large window that looked out across the bay.

"Ah, may I help you, sir?" the blonde asked. Clearly, she was not used to greeting strange visitors.

"Yes, is Mister Pavolli in?" Rick looked from the secretary to the man at the other desk. The entire office was one large room, sparsely furnished with some file cabinets, two desks, and a small refrigerator off in a corner and an old dining table under the second window. Movie posters littered the table.

"Ah," she hesitated, again glancing across the room.

"Now don't tell me that you're here alone, miss..." Rick looked around, no nameplate. He noticed that the desk held only the old typewriter and an old radial dial phone. Not even a message pad, paper clip or pencil graced the desktop.

"No, well, yes, he's here. I mean," She looked back again, flustered.

Pavolli came around his desk. He was a short man, barely clearing five feet. Rick guessed his weight at close to two hundred, maybe more. Sweat stains under the arms distracted from the man's loud floral Hawaiian style shirt.

"It's all right, Hon," the man said to his secretary. He held out his hand to Rick, "I'm John Pavolli, how can I help you?"

Taking his hand, Rick replied, "I'm Rick Prescott. I represent a magazine and I would like to talk to you about your films and some of your people."

"Oh, well now, that sounds interesting, what magazine is this?"

"Real Saucer. Normally, we only deal with UFO's and stories of supposedly true abductions, but I'm trying to talk the editor into a story on the impact of the Sci-Fi films on people's sense of reality."

"My, my, that sounds right down my alley. You already know, I assume, that my trade is high quality, low budget science fiction films. Have a seat, Mr. Prescott. How about something to drink? Hon, bring a couple bottles of brew over here." Pavolli motioned him to a cheap wooden straight back chair he dragged out from a corner.

Rick accepted the beer reluctantly, although he was surprised to see it was a little known import. Whatever else, John Pavolli had good taste in beer. He sat down and pulled out a small notebook.

"May we start with the interview? I don't want to take up any more of your time than necessary, especially since I came in unannounced."

"Go ahead, Prescott, you can see that I'm really not that busy." Pavolli said, waving a hand, taking in the large near empty room.

For the next ten minutes, Rick questioned Pavolli about his business. Finally he got around to discussing some of the people he had working for him.

"Do you have anyone in particular doing your special effects, or do you hire out for each film?'

Pavolli sighed, "Now-a-days I have to hire for each new production, but I used to have a damn good man. Let's see, I believe we worked together for five or six years, then suddenly, he said he had an offer too good to refuse and left."

"Really, who was the guy? Would I recognize his name in the credits of any movies?"

"Donald Dyba, one hell of a special effects, or FX man. He came straight from college into the industry. Before me, however, he worked for one of the big special effects shops in town but then had a falling out. He wanted his name to appear in all the credits. He said he was worth more than they were paying him, which was true, but then he really pissed off a big shot in the industry and was blackballed."

Rick's interest peaked. "Do you remember what he did? Do you have any pictures of him?"

"Yes, someplace around here. Say, Hon, find our photo album will you?" Pavolli snapped his fingers and waved at his secretary. "Now, what did he do? He was caught hiding the weenie with the guy's wife, mistress, and seventeen-year-old daughter. See what I mean. He was some kind of FX man," Pavolli laughed, finished his beer, and called for another.

Hon sat the fresh beer and the photo album on Pavolli's desk, then returned to her reception desk. As she sat down, Rick saw a movie magazine magically appear.

"Let me see now," Pavolli said as he flipped back and forth, sipping his fresh beer. "Did I tell you that Donald insisted on making all of his monsters near life-size? Yeah, he was freaky that way, almost as if each one was a part of him. He was always drawing different ones, but I kept telling him that his aliens were not scary enough. His looked almost childlike, while his other monsters were nightmares come to life."

Rick finished his beer and sat the bottle on the floor by his chair. "Did he actually make any of the aliens that you know of?"

"Here he is, with one of the screamer stars." Pavolli passed Rick the album. A young man stood facing the camera. In his left hand, he held what looked like a plastic or rubber monster with a hideous face and huge teeth. The man's other hand was around a pretty blonde wearing only the bottom half of a string bikini and a large smile.

"You said his name is Donald Dyba?' Rick said stifling his anxiety.

"That's him. He slept with more bimbos that anyone I know."

"When did you see him last? Do you know where he is now?"

"Three years ago. He said he was finally going to get paid what he was worth. Last I heard, he was in the Southwest somewhere."

"Do you know where?" Rick had recognized Dyba as their man. The one in the mirror. Now he wanted to know where the man was. "Any idea as to what state or city?"

"Wait a minute, Prescott. What is this? Suddenly we're not talking about me and my productions, but a burned out FX man. What is you story really on?"

Rick backpedaled hurriedly, asking more

questions about Pavolli's films. Twenty minutes later, Rick wrapped up the interview, promising to keep in touch. As he left the office, Pavolli told him that he had heard that Dyba now lived somewhere in New Mexico and wasn't working that much anymore.

## *12*

Ten minutes after three in the afternoon, the motel phone rang. Rick waited until the third ring to pick up the receiver. The same voice from the earlier call was on the other end. "I understand you're looking for me. I'm ready to meet you."

"I still need a name before we meet," Rick said.

"Don't you know it? I bet you do. Ten o'clock tonight. Your favorite seat on the pier." A click, followed by a dial tone.

Rick was sure Pavolli said Donald Dyba the FX man was somewhere in the Southwest, yet here was somebody professing to be Dyba. At the same time, from the statement about the pier, Rick learned that he had been under surveillance; his best guess would be since he came to Los Angeles. Only by showing up at the meeting could Rick be sure.

Two hours before the meeting, Rick checked in with Lawrence.

"Lawrence, have you heard from Sarina yet?"

"She's fine, Rick. Traffic kept her from calling last night. She has visited two separate offices. She doesn't have any leads yet, but she is still working at it."

"I've got our man. His name is Donald Dyba and he is or was a special-effects man. He is supposed to be damned good, according to one producer. Supposedly he is living in the Southwest, Pavolli mentioned New Mexico. That's all I have."

"Good enough, I'll get Beth and Layne on it as soon as they get in. Since they kept getting stonewalled, they decided to come back early. They should arrive here later tonight."

"I got a funny phone call a while ago. I'm not sure what's happening."

"Tell me about it," Lawrence said.

"Well, this male voice says he is the guy I'm looking for. Then he sets up a meeting out on a pier."

"He actually said that he was Dyba?"

"No. He never mentioned a name, just that he's the guy I'm looking for," Rick said. "Oh, he also said that we would meet on the pier I was on earlier."

"Somebody's been watching you," Lawrence said. "You better cover your ass. Do you have a weapon?"

"No. Didn't bring one since I flew out here."

Lawrence gave him a name and phone number to call.

After his discussion with Lawrence, Rick visited one of Lawrence's LA contacts and purchased a weapon. Although he had fired a similar pistol in the past, he wasn't as comfortable with it as he was with his .380 Beretta semi-automatic. By eight o'clock Rick was enjoying a light meal at the Lobster Shack. He shifted in his chair and felt the weight of the newly acquired thirty-eight-caliber revolver in his right coat pocket.

At eight-forty-five, Rick dropped some bills on the table and headed for the bathroom, but instead of stopping there, he went through the kitchen, exiting by the backdoor. Rick turned left in the alleyway and dropped behind the first trash bin he saw.

Hunched back in the corner created by the bins and the buildings brick wall, Rick waited for five minutes. The alley was littered with enough trash that anyone moving around would have to make noise.

Finally, deciding that no one was following him, Rick moved out of the alley and headed down to the pier. A fog was descending on the area and hung above the streetlights, lending the pier an almost esoteric atmosphere. As far as he could see, no one was watching the pier. Keeping to the shadows he moved pass the snack bar and into the deep darkness cast by the building.

Only two lights worked out on the pier. One was a low wattage bulb at the very end, and the other was a flickering overhead day glow. A man and boy were cleaning their catch across from Rick. Otherwise, the pier appeared deserted.

The father and son left shortly before ten. Their footsteps hardly faded when the existing lights flickered and went out. The fog obscured what little moonlight there was. Rick moved deeper into the shadows.

Twice Rick heard boards in the walkway creak as they accepted a person's weight. Waves lapping the pilings almost covered the soft footsteps. Faintly, the cough and sputter of a small boat engine whispered in from the bay. Running lights, one very faint green for starboard, or the right side of a boat, and one weak white light in front showed the position of the craft.

Rick made it out to be about twenty feet long

with a small cabin. Probably someone is returning from a day of fishing or heading out for night trolling. The boat took his mind away from the footsteps for a moment. Next thing he heard was very close. A gruff voice spoke softly, "What? Where?"

Cold settled into the pit of Rick's stomach as he heard the slide of an automatic pistol jacking a round into the chamber. From the sound, it was a large caliber weapon, not a small easily concealed handgun. His hand slid into his jacket pocked, withdrawing the revolver. Now, he wished he had bought more than six bullets.

Suddenly, the wood by Rick's left ear splintered with a thunk. A second thunk followed almost immediately. What the hell, thought Rick? Gunshots? If so, not from the man or men on the pier. The apparent angle was wrong.

Bright lights flashed up off the water into Rick's eyes, blinding him. Another thunk followed the first, only this time closer. The original powerful light was rising and falling while another from the opposite side of the boat was swinging back and forth trying to locate him. The motorboat was firing on him. Evidently, since the shooter came so close, he was using a night scope, which gathered all the ambient light and allowed the user to see practically in total darkness. Shaking his head, Rick became aware of more beams of light coming from behind him on the pier. Not only was he under attack from the boat, but apparently, somebody on the pier was also looking for him.

Rick dropped flat on the deck. Cocking the pistol, he slithered forward, trying to get between the boat and the men on the pier. He was hoping the bench seat would provide some cover. Two shots came from his left on the pier. One tore into the wooden decking, and the other creased the back of his right calf.

Stifling a yelp of pain, Rick grunted. As he neared the wooden seat, he rolled on his back, raised his head, sighted down his arm and fired twicc at the flashlight. The flashlight dropped and somebody grunted loudly. What sounded like a body thumped on the deck. He rolled to his right, away from his muzzle blasts. Immediately, he crawled behind the seat then fired twice more at the boat. More gunshots rang out, one splintered the backrest on the seat, and the others went wide of their mark.

Rick heard another moan then a body hit the deck, as he fired his last two bullets at the boat. The light went out with a shattering of glass. Turning to his side, he listened. No other sound came from the pier. Hoping that the man was alone, Rick rose to a crouch and scooted across the decking. Ahead of him two different shapes lay on the pier. He stood up quickly and limped over to the closest body. He picked up the man's Glock nineteen nine-millimeter semi-automatic pistol then rolled him to the edge of the pier.

He went back, retrieved the flashlight, waved it around, and in a deep voice he called out. "Prescott, give it up. Now." Rick shouted. "No, don't," then fired into the water. Again, he limped toward the body, flashing the light toward the men in the boat. He kicked the first body over the side. As it splashed into the water, Rick called out again.

"Damn, he rolled off the pier. I think I got him."

"You okay? We heard some more gunshots up there." A man from the boat asked.

"Yea, Prescott couldn't shoot worth shit."

"We'll look for the body. Catch you later," came the reply from the boat.

Rick figured he had made some time. Not much, but hopefully enough to get the hell out of town. He searched the second body, removing ID and money from his wallet. Not bothering to check either one at the moment, he stuffed them into his pocket. Almost everything he needed was in his Wagoneer, safely stored in Lawrence's garage. Only some clothing and toiletry remained in his room. His notebook with all his research in it was in a small carry case in the back seat of his rental car.

Sliding the automatic into the back of his slacks, Rick limped back to where he parked the compact car. The rental was gone. Rick knew where he parked it and it wasn't there. He looked up and down the street. He was sure this is where he left it. Damn, there went the notebook. Every bit of information he had collected. Somehow, he needed to duplicate it, but first he needed to get away from the pier and L. A., if possible. He slipped into the shadows of a building and leaned against the cool brick deep in thought.

Searching his pockets, he came up with a little over one hundred and fifty dollars in cash plus the seventy-five from the gunman on the pier. The ID listed the gunman as a security agent for a local detective agency. Rick thought it was probably bogus, or a cover agency for the government. He knew better than to call a cab to pick him up. Just as soon as those guys find the body, they would realize Rick's trick and be hot on his trail. Information on a taxi pick and drop would be simple for an agency to acquire. That left him only one alternative. Walk. He knew his wound was only superficial, but he could see that he had been losing blood. Two blocks away, his right leg gave out on him.

Rick moved into an alley and sat down with his back a brick wall. He pulled out his shirttail and ripped off a long piece of material. Rolling up his pants leg, he gingerly felt the wound. The area was very tender but not that painful. He pulled his handkerchief from his back pocket, folded it twice and using the shirt as a tourniquet, applied a pressure bandage to the wound.

Rats scurried around trashcans further down the alley. Rick rested for ten minutes then moved on. Whenever he saw a car approach, he ducked into the closest doorway. The only people out this time of night were most probably the gunmen looking for him.

A Bay Area Transit Authority bus was coming his way. Rick hailed the bus and climbed on. After depositing the correct change, he moved to a bench near the rear exit and slid low in the uncomfortable seat, facing away from the window. Only three or four other people were on the bus, each one either asleep or too involved in their own problems to pay him any attention.

Half an hour later, the bus passed an all-night discount store. Rick pulled the bell cord in the next block and got off. Trying not to hobble, he made his way back to the store. Looking around carefully, he hid the gun behind a large trash barrel near the entrance. Once inside, he bought a small travel toiletry bag, a change of underwear, a pair of jeans, western shirt and jeans jacket.

Almost as a second thought, Rick picked up a cheap spiral notebook, pen, backpack and Buck Boy Scout knife. Outside, Rick reclaimed the pistol and went around to the side of the building. He found a dark area where he changed into his new clothes.

Ten minutes later, Rick re-entered the store and went to the bathroom. Quickly, he shaved and washed up. A twenty-four hour fast-food shop was franchised into a corner of the store. There he bought a cup of coffee, borrowed a telephone directory, and made notes of everything he remembered.

Two travel services advertised cheap round trip gambling packages to Las Vegas. Rick copied down the numbers hoping one would have a trip leaving early in the morning. Many of them left late afternoon and arrived in Las Vegas around ten that night. Just to be on the safe side, he copied down the Greyhound number also. By now, it was midnight and Rick needed a place to stay. Rick's thoughts became fuzzy and suddenly he was very tired.

\* \* \*

"Hey buddy, wake up. Can't let you stay here any longer." A middle-aged man gently nudged Rick's shoulder. "The day manager catches you here, he's liable to call the cops."

Rick woke with a start. It took some time before he understood what the man had said. He looked at his watch. Six forty-five. He had fallen asleep in the store. "Ah, sorry. Mind if I have breakfast first?"

"Can't give it to you, friend. Sorry."

Rick pulled out his wallet and handed the man five dollars. "This should cover it, I'm going to splash some water on my face."

"Sure, friend. It should be ready in a couple of minutes."

Rick located a pay phone, and made some calls. When he returned, the manager was sitting at his table. A tray of food sat there, coffee steaming.

"Thanks, and thanks for letting me sleep here." Rick noted his change piled in a corner of the tray.

"You didn't look like the street people who usually try to crash here, so I figured as long as no one complained, I'd let it go. Sometimes we are all down and out. Isn't anything serious, I hope?"

"No, just a misunderstanding," Rick wasn't about to say how big a misunderstanding. "If I can get to the bus station, then I think I will be able to straighten it all out."

"If that will do it, I can drop you. My shift is over as soon as the day man comes in. Usually, he is twenty minutes late, not in a hurry are you?"

Rick wasn't sure if he was in a hurry or not. By now, they knew he was still alive and would be looking for him. If they knew enough to find him out here, maybe they knew he would return to Albuquerque. His biggest problem, was how to get back there safely, and pass on the information he had.

"No, I'm not in a hurry. Just holler and I'll be

123

ready."

"Sure thing," the manager patted him on the shoulder and went back to the counter, checking up on his crew.

Rick asked to be dropped close to the bus terminal, claiming a desire for some exercise as his excuse. Instead, he tried to look for another stakeout. Actually, Rick was not sure any more if he could spot one or not. Last night's near fiasco kept replaying itself in his mind.

After paying for his ticket, Rick moved to the most crowded section of the terminal, theorizing that whoever was after him would not want to create a scene in public. All he needed was to wait out the next two hours.

The motion and low vibrations of the bus quickly put Rick back to sleep. Since the seats next to him and on the other side of the aisle were empty, he relaxed. Most people boarding the Vegas bound bus were retired types living on a tight budget. Fare was cheap and the bus made one stop where those who were hungry could buy cold sandwiches and soda.

Once in Las Vegas, Rick bought a ticket for an all day excursion to Laughlin, Nevada, another fast growing casino town. From there, it was an easy trip across the Colorado River on one of the casino's courtesy boat shuttles to Bullhead City, Arizona. Connections were quickly made to get him on a Greyhound bound for Albuquerque, through Kingman, Arizona.

Looking out the window, Rick saw desolate areas of reddish desert. Hogans, Navajo Indian houses, dotted the isolated region. By now, he knew he was not being followed, but his sense of unease would not go away.

During the half-hour rest stop in Holbrook, Arizona, Rick walked two blocks away and used the phone at a Chevron station. Lawrence answered on the third ring.

"Rick, Rick. Where are you buddy? I've been waiting. Your call is overdue."

"It's a long story, Lawrence. I'll have to call back later. After my next call, pick me up where we all had dinner together."

"Okay, Rick." Lawrence paused. "The rest of the group is back. Sarina is fine. She's a real looker, Rick."

"Great. Say hi to everyone. Give Sarina a hug. I'll call again." Rick hung up, searching the crowd for anyone paying him attention

* * *

Dinner at the El Sombre restaurant was always good, but tonight Rick enjoyed it more than usual. Sarina sat across from him. He was more enthralled with her beauty then he was with the gourmet Mexican food.

Lawrence would not swear that they were not followed to the restaurant, although he agreed with Rick that a devious route back would most likely lose all but the most tenacious tail. Rick's story was unsettling. Everyone still found it hard to believe that the U. S. government would secretly try to kill one of its own citizens.

"I still find a lot of this hard to believe," Sarina said, going back to the Roswell story. "Our government forcing people to ignore something that happened to them, or worse, lie about it."

"You have to remember many of the Roswell crash witnesses swear that soldiers threatened them with death if they spoke out," Lawrence said.

"Threatened to kill them?"

"What would you think if someone told you that your bones would never be found in the desert?" Rick asked.

"That's pretty serious." Beth nodded.

"You're right. There were, and still are, airline pilots accused of flying while intoxicated when they report any aerial phenomena."

"Don't forget the air traffic controllers who try to substantiate a pilot's claim."

"They are usually accused of illegal use of a controlled substance." Lawrence sipped his beer.

"In New York, in three different cases, policemen and firefighters have had their jobs and pensions threatened." Rick held up three fingers emphasizing his point.

"Why don't they just come out and arrest you for murdering a police officer or government agent?" Sarina pointed to Rick. "You're now responsible for four or five deaths."

"Probably because then they would have to admit that this top-secret agency exists. Then they would need to explain why their agents can use extreme sanctions whenever somebody torques their crank," Lawrence said.

"They could just say you murdered some dumb jerk off the street, couldn't they? I mean, can't they make up some fake ID for those guys or something?" Sarina frowned.

"I think those guys already have some fake ID. Their ID probably shows them to be employed by the FBI, Treasury, DEA or NSA." Beth munched on the last of her food.

Rick nodded, flipping an ID card on the table. "Here's one."

"Those agencies probably just cut checks for these people but don't even see them. Even an agency like that is so bogged down in bureaucracy that the right hand doesn't know what the left one is doing." Layne turned the card over and over in his hand.

Conversation quickly moved on to Donald Dyba. Layne and Beth could not find anyone by that name in New Mexico. Their contacts at the Department of Motor Vehicles searched the whole state. Only one resource was left, and it wasn't very promising. State tax records. Since New Mexico had a state income tax anyone working in the state would be in their computer.

Should he be using an alias, they realized there would be no way to trace him. According to the movie producer, he was possibly living in southern New Mexico. Looking at a map, that left only a couple dozen towns. A list of these towns included Roswell, Alamogordo, Socorro, Lordsburg, Holloman Air Force Base, Corona, Vaughn and other smaller communities.

Rick snapped his fingers, "Well, well, I believe we can cut this list at least in half right now."

"Sarina's suppose to be the psychic one, not you. What do you base your supposition on?" Beth asked.

"I think I follow Rick," Layne nodded in agreement, "Yeah, I agree."

"Come on now guys. Fill us in. What gives?" Beth looks questionably to Sarina, who smiled vainly and shrugged.

Layne motioned Rick to go ahead.

"Many of these towns have had something to do with UFO's. So, I think we will find him in one of them."

"Why? Just because they are somehow mixed up with UFO's, why would he be in one of them?" Beth asked.

Sarina sat up suddenly, a smile beaming in every direction. "Yeah, I agree. Suppose, just suppose, he came across something while he was making that fake autopsy."

"Come on now. That's too far fetched." Beth slammed her palms on the table rattling silverware. "Here we go again. Insight into world mysteries. A burned out, special effects man puts together an alien autopsy film then suddenly, sees the light and comes out to one of the Meccas of flying saucers to wait for E. T. to return. That's bullshit."

"Maybe not, Beth. Look at if from his viewpoint. Donald may have talked himself into believing in aliens or flying saucers, or maybe whoever financed him might have shown him something to change his mind."

"For lack of any reasonable ideas, I'll play along. What sites do we have in New Mexico?" Beth sighed.

"There's Aztec, where a very questionable

crash occurred, but it is too far north. Dulce, even further north, where the ground is suppose to hum, possibly from an underground tunnel system containing aliens doing biological experiments," Rick said.

"Don't forget the Luna Area." Layne wagged a finger in Rick's direction.

"Yeah, there were three electrical blackouts that affected El Paso, Texas, and all the way up to central New Mexico. One even got us here in Albuquerque," Lawrence added.

"Los Alamos, still too far north, supposedly works on reverse engineering of alien technology."

"What's that, Rick?" Sarina asked.

"That's when technicians and engineers have a space craft and take it apart piece by piece to see the hows, why, etc. of the ship, hoping to learn enough to make one of our own."

"Can that really be done?" Sarina pushed her plate away.

"Yes, it can," Lawrence said. "The military has been doing it with weapon systems from other countries for years. Computer companies and other state of the art high tech businesses have also been at it, successfully too."

"It looks as if New Mexico is the capital of UFO sightings."

"Oh, no, but for a short period of time, when the early atomic bomb was being tested, there was an unusual amount of activity in the area. There are lots more places. Kirkland Air Base right here supposedly has a large underground hanger with a couple of saucers, but in reality people probably saw the Stealth bomber before it was released to the public.

"In 1964, a sheriff's deputy was supposed to have seen a landed saucer up close along with two aliens. This was in Socorro. Also in Socorro, back at the same time as the Roswell crash, there were reports of another crash on the plains of San Agustin, not very far west of the town," Rick said.

"Some people have said that that crash is or was related to the one in Roswell. Most Ufologists though say that the Socorro crash never happened. They say a guy named George Armstrong just made it up, or was confused with the Roswell case." Layne moved his drink around the table.

"That makes sense. Or Donald may be in Roswell. That would explain how the cammo dudes got on our tail quickly," Beth said.

"Possibly, but I don't remember ever seeing him around the museum and I'm sure if he went there very often, I would have seen him." Layne tapped his finger on the table.

"Well, we need to start our search someplace," Sarina looked around the table, "but I'm not too happy about going back to Roswell right now."

Layne and Beth decided to take copies of Dyba's picture and return to Roswell. Sarina and Rick would cover Vaughn, Corona, and other small towns all the way to Alamogordo, probably the largest town in their search area.

\* \* \*

Early the next morning, the group loaded both vehicles. Just as they finished packing, Lawrence approached Rick. Beth, Sarina and Layne were inside the house fixing lunches.

"Rick, I'm not sure what you guys are letting yourselves in for, but I want you to be fully prepared." Lawrence said, as he handed Rick a quiver of arrows and one of his compound bows.

Rick shoved them away, "I've got my survival rifle and the Beretta, Lawrence. Thanks anyway."

"Oh, no you don't. Sometimes the silent approach is better. You will take these." Lawrence shoved them into Rick's hands. "Oh, by the way, I've created some special fireworks for you." He handed Rick a bag.

Rick looked inside. He saw two cans of hair spray, a high-powered BB gun and a piece of paper. As he withdrew the paper, he could see a simple drawing of a gun, the line of a projectile striking the bottom of the can and the words "stand back!"

With a frown on his face, Rick took everything out to the Wagoneer, stowing it in the back under his frazzled blanket. "What ever you say, Lawrence, what ever you say."

## *13*

The narrow two-lane highway flowed against the eastern slope of the Manzano Mountains. Scrub Oak and Alligator juniper stood regal in otherwise short grassland. Gently rolling hills broke up the countryside. Back up the side of the mountains to the west, small stands of Ponderosa Pine led to more heavily forested canyons. Lone pines or juniper stood majestically on the crest, defying nature's wrath.

Twice, Rick had to slow down for cattle on the highway. He was still amazed at the health exhibited by cattle in this region. Scrub brush should yield scrawny cattle, but most of the animals he saw were shiny-coated with deep, full stomachs. That was just one more of the incongruities of the Southwest. Another was winter, itself. A Norther could blow across the high desert dropping snow and hail, then two or three nights later, a crystal clear night could offer temperatures as high as fifty degrees. Almost short sleeve weather in this region.

Cresting a hill outside of Corona, Sarina spotted a highway patrol car; the car flashed its headlights once, but did not pursue or take any other action. Rick told Sarina that quite often if the officer didn't have his radar operating, but thought you might be over the speed limit, you'd get a flash of light like that as a warning.

Corona was another one of the small highway

towns that dotted the southwest like many that spring up along the highway. Sometimes, they would stretch a couple of miles along one or two roads but would only be a couple of blocks deep to either side of the blacktop. This one grew along the highway and a railroad track that slanted across one side of town.

Corona's population couldn't be over a couple of thousand including farms or ranches surrounding the area. Sarina spotted the post office first, it's front a light tan stucco. Two large blue mailboxes stood curbside. Between them a flagpole proudly displayed the American flag, next to it hung the Zia of New Mexico. Five slots were painted onto the parking lot, overlooked by a large plate glass window. Inside stood a long bank of post office boxes. One narrow window could be seen from the parking lot.

Rick's Wagoneer was the only vehicle in the lot, but two Hispanic women stood in line at the window. Both were large, typical of women who spend a lot of time in the kitchen cooking and caring for a brood of children. One wore a long full dress that hid her bulk in its folds, while the other one wore tight fitting knit slacks with stirrups and a tee-shirt too small for her. The tee-shirt advertised a Ford dealership up in Santa Rosa further north on the highway.

"Look," Sarina whispered, "our pictures aren't on the wall." She giggled.

"Yet," Rick whispered back, frowning at her, "that's the operative word, yet." The two women moved off toward the post boxes speaking softly in Spanish.

"Hello," Rick looked at the postal worker's

nametag. "Alicia, I wonder if you can help me?"

"I'm here to help, when I can." Alicia smiled back.

Sarina spoke up, her award-winning smile entering the cordiality competition. "We need to find this man. He probably moved into the area two to three years ago."

"Why are you looking for him? I didn't catch that part."

"He is, or was, married to my sister, and we need to locate him. She's in the hospital and keeps calling for the creep," Sarina said.

"Then you should have his address, shouldn't you?" Alicia's brows furrowed.

"No one has heard from him in the last three years. He told a drinking buddy of his that he liked this part of New Mexico and wouldn't mind moving out here," Rick said.

"Let me take a good look at that picture."

"The picture is three to four years old. He's probably changed some."

"Well, young lady, I sure haven't seen this guy around here. If he gets mail, then it must be by carrier pigeon because everyone around here checks with me at least once a month. Our route carrier don't handle any large packages since his back went out on him two years ago this Thanksgiving, but he wouldn't know anyone I don't. So he would have to come here. I can pretty much say that he doesn't live anywhere nearby."

"Thank you," Sarina said.

They piled back into the Wagoneer and headed south. The highway wound its way over a series of hills and finally dropped to the edge of a long, wide valley. Hugging the western slope of the mountain range to the east, the narrow two-lane road snaked into the town of Carrizozo.

Rick pointed out the crossroads that led back into the mountains to Capitan and eventually to Roswell where their odyssey began. The Wagoneer steered past the small cafe where the four of them met after fleeing Laynes home.

"Let's find some place to get a drink," Sarina said.

"There is a Tastee Freeze back near the Chamber of Commerce," Rick said.

A small white building with large picture windows on three sides advertised floats, shakes, burgers and fries. A metal awning extended fifty feet in front of the building, which sat sideways to the road. Any resemblance of paving disappeared long ago, leaving gravel and dirt in the parking area.

Inside were a booth and two small tables with three chairs crowded around each one. Two girls stood behind the counter. One was talking to someone on the phone, the other one wiped down a piece of equipment, while aggressively chomping on a wad of gum.

"Can I help you?" the gum chewer asked.

"Yes, how about a strawberry shake and..." Rick turned toward Sarina questioning.

"Some fries and a diet coke," Sarina finished.

"OK, it'll be a couple of minutes on the fries," the girl rang up the order. "That'll be four-eighty-six. Have a seat and I'll bring you your order."

Rick paid while Sarina chose a table and sat

looking out the window. When Rick joined her, she pointed across the street. A building faced the street. Two small poplars sat on either side of a flagpole. Raised white letters spelled out County Sheriff. An old beat up Ford station wagon sat out front.

When the waitress brought their order, they noticed the other girl was still on the phone.

"Thank you, do you know if anyone is at the Sheriff's? There's only one car in the lot," Rick said.

"Oh yeah, Mrs. Casavantes is there all day. That beat up old car is hers. She's had it forever. Why? You got a problem?" the girl asked.

"Not a problem, but we need some information. We're looking for an old friend," Rick said.

"In that case, you want to talk to ol' lady Casavantes. I think she saw Billy the Kid ride through here. That's how old she is."

Sarina chuckled. Shaking her head, "Now that would be old. Well over a hundred years old."

"Oh, she's not that old, I mean..."

"I know she's old like your grandmother, right?"

"Yeah, that's it, if she was alive, that's how old she would be. Anyway, she knows everything and everybody for at least a hundred miles around here."

Thanking the girl, Rick and Sarina shared the fries and since it was getting to be mid-afternoon, discussed where to spend the night. They figured they could probably visit everyone they needed to here and in Tularosa before dark, then drive into Alamogordo for the night.

Rick and Sarina watched an old lady, possibly in her seventies, step out of the sheriff's office and close the door. She wrapped a long tweed jacket around herself before cautiously crossing the highway.

The girl who served them called out an order to the other girl, ending the order by announcing the eminent arrival of Mrs. Casavantes. When the old lady entered, their waitress handed her a steaming cup of coffee.

"Hiya Mrs. C. How are you doing today?'

"Fine, honey, fine. Things are little slow right now, you know." The old woman's voice quaked.

"These folks are here to see you. I told them how you are the expert on everyone and everything in the whole area."

"You called me a big ol' gossip, did you?" Mrs. Casavantes turned to Rick and Sarina and gave them a wink. The woman's eyes twinkled.

"No, not big, just an old gossip." The girl countered. The other one was back on the phone after warming a large brownie.

"Here you go, Mrs. C." The waitress said set the plate at Rick and Sarina's table.

"And what if I don't want to sit with these folks, huh?"

"Sure you do. You know how much you like to talk about the town and its people."

"There you go again, hon, calling me an old gossip." Mrs. C. winked again.

"You just be nice and talk to these people here, but if you start in on some of the juicy stuff, call me, okay?"

"Honey, you're way too young to hear that stuff. Why, one of us would blush something fierce."

"It wouldn't be me, Mrs. C." The waitress bussed the woman's cheek, then went back to the counter.

"Kids these days." Casavantes, said, shook her head but with a grin extending from ear to ear. She turned to Rick and Sarina. "Do you want to talk to the Sheriff's office, or me?'

Rick was amazed at how quickly the woman switched from fun to serious. He turned to Sarina, waiting for her to answer.

"Mrs. Casavantes," Sarina began.

"Mrs. C, hon, everyone calls me Mrs. C."

"OK, uh, Mrs. C., my friend and I are looking for an old acquaintance that may have moved into the Carrizozo area about three years ago." Sarina slid the photo from her purse.

"Oh, I left my glasses in the station, hon. Put that away. Describe him to me. I can follow descriptions very well. I work over the radio and phone a lot, you know."

Sarina gave the woman the best description she could. She had to guess at height and weight since they had never seen him in person. Mrs. C. hesitated a few minutes, sipped her coffee, and thought with her eyes closed.

"Hum, no, I don't recall anyone fitting that description moving in around here, no. Two young couples have moved onto ranches in the east of town but nobody like that."

"Well, thanks for your time, Mrs. C. We really need to find Donald. Guess we'll have to head on down to Tularosa," Sarina said.

"Oh, dear, I can save you some time there, my sister's niece, Anna lives there. Let me run back to the office and call her. Then in half an hour or so, we'll know. Give me the photo, hon." Mrs. Casavantes picked up the picture and wrapped her coat around her thin body and left.

Rick and Sarina discussed their next move. Evidently, Mrs. Casavantes could save them time, but she would probably want them to keep her company. Sarina preferred sitting here drinking diet Coke and having a pleasant conversation with the lonely woman to getting in and out of the car every five minutes.

Clouds were scudding across the sky. A cold wind was rustling leaves in the skeleton of the surrounding cottonwoods. If the wind picked up any more, whole armies of brown leaves would scamper across the highway invading the well kept lawns on the other side.

Their waitress called over to their table, "Hey, lady, Mrs. C. is on the phone. She says to stay put for a while. She has an accident to take care of."

"Hey back, thanks," Sarina said, and turned to Rick. "Well, it's better than getting out in that weather. I can feel the cold in here."

"You're right, but I'd rather be stuck someplace with a better menu."

An hour and three cups of coffee later, Rick was on edge, from nerves or caffeine, he wasn't sure. "Why doesn't she call? We could have been down there already, instead of sitting around here wasting time."

"Calm down, Rick. Do you really want to get out in that weather? It must have dropped fifteen degrees out there since we came in. Look at that wind whipping around."

"Let's give it ten minutes then we'll cross over to the office and check with Mrs. C. Depending on what she says, we're out of here." Sarina patted his hand. "We need to get the picture back."

"No, Sarina, I still have a couple more copies."

Minutes later, the phone rang. Their waitress called them again, "Hey folks, Mrs. C. says her sister's niece doesn't know of anybody fitting the description."

"Tell her thanks, we need to hit the road to Alamogordo now." Sarina said as Rick stood, dropping five dollars on the table.

Wind buffeted the Wagoneer as it headed south on highway fifty-four towards the moderate sized town of Alamogordo. Heavy dark clouds filled the heavens, casting forbidding shadows into every nook and cranny in the long north south valley.

"Rick, is the road to Alamogordo any better than what we came here on?" Sarina asked.

"No, it's even worse. It's narrower and there are no shoulders on most of it. Why?"

"Well, with the weather deteriorating the way it is, and a bad road ahead, why we don't just find ourselves a motel to stay warm in?" Sarina asked.

"That suits me fine." Rick said, wondering about her suggestion.

As if in answer, a sign advertising an RV Park and motel one mile down the road caught their attention. The motel sprawled on a hill overlooking the valley to the west. Two motor homes and a couple of travel trailers looked as if they were staying for a while. One man was fighting the wind trying to put his awning away. The backside of the building was exposed to the full force of the brewing storm.

Rick took the last room they had. One queen sized bed. Well, he thought, Sarina gets the bed and he gets a quilt and the floor. There have been playful insinuations, but nothing more. This night was going to be eventful, one way or another.

## *14*

Beth turned to Layne and stomped her foot, "You're not helping the situation."

"What do you mean?"

"Flashing Dyba's picture! That's what," she said. "If a friend of his sees we're looking for him, they'll tell Dyba. Then he's outta here."

"All right, Beth," Layne sighed. "We'll try it your way."

Three hours later, they were back at Layne's house with no better luck than before. Their visit to the Roswell Daily Record, the newspaper, was useless. Layne's friend couldn't find Dyba's name on the circulation list. The post office refused to help without more information, and city records revealed nothing. Beth took two Dos Equis beers from the refrigerator and opened them.

"I should kick your ass, Layne." Beth spat.

"Why?" Layne said.

"For flashing that picture. That was stupid."

"Drop it, already. We've been through that. Sorry." Layne rolled his eyes.

"If he's around here, you've scared him off."

"Beth, I told you before, he's not here. Hell, I've lived here almost forever, I'd know." Layne accepted the opened bottle and took a deep swig.

"You know everyone here in Roswell? Is that what you're telling me?"

"No, but if he were here, I'd have seen him. That is, if our supposition is correct."

"Our supposition? Rick is the one who came up with this stupid idea, and you agreed. Without any argument, I might add."

"I don't remember you coming up with anything better, Beth. You went along with it too."

"I'm saying that if he's here, we're going to scare him off. There are other ways besides shaking trees. We can try the county clerk's office, post office, and sheriff to name a few."

"All right, we'll do it your way, Beth. Stop bitching."

"Dammit, if I were the suspicious kind, I'd think you were doing this on purpose. After all, we didn't have any trouble out there on the debris field until you joined us. Then wham bam all hell broke loose."

"Yeah, who's the one that tried to talk on the radio while the cammo dudes were listening? We're trying to sneak away from them, and then you start squawking on the radio, with them only a block away."

"Why you." Beth launched herself at Layne, fingers outstretched like the claws of a Peregrine falcon.

Beth's attack threw Layne across the kitchen table. The two of them slid off the other side of the table onto the floor. Two long raking scratches appeared over his left eye. Drops of blood welled into the furrows.

Too late, Layne grasped her wrists. Beth's twisting and turning only served to draw their bodies closer together. Her hot breath scorched along Layne's cheek. Her breast jabbed Layne's chest.

Beth's legs tangled between Layne's. Her thighs pressed against Layne's groin. She was surprised to feel him aroused. Her anger slowly melted as she sensed her own desire rising from within her private self. It had been a long time, she remembered, since she had succumbed to those deep inner desires.

Afterwards, Beth picked up her shirt, covering herself as much as possible. Embarrassed, she hurried down the hallway. Layne heard the shower running. Confused, he collected his clothes then used the other bathroom.

The sweet aroma of Amaretto coffee filled the kitchen. Layne was busy setting out an assortment of cheeses, breads and lunchmeats as Beth entered the room. She stood in the doorway, dressed as before but using a towel to dry her still damp hair.

"Mmm. Smells good. I am hungry, thanks."

"It'll be ready in a couple more minutes. If there is anything you need, we'll go to town later. Another storm is forming up to the west."

"Aren't Rick and Sarina out there?"

"Yeah, they should be near Alamogordo by now," Layne said

Beth hung the towel around her neck and using her fingers, fluffed out her short bobbed, black hair. She poured two cups of coffee, preferring hers black, she assumed Layne took his the same way.

As they threw together a couple of sandwiches, they discussed where they would start their new search for Donald Dyba.

\* \* \*

Together Layne and Beth worked through the records in city hall. The search produced seventy-five names worth checking. Hopefully one of them would turn out to be Donald Dyba. Another twenty they discarded for various reasons. Chaves County records showed two men who could possibly be their man. One, a Billy Kirkland moved onto the old Ortega ranch to the northeast of town about fifteen miles out, while the other, Jesus Villasenor, started an ostrich ranch south by the Pecos River. Both men had been in the area less than three years.

Wind whistled across the chimney while Layne started a big fire. By eight that evening, the storm was rampaging through the Roswell area, with a forecast of heavy rains with possible hail before morning.

While Beth cleaned away the dinner table, Layne looked up the names in the phone book. He handed Beth the numbers, and she called them claiming to be a pollster investigating the possibility of introducing another large chain store in the town.

Twenty names were left by ten o'clock. Most of the list was eliminated by the question of age. According to John Pavolli the producer in Los Angeles, Donald Dyba could not be much over thirty years old, if that. Layne set his list aside and poured two cognacs, handing one to Beth then settled on the floor watching flames leap and dance in the fireplace.

Beth sat down next to him sipping her drink. Their shoulders barely inches apart. Both of them were aware of their closeness across a gaping distance.

Quietly, Beth moved to the couch as the fire died. Layne was preparing to move with her when she drew the Indian blanket used as a dust cover, over her body. Dreamily she whispered, "Goodnight Layne, and thanks."

Layne dropped more firewood on the grate then prepared the coffee maker for morning. Crawling under cool sheets, he hoped Beth would join him after the logs burned through.

The aroma of fresh coffee, sizzling bacon and fresh bread brought Layne awake. Red numbers silently told him it was seven-fifteen. Outside, wind rattled the windows. He splashed water on his face, gargled and ran his fingers through thinning salt and pepper hair. He went to the kitchen and saw bare legs extending below the tail of one of his cast off shirts. With Beth being very close in stature to him, the shirt barely made the view decent.

"Hi there," Layne called. "Good morning."

Beth jumped and turned. "Hi yourself, sleepy head." She sat down the spatula she was turning bacon with and buttoned the front of the shirt until her breasts were covered.

Rain pelted the ground, turning all the dirt roads surrounding Roswell into quagmires. Telephone lines were still operational, so they finished their phone calls, preferring to wait out the storm. Layne figured they would brave the storm around noon and visit everyone still remaining on their list. By midmorning, the wind died down and the rain had slowed to a drizzle.

Tires sloshed as Layne's Blazer rolled through ruts filled with water. Once on the hardtop, the

Blazer's tires sang all the way to town. By dinnertime, all but the two ranchers were eliminated from the list. Layne figured that by morning the long dirt tracks leading out to the ranch houses would be dry enough to travel. As they walked back into Layne's living room, he noticed a message on the answering machine. It was from Rick and Sarina. They too had little luck and were staying in Carrizozo before driving to Alamogordo.

Beth dialed the number Rick left on the machine.

"Hello?" a woman's voice responded.

"Sarina? That you?"

"Yes, Beth? Did you get our message?"

"How do you think I got your phone number?" Beth snickered. "We've struck out here in Roswell. We even hit up the surrounding burgs."

"Same here. We're on our way to Alamogordo."

"We'll visit Hondo, Lincoln and Capitan on our way to Alamogordo, but we really don't expect much. I think our best bet now is in Alamo. The International Space Hall of Fame is there."

"So? What's so special about that?"

"Layne says that they may have reports about aerial phenomena there in their library, and Holloman Air Base is also there."

"Okay, Rick says to meet at the Mexican restaurant right on White Sands Boulevard. He says that you can't miss it."

\* \* \*

Beth and Layne beat the others to the restaurant. The ranch house exterior intrigued them.

A subtle western motif also prevailed inside. They sat eating chips and a deliciously mild salsa while they waited for Rick and Sarina. The weather had cleared, but continued to be chilly, promising more winter antics.

Halfway through the bowl of chips, the door opened admitting a gust of cool air as Sarina and Rick shuffled inside. After drinks were ordered, the four discussed their future actions.

Although there were setbacks, everyone was willing to continue. Proof still existed of the fraud involved in the autopsy film. Each one of them was firmly committed to locating Donald Dyba in order to not only gain solid proof, but also to uncover an exclusive story on why it was done. One day soon, they hoped to corner their elusive prey, then their troubles would be worthwhile.

Beth and Layne decided it would take them a few days to eliminate all the leads in Alamogordo and Las Cruces. During that time, Sarina and Rick would move on to their next town, Socorro. Which was the 1964 location of a local police officers flying saucer sighting. The sighting, after intense investigation, helped convert Allen Hynek, a scientist and leader of Project Blue Book from being a skeptic.

In 1947, just about the same time as the Roswell incident, there were reports of a saucer crash west the town. Most people considered it to be a hoax or thought that someone confused the town with Corona, often associated with the Roswell crash. Some people believed that the Very Large Array radio telescope system was placed on the Plains of San Agustin because that was the location of the crash, thus making it some sort of energy source.

As they left Alamogordo another cold wind whipped out of the west, down from the Organ Mountains and across the flats that made up part of White Sands Missile Range and White Sands National Park. Rick slowed once they passed Holloman Air Force Base to allow Sarina a chance to drink in the natural simplistic beauty of the desert. Off to their right low dunes of pure white sand covered in cactus gave way to larger dunes bare of any vegetation.

"Once, a few years back, I brought my dog up here in the winter," Rick said, a soft smile on his face. "Actually, we started up in Cloud Croft, which is about forty miles behind us and over seven thousand feet in elevation. The whole area was covered with snow. We had a grand old time, until finally her feet got extremely cold."

"Can dogs get frostbite?" Sarina asked.

"Yeah, they can. I got her back into the car and cleaned her feet up and dried them off. Then we headed for White Sands. That dog looked at the white sand and refused to get out of the jeep. I held a hot dog in my hand trying to coax her out of the car. She looked from the hot dog to the sand and back, over and over. I suppose she thought the sand was snow. She sat on the front seat and whined."

"That's mean. Cute, but mean," Sarina laughed.

As they crossed San Augustine pass, they were greeted with a breath-taking view. Straight ahead were the tops of clouds. They glowed with the whiteness of cotton balls. Miles and miles of cotton balls, white on top but gray black in the creases between them. Visibility dropped to mere feet. Slowly they made their way down the west slope of the Organ Mountains toward Las Cruces. One thousand feet lower, the Wagoneer broke out of the clouds.

Darkness had settled over the entire region. The few streetlights in the village of Organ were on, as were headlights of all the cars.

"This is totally amazing," Sarina said. "Does this happen often?"

"Not really, as a matter of fact, I believe that I have only seen it once before." Rick said. "I'm glad you could see it."

They picked up the interstate heading north and left Las Cruces behind them. The clouds hung low all the way to Truth or Consequences, a town named after the television program. Previously, it had been known as Hot Springs, New Mexico, and then one year, Bert Parks, the master of ceremonies of the Truth or Consequences television program, had a contest. The town that would be willing to change its name permanently would be the winner. Some of the program was filmed there and Bert Parks visited annually to join the festivities.

Today, there's a museum dedicated to the town, and a park named after the television personality. The sign for the museum overshadows one of the hot springs that the town was originally named for and says something about Geronimo having used it whenever he passed through the area.

Just to the east of the town is the largest lake in the state of New Mexico. At the bottom of

Elephant Butte Lake rests two small old western towns. Speedboats flash by overhead today, while once in while a fisherman snags a line on part of the town's ruins which rest deep below the cold, dark water. Close to the dam is the Butte, which the lake is named for. An early settler felt the butte resembled an Elephant, creating the name.

This time of the year, Rick knew the Elephant Butte Lodge would be open with many vacancies. After checking into one of the cabins overlooking the lake, the couple strolled along the walkway above the water. Most of the cold wind was deflected by the surrounding hills that choked off the river. The choke point was where the Army Corps of Engineers built the dam to provide a year round supply of water to all the farmers south, as far as a hundred miles to El Paso, Texas. Hand in hand, they walked into the restaurant.

Sarina looked out the dining room window. Weak sunlight painted the far shore in a picture of soft yellow, and oranges with a slight rose tint. Two foot tall white tipped waves were crashing into the rocky shore below, like rows of dark green uniformed soldiers being consumed in battle.

"Beautiful, absolutely beautiful. The scenery and the dinner." Sarina said folding her hands above her plate.

"So is the company," Rick said.

"If I didn't know better, I would think you are trying to seduce me."

"Maybe you don't know better."

"My, my, maybe I should be on guard to protect my virtue."

"I'll take care of your virtue for you."

"Well thank you Mister Prescott, I'm honored to be in such good hands."

Rick smiled as he laid a couple of bills on the check. "Soon, you will see just how good those hands really are."

The couple walked arm-in-arm across the parking lot. Suddenly, Sarina faltered. Rick heard her gasp and looked around. Parked all by itself against a rock retaining wall was a white Jeep Cherokee. Rick could tell the windows were tinted a luminescent purplish color even in the dim light provided by a lone overhead light hung from a tree.

"Is it?"

"I don't think so. I don't remember any window tint on the two jeeps that chased us."

"Sure?"

"From here it looks like Arizona plates on the car. I need a closer look." Rick moved closer to the vehicle.

A man climbed out of the driver's door, buttoning his shirt. "You got a problem, buddy?"

"Ugh, no, sorry. I was looking at your license plate. We're curious, that's all." Rick backed away holding both hands up in front of him in supplication.

"Well, move on, dammit. You're interrupting something."

"Again, sorry. We didn't mean any harm." Rick grabbed Sarina's elbow and steered her quietly toward their cabin as the jeep's door slammed behind them.

"Do you think he was trying to do what you're planning to do?" Sarina giggled.

"That depends on what you think I'm planning to do." He smiled.

"If we were interrupted like that, would you have behaved like he did?"

"No, I probably would have driven off cursing myself for being too cheap to get a motel room."

"Maybe he isn't lucky enough to have an expense account."

"Unless we can come up with something solid, I may not either."

With a wicked smile, Sarina said, "Oh, I think we can come up with something solid."

"I believe you took my comment out of context."

'That's not all I plan to take out." Sarina said, closing and locking the cabin door behind her.

* * *

Breakfast was buffet style offering a variety of eggs, meats and breads. Clouds still hung heavy, practically dripping humidity, resting against the mountains east of the lake. A sullen atmosphere hung in the air. Chill air radiated from the large plate glass windows overlooking the Butte and the south end of the lake.

"How long before we reach Socorro?"

Rick set his coffee cup down and figured quickly. "A little over an hour, depending on traffic and weather."

"What are we going to do once we get there?"

"First thing is a motel down town close to a restaurant. Next, I think we will try the phone book, then maybe city hall."

"Do you really believe that we'll find this

guy? I mean, New Mexico is kind of large and we're only concentrating on one area."

"From what I was told, he has to be around here someplace. My guess is that while he was working on the bodies for that autopsy film, he accidentally discovered something to change his mind about the whole concept of aliens and flying saucers."

"Okay, but what would it take to change his mind? I mean, well, what would he learn that would convert him?"

"You tell me, Sarina," Rick said as he paid their bill. "What would it take to convince you?"

"That's not fair. I almost believe already. My sister swears that she was involved in an abduction and sometimes I've received very weird feelings. Although I haven't had any psychic experiences that directly relate to UFO's, in the past if a sighting happened within twenty miles or so, I've felt, well, electrified. It's as if my body becomes charged with some kind of particles or something. That's why I wanted to visit Roswell and the debris field."

"Did you feel charged there? We know you fainted, but you said that was a shock from human and non-human feelings in the area. Was that being supercharged?"

"No, those feelings were definitely human like, not clear, but almost human. The non-human feelings were more like an animal of some sort. Once, as a kid I remember receiving feeling of shock and sadness from a neighbor's dog, just before it died. A car had run it down."

"So you believe that you had human and animal feelings from the crash sight. You don't think that the animal feelings were from alien thoughts. That's pretty mixed up. Could the feelings be, say, two different channels of the same being?"

"You mean like a radio station broadcasting two different programs at the same time? Maybe, but how would that fit an alien being?"

"I don't know," Rick said, "they have supposedly been visiting earth for so long, maybe they can think like us."

"Sorta like being bilingual? That might be. I'll have to think about that for a while. Yeah, strange, but possible."

## *15*

Socorro, nestled on a rise overlooking the Rio Grande valley to the east, rests at the entrance to a long wide valley leading westward to a large plain. During the 1800's, mining was the most important industry in the area, along with cattle. Mine shafts, tailing, and ghost towns dot the mountainous area behind the town of Socorro and the entire region south of the plains. Although man has lived throughout the valley for thousands of years, it still has remained a desolate, lonely region.

Thirty-two miles to the west of the closed mines lay the Plains of San Agustin.

A large radio-telescope observatory sprawls across the widest portion of the plain. Twenty-seven huge dish antennae rest on cement pillars and move by powerful electronic trucks which slowly relocate them from one fixed position to another. The effect is similar to a zoom lens on a camera. All twenty-seven antennas can be grouped close together or spread out clear across the valley, depending on what object in space is being studied.

Rick pulled the Wagoneer off the highway at the southern exit to the town. As they crossed over the highway, Rick pointed back to the southwest. "See the RV campground over there? Just before you get to it, there's a dirt road heading toward the west. Up that road is a long, low hill. Beyond the hill is a fairly flat area at the edge of an arroyo or dry streambed. That's where the deputy reported seeing his flying saucer."

"When was this?" Sarina asked.

"Back in 1964. That's one reason I feel that we will find Donald Dyba around here. We have two separate unexplained UFO cases here."

"Two cases? What was the other one?"

"At the same time as the Roswell crash in July of '47, there were reports of a separate crash here."

"Then why don't we hear more about this one? What happened here?" Sarina asked.

"Supposedly, it happened way back behind the town close to where the VLA or radio telescopes are. Only one or two people actually reported it, but there was no evidence found."

"How is that different from Roswell?"

"Okay, first Sarina, at Roswell we have twenty or so people telling a very similar story only from different viewpoints. Here, we have only one or two and the story has changed over the years repeating some information almost identical to Roswell. In Roswell we have few changes to the story, but new information that enhances the existing story. Also, more witnesses are coming forward."

"That seems to make the Socorro case weak. How can you say that you have two good cases if one is so poorly documented?"

"Good question. Ufologists, some anyway, say that these two cases are why the government established the Very Large Array observatory there. The Plains of San Agustin, according to them, is a power hub or something similar for flying saucers.

Actually, I believe what the brochure says."

"And what is that, Mr. know-it-all?"

"According to sources, the reason VLA was built there was because the whole area is sparsely populated. There is very little radio traffic in the region to cause interference or spurious radiation that would affect reception at the observatory. Even amateur radio operators near the telescopes are limited in the amount of power they can use. Mountains protect the plains from unnatural interference."

"That makes sense. Other places have a lot more UFO activity then here, like Gulf Breeze in Florida, but those areas are also a lot more populated. Creating more interference," Sarina said. "Can we go there sometime?"

"Sure," Rick replied. "Anyway, that is why I think Dyba is around here someplace."

"Why didn't we just start here? If this is the best place to look. Why waste time every where else?"

"Since the film is supposed to be of the Roswell aliens, if Dyba discovered something, it seemed logical that he would be in or near Roswell. Now that we have eliminated that, we are moving on to the next best place: Socorro." Rick pointed to the Zia Motor Lodge. Across the street was a small family owned diner. "Home for the next few days."

As expected, the couple drew a blank searching the phone book. Outside, a large circular thermometer indicated the temperature was in the low fifty's. Clouds settled on the mountains just to the west and a cold drizzle developed. Rick and Sarina dashed across the street into the diner.

After ordering coffee and *empanadas*, a dessert similar to a fruit turnover, Sarina engaged the waitress in conversation. No one else was in the diner at the time and Mayra, the waitress, seemed chatty.

"Yeah, this is a pretty quiet town all right," Mayra said around her gum. "People come and go, but slowly, ya know."

"What about you? How long have you been here?" Sarina asked.

"It seems like forever, but I moved here about four years ago with my boyfriend, you know. We were going to get good jobs and get married." Mayra shrugged, the rest of her statement understood.

Sarina and Rick exchanged questioning glances. The time fit, but somehow, Mayra didn't seem to be the type to move from Los Angeles to here, looking for a good job.

"Where are you from?"

"Nowhere," Mayra popped her gum, looking blankly out the window. "A little town called Weed. It is in southern New Mexico. We were high school sweethearts."

"What happened?"

"After a year, Jay decided the army was better than here. Left me stranded alone. Good news, I was not pregnant. Then someone else came along and things got a little better."

Near freezing rain drove more people into the small diner. Rick paid their bill and asked directions to the city tax assessor's office. The two dashed back to their motel but decided to wait out the storm. After changing clothes and drying off, Rick went down to the motel lounge. Fresh coffee was brewing as he looked at a wall map of central New Mexico.

"There are much better maps than that one, mister," a deep Hispanic voice said.

Rick shook off his thoughts. "Excuse me."

"That map is good enough if you are just going up the road, but if you are interested in this area, there are much better ones around," the man repeated. Behind him on the wall were three certificates. One looked like an engineering degree with drawings of early day engineering instruments decorating the corners.

"Are there a lot of interesting things around here?" Rick asked.

"Chure. We have ghost towns, old mines, dried up lake beds, beautiful national forests, and historic buildings dating back to Spanish times. There is hunting, fishing, just over the hill is a game reserve for people who like to take bird pictures. Oh yeah, even space aliens for people who are bored with real stuff." The man snickered at his last comment.

"Sounds like a wonderful place," Rick said, adding, "You don't put much stock in UFO's then."

"You kidding? I don't see how anyone with two bits of common sense can take them seriously. Unidentified flying objects my ass. People just don't know what they are looking at."

"What about that deputy that was on TV some time back, telling about what he saw around here?" Rick asked.

"Well, he's a friend. I can't say anything bad about him, but it does get awful hot in the summer around here. People have been known to see some mighty strange things."

"How would I go about finding a map that shows those things you mentioned?" Rick asked.

"The Chamber of Commerce used to have an illustrated map that showed most of it, but even better was the one produced by a bunch of the college students. They created a cartoon version of the Chamber's map that was a real hoot."

"That sounds like what I'm looking for," Rick said.

"Well if you're going to be around here long enough, try the college library tomorrow, or the campus print shop."

"All right, thanks for the information." Rick took two Styrofoam cups of coffee back to the rooms with him.

Sometime during the night, the freezing rain turned to snow. After a lazy morning consisting of breakfast and watching traffic from the warm comfort of the diner, Rick and Sarina decided to brave the elements and drive down to the courthouse.

Surprisingly, the hall of records was housed in a new orange brick building across the street from the courthouse, a tall solidly built structure of gray stone. Typical of late 1800's buildings, the courthouse looked officious and slightly intimidating. Swamp coolers, large square evaporative coolers, clung to the exterior walls, like overweight rock climbers suspended from ropes. Large cottonwood trees surrounded the building stretching their bare branches toward the sky.

Rick and Sarina were sent to the basement of

the courthouse. Even during the cold, damp weather, the room felt and smelled dusty. A Dutch door greeted them, the upper half opened, revealing a shelf holding a small bell and a sign-up sheet on a clipboard. A gnawed, stubby pencil was attached by a grimy piece of twine that had originally been white.

Judging from the last date on the sheet, early last month, the office wasn't very busy. Sarina pinged the bell and they waited. After a brief wait, they could hear a shuffling sound from behind the shelves that filled the room.

An elderly lady appeared from behind the shelves, just as Sarina was about to tap the bell again. She peered over a set of wired-rimmed glasses that for her were appropriately thought of as granny glasses. Her gray hair was piled on her head in what used to be called a beehive. Ends stuck out in every direction, giving her a halo-ed appearance. When she spoke, a slight Hispanic accent was detectable.

"Young people these days, always in a hurry. Ding, ding, ding. Hurry, hurry, hurry. You need patience."

"Yes, ma'am, I guess we do." Sarina hung her head slightly.

"Well now, kids, what can I do for you?"

"Across the street, they told us we needed to get a form from you before we can search city or county records," Rick said.

"Yes, that's right. You have to explain your purpose for the search, and then pay a filing fee, and then I can release the information."

"Great. May we have the form?"

"Why do you want to look at the records?" the

clerk asked.

"We're looking for someone who moved here sometime in the last three years," Sarina said.

"Was it a he or a she?"

Exasperated, Sarina's voice rose, "A he, now may we have the form?"

"Always in a hurry, young lady?" The clerk's eyes cut sharply to Sarina. "How does your young man feel with you always in a hurry to do everything?"

"She's not in a hurry to do everything, just some things." Rick placed his hand on Sarina's shoulder smiling.

"Well, I hope she knows the difference. Now, what is it I can do for you?" A faint smile crossed her face then disappeared.

Sarina cleared her throat, put on her nicest smile and said, "We're looking for a fairly young man that moved into the area sometime in the last three years."

"What's fairly young, dear? To me even Moses can be considered young."

Rick caught the fleeting twinkle in her eye and gently, warningly squeezed Sarina's shoulder again.

"Let's see, he's probably in his early thirties."

"Okay, now, where did he move here from?"

Sarina sighed. Trying to maintain her composure, she said, "California."

"Nope. Not here," She said triumphantly.

"How do you know?" Sarina sounded exasperated. "Just from what I told you, how do you know?"

"Them people from California have a certain

way about them.  Anyone with a little bit of sense can tell a Californian after seeing one for five minutes. Now you, you must be from somewhere back East. They can hurry up and wait all they want back there, but once they leave, they forget the wait part."  The clerk's smile grew almost glaringly in intensity.

Rick squeezed Sarina's shoulder hard, "You pegged Sarina right.  She's from New York.  That's amazing.  I bet you study people a lot."  He shook his head in amazement.

"As a matter of fact, I do.  I can tell quite a bit about a person from just talking to them.  I was going to say, New York."

"But..." Sarina stammered.

"Yes, but.  Would you mind terribly if we filled out the form and spent some time looking through the records?  Our boss sent us all the way here and I don't think she would approve of us going back this soon.  She might not feel that she was getting her money's worth," Rick said.

"I guess so.  I can see your point.  It's your time, you know.  Sign in."

Sarina and Rick exchanged glances.

"Sign in, you know, the log.  I can't do anything without you signing in."

Sarina signed for them.  Then the clerk produced the form from a basket hanging on the wall just inside the door.  "Ring for me when you're done filling out the form."  The clerk disappeared behind the shelves just as quickly as she had appeared.

"I'm not from New York!  Why'd you say that?" Sarina whispered.

"Wouldn't you rather deal with a contented

old lady, than an old bitty?"  Rick answered softly.

"Yeah, but..."

"Well, shh.   She may have very good hearing," Rick said.

Ten minutes later the couple again braved the storm, crossing the street to the Hall of Records.  The storm let up a little while they were down in the basement of the courthouse, but it was still blowing a light snow and the air was frigid.

By closing time, Sarina had a list of twelve people to check on.  Scanning the phone book, three of the names were not listed.  Sarina tried Beth's ploy of acting as a phone pollster and quickly eliminated all nine names.  Tomorrow they would check the unlisted names.

# *16*

Only one more name after this one. Rick and Sarina stopped on the street, checking the fading numbers on the beat up mailboxes. There were only ten houses on Kachina Road. Six stone buildings on the east side and four mobile homes sitting on larger lots on the west side. Desert led off toward the mountains behind the trailer houses.

The outdated mobile home sat in the middle of a large, fenced off section of land. A chain link fence closed off the land. In places, top rails were bent causing the material to sag, while the gate lay in weeds out of the way of any cars entering the drive. Bare trees and dead weeds littered the yard. An old rusty pick up sat under a tired carport cover. Next to the front steps Rick recognized a Harley-Davidson Rebel motorcycle partially hidden under a tarp.

Knocking on the front door, Rick and Sarina noticed peeling varnish on the wooden surface. The rest of the exterior was just as poorly kept, including the rickety stairs they stood on.

A harsh voice called out from inside telling them to wait. From the sounds coming through the closed door, someone was having a hard time moving around or was trying to clean the place up.

A brass security chain stretched tight across the opening obscured the man's face. His eyes were bloodshot, hair totally disheveled and he had at least a few days' growth of beard. "Yeah, watcha want?"

"We're looking for a Donald Dyba," Sarina said. She looked at Rick and nodded. Yes. Her nerves were tingling. This is the man. She knew it.

"What for? I don't know you. I'm David Smithers. Don't know who you're talking about."

"We're from the local paper and are working on an article about people who have re-located here from other places. You know, how successful they are, were their expectations met, that kind of thing." Sarina smiled.

"I don't think I want an interview. Go away," Smithers said.

"We really would appreciate this chance, sir." Sarina kept smiling.

"Otherwise, I think we will have to call NSA and ask their permission for this interview. The National Security Agency might not appreciate that," Rick said.

"Who the hell are you people?" The man's eyes swept back and forth between them. "I don't know what you're talking about. Get out of here and leave me alone." The door slammed in their face.

"That sure looked like him to me. Older and tired, but I'd swear that was him." Rick said. Sarina nodded in agreement.

"Especially after his last comment," Rick added.

"Donald Dyba, we need to talk. We're not with the military. Talk to us," Rick shouted.

Sarina whispered to Rick. "I know it's him. I feel it."

The couple stood on the stoop for a minute.

No noise came from the interior of the mobile home.

"That's it. I guess we're out of luck." Rick shrugged, ignoring Sarina's statement.

"What are we going to do now, Rick? After all the trouble we went to, to find him. How can we just stop now?"

"If the man won't talk, then we don't have any choice." Rick took Sarina by the elbow and steered her off the stoop and back to his Wagoneer.

Suddenly, the door opened. Dyba stood there, a shotgun cradled in his arm, a mean look on his face.

"You two get the hell out of here and don't come back." Dyba jacked a shell into the shotgun's chamber. "Or else."

Sarina hurried to the Wagoneer and climbed into the passenger seat. Rick turned, resting his right hand on the vehicle's hood.

"Dyba, if we found you, so can they. Either way, your best bet is to talk to us. We're the only protection you have." He pulled a card from his wallet, one he picked up at the motel, and wrote his name and room number on the back.

"Change your mind, this is where you can get a hold of us."

Rick placed the card on a piece of scrap metal near the Wagoneer then slid into the driver's seat. After they pulled back onto the street, Rick thought he saw Dyba go over and pick up the card, but he wasn't sure.

Rick headed for the college, to see if they could locate a copy of the student's map. That would make a good afternoon's work. Then it would be time for an early supper.

The campus press, a small building nestled between two larger structures housing the physical plant, was noisy. Even with the door closed, Sarina and Rick could hear the thumping of a press. Inside, the noise level was almost uncomfortable. To the left of the door was a small office. Just inside the office was a desk with a nameplate identifying the young man as the receptionist. J. Moody was typing away, apparently oblivious to the noise and their presence.

Moody's right hand fluttered in their direction in acknowledgment. The two shuffled out of the way of the main door and waited until he finished typing. Quickly his hand shot out, grabbing a pencil and starring the last word he typed.

"Hi, can I help you?" Moody asked.

"Yes," Sarina smiled her award-winning smile. "We were told that you might have some copies of an old Chamber of Commerce map. The one we are interested in was done as a spoof of the real one."

"I don't remember that one, but let me ask the printer. He's been here since the presses were installed."

Moody moved around the desk, passed Rick and Sarina then into the center of the room where the sound was loudest. Large pieces of machinery filled the room. Rolls of paper lined one wall, while a computer occupied the far corner. Several people appeared and vanished in and around the presses like busy ghosts visiting a favorite haunt.

Several minutes later, an older man in bib-overalls came toward them. He introduced himself as Walter, the resident pressman. Walter herded them outside and around the corner of the building and away from the wind.

"Hope you don't mind," Walter said, lighting a cigarette and taking a deep drag. "All these damned new rules about smoking and stuff really suck. What was it Jay was saying about a map?"

"I'm Rick and this is Sarina. I work for a magazine and we're just passing through. Thought we'd do some looking around. The man at our motel said that the college produced the best map of the area. We wondered if you still had any?"

"Glad to meet you," Walter said shaking hands with both of them. "Yeah, I remember that one." The man chuckled. "Some kids just about got their ass kicked out of school because of it. Only thing that saved them was some letters written by tourists about how cute it was."

"That's the one. We were told that the college would be the only place to have a copy now," Rick said.

"You know what? It's possible we do have a couple stashed some where around here. Where are the two of you staying? I'll look for it and drop it off tonight if I can find one."

"That'd be great, Walt," Rick said, digging another motel card from his wallet. "If you come by about five or so, we may be at the restaurant across the street. Stop in. Dinner will be on us," Rick said.

"Is there anything in particular you're looking for? That map had a lot of strange things shown on it," Walter said.

"Actually there is. We're interested in the supposed flying saucer sighting around here," Sarina said.

"We have only had two nationally know cases. Both of them are shown on the map. Accurately, I might add."

"Well, I work for <u>Real</u> <u>Saucer</u> <u>Magazine</u>. There have already been many articles published about both of them. I'm just in the area and thought we would visit the sites. You know, 'been there, done that'. That sort of thing," Rick said.

"I think I know what you mean. It's sorta like visiting a religious shrine or historical site of interest," Walter said.

"Exactly," Sarina smiled, touching Walter's elbow lightly.

Walter shook hands with both of them again, and said he would drop by. He lit his second cigarette as Rick and Sarina walked back to their jeep.

"Well, I'll catch you later. It shouldn't take too long to find that map for you."

"Thank you, Walt. We'll see you at supper," Sarina said.

Sarina and Rick had their hands in each other's back pocket as they walked across the street to the cafe. Out front, just to the side of the door they saw a motorcycle. It looked new. Rick said something about having seen it before, but shrugged it off.

Inside they saw Mayra, the waitress they had spoken to earlier. A man wearing a black leather jacket was hunched over the counter in front of her. They could not see his face, but something seemed familiar about him.

As he turned to leave, Rick and Sarina

realized the man was Dyba. He finally saw them as he opened the door. Hatred filled his face as it turned a glowing red. Rick was surprised that Dyba didn't turn back to them and confront them after their earlier meeting.

Rick chose a table away from the window. A breeze was picking up and the chill could be felt oozing through the window glass. When the waitress came over, Sarina tried to start a conversation with her.

"Hi, was that the guy you said changed things?" Sarina asked, nodding at the man in the leather jacket leaving.

"Huh, oh, yeah, that's him. What have you done to him? He was telling me about some people coming out to his place hassling him. From the description, I figured it had to be you two," the waitress said.

"We're looking for someone and he resembles the man very much. We're not with the government or any other organization like that. He won't get in trouble by talking to us," Sarina said.

"He was upset when he was telling me about it. He also seemed to be scared about something."

"He has no reason to be scared of us. All we are is journalists for a magazine. Do you know him well?" Sarina asked.

"For about three years now, we've been going together off and on. We have gotten close, if you know what I mean," she shrugged.

"I wish you would talk to him and see if you could get him to sit down with us for an interview," Rick said handing her one of the hotel cards. At this rate, he reminded himself he would need to pick up another handful of cards.

"I'll try. But you must promise me that you'll not get him into any kind of trouble."

"Well, I can promise that we'll not cause him any trouble of any kind. All we want to do is ask him a few questions," Rick said again.

Walter walked in and looked around for Rick and Sarina. When they waved at him, he walked over and sat down. The waitress took his order for coffee. No need for a menu, because he knew what he wanted. A plain old hamburger. Nothing else, just a plain hamburger. Not even an order of fries.

The old man smiled at them as he reached inside his jacket for a paper. The map was rolled into a one-inch diameter tube.

"No trouble, like I said. Just had to remember which drawer the damn thing was stuck in. There are some more in case you would like another." Walter handed the tube over to Sarina with a wink.

"Hey thanks," Sarina said. She unrolled the paper, flattened it out on the table and scrutinized the map. "Whoa, this is real neat. Think I'd like to have a copy of my own."

"No problem for a pretty lady like you," Walter said.

"Oh, oh, talk like that will go to her head and then no one can get anything out of her," Rick said with a smile.

"Your problem, bud, is that you don't know how to treat a lady."

As the waitress approached the table, Sarina slid the map off onto her lap. Walter's forehead knitted as he watched the waitress place a cup of coffee in front of him. When the three of them were alone again, he asked. "What was that all about?"

"Oh, nothing. We want to talk to her boyfriend, but don't want them to know that we're interested in UFO's," Rick said.

"You want to talk to him about saucers, huh? Why him? I am familiar with almost everyone and everything happening around here, but him. I don't know," Walter said.

"Well, it goes back a long way. Not around here, but someplace else. I don't know if he's the right person or not, but he resembles the man we're after," Rick said.

"Sarina, mind if I call you that?" Walter said with a fatherly smile. "Sarina, scoot that map up here and I'll show you the places you guys are interested in."

Sarina spread the map out again and both her and Rick looked on as Walter poked his finger here and there describing the area that the supposed crash of 1947 happened and the place that the Deputy had his encounter. In both cases, roads led to the location or within a short walk of it.

Small talk followed as everyone ate supper. Walter thanked them and left, promising to get Sarina another copy of the map.

Rick reminded the waitress to talk to her boyfriend and left her a sizable tip.

The message light was lit on Rick's phone. He called the office and the night clerk told him Layne Gunther had called and left a phone number.

Layne answered on the third ring.

"Layne?  Rick.  How's everything?"

"Not so hot.  We struck out.  Again."

"No problem.  We found Dyba.  He's here in Socorro.  Come on up."

"You're kidding.  Really?"  Layne asked.

"Yep.  I thought we should have started here in the first place."

"Yeah, but Roswell made just as much sense," Layne said.  "Where is he?"

"He's living in a mobile home.  The last one on Kachina Street.  Tomorrow we plan on getting a video recorder and filming an interview with him.  He should have some amazing things to say."

## *17*

Rick and Sarina drove out to the Deputy's landing site and looked around. A shallow ravine dropped away from the rutted tracks on the left. The Sheriff's Deputy had seen his flying saucer down in the center of the depression. Rick pulled his Wagoneer off the road and both of them got out.

Early cloud cover had dispersed and now the sun was shining. Weak waves of heat rose from the sandy floor of the arroyo as sunlight warmed the ground. Rick wiped his brow in frustration. He hadn't found any visible evidence after searching the rocky area.

Sarina stood at the center of the area, closed her eyes and tilted her head back. Her arms rose parallel to the ground. Rick paused, not wanting to make any noise to distract her. For close to three minutes, both of them stood as still as granite statues.

"Nothing. Nothing at all." Sarina whispered. "I thought I'd get some sort of feelings. After all, this is suppose to be one of the most documented cases there is. According to you, even Doctor Hynek became convinced of UFO's because of this case."

"Maybe you're not really attuned to aliens," Rick said. "Or maybe you're just tired and out of focus."

Rick watched as pools of liquid silver filled Sarina's eyes. "I'm a good psychic. I know because

I've found things in the past and been able to describe places and things that I've never seen. But for some reason, right now, I'm getting nothing."

"Sarina, maybe it's because you had that bad experience in Roswell. Maybe you're afraid that it'll happen again and you aren't really tuned in to everything."

"That's possible, but I should be at least getting some indication. Just a slight tingling or something."

"Well, I'm not going to worry about it. I feel that you'll come out of it soon and everything will develop normally." He patted her on the back.

They turned back toward town. On the way, they discussed the possibility of running out to the other site beyond Socorro. Since it was all the way across the San Agustin plain, Rick figured it would take the rest of the day. He would rather spend the time with Layne and Beth.

Sarina suggested stopping by the cafe for a snack and seeing if there was any news of Dyba. Layne and Beth weren't going to arrive before dinner anyway. After driving across town, Sarina ordered a large vanilla shake and side order of onion rings. Rick stayed with a coffee and Danish.

A different waitress served them and told them that the girl they were interested in had called in sick earlier. Rick thought they should make a trip out to the Dyba place in a few minutes.

The same motorcycle they had seen at the restaurant was parked out front of the mobile home. As they pulled up, Sarina noticed that the front door was open. Rick reached for his gun, but Sarina stopped him. She didn't want any weapons around. Rick approached the door first, careful to shield Sarina. Screams blasted from inside. Rick bolted through the doorway into the living room, looking in all directions.

He heard a man's voice coming through the arched doorway behind the living room, followed by a woman's voice. Rick stopped in the archway separating the two rooms. He recognized both voices. One was Dyba's and the other was his girlfriend's.

"I can't take you with me. They'll find both of us and kill us."

"Who are you talking about? Not those two at the cafe. They are from some magazine. Who would want to kill us?"

"You don't understand. They'll come after us and kill us."

"Who, dammit, who? Tell me what's going on."

"That is just it, if I tell you, then you're in just as much danger as I am," Dyba said.

"I love you. I want to be with you."

"No, leave before someone puts us together," Dyba said.

"Too late." Rick said. "Donald, sit down and let's talk about this."

"Donald? Who's Donald?" Mayra said.

"Mayra shut up." Donald said. He turned to Rick, "What the hell are you doing here? I told you yesterday to leave me alone."

"David, tell me what's happening." Mayra shouted. "Why are we in danger?"

Donald took Mayra by her arms and shook

her. When she quieted down, he steered her into a kitchen chair and knelt in front of her and put his hand gently over her mouth. "Honey, just sit there quietly for a few minutes and I'll get this all straightened out."

She nodded, her saucer-sized eyes glaring over the top of Donald's hand. Mayra leaned back in the chair and breathed deeply when Donald removed his hand.

"Okay, now, why are you two here? What is it you really want?"

"Donald, I'm from Real Saucer Magazine. I was contracted to view the newest of the autopsy films for the magazine. Somebody's trying to sell the film and we have first choice. During our investigation, we discovered it was a fake."

"How? I was very careful. I researched every detail. The military helped me on getting all the correct instruments. They're the ones who transformed the video onto that old film."

"You used two cameras to film, didn't you?"

"Yeah, geez, you know the whole thing. How?"

"You should be very proud of your film. It took us quite a few hours of intense study to finally find a flaw. It was in the window. In only a couple of frames, you cast a faint reflection. It was enough for our analyst to get an image of you. Then, through computer enhancement, we came up with a picture."

Sarina took one of the pictures from her purse and dropped it on the table in front of Donald. Donald's face slumped like a California mudslide. He was shocked at the clarity of the photograph. No doubt about it, it was a picture of a younger Donald.

"Damn, that's a pretty good picture to come off a reflection in a window. I don't know how we missed that. I only got to see the finished film once, but their people went over it with a fine toothcomb. They analyzed it from every direction."

"Well, evidently they missed the reflection in the mirror," Sarina said.

"Why did you move way out here?" Rick asked.

"I wanted to be close to where everything happened. Before I got involved with the military, I thought the whole thing was a bunch of bull. Then I saw for myself what was really going on. It scared the hell out of me."

"What do you mean out here where everything happened? There's no solid evidence that anything actually happened around here," Rick said.

"While I was working on the autopsy, I heard that some really important things happened here. It was hinted that it was bigger than Roswell."

"Why don't you tell us about it from the beginning so nothing's left out?" Sarina suggested.

Donald nodded motioning everyone to a seat. He finally sat down, ran a hand over his face and drew a deep breath.

"While I was in Hollywood, nobody really recognized my work. Out there, unless you get proper credit for your work, you're nothing. I was the best at my job. Hell, I created monsters that gave the film crews nightmares. There was one of the scream queens that would not get within twenty feet of any of my creations."

"Excuse me," Sarina said, "scream queen?"

"Yeah, oh, that's a slang term for an actress in those B grade films. You know the ones that run around in their underwear screaming every time they hear any sound."

"Okay, yeah, I know."

"Anyway, that's how good a job I did. No one gave a damn, they just wanted the masks, dummies, and bodies to look real. Mine were better than real."

"One day, I got a phone call from a captain in the army. He wanted me to meet him at some restaurant out in Twenty-Nine Palms. I asked him why way out there. He said because he had something I would be interested in. I said, 'Yeah, whatever.'

"The next day, about nine in the morning, he called again and reminded me of our noon appointment. Once I got there, all he wanted to know was if I would be willing to work for the government, and if I had any important jobs pending for the next couple of months. My calendar was blank, so I said why not."

"When was all of this?" Rick asked.

"Four years ago, next month. Two days later, I was on an airplane going to Dayton, Ohio. When I got off the plane, there's the captain. He hurried me out to a staff car and we were off. My bags would follow, he said."

"I ended up in some general's office out at Wright-Patterson. Just the two of us. He asked me if I wanted to make a half mill. That's more than I ever made on any job. Of course, I said. He gave me a form to sign. I read the form carefully. It dealt with national security. According to the paper, if I ever divulge any information about what I did or heard or saw, they could hang my ass out to dry."

"What's the general's name? Do you remember?" Sarina asked.

"Something like Smith, with an English accent. Smythe. I never saw his name in print. He asked me if I understood what I read. I said sure. He said sign it or fly back to LA, so I signed." Donald got up, shook his head and went to the refrigerator. He offered everyone a beer, then took one for himself. In one long swallow, he drained off half the amber liquid.

Sitting back down, he continued. "Once again after I signed, he asked me if I was willing to continue. I said yeah, then we got into a jeep and drove half way across the base. There were three large old hangers isolated with chain link fence topped with razor wire. We went into one with the number 58 on it, I think. There was an armed guard out front who even asked the general for his identification. Geez, even the general had to show a pass."

Donald wiped his face before continuing. "Inside, the building was divided into three sections. Each had a heavy door with one of those devices on it where you have to enter the right number on a keypad. A sign over the pad said there was no second chance." He threw his empty bottle in the trash and took out another beer.

"Inside the room, there must have been twenty or thirty large vats. Tubes and wires came out of the top and side of all of them. Each one had a curtain hanging on the side. Behind the curtain was a window."

Donald started to visibly shake at this point. He seemed close to loosing control. Rick asked him if he wanted to take a break, while Mayra stood behind him massaging his shoulders.

Donald shook his upper body then started again. "When General Smythe opened the curtain, I almost lost it. I was not prepared for what I saw. It was a body. Not human, almost, but not quite. The body was suspended in some kind of liquid. He was looking at me."

"He? How did you know it was a he?" Sarina asked.

"It was a he. I knew because down between his legs a small tube thing stuck out about two inches. Others I saw later had little holes there, not like a woman's vagina, just a little hole. This one had evidently been in a crash as one side of its head was lopsided. Smashed-in, sorta. There were also burn marks all over the body."

"General Smythe took me around to the other vats. Inside were other aliens, but not all alike. A few were reptilian-like and some real small, gray, and thin. Most were in between. The general told me not to make any drawings or take any photos in there, but that I could visit here whenever I needed to."

Donald got out a third beer before continuing, "The General took me to another hanger. Inside was a large work area. Two oversized drafting tables were in one corner under fluorescent lights. More worktables were scattered around the room. He told me that I would work in there. I could do all the drawings I wanted, and then I noticed that the drawing paper was numbered on each page. A guard stood by the door and another uniformed guy sat drinking coffee at one of the drafting tables. He was introduced as The Major. The two of us would be working together."

"What were you suppose to work on, honey?" Mayra asked.

"We were supposed to produce five composite alien bodies. Each one had to have internal organs that could be seen. It took us a while, but we finally came up with a way of making them look pretty realistic." His footsteps faded down the hallway. Donald excused himself and left the room for a few minutes.

Rick heard a thump followed by a soft drawn out screeching sound. Then footsteps and shortly a toilet flush. When Donald returned, he was holding several small pieces of paper. He waved them under Rick's nose. "Here, I saw your face. You didn't believe me." He pointed a shaky finger at the drawings, "This is what I saw. Look at these."

Rick took the papers from Donald. As he spread them on the kitchen table, he noticed they were warm to the touch. Each one was a portion of a diagram. The designs looked like bodies. They were different than human bodies.

"It sure looks like somebody was drawing aliens." Rick said.

"Not only did we draw them, we actually made five bodies. To get the internal organs correct, we used real ones. From people and animals."

Mayra moaned and silently left the room;

Sarina followed her out into the living room and sat beside her on the couch. She had just received a jolt. Nothing was what she imagined. Her boyfriend was nothing like she expected.

Back in the kitchen, Rick asked incredulously, "Actual human organs?"

"We would take them and cover them with a rubbery substance that would harden into the exact shape of the organ. We peeled it off after it hardened and threw the organ away. From that mold, we would pour a gel that would take the shape of the organ. It was for black and white film. We shaded the gel to give the final results more definition in the picture."

"I don't get it, why use these organs? I mean, it was suppose to be an alien and no one knows what an aliens insides look like."

"Yes they do, they have performed many autopsies. But, you see we weren't making a real one, we were making a fake. It was suppose to look like the real thing."

"If the army had the real thing, why did they need your dummies?" Rick asked.

"They said something about being in control." Donald wiped his brow. "You know, the dummies looked real enough to be used at a crash site or whatever, but at the same time they could easily be shown to be a hoax. That was the General's story."

Suddenly, Donald stood up. A shadow fell across his face. "I don't want to talk about it any more. Damn, I told you more that I should have. I could be in trouble now."

"I don't think they're after you. Why should they be?"

"I skipped out without giving anyone notice. I cleared out my bank account in cash and bought an old pickup from a kid. No one was supposed to know where I am. I don't even deal with the bank here in town. I thought I was safe here. I got a new drivers license and ID card. How the hell did you find me?"

"For some reason, one of the Hollywood directors you worked with thought you may have moved out to the Southwest, New Mexico in particular. We took it from there and finally came here looking for you."

"That had to be Pavolli. He's the only one that I told about New Mexico." Donald said.

"I hate to tell you this, but somebody tried to stop me from finding out about you in L. A. They tried using lethal force. I don't know if I'm being followed, or if I stumbled into something. That's why I told you that you need to talk to us. We want to get you on videotape tomorrow. You know, repeat the story you just told us and show the drawings. We'll zoom in on them. After that, there should be no reason to harm you," Rick said.

"I hope so, because that general told me that they were serious about that secrecy shit. I don't want to end up out in the desert," Donald said.

## *18*

During breakfast, Layne and Beth caught up on the latest events. They were on the edge of their seat while Sarina filled them in on Donald's story. Every once in a while, Rick would stop her and add a forgotten detail.

"I want to meet that guy," Layne said. "Maybe he has some information on the Roswell crash and alien bodies recovered there."

"According to him, something a lot more significant happened here than over in Roswell or Corona," Rick said.

"That can't be. I've spent hundreds of hours investigating that case. There's too much overwhelming evidence. Too many witnesses," Layne growled.

"Whoa, Layne, I'm just telling you what Donald said. He didn't say that it never happened, just that it wasn't as big a deal as what happened here around Socorro."

"Well, I still want to meet him. According to everything, and I mean everything, the whole report from this area was denounced as a fake." Layne said.

"I guess we'll see him pretty soon. We'll head out that way after we finish breakfast. I wouldn't mind hearing the whole story for myself," Beth said.

Sarina nudged Rick. When she got his attention, she raised her eyebrows and looked around.

Her gaze settled on the waitress and the counter lady, then back to him. Rick frowned, and nodded questioningly at her. Again, Sarina repeated the action, only this time she jutted her jaw at the waitress. Rick's attention, drawn to the other waitress, became apparent. Mayra was not here.

A cold damp chill filled the air as they left the cafe. Everyone returned to his or her rooms to clean up and get a warm jacket. Fifteen minutes later, they were on the road. Low clouds rested against the mountains west of town, threatening yet another winter storm. Rick used his headlights in the semi-dark. Normally, by seven in the morning, even deep into winter, a weak sun would poke its face over the horizon around six, causing the Southwest to glow in its meager warmth.

As the jeep drew near Dyba's house, Sarina became uneasy. "Something's wrong. I can feel it."

"Here we go again. Just don't pass out on us this time," Beth said.

"This isn't the same kind of feeling. I just know something is wrong," Sarina said.

Dyba's front door stood wide open. Rick's first thought was that it was too chilly for that. He pulled to a stop half way across the yard, telling Sarina to move into the drivers' seat as the two men got out.

"You two remain here until we call for you," Rick said.

"Be careful." Beth echoed Sarina's comment.

Rick quickly explained the layout of the house trailer to Layne as they approached. Just inside the door, the men were greeted by chaos. Somebody had ransacked the living room thoroughly. Shelves were bare, tables, chairs and two short couches were turned over. Stuffing spilled from every cushion.

The inside of the house felt almost as cold as the outside. Evidently, Donald did not turn on the heat last night. Rick looked at the thermostat on the wall. It was set for seventy-six degrees. Next, he tried the light switch. There was no light. Whoever searched the house must have turned off the electricity.

Layne pushed through the mess into the kitchen, calling Dyba's name. Evidence on the floor suggested the searchers were still energetic as they tore through the room. "Nobody here," Layne said.

Both men started down the narrow hallway leading back into the bedroom area. Both bedrooms were in total disarray. None of the furniture in either room would be of much use to anyone but an upholsterer. Layne heard cars pull into the gravel drive.

"Somebody just pulled in. Maybe it's Dyba." Layne said. They headed back toward the living room.

Heavy footsteps pounded up the stairs and into the living room. Two police officers stood with their weapons drawn.

"Hold it. Hands over your head," the officer with sergeant stripes said. The younger officer was slightly behind and to the sergeant's left. His constant shifting of weight from one foot to the other telegraphed a nervousness that was not apparent in his face.

"Hello, officers, glad you showed up," Layne

said, stepping forward.

"Hold it! I said." The sergeant's weapon centered on Layne's torso.

"You don't think we are responsible for this, do you?" Layne said, swung his arm to encompass the living room.

"Don't move, dammit," the younger officer said. A nametag announced him as Officer Wainwright. The sergeant was Gomez.

"Calm down, Wainwright," Layne said. "We just got here ourselves."

"Shut up, Layne." Rick said. "Just do as they say."

"Do as your friend suggests...Layne," Gomez said. His deep gravely voice gained control of the situation. "Just put your hands over your head and wait."

"What about the girls outside? Are they okay?" Rick asked.

"Of course, I have another officer watching them. Now, move over against that wall and do as Wainwright says. I'll finish searching the house."

"Nobody here but us, Sarge," Layne said.

"We'll see," Gomez growled, conducting his own search.

Five minutes later, Rick and Layne were guided down the stairs and toward the second patrol car. Both cars had flashing light bars and head lights. Another officer already had both women sitting in the back of his car. Beside the officer stood an elderly woman pointing to the two men.

"That's them. Yep. That's them. I saw him yesterday and the day before that. He was run off the first time. David pointed his shotgun at him," an elderly woman with a smoker's scratchy voice said. She stood wrapped in a heavy ankle-length coat. Only the pink toes of her slippers showed. Hair curlers decorated her thin silver strands of hair. A pair of horn rimmed glasses sat precariously on top of two fat yellow curlers above her hairline.

"Are you sure, ma'am? These are serious charges," Sergeant Gomez said.

"Yes, young man. I'm sure. I live over there across the street. I was standing there looking through a break in the curtains and watched him and his woman friend drive up and go to the house."

"When was this, ma'am?" Gomez pulled a notebook from his left breast pocket, clicked his pen and started writing. "Can you identify the woman who was with him?"

"Sure can, she's one of them you have in that police car over there."

"Which one, ma'am? Can you tell me which one?"

"I'm going to catch my death out here. I need to get back inside and warm up. I'll get dressed proper and be right back. Oh dear. I still have those blasted curlers in my hair. You know my little grandson calls them antennae. Isn't that a cute thing to call them?" The old lady turned on her heels and marched out the gate and back to her house.

"Wainwright, after we get these people down to the station, come on back and wait for Mrs. Hargrove. Then bring her on down. We'll want to write up her testimony."

"Right, Sergeant," the young officer

responded. He gently pushed Rick into the back of his patrol car. Gomez did the same with Layne.

* * *

The two men were kept separate from the women after arriving at the station. Rick and Layne were placed in a holding cell while Sergeant Gomez and another officer interrogated Sarina and Beth. Their nostrils were assaulted by the sour smell of sweat that lingered in the cell. An open toilet was half full of dirty water, and an acidic urine odor floated like a banner over a drain. Evidently, some previous occupants of the cell did not trust flushing the toilet and used the drain instead.

Paint was peeling in strips from the bars of the cell, exposing dull metal underneath. The wall covered in graffiti, was indecipherable to both men. They sat side by side on the lower bunk, elbows on knees, their heads cradled in their hands.

"What do you think they're doing with Beth and Sarina?" Layne asked, keeping his voice low.

"They're going over everything that has happened. The girls don't really have much to say. Beth just got here late last night."

"I don't think Sarina would tell them why we're interested in Dyba, but I'm not sure. What did they say the charges were?"

Sergeant Gomez entered the cellblock and approached the two men. "We're just about finished with the women. You two are next."

"What are we charged with? You have to have a charge to hold us," Layne said. "We also get a phone call."

"You are not charged with anything yet.

We're just discussing the events that led to Smither's disappearance. The eventual charge may be murder, but right now we're just interrogating witnesses."

"Do you usually bring witnesses down to the station in cuffs? Dump them in a cell?" Layne asked.

"Under the existing circumstances, yes. You have to admit that we found you in a compromising position. Plus, ol' lady Hargrove witnessed most of the events."

"When is she going to show up? I would like to talk to her. Beth and I weren't even in town until last night. We have receipts tracing back three or four days and stretching half way across the state," Layne said.

"Now where might those be? That might help, but your two friends have been here a couple of days and could have set everything up, then waited for you two."

"What motive would we have to harm Dyba?" Layne asked.

"You may have given me one right there, friend. We know him as David Smithers, but you're calling him Donald Dyba. Somebody has a lot of explaining to do."

"When we first came across him, his name was Donald Dyba. We lost track of him out in L. A. and conducted an intensive search. When we finally caught up with him, he was living here in Socorro. He changed his name to David Smithers," Rick said.

"Sounds like you're conducting an investigation of your own. If you were a P. I., you would have flashed your ID. Somebody from the government would be pushy or snotty about the whole thing. Who are you guys?"

"We're here representing <u>Real</u> <u>Saucer</u> <u>Magazine</u>. Beth and I actually are the only ones on assignment with them. Layne is tagging along because of a strong interest in the Roswell crash and Sarina is our resident psychic."

"That's a tangled bunch," Gomez said. "What put you onto this Dyba guy?"

"There was strong evidence that he was involved in a sighting of a very unusual sort. It would broadly fit Doctor Allen Hynek's CE-two category," Rick said.

"Don't quite understand that last part, but go on. So you wanted to talk to him about the sighting?"

"Actually, we talked yesterday evening and we came back this morning with some last minute questions. Are you familiar with the Deputy's story of his saucer sighting? If so, his case would be a category CE-three."

Officer Wainwright opened the door to the main office and called the sergeant. Gomez excused himself and left. The two men held a quiet discussion in the doorway. Sergeant Gomez shook his head in disgust and turned back to the men in the cell.

Gomez unlocked the door and swung it open. "Come on out you two. After a short talk with Officer Wainwright you will be released."

"It seems that our star witness can't identify either of the women. Seeing as one is blonde and the other has black hair, I don't feel she's a dependable witness. But, I must insist that you don't leave town without consulting me first."

\* \* \*

An hour later, the group was released. Gomez drove them to their motel where they picked up Layne's Blazer. "Where to now?" Layne climbed behind the wheel as the others got in.

"Drop us at Dyba's trailer, Layne," Rick said. "We'll meet you at the room later."

"What are you going to do? You can't go in there. That's a crime scene," Layne cranked the ignition and pulled out of the lot.

"We have to. The people who got Dyba were looking for something. Hopefully, they didn't find it. Anyway, I want to check."

"We're still not clear of this, Rick. You get caught and our combined asses are back in the sling," Beth said.

"We'll be quick," Sarina said. "Besides, the Wagoneer has been there all morning, and no one will notice, if we move quickly. Just pull up next to the jeep. We'll jump out, then you take off."

"Okay, but don't take too long."

Rick moved back to the doorway and called Sarina. Sarina closed the door behind her and stared at the mess the searchers left behind.

"No bodies or blood, but a real mess." Rick said.

"What do you think happened to Donald?" Sarina asked.

"I couldn't find any signs of a struggle, but we can't rule out the idea that he's been taken away and possibly killed, although I don't know why, after all this time, they would want to kill him."

"Did they get Mayra also?" Sarina asked.

"Don't know I haven't seen any signs of her

being here, but I don't see many signs of Donald being here either."

"What are we looking for, Rick?"

"Let's try to find those drawings that Donald showed us, maybe there are more of them, or other papers."

"How do you plan to do that? This place has been torn apart already. There can't be any other hiding places."

"Well, let's give it a shot anyway. We'll look for thirty minutes then leave as quietly as possible."

"Where do we start looking?"

"Do you remember which room he went to after leaving the kitchen yesterday?"

"It sounded as if he went to the first bedroom, right here. He went inside but he was only there for a few minutes. Oh, yeah, I also remember the sound of a flushing toilet."

"Okay. Now think. Did you hear anything? Did he move any furniture or anything? What do you remember happening?"

"I don't know, give me a minute." Sarina stood for a minute, a deep frown clouding her face. "Yes, I remember some sound. A loud noise."

"I remember it being like a thump. It wasn't as loud because of the wall, but it was a thump."

"Let's go into the room and see what could cause that."

Both of them stood in the middle of the room. There was a small dresser, a nightstand, and a small couch that turned into a bed. The couch was upside down, the inner springs twisted to the side.

"Any of the furniture would thump if moved.

Anyway, the thump could be from moving a chair to climb on to reach something high. It could be from moving it out of the way for something underneath."

"Look around, Sarina, there must be someplace to hide things."

"Rick, was there any other sound?"

"Yeah, there was a faint screeching sound, like metal against metal."

"What else, Rick. Is there anything else? God, it's chilly in here. Isn't the heat on?"

"No, the electricity's off for some reason, so the thermostat won't work. Those doors may have been open all night, draining all the heat. Wait a minute! The papers Donald handed me were noticeably warm. That means that they were someplace warm."

"Metal and warmth, could Donald have hidden the papers in the heating vent?"

"Up there." Rick pointed to a metal grill in the ceiling. He turned a chair over and placed it under the vent. Straddling the seat, his feet rested on the arms, giving him extra height. The vent was still screwed into place. No matter how much Rick tried to pry it loose, the metal grill resisted. "I don't think they are hidden behind this grill."

"Let's keep looking. I'm sure Donald came in here." Sarina said. After moving more overturned furniture, they discovered a floor vent. Sarina bent down, reaching out to lift a corner of the vent. "It's screwed down tight."

Rick stepped into the hallway and surveyed the area deciding to search the bathroom next. They found the floor covered with dirty clothes. The wicker hamper lay shattered in the tub.

"Moving the clothes hamper would make a thump, but what would it be hiding?" Sarina asked.

"Another vent, maybe?"

Sarina kicked jeans and western shirts across the floor. Finally she found a metal vent. One edge was almost unnoticeable bent.

"Rick, here. Check this out."

Rick knelt down curling his fingers under the bent edge of metal. It took three tries, but finally the grill moved. As the grill came away from the floor, it screeched. Screw heads had been sawed off and glued in place. "That's it, Sarina. With the heat working properly, the papers would be warm to the touch." Rick reached down into the aluminum ducting. Feeling around, he drew a blank. "Nothing, damn. I'm sure this is where he kept the papers."

"Let me try. I bet if those other guys found the papers, they wouldn't replace the vent cover." Sarina said. She knelt beside Rick, pushing her thinner hand and arm further into the ducting. Just as she was about to give up, her fingertip brushed against something. Feeling around blindly, her fingers felt a thin strand of wire.

Deftly, her index finger curled the wire around a knuckle. Slowly, she drew the wire toward the opening. An envelope emerged in the bottom of the vertical opening attached to the wire. The couple looked at each other in surprise and awe. Here were the papers Donald had shown them.

"Thank you. I'll take that," said a familiar voice.

## *19*

"Thank you, Rick." Repeated a voice from the doorway. "I knew you would find 'em. Donald just wouldn't cooperate." The familiar voice belonged to Layne.

"What are you doing here?" Rick asked, staring at the business end of a Desert Eagle forty-caliber revolver in Layne's hand.

"I'm after those papers Sarina has in her hands. Too much information too quickly is not healthy for the general public." A superior smile crossed his face. "Now, Sarina, hand over the papers and come with us."

For the first time, Rick noticed two men in black suits standing just behind Layne. Both men also had drawn weapons. For the second time today, Rick raised his hands over his head.

"Is Beth in on this with you? Who do you work for?" Sarina handed Layne the envelope.

"Beth, no, I don't think so. Let's just say that she is temporarily occupied right now." Layne laughed. "Just think of us as protectors of the common people."

Layne opened the envelope, looked at something inside, nodded with a grin, then placed the envelope in his jacket pocket. Next, he motioned the couple to move into the living room. Once there, both of them had their hands drawn behind their backs and plastic restraints tightly wrapped around their wrists.

One of the men escorted each captive to a black Cadillac parked beside Rick's Wagoneer. Before shoving them into the back, Layne reached for Rick's car keys, which he kept on a snap spring clipped around a belt loop on his jeans.

They got into the Cadillac and followed Layne driving Rick's Wagoneer through the town of Socorro. The two vehicles headed west on the road leading to the VLA observatory and the small cross roads town of Datil, New Mexico.

Just outside of town a quarry nestled the hillside off the road to the right. The small caravan wound its way through the quarry until piles of rock hid the two cars. Rick and Sarina were forced out of the Cadillac and into Rick's Wagoneer. Layne and the driver of the Cadillac exchanged words then the Cadillac drove off, leaving Layne with his two prisoners sitting in the back of the Jeep.

The Wagoneer continued its way west until it reached the small town of Magdelana. Half way through town, they turned south on a well-maintained dirt road. One mile outside of town, the road deteriorated into a rutted trail.

Through the windshield, Rick noticed a huge mound of mine tailings or discarded rock from an old mining operation. The rutted road twisted against the mountain, climbing almost two hundred feet to the mine entrance.

Three poorly maintained buildings stood around an open area the size of a football field. Rusty girders held up sheets of corrugated tin that at one time were the exterior walls of the stamp mill, machine shop and probably the office and bunkhouse for the mine workers.

The Wagoneer stopped in front of a metal door. A cement casement stretched away from the rock wall. From what Rick could remember, small buildings like this were used as powder houses. A short tunnel was scratched out of rock. When the miners encountered hard rock, they would extend the size of the powder room by building a concrete or rock room with a heavy metal door.

A white Cherokee pulled next to the Wagoneer. The driver dressed in three-color cammo-fatigues climbed out, saluted Layne, then moved over to the door and slid a bolt on the door. A hair-raising screech came from the door as it was forced open.

"Everyone out." Layne pointed the gun at Sarina's head. "You'll be safe here while I clear up some last minute arrangements." He clubbed Rick with the heel of his hand. "Then we have other things to discuss, such as the location of the pieces of metal, the note and videotapes."

The driver motioned the two captives toward the opening. Slowly, they ducked into the tunnel. The heavy metal door screamed on rusty hinges as it was pushed closed. Sarina winced as they heard the snick of the bolt being driven into place.

In a muffled voice, they could hear the driver talking to Layne from outside. "You need me to stay and watch, Sir?"

"Naw, there's no way out, and without weapons, the guy's harmless."

"Yes, Sir."

Rick and Sarina heard two doors slam shut then a vehicle drive off.

Narrow swords of light cut the darkness from small chinks in the wall. Motes of dust drifted across the silvery shafts. Sarina stumbled over an object on the floor. The object moved. Rick had to give the door a token shove before joining Sarina kneeling next to a person on the floor.

"Mayra. What happened?" Sarina called out, recognizing Dyba's girlfriend. "Where is Donald?"

Mayra moaned as she rolled onto her back. Her clothing had been torn in places, exposing her undergarments. The remnants were part of her waitress uniform. "Donald, oh Donald. Where is he?"

"Mayra, it's Sarina and Rick, Donald isn't here. How do you feel?"

"I'm just bruised, that's all. They kept threatening me to make Donald give them something they wanted badly. They beat him real hard, but he wouldn't give it to them or tell. Then they started on me. They ripped my clothes and threatened rape. He still wouldn't tell. That bastard."

Rick wasn't sure who that last epitaph was aimed at, but he didn't have the heart to tell her that he ended up handing those same papers to Layne without any fight. After their valiant struggle, he felt that the news would be too disheartening. Instead, he vowed to find Donald, get him, Mayra and Sarina to safety, then even the score.

Sarina sat in the dirt with Mayra. Although the bunkers' walls were thick concrete, it was almost unbearably hot, with the sun to the west pounding relentlessly against the metal safety door.

Rick examined every inch of their prison. A few cracks existed in the seams of the concrete, and around the doorframe, allowing the bright spikes of light to penetrate the darkness surrounding the prisoners. Rick's foot encountered a thin object buried in the dust of the floor. Digging in the fine dirt and gravel, he discovered a bent two-foot long steel rod, jagged on one end.

Rick placed his ear against the hot metal door, listening for any sounds from Layne or the soldier. A few moments later, he was rewarded with the faint whine of an engine and clattering of gravel. Rick was sure Layne had driven off.

Rick remembered the Boy Scout knife he bought in L. A. It was still in his pocket. He pulled it out and opened the secondary blade, the one with the emery board. Quickly he got to work trying to enlarge one of the cracks large enough to push the rod into.

Five minutes and three scraped knuckles later, Rick had a crack enlarged to accept one end of the steel rod. "Sarina, you and Mayra move off to the other side. I'm going to use this bar and try to break through the concrete."

"That wall must be over a foot thick. Do you think it'll work?" Sarina asked.

"There seems to be no other choice. Look around. I don't want to just sit here."

"They...they may come back. That one guy said they were not finished yet." Mayra spoke half-heartedly.

"I'm going to try anyway." Rick grabbed one

end of the pipe with both hands and attacked one of the cracks, gouging at the concrete. "I don't think we want to be here when they return."

Pieces of concrete started to fall away within minutes, driving Rick all the harder. Twenty minutes later, Rick paused, sweat pouring from every pore. His shirt was plastered to his back. His short hair was soaked, while his eyes burned from the sweat flooding them. Blisters formed on his palms and quickly burst, causing excruciating pain. Sarina tore the sleeves from her blouse and wrapped them around Rick's hands as bandages. She then took a turn with the pipe, but wasn't making progress. Just as she was ready to give up, a large chunk of concrete collapsed, exposing natural rock.

"Rick, a large rock is showing through. Is that good?"

"Let me see." Rick moved next to her, running his swollen fingers across the rocks surface. "I think so. We need to chip out the cement around that rock, then see if we can pry it loose."

"Let me try," Mayra said, reaching for the tool. "Both of you have been doing all the work."

For the next hour, they took turns chipping away at the cement still covering the exposed rock until finally they could see the mortar binding the rocks together. Rick continued to work his shift with bandaged hands. The winter sun still beat on the metal door and the temperature in the confined bunker continued to climb.

Outside, the afternoon sun became weakened as it slowly crept behind a tall hill to the west. Small relief came from a lack of pounding sunlight against the door. Inside, the bunker grew even darker, making it difficult to see what they were doing. Most of the scratching and digging was being done by hand until Rick, frustrated, placed his foot against the exposed end of the rod and kicked.

Mayra was holding the pipe steady as Rick jammed his foot into the rod again and again. He shifted his position until his back was braced against the opposite wall.

Suddenly, Mayra shouted. She almost lost the metal rod as it broke through. A large three-inch hole gave them their first peek at the outside. Cooler air slowly dripped into the bunker. Mayra moved the rod six inches around the rock. He kicked again, renewed strength from their minor victory spurring him on. Sarina took his place after four or five kicks. The next victory was hers. Another fist sized piece of mortar and concrete covering fell away.

Mayra twisted and shoved at the piece of metal between the two holes, creating a large opening. She set beside Sarina and together they shoved against the rock. Kick. Shove. Kick. Shove. Finally cracks appeared in the remaining mortar collar. The rock and mortar slowly gave way, creating a hole two feet wide.

It wasn't much longer, before Sarina, being the thinner one, shimmied out. She looked around but saw only Rick's Wagoneer. Sarina went around to the front and tried the door. A makeshift lock had been put on the slide, making it impossible for her to open the door. Working from both sides now, the opening was enlarged so Mayra and Rick could escape the bunker.

Rick inspected the Wagoneer. It was unlocked, although his keys were missing and he had never learned how to hot wire a car. He promised himself that he would learn as soon as possible. Not only could he not start the car, the missing keys meant he could not access the weapons compartment. Normally he kept it locked in town denying potential thieves his weapons.

In the cargo area, his old ratty army blankets were still haphazardly strewn about. Underneath were a plastic gallon jug of stale water, a traveler's first aid kit, two tins of Swedish cookies, a flashlight, and a roll of duct tape. Lawrence's bow and quiver of arrows were jammed between the back seat and cargo bay.

Retrieving a piece of pipe, Rick opened the three and a half inch blade of the Scout knife. He then pulled the end of the duct tape loose and started to unroll it. When he had over a foot unwound, Rick used the razor-sharp blade to slice off the tape.

Slowly, he wound the duct tape over the handle of the knife and the end of the rod. When he was finished, he presented the crude spear to Sarina. "Only use this to stab with. Be sure to get close and hold on tight."

Forgotten until now was the bow and quiver of arrows Lawrence made him accept. Rick remembered his last instructions for Lawrence. His friend told him to be careful who he aimed at because unless he watched what he was doing, more than the target would be surprised.

Rick had the women eat some of the cookies and wash them down with a little of the tepid water while he looked around. Then Sarina kept watch while he had his own snack. There were two blankets in the back. He could not use his knife, so carefully he reached into the quiver for one of the arrows, knowing how sharp the steelheads were.

The first arrow he withdrew was blunt. There was no metal arrowhead. In place of it was a B-B glued to something. Closer inspection showed it to be glued to a primer, the cap that fires into a shell to set off the powder that drives a bullet. Now it dawned on Rick. Back in Albuquerque, Lawrence had showed him one of his secret weapons, the exploding arrow shaft that shredded a tree's bark and damaged the surrounding branches.

Altogether, he had a dozen arrows. Six blunt ones and six with razor sharp metal heads. With one of these, he cut one blanket into two pieces. Now that the sun was dropping, so was the temperature outside. Hopefully, they could stay warm with the blankets.

Before dark, Rick sent Sarina to find a sheltered area where they could build a fire. In the meantime Mayra gathered firewood. Since it would be too dangerous to hike to town on foot, they would camp at the mine then in the morning try to walk the five or six miles back to Magdalena.

Ironically, the mine sheltered them again. This time the group retreated into the main shaft about forty feet, and started a fire behind an overturned ore cart. The metal cart reflected heat back to the group and would also hide the majority of the flames from the fire. Mayra collected an impressive pile of wood, enough to keep a strong flame burning all night. They moved all their meager possessions inside and settled down for the night.

Rick made a tour of the entire mining camp before dark and came across Donald's body. Layne or one of his henchmen had beaten him badly, almost beyond recognition, then thrown him down one of the open vertical shafts.

Donald's body was draped over a crossbeam about fifteen feet down. Rick was sure he was dead, but in the poor light of his flashlight, even with the body on its back, he could not tell for sure. No rope was available and Rick could not find sufficient cable or wood to make a ladder.

"I'm sorry, but I'd swear Donald was dead. His head was twisted at an impossible angle. Somebody used him as a punching bag. His arms and legs were also badly bent," Rick said.

"Can't you get down there and check? My God, he might be alive," Mayra asked, tears welling up in her eyes.

"It's too dark, besides, I couldn't find any rope or anything that would make a ladder."

Sarina said, "Shh!" She cocked her head to the side, listening hard. "Hear that!" The deep growl of several small engines under full power echoed into the mineshaft. Rick grabbed the bow and quiver. While he could still see by the firelight, he notched an arrow with a point to it to the bowstring. Then he slid silently out into the dark openness of the night.

Twin headlamps glowed like angry eyes, their beams madly slashing back and forth. Two all terrain vehicles were approaching, first up a gully, then between hills of rock tailings or debris. Rick moved into the shadow of a ruined building. A quarter moon was rising somewhere to the east but would not be much good yet.

As the two machines drew near, Rick took aim. Rhythmically, the second ATV's headlights would sweep across the first vehicle, exposing a driver and passenger both armed. Coming over a rise of ground about thirty feet away, Rick took his chance. He released the first arrow.

Silently, it struck home in the driver's left shoulder. With a groan, the driver lost control of his vehicle. It turned against the rise as the driver slumped sideways. The rider, tried to get off by standing up. His leg was caught under the right rear wheel and he was dragged forward as the three-wheeled ATV tipped to the right. The rider screamed as the vehicle rolled across his body. The second driver stopped his ATV just short of the rise.

Using the handlebars as a lever, he swept the area with his headlight. Since the ATV was on a rise, the beam went over Rick's head. As the beam swept back and forth, Rick noticed another man standing beside the front of the ATV, a rifle in his hand.

The first vehicle stopped rolling upside down, the headlight beam pointing down the tailings. A faint whiff of gasoline drifted up to Rick. He drew out an arrow with a blunt tip and moved to a better position, one where he was looking almost straight down at the overturned vehicle. In the faint light, he made out the blackness of a body moving.

The light rocked back and forth as one of the men tried to right the vehicle. Again Rick drew a bead and took his shot. A bright flash exploded, filling the night with a sudden glare of light just below the ATV. Then with a whoosh, the gasoline ignited. Rick saw the man turn and start to limp away from the burning fire as the gas tank exploded.

When the explosion died away, the man lay next to the ruins of the vehicle, his clothes smoldering.

"Prescott. Dammit. I know it's you. Come out and give yourself up." Layne's voice bellowed against the rock wall behind Rick. "Lawrences' toys are cute, but won't help you any."

After a minute of silence, "I don't know how you got out, but you can't go around killing people. Give yourself up."

Rick moved back, away from the tailing's rim. Swiftly he slid back into the blackest shadows provided by the buildings. He was not about to talk to Layne, knowing that the sound of his voice would locate him, and probably draw gunfire.

"Layne, over here. Help me. This damned arrow hurts like a sonna bitch."

"Pull the damned thing out, Frank," Layne shouted back.

"It feels like its got barbs on it. Oh. oh, God."

"Where were you hit? Can you come over here?"

"Left shoulder, high by the bone. Flash your light so I can see where you guys are."

"Frank, just work your way down slope, we'll find you. I'm not going to shine any lights around here. I've seen that bastard shoot. He's accurate. Look what he did to you in the dark."

"He must have some grenades or something, to blow up that ATV the way he did," the other man said.

From their conversation, Rick located three of the four men. The fourth one was probably dead and Frank had lost his will to fight, at least  for a while. That left Rick facing Layne and one other man.  Rick hefted a chunk of rusty metal and threw it low against the side of the next building.  As it skipped across the ground, it almost sounded like somebody running.

Automatic gunfire roared like an angry chain saw through the night.  Dirt, pebbles and other debris kicked up around Rick then off to his left in the direction of the thrown metal.  He loosed another pointed arrow at the flame growing from the gun barrel.

"Jeez, you're right, Layne.  An arrow just flew by me.  Couldn't have been a couple of inches away."

"Shut up, Carl.  You are giving him information.  Just shut up.  Wait for me." Layne called.  "Frank, say something."

Rick heard a scrambling sound as Frank moved.  Layne must be crawling about looking for the injured man.  For a short while, all he needed was to watch out for Carl.  He hefted another piece of metal, only this time he rolled it towards Frank's last known position.

Again, automatic gunfire ripped across the ground, throwing rock chips in every direction.  One caught Rick over his left eye, digging a furrow above his eyebrow.  The arrow Rick had notched slipped, skittering off down the tailing pile.  Luckily, it was not one of the explosive arrows.

Rick felt a damp sticky fluid roll into his eyes at the same time as he registered the pain.  Using the back of his hand, he wiped the blood away. He had missed his shot. Carl's random fire was getting too close. Rick decided to move to another position where he could keep an eye on the mine entrance.

Off to Rick's right stood a large metal cylinder left from an old steam plant. The steam was piped to an engine that ran a small stamping mill. At one time, ore from the mine was crushed into dust and small gravel before being moved. It was a good thirty yards away. It took Rick two short sprints to cover the distance to the drum.

From his new vantage point, he could see Layne's form moving diagonally down the tailing slope to Frank illuminated by the faint last flickering of the fire. Rick wiped the blood from his eyes again and aimed at Layne. The arrow dug into the dirt between the two men. When it exploded, shrapnel flew upward, the ground deflecting most of the downward blast. Rocks and pieces of aluminum struck Frank in the face.

Screams from Frank startled Carl enough to cause him to fire another burst up the hill. Layne collected minor wounds in the shins, effectively dropping him to his knees.

"You bastard. There was a chance to live, but not anymore. You're dead now," Layne said. "Carl, get over here, we need to take care of Frank, then we're going to kill that bastard."

## *20*

Silence shrouded the mining camp. No matter how hard Rick tried, he could not hear any sounds from down slope. Suddenly, he felt a brief puff of air against his neck and someone was beside him.

"How's it going?" Sarina whispered in his ear. "I let the fire die down to keep reflecting flames from illuminating the walls."

Rick jumped, startled by her voice. "You scared the hell out of me!"

"Sorry." She pecked him on the cheek.

"They drew back about fifteen minutes ago. I killed one and wounded another. Now it's just Layne and some guy named Carl."

"I heard him yelling about killing you. Do you think they'll be back?"

"I believe so. My last arrow hit Layne, so I don't think he'll leave it alone now."

As the moon rose over the towering rock cliff directly to the east, Sarina finally saw the cut over Rick's eye. She reached out and touched the wound tenderly. By now, it had stopped bleeding.

"Sarina, you need to get back in the mine. Now that the moon is up, Layne's probably preparing another attack."

"Can't I help you? You've been wounded."

"No, I'd feel better with you safely hidden. That way, anyone moving around up here is a bad guy."

"Okay, but help me locate a club or something. I gave my spear to Mayra."

Rick helped her find a two foot long metal pole she felt comfortable using as a club. Rick pointed out three positions he might try to occupy when the next attack started, and then he shooed her back to the relative safety of the mine.

Time stood still after Sarina left. Night noises returned to the mining camp. Rats busily scurrying back and forth startled Rick several times. The noise was unnerving, but tended to keep him alert.

A tinkle of glass shattered the quiet for a few seconds, then the shroud of calm settled again. Rick was not sure where the sound came from, but he knew it was not close by. Something was moving, he could hear a crunching of gravel.

It sounded as if someone was walking down the gravel road, crossing from right to left about a hundred yards out. Then it was quiet again. Rick imagined what it was like out here a hundred years ago. Indians or claim jumpers harassing a mining camp.

The miners must have been scared to death. His weapons were more sophisticated then the Indian's, but that didn't matter after dark. How ironic, Rick thought. Here he was, defending the remains of a mining camp with a bow and arrow while the attackers had rapid-fire weapons.

The sudden roar of an engine startled Rick. His thoughts turned to the remaining ATV. The sound came from his left. Parts of the puzzle fell into place. The shattering glass and the crunch of movement. Someone broke the headlamp on the vehicle and would depend on moonlight to illuminate the area. Layne had moved. The new attack would come from the other side of the camp.

Down to seven arrows, Rick became cautious. As quietly as possible, he moved to the middle building. Beside the uprights, there were only three large sheets of bowed corrugated metal defining one wall. Half way to the buildings' shelter, shots rang. It appeared that Carl was still in his original location with the automatic rifle. Dirt sprouted all around Rick's feet. He went into a zigzag pattern cutting to the far building, changing his other plans.

Bullets pranged off the corrugated iron or punched their way through it, spreading small shards of shrapnel in every direction. Rick knelt behind one of the vertical girders for protection. He withdrew an arrow from the quiver, looking for a metal tip.

Rick drew the arrow three quarters back and scanned the ground in front of him. Trying to remember Lawrence's training. A noise close against the rock cliff to his left drew fire from down slope. A soft moan came from the dark, followed by more scrambling across rock.

Rick was ready, bow bent to its extreme. As gunfire again erupted, he released the arrow. Moments later, Rick knew the results. The muzzle flashes were moving upward in an arch. Cold metal touched his skin, directly behind his right ear.

"Another good shot, Rick. I'm continually surprised at you. You never showed this blood lust when we were together. I had you pegged for a wimp, even after the shoot-out with the cammo dudes. Drop the bow and slip that quiver to the ground," Layne nudged Rick's ear with his pistol.

"What's going to happen now, Layne? Donald is dead and you have the rest of us captive."

"Since you managed to kill off my associates I'll have to work out some new arrangements. Now where are the women?"

"You figure it out, asshole."

Layne slammed the barrel of the pistol into Rick's temple. Rick staggered back two steps, his hand held against his right ear.

"Now, I will ask you again. Where are the women?"

Rick dropped drunkenly into a fighters stance before replying. "You figure it out. Asshole!"

Layne moved forward, but remained out of Rick's range. "I would just as soon shoot you now, but I'd prefer to have your co-operation." He leveled the pistol at Rick's forehead. "You still have information I need."

The two men stood still as statues, neither one willing to give in.

"From the way you were shooting, you knew the women would not be in the line of fire. That means they are secreted safely out of the way. There are only two places that would be safe. The bunker or the mineshaft. I don't think they would go back into the bunker. That leaves the shaft."

Layne pulled out some plastic strapping and tied Rick's wrists behind his back. Staying three feet behind Rick, the two men limped back to the mine entrance.

"Ladies, come on out now. I've got Rick."

Silence drifted from the mine.

Layne paused for a couple of moments.

Gunfire erupted down the mineshaft; one bullet ricocheted off the overturned ore cart. "Now, Goddam it!" Layne barked.

A rustling sound greeted the men, followed by a soft frightened voice from Mayra, "Please don't shoot. Here I am."

As Mayra emerged into the moonlight, Layne looked over her shoulder searching the blackness for Sarina.

"Where is Sarina? Tell her to get her ass out here, too."

"She left just before the shooting started this last time."

"Where is she, then?" Layne poked Rick in the back.

"I don't know. She came out to talk to me during the lull, but I had her come back here."

"She came in and told me what happened earlier, then she left again," Mayra said.

As Layne strapped Mayra's wrists behind her back, Rick was sure he knew what happened to Sarina. His heart dropped. The gunfire directed away from his position meant Sarina drew their attention. The last sounds he had heard were ones of pain.

"Sarina, come out here girl. Come out before I have to hurt one of your friends."

Layne patiently waited a minute or so, then called again.

"Last chance, Sarina. I'm going to shoot somebody. Maybe I'll shoot Rick, your lover boy, or maybe Mayra."

A shot rang out, Mayra screamed, startled from the noise as the angry wasp, like sound of the bullet passed her ear.

Angrily, Layne pushed Mayra next to Rick. Sarina was not coming out. He could not afford to kill either one of them right here. That would have to wait.

Layne marched the two prisoners down the rutted road to the ATV, which was still running. A body lay five feet off to the side. An arrow protruded from the lower part of the man's solar plexus.

"Damn, Rick. Lawrence said you were good with a bow. How did you manage to shot like that in the dark?"

"Didn't you know, luck is always with the good guys," Rick said.

"Your luck is going to be good and dead in a little while, smartass, just like you and your friends." Layne clubbed Rick's ear with the pistol barrel again.

Rick grunted in pain, tucking his injured ear against his shoulder. Layne turned them around, and walked them back up the hill. As they neared the mineshaft, he pushed the two prisoners against Rick's Wagoneer. "I know I kept your keys for some reason."

"Layne, no one has mentioned Beth. Is she dead, or is she in on this with you? Are you both government agents?"

"Beth. She's a different story. I will regret killing her, but at this point, there is no choice. What I need from you Rick is the real pieces of metal we found, and the original tapes."

"Layne, you aren't going to get them, and that's all there is to it."

"We'll see about that."

"What do you plan to do with Beth? Where is she?"

"At first, the two of you were to be lost in a cave-in, looking for something. Maybe more ghosts for Sarina to communicate with. Beth and I would come out tomorrow in search of you and she would fall down another mineshaft, leaving me. After dealing with the authorities, I would quietly return to Roswell and my job."

Using more plastic strips, Layne tied both of them to the spare tire mount on the tailgate.

"Don't go anywhere, you two." Layne said as he headed back toward the mineshaft.

Flashing the light in front of him, Layne entered the mine. He came across the remains of their bonfire and saw pieces of blanket lying on the ground. Working his way further inside, he found a spot covered with fine dust. No footprints were in the dust, so Layne turned back to the entrance.

Outside, Layne swept the powerful flashlight beam across the ground. The bright light stopped on the Wagoneer, then passed on. With his pistol in one hand and the flashlight in the other, Layne searched the entire mound. Close to where he captured Rick, Layne spotted a puddle of blood.

Layne found one arrow on the ground. It had a blunt point and a B-B glued to the end. A few moments examination showed him Lawrence's ingenuity. The search extended back down the hill to the two bodies. Both of them had their weapons nearby.

"Sarina, Sarrrinna," Layne called. "I know where you're hiding. Come on out."

Again he was answered by a gloomy silence that added to the cold to drive fear deep to the bone. "Come on out and we can get into the jeep. Wouldn't you like to get warm?"

Layne circled the tailings and approached from the direction of the original attack. Maybe Sarina would be trying to free her boyfriend by now. He swept the area with the beam of light, hoping to catch the woman out in the open.

"Hey, Layne. Come here," Rick called.

Layne ignored him and continued his search.

"Hey, Layne, come on. You tied Mayra's wrists too tight, the circulation's cut off. She's loosing all feeling in them," Rick called.

"What does it matter, Rick? You're both going to be dead before the sun comes up."

"At least let her be comfortable until then. There's no sense in needless suffering."

"Yeah, yeah, I'll be there in a couple of minutes." Layne cautiously approached the vehicle, the beam of light constantly dancing back and forth.

When Layne reached the back of the Wagoneer, he paused. There should be little cause for alarm since he toured the whole area and could not find Sarina. Wounded, she probably headed back to town for help. In her condition, it would take a couple of hours, at least. He had plenty of time to find her.

A scream of fury erupted directly behind him. Twisting around, Layne saw a glint of steel.

Reflexively, his left hand swung up protectively. Laynes' arm deflected the knife, causing Sarina to crash into the side of the jeep.

"God damn you," Sarina shouted. "Damn you to hell." She turned to strike again, but Layne slashed out with his right foot knocking her off balance.

As Sarina fell, Layne raised the pistol and took aim.

Sarina rolled onto her back, clutching the spear to her, then she kicked out, barely missing Layne's groin.

The bullet tore into the ground at Sarina's side, as Layne bent sideways in pain.

Sarina struck out at Layne with the spear, only noticing at the last minute that the taped knife had turned sideways. The blunt end of the pipe struck him in the chest.

The wind was knocked out of him. Layne blurted, "Damn, girl. Now I'm gonna get you good." He backed off, trying to give himself some room for a decent shot.

Sarina scrabbled toward him on heels and elbows, kicking out when she could to trip him. The spear fell to her side. Layne fired again wildly, missing both Sarina and the vehicle.

Sarina rolled on her side, grabbing the spear. Layne took the chance to get his balance. Clutching the spear with both hands, Sarina rolled further, onto her elbows and knees, then tried to stand, her back to Layne.

"Hold it right there, bitch," Layne growled. "I've had enough of you."

"I don't think so, asshole," Sarina hissed,

trying to catch her breath.

"Turn around and drop that ridiculous spear of yours."

Sarina dropped into a crouch and twisted around, swinging the pipe as a club. Layne screamed as the knife blade tore into his arm. Reflexes took over as he jerked his arm back, tearing the knife away from the handle. With his other hand, he drew the Scout knife from his arm. Warm blood gushed from the wound adding a coppery smell to the dust kicked up by their struggling.

"You bitch, you're gonna pay for this." Layne screamed, bending to recover his gun.

Sarina took one last chance. Grasping the rod with her remaining strength, she brought it down on his neck. The blow glanced off the back of his skull and slammed into his neck.

Layne dropped like a sack of concrete, one faint moan escaping his lips.

"Oh, my God. Rick. I think I killed him," Sarina sobbed.

"Come here, hon, bring the knife. You did what had to be done."

"I can't, he threw it someplace."

"Hon, listen to me. You have to find something to cut us loose with. Can you do that?"

"Ye...yes. Rick, I hid the arrows, one of them is sharp." Sarina picked up Layne's flashlight and tried it, but the bulb had broken in the fall.

Minutes later, Sarina was back, bow and quiver in hand. She cut both of them loose, then collapsed. Rick and Mayra lifted her into the back seat.

Layne's body was face down in the dirt, making Rick cautious. He held the dead man's gun in one hand as he rolled the body over. A quick search of the man's pocket produced the keys to his jeep. Rick rolled him back and took Layne's wallet and keys from the back pocket.

After starting the jeep and the heater Rick made his own tour of the mining camp. He collected another Glock 19 9mm automatic and three clips from one body, but left the AK-47. By the time he returned to the jeep, the heater was running full blast.

The warm interior was a welcome after the cold of the night. Rick drove back twenty-three miles into Socorro. As they prepared to drop Mayra at her place, she talked them into spending the night with her. Settling down on the couch in her living room, Rick took out Layne's wallet, searching for some ID.

A New Mexico driver's license, two credit cards, and a library card all identified Layne as the man they knew. There was two hundred dollars in cash. One business card presented a question. In plain script it had a phone number with area code, nothing more.

Rick walked down to the Stop-n-Go station and used their phone. When a machine answered, he left a simple message at the tone. "You have a mess to clean up out at Kelly."

Rick put the receiver back in its cradle.

## *21*

Early the next morning, on their way to the motel, Mayra and Sarina talked in hushed voices as Rick listened. He cleared his throat when he spotted the flashing emergency vehicles lights in the parking lot of the Zia Motor Lodge.

"Wonder what happened here last night?" Rick pointed at the commotion.

"Drive by slowly, Rick." Sarina leaned across the seat. "Maybe I can see what's going on."

The Wagoneer slowed almost to a halt. Rick's eyes kept darting from the flashing light bars to the road ahead of him.

"It's our room. Somehow they must have found Beth."

"I'm going to pull in. Sarina, you go up to the room and find out what's going on," Rick said.

Sarina climbed out of the jeep and walked over to the room. "Hey, what's going on here?"

"Who are you?" a paramedic asked.

"I'm Sarina Lake, Beth's roommate." Sarina looked at the still form lying on the bed. She saw loose strands of rope at the corners that looked like they were used to restrain Beth.

"Oh, my God! Is she dead?" Sarina asked, holding a hand over her mouth.

"No, we think somebody gave her a strong sedative of some sort." The young officer pulled a notebook from his jacket pocket. "The maid found her."

Sarina answered questions until the EMS unit took Beth away. The officer on duty called the station, and after a brief discussion with someone there, told Sarina that Sheriff Gomez would be around to take her statement personally.

"It's all yours, lock up when you're done." She turned back to the parking lot and returned to the Wagoneer.

"Tell us what happened over breakfast," Mayra yawned.

The three were sitting at the diner across from the Zia Motor Lodge, when Gomez appeared.

"Well, well. Mayra. I don't ever remember seeing you as a customer here before." The policeman pulled up a chair, sitting at the end of their booth.

"Good morning, officer," Rick said.

"That depends. For me, every morning I wake up is good. If the wife is in the mood, then it is a very good morning. I think that if I had just survived a life and death ordeal, then it would be an excellent morning." His eyes traveled from one to the other, taking in their bruises and bandages.

"Oh, good." Sarina smiled. "That means Beth's alive and well."

"Cut the shit, sweetheart, you know exactly what I'm talking about." Gomez touched his forehead in the exact location a small ugly bruise highlighted Sarina's hairline.

"What else could you be referring to, Gomez?" Rick tried a cheap imitation of Sarina's smile, ignoring Gomez' motions.

"The paramedics wouldn't tell us anything when they found Beth. I just thought you were being nice and letting us know how our friend is." Sarina cranked up her smile a notch.

"Oh, my God. Then you found David. Is he dead?" She didn't wait for an answer. Her head fell forward into her arms as loud sobs wracked her body. She had cried silently for half an hour when Rick broke the news last night. Now, it was hard to tell how much of Mayra's reactions were real. Possibly, Rick thought, this was a delayed reaction.

"No, Mayra, we haven't found any bodies. Yet. But we're still looking. There was a complaint from the town of Magdalena, which's west of here, about hearing loud noises south of town way late into last night."

"What is south of that town, officer?" Rick asked.

"Some old mines and grazing land for a ranch or two," Gomez replied.

"Did any of the ranchers report mysterious noises?"

"No, Mr. Prescott, they didn't."

"Why are you here, then? Are we suppose to be interested in the noises?" Mayra perked up suddenly, wiping away a tear.

"From the looks of you, I'd say you were involved in making the noises. Especially Mr. Prescott here and his lady. I should run you all in for questioning."

"Just on a report of noises? Nothing more substantial? I may have to contact the magazine's lawyers to see if I have grounds for a harassment charge," Rick said.

"Stop bothering us," Mayra said, "and go find my David."

"You should ask your friends where he is, Mayra. They can tell you a lot more than I can." Gomez got up and headed for the door. "Don't leave town for a while, ya hea'." He pointed his hand like a gun at the group.

The three sat there, thinking about what Gomez said and didn't say. The waitress stopped at the table checking drinks, breaking the spell.

"Evidently some one cleaned up the area very well," Rick said.

"Yeah, but who? Do we have any ideas?" Sarina asked.

"It could be anyone, the FBI, CIA, NSA or a secret military group." Rick shrugged.

"I don't believe it. I lived through last night and I still find it hard to believe," Mayra said.

"Oh, yeah, well let me tell you about an incident that happened while I was in college," Rick said.

During his sophomore and junior year of college, fifteen years ago, Rick worked as a night watchman at a large gravel pit. In the back of the yard, against the side of a mountain, the company had a dynamite bunker similar to the one they had been held prisoner in.

For a year and a half, he carried a gun, his .380, in a holster at the small of his back. Several times, he had to draw the weapon but he never fired it in anger. Some weekends, other security men would stop by with burgers and beer. Everyone would head for the back of the quarry, killing each beer can at least twice.

One day, Rick received a call from the chief of security, informing him that all the night watchmen had to attend a special meeting. When Rick got there, two men in dark suits took over the meeting.

A dangerous political activist was due to arrive in town the following day. For the next three nights, if any night watchman found a person tampering with the dynamite bunker, he had orders to shoot to kill.

One of the men in suits handed out white business cards with a telephone number boldly printed in black. As he passed out the cards, he said, "Kill the bastard, then call this number. After that, don't do a damned thing. Everything else will be taken care of."

On the way out of the office, the other man said, "Follow our instructions and everything will work out fine. Any variation and I promise you, you'll end up in shit so deep it'll take you a month to touch bottom."

"You're kidding, right?" Mayra asked.

"No. That's exactly what he told us," Rick nodded an affirmation.

"Come on, tell us what happened." Sarina said, shaking her head sadly.

"Well, our chief of security told us to stay away from the bunker. We were to take care of the rest of the place, but leave that area to him. He would assume personal responsibility for the dynamite."

"And?" Mayra asked again.

"We found out later that this guy had been a sniper in Vietnam and managed to bring his rifle with a twilight scope back with him. The twilight scope made it possible for him to see everything around the bunker in pitch dark. He spent the whole night, three nights in a row sitting on top of a hill watching the bunker."

"Did anyone approach the dynamite?" Sarina asked.

"No, but I believe he was weird enough to shoot anybody who would have gone to it, even one of us," Rick said.

"So, were the guys FBI or what?" Mayra asked.

"We never found out. They didn't identify themselves, except as working for the government. I even tried to call the phone number about a week later. It had been disconnected," Rick said.

"That means that it's possible for somebody in the government to go around killing people." Mayra sipped her soda.

"Rick, tell her about our experience at the debris field. That may help explain even more," Sarina said.

Rick went back over everything that happened to them, including his trouble out in L. A. Mayra interrupted him many times with questions, but overall she accepted their story.

"What you're saying, Rick is that it appears to be the military or a government agency doing all of these horrible things, but there's no definite proof," Mayra said.

"True, none of the men wear any standard

military uniforms with insignia, nor do the vehicles carry any known government plates. When we saw the wreckage of the jeeps being brought out, the semi's and flatbed trailers had vague military-like symbols and numbers, but there were no military police vehicles around, just local police officials who could be intimidated with a couple of phone calls from higher up."

"Don't forget the white Jeep Cherokees," Sarina added.

"Oh yeah, they were there also, but back on the fringe."

"So what we have is a group of para-military people involved with some sort of government or private organization running a cover-up of UFO's, space aliens and all that."

"Well, not all of it, Mayra. Look at the abduction stories. Many people believe them and they continue to receive a lot of attention. Doctors say that the regressive hypnosis experiments that are being conducted actually lead the patients into his or her story," Rick paused.

"In reality, no one is sure what happened to the abductees, or experiencers, as some investigators are calling them. There's evidence that if a person believes in something enough, then even that belief can influence his subconscious," Rick said.

"Many people scoff at the idea of abduction and feel that the whole idea is absurd. Others, especially the people personally involved in one, are very serious. If you compare abductions to crashes or crash retrievals with or without alien bodies, there seem to be a stronger case for the crashes. The government would try to counter the more serious threat, the crashes, while allowing the general feeling of humor to handle abductions," Sarina said.

"Along with the abductionist or experiencers, is a group of mental telepaths. All of this is considered to be laughable. Probably aided by the government through press releases of the more bizarre cases. All of this misinformation destroys the credibility these people are trying hard to build," Rick said.

"You mean some people actually believe that they have communicated with aliens using their minds?" Mayra asked, frowning.

"See, that is the exact reaction the cover-up people are hoping for. People who have had experiences like that will not talk about them. They're afraid of ridicule," Sarina replied.

Rick said nothing of Sarina's own experiences, waiting for her to make the choice. He looked into Sarina's eyes and saw her strength. She would tell Mayra, he was sure of it.

"Come on guys, you are kidding, right? Mental telepathy with flying saucers. Come on now."

"Mayra, what would it take to convince you? Would it take a personal experience or would you accept another person's word?" Sarina's voice had an edge to it.

"Depending on the person. I could probably accept their word. Why?"

"Let me tell you. My sister had an experience as a young girl. She saw an object in the sky then lost two hours of time. This was close to dinner after school one afternoon. Our mother sent me out to look for her." Sarina's face was blank, without any trace of emotion, her eyes appeared hollow. Rick thought she appeared to be in a low state of a trance.

"I looked everywhere. All up and down our street and in the fields behind our house. I even called our friends to see if she was visiting. Nothing. My sister was gone." Tears welled in her eyes and flowed slowly down her cheeks as she remembered the experience.

"Mother got scared and wanted to call the police. Daddy finally got home from work and calmed mom down. I called our friends again with no results. Suddenly, I felt a strong impulse jolt through my body, like an electrical shock. My parents say that I stood still and my entire body vibrated, then I returned to normal. No more than five minutes later, just as we were about to call the police, Tabitha, my sister, walked through the door as if nothing had happened."

"Surely you don't think the two are connected, do you?" Mayra asked.

"Yes, yes they are. I mean, we thought it was nerves, Tabitha was not aware of the missing time. That worried all of us, so my experience was forgotten. Until..." Sarina's tears slowed as her forehead furrowed deeply. Rick was afraid she was in pain.

"Until two nights later. Just after dark, I had another one of those seizures, like a tremor moving through me."

"What was it?" Mayra asked, her forehead creased with worry lines. She studied Sarina's face.

"No one knew. It happened again about an

hour later. Mother gave me a warm glass of milk and made me go to bed. Then my parents quizzed Tabitha for another hour on her whereabouts. My sister was just as startled as they were worried about the missing two hours." Sarina sighed, leaned back into the booth's cushion and tried to relax.

"The next morning, we heard about people seeing flying sauces twice during the night. I had my spells about the same time. Our folks were scared. Tabitha said something about seeing a bright light then she sorta woke up as she walked into the house. After reporting it to the authorities, we were visited by a guy in a military uniform and were told never to mention anything about this." A tired look settled over Sarina's face, as a deep sigh escaped from deep within her.

"I'd have one of my spells every time a UFO was reported nearby," Sarina said. "My sister, Tabitha, had several more encounters over the next three years. There were at least two more times where she lost as much as three hours of time."

Slowly, over the same period of time, Sarina noticed that she could find things. If a key fell off the hook just inside the back door, Sarina's mother wanted her to look for it. Often her reply was simply to look behind the refrigerator. She knew the key had bounced over five feet from where it should have been.

Another time, Sarina felt a car crash. She was walking home from school thinking about her best friend Helen Schmitt. Suddenly, a shock coursed through her entire body. Sarina heard Helen calling for her mother. The screams deafened her. Moments later, the screaming slowly faded, seeming to rise above Sarina as Helen's call for her mother became fainter and fainter.

When the noise in Sarina's head was finally silenced, she felt a great emptiness all the way to the pit of her stomach. She knew what it was like to be in a black hole in space. Sarina's insides were being sucked in just as light would be pulled into the vast void of a black hole.

Later that day, she discovered that her best friend had been killed in a car accident approximately at the same time Sarina had her experience. This was only the beginning. Whenever some one she knew underwent a traumatic experience, she knew it. Whenever flying saucers were near, she knew it.

It took her most of her high school years to learn to control these emotional intrusions. Finally, Sarina learned to block out the experience. She compared it to call waiting, where her mind is actively pursuing a subject, then her thoughts are interrupted by a brief tingle.

Sarina swore that the two events were tied together. She could not remember even the slightest psychic activity before her sister disappeared for two hours. Then suddenly, she had unwanted powers.

"You mean that you actually feel what is happening to other people around you. That you sense any flying saucers that zip by?" Mayra asked.

"Under certain circumstances, yes. With those people, they have to be people that I know well." She glanced at Rick, her eyes softened. "Finding things is a bit different. Someone will ask, do you know where the is item is? Almost simultaneously I'll see a picture of it laying someplace. The question and image are practically instantaneous. If I have to think about a lost object, it usually stays lost." Sarina shrugged.

"Anyway, that is where we're come from on this, Mayra." Rick said. "We still don't know which agency or agencies are behind all of this."

"Tell me about this Layne guy. I thought he was on your side."

"Yes, Rick, did you find anything on his body or in his room when you searched it? Do you know if Sheriff Gomez had been there yet?" Sarina asked.

"I don't thing Gomez can search the room until he has some kind of report or suspicion that will give him just cause. I took Layne's room key and his wallet. His wallet had some money, a couple of business cards of his from the museum and a card with only a phone number on it, plus his driver license and two credit cards.

"There were no clues as to his true identify in the room, at least I didn't find any. Both the driver license and credit cards were in the name of Layne Gunther. The phone number was a recording using what sounded like a computerized voice. By the way, I called the number again and it was not an operating number."

"Who was Layne?" Sarina asked.

"The best I can figure is he was a mole. You know an agent that is put in a certain position to see what is happening. Remember Beth saying that anyone seriously interested in UFO's should Layne because he knew all about the Roswell story and was their resident expert." Rick reached for

Sarinas hand. "If everyone who had any real interest worked with him, then he would be able to keep track of their investigation and if they turned up anything important, he would know about it."

"That's right, Rick. Look, shortly after we started searching the rock cairns instead of the surface out there at the debris field, the cammo-dudes show up. Then the day we actually discover two pieces of metal, the cammo dudes try to kill us." Sarina paused. A confused look filled her face. "Rick, if they stole the metal from us at Lawrences', then why were they after us? Why would they try to kill us?"

"They attacked me, not you. I guess those guys could easily tell the difference between two slivers of tin off a Campbell's soup can and flying saucer pieces." Rick smiled.

"What!" Sarina almost shouted, drawing heads her way. Softly, she asked, "You mean you substituted the real metal for fake ones? Why didn't you tell...never mind, I see."

With a sad look on her face, Sarina frowned and said in a low husky voice, "but, still, you didn't even tell me. After what we have become?"

Mayra blushed slightly, cleared her throat and asked. "You actually have pieces of a flying saucer? Where?"

"Yes, Mayra, we do. They're in a safe place." Looking at Sarina he smiled. "I really don't want anyone to know because that would endanger his or her life also. But, seeing as how you accidentally got involved, I'm taking a chance."

"Wow, we still have them. Now it all makes sense. Every time we turn around and discover something, boom, the bad guys show up," Sarina said.

"That was why Layne insisted on nightly reports to Lawrence. So he could keep up to date and pass on the information. Those guys out there in LA were looking for me."

"Oh, my God, Rick, you mean that if I had been the one who found out who Donald was, then somebody in Washington would have tried to kill me?"

Rick grabbed her hands and looked into her eyes. "Yes, I think so. Now I am twice as glad that they were after me instead. I wouldn't want anything to happen to you."

"What would have happened if he and Beth would have discovered anything?" Mayra asked.

"I think that up to last night, Beth was probably the safest one of us. I can't see Layne actually releasing any real information to us."

"Why didn't he turn on us at Capitan while we were waiting for the cammo-dudes with the truck? Beth is the one that almost gave us away."

"You know Sarina I thought about that. Maybe he was hoping that Beth would succeed, or maybe he became curious about our next step. Also, their attempt had failed in killing me and recovering the metal. He was probably hoping that he could find out where it was."

"Yeah, you're right," Sarina said. "That explains why Lawrence's place was suddenly searched. Again, after we found out the movie was a fake, and finally why nothing happened to Dyba until after Layne and Beth showed up."

"Now, maybe we can continue in peace. If

they were going to arrest me for murder, it would already have happened. Gomez could not find any evidence of last night. The only thing now is to see Beth and get her side of the story," Rick said.

## *22*

Beth anxiously awaited Sarina and Rick's arrival at the hospital. She couldn't wait to leave. The doctor expressed some concern about the early release, but Beth politely brushed him off.

On the drive back to the motel, they filled her in on the previous night's events, concluding with their discovery of Beth in her room. Tears came to Beth's eyes briefly at the mention of Layne's death, but anger quickly dried them up.

"Good. That son of a bitch deserved it. He, we, well, you know. We were together for a while, then last night, we made love again before he drugged me, and I woke up in the hospital. What was he going to do?"

"Whoa, we didn't know you two were lovers," Rick frowned. "I'm sorry to say that he was going to kill you. This morning he would take you out to the mine where you would help him look for us. Sometime during the search you were to have an accident."

Sarina placed a consoling hand on Beth's shoulder and mumbled an apology.

Beth sighed, "That's my life story. Every man I meet is an asshole," looking at Rick, "present company excluded. Well. What do we do now? Our star witness is dead. Everything else has been stolen. This is beginning to resemble a disaster movie."

Rick pulled into the Zia Motor Lodge parking lot. "I, for one, want to sit back and think for a while. Why don't we meet for dinner and see what everybody wants to do at this point."

Later that afternoon, Mayra stood behind the counter as she served Rick a cup of coffee. Beth and Sarina came in, nodded in their direction and settled into a booth at the back. Rick picked up his cup and saucer, rose and headed their way.

"If anybody wants to quit and go home, there will be no hard feelings. Me, I'm going to nose around at least one more day."

Both women agreed to stay. They also decided to continue to share a room, mostly to ease Beth's nerves. They were unsure what to do next, but were not ready to give up.

"I want to visit the mine. See for myself how good a job the agency did of hiding all the evidence. Why did he choose that mine? There are a lot of others closer to Socorro that are just as isolated, I'm sure."

"You're right, but how do we go about keeping Gomez from being suspicious?" Sarina asked.

"I'm not sure, yet. Let me think about it. Sarina, do you still have that map Walter gave us? The one with area attractions on it?"

"It's back in the room, want me to go get it?" Sarina got up and left.

"Please, it may be helpful, real soon. Mayra, didn't you say that Gomez stops by here almost every afternoon for dinner or coffee?"

"Yes he does, Rick." Mayra turned to look at

the clock in the Coca-Cola sign. "He should be here within the next ten minutes or so."

Rick had a plan. "When he comes in, ignore him. Beth, don't even look his way. I'll keep Sarina's attention if she's back before then and Mayra, you pay him as little mind as possible. If he sits at the counter, grab the coffeepot and bring it over to our table. I want him to focus on us. I'll get him over here to the table."

Sarina returned, handing the rolled up map to Rick as she slid in beside him. He spread it out on the table and anchored the corners with the salt and pepper shakers, his coffee cup and the sugar container. Gomez walked through the door just as Rick located what he was after on the map.

The policeman barely looked around the room as he headed for the corner counter stool. Before he sat down, he reached behind the counter, grabbing a coffee mug.

Mayra moved to the far end of the counter as Gomez crossed the room. She looked at Rick. He nodded. Mayra picked up the coffeepot and holding it in front of her, walked past the sheriff straight to Rick's booth. She stood off to the side while refilling his cup. With a wink and a grin, she turned. Gomez had a scowl crowding his face.

"Oh, it's Sheriff Gomez. Want some coffee?" Mayra moved slowly toward him.

"Hey there Gomez, grab your cup and come on over. We are planning a day of sight seeing and you should be able to help us out," Rick said.

Gomez continued to scowl at them as he lifted the cup to his lips. Just as he took a sip, Sarina called out.

"You know anything about Kelly. The old mine? It's on the way to VLA."

Gomez sputtered coffee every where. The officer grabbed a napkin and patted his chin, then the front of his uniform. Mayra grimaced, holding a straight face as she helped clean up the countertop with a towel. Gomez gasped. "Kelly, what, yea," a look of shock and disbelief crossed his face. "It is an old mine, it can be dangerous out there if you don't know what you are doing." Gomez growled. "That's not a safe place to be, you should know that already."

"Well, we promise to be careful and stay out of any trouble, officer," Sarina smiled, her eyes fluttering.

"What kind of trouble should we watch for Sheriff Gomez?" Beth asked, injecting a serious note into the conversation.

"There are some open vertical shafts out there and many of the others have weak shoring or supporting timbers. Personally, I wouldn't go into any of them." Gomez replied. "I'd go on out the VLA then maybe visit the dry lake beds."

Looking from one to the other, Rick winked. "That sounds like a plan. Thanks."

The second trip through Magdalena to the ghost town of Kelly was much more enjoyable for Sarina and Rick. Sarina led Beth from place to place, looking for signs of last night. Little evidence remained, the charred wood from their fire, and footprints in and around the dynamite bunker were all Sarina could see.

Rick looked for the scorched ground where

the ATV burned. Even that had been raked over. Cautiously he moved to the lip of the pit where he found Donald Dyba's body. Peering over the edge, he could not find any sign of the body.

The first cross bracing was down about fifteen feet. That was where Rick remembered Dyba being. His body was stretched out across most of the wooded crossbeams. Now, with sunlight, he could see a horizontal shaft a little way below the beams.

Rick returned to his Wagoneer and found the hemp rope he usually kept there. Throwing it over his shoulder, he returned to the shaft calling for the two women. As he knotted the rope every three feet, he explained to them what he intended to do.

Sarina and Beth were free to explore the horizontal shaft after Rick disappeared into the vertical one below. Moving past the overturned ore cart, they were amazed at all the hard rock drilling that went into the tunnel. It had to be six feet wide and eight feet tall along its entire length. Twice they stopped when they discovered wooden flooring.

Sarina got down on hands and knees to peer through a long crack between the planks. She couldn't see the bottom for all of the trash resting about twenty feet below her. Cans, bottles and scraps of metal and wood were everywhere.

The women hesitated again at the second plank flooring, this time; the hole below them appeared bottomless. At least ten seconds passed before a weak splash returned to them. Approximately a hundred feet with water at the bottom, Sarina and Beth judicially worked their way around the edge of the flooring.

Rough rock showed where the miners stopped working on the shaft. A smaller shaft about half the size of the main one dropped four feet to the right before continuing deeper into the mountain. Here, the floor was littered with rocks of all sized. The two women followed the tunnel.

Veins of a bluish crystalline hue followed them. The rocky material appeared rotten to Beth. When she scraped it, chunks would fall off leaving loose flakes around the new scratch marks. Sarina noticed that the mineshaft now had a decided declination to it.

Gradually the angle became more noticeable as the women had to scan the floor to be sure not to step on any slippery surfaces that would sent them cascading downward.

Ahead, they noticed another sharp turn and from appearances, the flooring leveled off again. An echo grew louder the closer they approached the turn. Rounding the corner, wooden slats blocked the way. Sarina could not find any sign of pending danger.

Together, the women peered through the slats. Beyond was a large chamber with a fairly even floor. Back to the left, farther into the mountain they noticed a blacker area that seemed to absorb their flashlight beams.

"Sarina, look!" Beth's voice echoed loudly.

"What is it?"

"Check out these nails. Don't they look fairly new? They do to me."

Sarina flashed her light across the nail heads catching a faint glitter of light when the nail head had been struck. "You're right. This is new."

"Maybe this is where they hid everything." Beth peered through the slats waving her flashlight around.

"You're right, let's go get Rick."

"No, not yet. We'll explore some more, then if necessary we can go get Rick."

With that comment, Beth lifted her right leg, drew it back, and kicked the rear plank as hard as she could. They heard a faint squeal of nails leaving the wood. She kicked again. Sarina joined her. Three more kicks and one plank ripped away from the other, flying into the chamber.

Now there was enough room to duck under and enter the chamber. Beth and Sarina agreed to work side by side circling the room from right to left, leaving the darkest part to last.

Above their heads, the ceiling rose at least twenty feet. In one spot, it looked as if a narrow ledge were hiding another possible hole or shaft. Shallow indention's showed where the miners searched for ore, but no other exits presented themselves.

The closer the two got to the darkness, the more a gentle downward slope became apparent. Beth mentioned that the dark area resembled a small wind blown cave. As they swept the floor with their flashlights, they picked up the smell of age. Musky age.

Laid out against the back wall were two bundles of ivory colored sticks covered with what appeared to be burlap. Cautiously, they women stepped nearer. One of the whitish sticks ended with a knob of some sort.

"Oh my God!" Sarina said. "Oh my God." The beam of her light quivered.

"What Sarina?" Beth looked closer.

"Bones. Those are bones." Sarina's beam of light fluttered even more.

"They're human beings or at least at one time they were. Look, they still have clothing. Two people. Dead a long time I'd imagine." Beth said, gently nudging one of the piles.

"Let's get Rick."

"Rick, Rick, Rick. That's all you can thing about girl. We can handle this. Damn, it's only a couple of dead people. How messy can a couple of skeletons be?"

"But Beth. Don't you think Rick wants to know what we found?'

"Let him keep exploring, maybe he will find something else. He might find where they dumped all that evidence you two keep talking about."

Sarina turned toward Beth and shined the light in Beth's face. "You talk as if you don't believe us. After what happened to you, how could you doubt our story?"

Beth shoved the flashlight out of her eyes. "Girl, don't you ever do anything like that again. I believe most of your story, but I don't get how the two of you could have killed four soldiers or whatever they were. You're a wimp and Rick, well, he's a mild mannered fool."

"That's not true."

"You're a wimp." Beth shoved Sarina's shoulder lightly.

"Shut up." Sarina dropped her light and

shoved Beth back.

"Come on now Sarina, is that all you can do?" Beth sat her light on the floor to one side, illuminating Sarina's legs. "If you are going to do something, do it right." She grazed Sarina's shoulder with her knuckles.

Sarina moved backward reflexively at the touch and stumbled over a large rock. She went down hard, landing on her butt.

Beth was there almost immediately. "Oh, baby, you OK? I was just fooling around." Her hands went to Sarina's shoulder to steady her. "Sometimes I can get carried away."

Trying to shake off Beth's hands, Sarina said, "I'm OK, but it didn't sound like you were playing."

Beth gasped, "Look, here we're talking about these two piles of bones and you go sit down beside them."

Sarina scrabbled around on the floor, trying to move away from the bones. Her searching hand located her flashlight, which by some miracle still worked.

"Come here, Sarina. Look, I think these were two men. Few women wore men's clothing as long ago as it took for these two to melt down like this."

"I wish you'd stop making jokes like that. It's not, right."

"Decompose sounds a lot more gross then melt. Anyway, lighten up. There's nothing we can for them except report their remains to somebody and maybe see if family is still around. They can bury them. Let's find out who they were."

Beth went through the remaining pockets in

their clothing.  She found two wallets, a leather billfold under one of the remains and a canvas wallet still tucked into the other man's pocket.

Shining her light so Beth could see, Sarina stood mesmerized by the other woman's casual actions.

"Holy shit!  This one was born in 1949.  The picture shows a cute youngster with a cuter young girl.  Maybe high school sweethearts."  Beth held the picture up for Sarina who only grunted.

"Now this one.  He was born in 1947.  Must have been the older bad boy influence on cutie-pie here.  How else would the pair of them end up way the hell back in here."

"Does he have any pictures?  It's kind of sad to think that someone that young just disappeared like this and nobody knew what happened to them.  Do you think any of their family is alive?"

"Come on Sarina.  This happened a long time ago.  Any parents would be close to eighty or so by now.  My guess is that any family probably left here themselves.  Or, hey, these guys could be drifters from anywhere."

"Come on Beth, I'm getting the shakes.  Hurry up and look through their stuff."

"Here we go again.  Do you have the shakes because you are getting scared or overcome with sorrow or are you starting to get messages from beyond telling about these poor boys lives?"

"Shut up, Beth!  Just shut the hell up!"

"OK, OK, geez you're touchy."  Beth flipped through the crumbling plastic photo container.  A small piece of yellowed paper fluttered to the dusty floor. "Hey, hey. Look what I found."

Sarina leaned closer, "What is it?"

"A note, dummy." Beth carefully unfolded the paper. On the inside smudges in pencil were the words 'Bat Cave'. "What does that mean?"

"Bat Cave. Maybe it is someplace around here."

"Or maybe it is just a nickname for their favorite cave or even mineshaft."

\* \* \*

Rick's hands burned by the time he reached the first side tunnel. Looking down, he had seen the blackness that identified at least one more shaft. Trying to step off the knotted rope onto the floor, he realized too late that it was a bad idea. His foot slid out from under him twice, almost causing him to tumble into the void below.

Finally, Rick swung far enough into the mouth of the shaft to drop off onto the rock-strewn floor. He pulled the rope behind him until he found a place to tie it off, reassuring himself of an exit.

Seventy feet into the shaft, Rick found nothing but gravel on a loose dirt floor. The miners followed an ore vein until it petered out or changed direction. A narrow alcove led off to the left of the dead end. Two long timbers protruded upward from a hole. Flashing his light down into the hole, Rick saw a wooden ladder descending into the darkness. He estimated twenty-five feet to the next lower tunnel.

Checking the wooden cross bars, Rick believed it was still sturdy enough to take his weight. The dry desert climate and constant temperature in the mine preserved most objects left there. Slowly,

Rick placed most of his weight on the first rung. It groaned some under his bulk, but held.

Rick's sore hands screamed at him as he tried to distribute his weight evenly. He stepped lower. Descending into the near darkness was unnerving. To keep both hands free, Rick shoved the long cylindrical handle of his flashlight through his belt. He had a good view where he had been, but not of where he headed. Five rungs and stop, drag out the light and look down, check out the next five steps. Then he repeated the procedure again.

Someplace around the twentieth rung, one snapped. Rick's foot went out and down. His body fell against the wooden ladder as his chin came in contact with one of the steps. Fear more than anything else kept Rick from a serious fall. Both hands gripped the wooden uprights. Pain seared his brain.

What felt like hours passed. Hanging by his hands and one foot, Rick's mind cataloged each place that ached. Both hands hurt, his chin was tender and to top it all, he bit his tongue. His left knee ached as it passed through the broken rung. His ribs throbbed from slamming into the ladder.

Then, total darkness enveloped him. Somehow the flashlight he was carrying came out of his belt and fell. Rick was trapped, halfway up the decrepit ladder with no way to see what lay before him.

Taking deep breaths, Rick slowly righted himself below the broken rung. He lowered himself further, sweeping his foot back and forth, searching for the next rung. Twenty minutes later and one more missed step, Rick was at the bottom of the ladder. Feeling around, he found a place to sit.

Only after the strenuous trip down the ladder did Rick allow himself five minutes rest. He was afraid that he would suffer muscle cramps and be stuck here. He moved toward the circle of weak light that winked at him from the mouth of the tunnel.

This opening was even smaller than the one above it. Rick practically crawled the entire length on hands and knees. The air was fresher and cleaner at the entrance of the vertical shaft, but the end of the rope barely protruded from the upper tunnel and dropped within about fifteen feet above him.

* * *

Beth and Sarina stood in front of the mineshaft gulping in the fresh air. They could not believe that they just spent two hours underground. A fine dust had settled in their nostrils that was hard to remove. The two women crossed to the Wagoneer and took out a gallon jug of water. Taking turns, they splashed the water on their faces, arms and necks. At least now, they could feel a little cleaner.

From the vertical shaft, they heard Rick call their names. Distortion made it hard to hear distinctly, but they hurried to the edge. After a quick discussion, Beth grabbed the rope ladder Rick had tied to a standing pipe and jerked it several times before it came loose from the rock Rick had secured it to, dropping the lower end within Rick's reach.

Rick painfully pulled his way out of the pit. A deep drought of water helped revive him as he listened to the women's story.

"I'll tell you right now, I am not going back

down that damned hole, but I would like to see the two bodies before we go back to town," Rick wiped his forehead.

"If it is all the same to you, I'll let Beth take you back in there. It really gave me the willy's being close to those two poor boys."

"She means, willy's as in spooky, not as in psychic experience," Beth said.

"Come on, Beth, let's get this over with. Leave Sarina alone." Rick picked up Sarina's flashlight and flipped the switch a couple of times to ensure it worked properly. He did not particularly want to end up in the dark again.

Rick and Beth took a quick look at the bodies, their clothing and the contents of both wallets before heading back out into daylight. Sheriff Gomez was leaning against the hood of his patrol car as they exited the mineshaft. Sarina stood solemnly to his right sipping on a luke warm coke.

"Well hello again. Heard you found something different than what brought you out here."

"Don't know what you thought we were looking for, but we sure did find something unusual." Rick thought of the piece of paper securely tucked into his wallet.

## 23

"Called the diner and found out you folks were still in town," Walt said, sipping a glass of beer. "Boy, you sure lead an interesting life." The printer chuckled and swirled the liquid in the glass.

"Walt, glad to see you," Rick said from the doorway. He ushered Beth and Sarina into the dining room and over to Walt's table. Mayra came over quickly, took drink orders, and exchanged greetings.

"Word got around you found some bodies out by Kelly."

"Where did you hear that, Walt? We only got back in town a couple of hours ago."

"I've been in the printing business here since Gutenberg invented the damn things. Everything interesting, and some things not so interesting, reach my ears, especially after I put a claim on somebody. Anything I can help you with? Gomez trying to charge you with a crime?"

"He's very angry with us for various reasons, but he really doesn't have a shred of evidence of any crime," Rick said.

Sarina looked at Rick then cleared her throat. "Walt, if you have time, I'd like to tell you what we saw and see if you can help."

Rick nodded in agreement, while Walt sipped his drink. Mayra came back delivering drinks to the others and taking food orders. Slowly, Beth and

Sarina took turns describing their experiences in the mine. Walt's interest perked up at the mention of the bodies.

"Do you know any names? Ages? What about their belongings?" Walt asked.

"We don't know," Beth said.

"What did the Sheriff's Department have to say?"

"Walt," Beth said, "I told you, we don't know anything."

"I vaguely remember a story about two young men, but they weren't missing. Is there anything else that would help?" Walt leaned back into the chair, finishing off his beer.

"Only this," Rick said, opening his wallet and taking out the scrap of yellowed paper. He tossed it to Walt.

"Bat Cave," Walt read, "Yeah, I remember a news story. Tell you what, I'll check it out and get back to you."

Rick, curious about the two bodies, called the Sheriff's office the next day and talked to Gomez. It was too early for any lab results according to him. Gomez went so far as to say that they only had tentative ID on the bodies, and since they found the bodies, he would contact Rick as soon as he had any positive results.

During the morning, Walt left a message at the motel and diner. When Rick returned the call, Walt was still excited.

"I found them. You won't believe this, but I have some stuff right up your alley."

"Where do we meet? Can you get away from

work?"

"Come over here, then I'll take you to the college library," Walt said.

Twenty minutes later, the Wagoneer pulled under the large cottonwoods that shaded much of the large luscious grass lawns interspersed between the earth tone buildings comprising the College of Mines. Few cars were in the lot next to the physical plant. Rick squinted, the college press building appeared deserted. That wasn't a good sign.

"Wait here girls. I don't like the looks of this. Walt's truck isn't in the parking lot and I don't see any light through the window."

Looking around, Rick noticed a Sheriff's patrol car slowly cruising down the street just off campus. It stopped behind one of the towering cottonwoods.

"Look like we may have a tail, back on the street, by that second cottonwood."

"Why are they following us?" Sarina asked.

"In the last two days we've been involved in a shoot-out, kidnapping, and discovery of two bodies. What do you think, Sarina?" Beth made a face at the other woman.

"They can't prove the shoot-out. It is only supposition on their part. There's no logical way to associate us with the bodies," Sarina responded.

"Somebody put a bee in their bonnet," Beth said. "Otherwise they wouldn't be wasting their time on us."

Rick reached the door to the print shop. It was unlocked. As he stepped through the doorway, he noticed the only light was coming from a small desk lamp in the main office. "Hello?"

Silence answered Rick. The total quiet added to the eeriness of the situation. Rick remembered his last visit. The sound had been deafening. Presses that normally ran full blast now sat idle. As he sidestepped into the office, Rick felt a presence behind him.

Rick dropped and swiveled around quickly, moving further into the office.

"Walt! God, you scared me nearly to death. You said you'd be here waiting for us. When I saw the place empty, I got worried."

"At the last minute, I figured I'd go ahead and copy those newspaper articles and a map that I found. This way we wouldn't have to go traipsing back over there to the library. I'm hungry, buy me some lunch and we'll call it even." Walt waved a thin manila folder under Rick's nose.

The newspaper articles were thirty some years old. Two young men in town tried to form a caving club. Evidently, according to the first of several articles, the pair were moderately successful. On the club's third field trip, two other members were caught in a minor cave-in at a mine just west of Socorro.

Both men were brought out alive, but one remained in serious condition for a month in the local hospital. Many people in town, notably parents, clambered for the club to close down. Caving one thing, going into closed mines was another.

The next article was printed three months later. Two locals reported visiting a cave the other side of San Agustin Plain, south of the town of Datil. In the cave, they reported seeing unusual machinery.

At this point, the reporter seems to have twisted the story.

Laughingly, the reporter hinted that the two youths swore what they found was unlike anything they had ever seen. Possibly a flying saucer. How the huge, flying saucer first got into the cave remained a mystery. The youth's had described the entrance as being little more than a crawly hole on the side of a mountain.

A follow-up article made the young men out to be the laughing stocks of the community. Surprisingly, the last article mentioned that both young men were on their way back east, having received scholarships to different universities. Nothing more appeared in the Socorro paper.

Walt and Rick knew why the last article concerning these two men would be close to thirty years in the writing. Now they would wait and see. Gomez should search missing persons, but the men's names would not show up there. Rick discussed copying the first newspaper story and sending it to Gomez anonymously.

"If we can get the names then he should also have them and be able to come up with the same information we did," Walt said.

"You're right, let's wait and see how Gomez handles this." Rick nodded in agreement.

The afternoon edition of the paper carried the news story. Two bodies, still unidentified, were found in an abandoned mine. Further investigation would continue.

Sarina was furious. For some unknown reason, the paper had written a mostly fictitious story about finding the bodies. No names, no mention of her or Beth discovering the bodies. Even the location was ambiguous. She called the Sheriff's office and talked to Gomez.

"Gomez, why'd you let them print that article? You know a lot more than what was said, why not tell the real story?"

"Miss, we are in the middle of an investigation. We don't want the perpetrators to know how much information we really have."

"Investigation? You mean you guys are treating this like a murder investigation?"

"Yes, ma'am, we are. I don't expect you to know how important it is to keep a lot of the information private in a case like this. We don't want to spook the person who did this."

"Spook them, hell. The guy who did this is liable to be a spook himself after thirty years. This is ridiculous. Since you know the boy's names, you should get in touch with the family and see what they can tell you."

"Miss. Don't tell me how to do my job," Gomez growled. "I don't tell you how to hold your seances, now do I?"

"I don't do seances!" Sarina slammed the receiver down. Turning to Beth she exclaimed. "I cannot believe the audacity of that that, boob."

Beth shook her head and "hummed" and "hawed" at the correct places. She agreed with Gomez being a boob, but she did not agree with Sarina's idea of going to the paper with the real story. She felt that the group had enough trouble without actively looking for more.

When Rick heard Sarina's idea, he squelched it quickly, then turned his attention to the map. After an hour of research, he found a mention of Bat Cave.

It was off in the middle of nowhere close to a spring. An old army map showed Horseshoe Spring at the end of an unimproved jeep trail twelve miles south of Datil. One mile away to the east was a symbol showing a cave and the name.

Walt and Rick searched other maps. But none of the updated ones showed the cave, while another one didn't even show the spring.

Rick got together with the women and they made plans to head out to Bat Cave. Walt begged off, saying that he was too old. Anyway, according to him, who would let the magazine know what happened to its star journalist if they were abducted and never returned?

Rick purchased three powerful flashlights, as well as extra batteries, snack foods, bottles of water and lightweight packs to carry all of the supplies. He threw in more rope and a compass for good measure.

## *24*

Standing at the base of a large rockslide, Rick felt tired, yet invigorated. The mile hike from the spring was across dry arroyos, sand dunes, and through scrub brush. Sarina and Beth stood at Rick's side panting.

While he waited for the women to catch their breath, Rick scrutinized the surrounding terrain. He pulled out a piece of paper with the boy's story on it.

"Ladies, as soon as you're up to it, we have a climb to make." Over their groans, he continued, "It seems that we must go up the left side of this slide. How far, we don't know."

Moving slowly toward a large rock with a flat upper surface, Beth moaned, "I know how far I'm going." She pointed at the rock.

"Me too." Sarina gasped, following Beth.

"Here," Rick said, sliding his pack from his back. "I'll leave this with you two. While you powder your noses, I'm going to scout the area." With one flashlight in hand, he made his way up the slope.

"I'll powder you in a minute." Sarina picked up a pebble and tossed it in Rick's general direction.

Rick looked behind each large boulder he came across, hoping that the entrance was hidden from view. He almost passed over it when he did discover the opening. Two thirds of the way up the hill, he spotted a large flat rock lying across two smaller ones. The crawl space between them was comfortable. Off to one side near a supporting rock, was an area darker than the rest.

Rick's flashlight beam disappeared into the blackness. A small waterway had been cut into the dirt from the high side. Rick reasoned that after a rain, water poured down to this point and into the hole. Rick edged nearer the vertical shaft. He rubbed his right hand down along the edge of the darkness. The ground was slick. He called out for the women to join him.

Rick waited twenty minutes for the women to reach him. They sat down just outside the crawlway, rested, and talked.

"Do you think this is the entrance?" Beth asked.

"Don't know for sure, yet. I plan on tying one of the flashlights to the rope and lowering it down to see how deep the hole is. Maybe that way we can find out without having to get dirty ourselves," Rick said.

"While you do that, I'll look around some more."

"Good idea, Beth. Be sure to search behind all the boulders. The entrance could be hidden just like this one," Rick said.

Sarina fumbled through her pack, pulling a thin rope out and handed it to Rick. Accepting it, Rick snagged a knot around the handle of one of the big flashlights. The two of them snuggled close in the cramped quarters. Light beams brightly lit the sides of the hole. They could see that for at least twenty feet they would have a slide. The dirt was still damp and resembled clay.

Just at the last reaches of the beam, it looked as if the floor evened off and a tunnel led away to their right. Rick leaned a little further outward and twisted the rope, spinning the light at the other end. He could clearly distinguish three solid walls, and a floor littered with small plant-like debris.

As Rick and Sarina emerged from their cubbyhole, Beth was stuffing something back into her pack and pulling out a bottle of water. "You were right, Rick. Come over here. I found a long piece of pipe. It looks as if a piece of rope had once been tied to it."

Rick and Sarina called out their news in return as they crossed over to Beth who was leaning causally against another rock. The pipe was five feet long at least. In its center pieces of fibers still clung to the rounded surface where something had rotted off. Rubbing it with his hand, Rick scrubbed some fibrous flakes of rust off.

"You're right, Beth. Sure looks like somebody tied a knot around this. Had to be quite long ago too."

"Rick, if you look back to the hole, this is just about as far as a man could fling the rod away from there."

Slowly, Rick nodded as he visually took in the distance implied. "Yep. Sure looks that way. Let's go back up there and get ready. I'm going down the hole. You two can wait here and prepare to follow me if I find anything interesting."

Preparations required fifteen minutes of work.

Half of the time was spent lodging the pipe into the rock to hold the rope Beth was lowering into the hole. Rick put on a pair of gloves and took two lights. After his last experience in a tunnel, he wanted to be prepared. He backed down the sixty-five degree incline trying to maintain his balance on the clay-like slippery surface.

A mound of dirt, gravel, small sticks and the semi-petrified remains of a generation or two of rodents covered the bottom of the hole. A jagged fissure, narrow at the tip but fairly wide led off to one side. In the other direction, the fissure seemed to have been filled in naturally. Flashing his light through the opening, Rick watched the beam disappear into the void. There was no reflection from a nearby dead-end.

Rick called the women. "I'm going to explore the shaft to see if it's worth your efforts to come down." On hands and knees, he worked his way down the tunnel. Every once in a while, he would bang his head on a rock overhead as he looked up to check his progress.

The crack ran on and on, heading downward at a slight angle. As Rick followed it, he became aware of a faint musty odor. Rick knew it was familiar, but could not place it. Rick knew at some point he would have to decide whether to keep going or return to the surface for Beth and Sarina.

Rick's shoulder glanced off a protrusion to his left. He lost his balance and started to fall to the right. What he saw as a small alcove in that direction turned out to be the entrance to another downward shaft. As Rick fell toward it, he splayed his arms and legs apart. The fingers of one hand grabbed a narrow rock ledge as the dirt crumbled under the pressure of his fingers on his other hand. His flashlight tumbled and bounced downward fifteen or so feet before blinking out. Inch by inch, Rick wormed his body away from the drop off.

Now was the time Rick realized, to stop, and return for the women. Gripping the barrel of his only remaining flashlight, Rick turned and headed for the opening. He was surprised that he couldn't see even a faint glow from the entrance.

Finally, the darkness in front of him paled. For the first time, he looked at his watch and realized he had been crawling around for over an hour. It didn't seem to Rick that it had been nearly that long.

As he reached the rope, he called out to the women. Sarina's voice sounded frantic, while Beth almost sounded surprised to hear from him again. Rick was near exhaustion as he crawled out of the hole and into the open air. He sat panting and drinking in deep gulps of fresh air. It never tasted so good. Even when he was underground at Kelly, he had not been totally submerged in the mustiness experienced here.

It was too late in the day to go back in, besides, Rick wanted to replace his lost flashlight. He expected that they might end up spending all day tomorrow underground, so he wanted them to have plenty of snacks and a lightweight blanket or jacket.

* * *

The next day, they left the spring at sun up, better prepared for the hike and climb. Rick descended first, then the gear was lowered. Finally,

Sarina and Beth dropped into the darkness. Today would be an interesting day, Rick was sure.

Rick took the lead, Sarina in the middle and Beth brought up the rear. Most of the traveling was done on hands and knees at a slow steady pace. It took the group an hour to reach the drop off that Rick had nearly fallen into the last trip.

"Whoa, ladies, we may have come to the end of the trail."

"What is it?" Sarina asked, passing the message back to Beth.

"The floor drops off here. I'm going to move off to the right. There may be enough room for you to slide to the left."

"OK, hold on a minute."

"What's going on up there?" Beth called out. Being last in line, she missed most of the conversation.

"Hold on, Beth. Take a break while we figure out if we can go any further," Rick called back.

Rick and Sarina shuffled around. There was a lip extending half way around the drop off. Beth could never move forward enough to join the other two. Two lights shined downward into the hole.

Rick could not find any place to tie off the other rope. The lip was made up of jagged rocks jutting outward. Smaller rocks seemed to be lodged between the larger ones, making footing dangerous.

"I'll go down first," Sarina said. "I'm smaller and lighter than you are. Once I'm over the ledge, Beth can move up. With both of you shining your light on the ground, I'll be able to use both hands."

"Good idea," Beth said. "We'll watch where

you place your feet. That may help."

"You be careful, Sarina. Check your footing and each handhold before you put your full weight on it."

"Rick, I know how to climb. You two, watch my steps." Sarina smiled as she slowly slid over the lip. She placed her toes against protruding stones.

Sarina made her way lower and lower. Once, one foot slipped, dropping her three feet down the shaft. Frantically, she reached around grabbing for hand holds. She came to rest against a large rock sticking out of the side of the shaft.

"You all right?" Rick called down.

"Yeah, yeah, my hands and arms are scraped up some, but I'm okay." Sarina called back. "Flash your lights below me. Maybe I can see the bottom."

Beams of light flashed back and forth, slashing at the blackness below her. She saw the bottom, but also noticed some interesting marks slightly below her.

"The bottom is ten or so feet further down, but could one of you shine your light down about two feet under my right foot?"

"Hold on," Rick called shuffling for a better position. "What is it?"

"I'm not sure. Hold that light on the spot. Lower, lower, more to my right. Whoops, back just a little. There, there. Nope, up. Down. Hold it. Steady, Rick."

"What? I can't see anything from up here, just a rock," Rick said.

"Well, keep your light on that spot. Beth shine yours down, but to my left. I need to find a way to get close to the other spot."

"How's this?" Beth slowly swept her light in the desired direction.

"Good, Beth." Sarina sounded out of breath as she searched for other footholds. Her left foot swept back and forth in an arch until it contacted a rocky lump. Cautiously, she tested the next foothold, and then lowered herself.

"Here, I can see something! Somebody had been down here before. There's a good boot print here in the dirt. You can see where the boot kicked around making a foothold."

"Do you think those two boys we read about were here?"

"Sure looks like someone was," Sarina said.

"If the clipping was correct, then that has to be their footprint or somebody who followed them," Rick said. "Down here, things stay pretty well the way they were left. There is no wind or anything to destroy them."

"Shine your light lower but to the left, Rick. Maybe there's another foothold." Sarina said.

It took Rick three slow sweeps of the flashlight to finally locate the next step down. Sarina lowered herself to it carefully, and then her foot located the next one.

"Geez, this is almost like a set of stairs. Keep those lights below me, I think I can locate the rest."

Now Sarina was descending quickly. Thirty feet down, she reached the bottom. Sarina pulled out her flashlight and scanned the area. A small hole went further, deeper into the mountain.

"Come on down, I think all of us can make it

through the hole down here."

"What about steps up here at this end?" Beth called out.

"I never saw any. I think the ground is too loose."

"Rick is going next," Beth said. "This way, if I start to slide, then there is a strong set of arms to catch me."

Silently, Rick lowered two packs to Sarina then started down. He slipped and slid, working his way to the ledge that Sarina landed on. From there, it was a swift decent to the bottom. Rick shined his light up toward Beth. He thought he saw her holding something to her ear.

"Beth? Hey, girl." Rick called. "Your turn."

"No, oh, no!" Beth screamed.

Rick saw her start to stand, flashing her light back the way they came.

At the same time, he felt the ground shake, hearing a dull thump then a rumble. Immediately, he thought of an earthquake, but that thought was dispelled almost as quickly.

The air compressed, almost bursting their eardrums. Then in the beams of their lights, Rick saw dirt and debris blow across Beth from the direction of the entrance. Beth screamed as the blast encompassed her, throwing her off balance.

Beth was tossed into the mouth of the vertical shaft, her head and right shoulder bounced off the far wall. Her body rebounded and slid down the graveled slope. Rick and Sarina tried to reach Beth as her body slid toward them, but they couldn't catch her. She landed head first, her body collapsing into a pile of rags.

Sarina sobbed, looking at the body at her feet. Her flashlight beam slid across the body as she continued crying. Rick knelt, searching for a pulse. Dirt and debris sprinkled down on them, dusting their heads and shoulders.

"Oh my God, Rick. What happened?" Sarina cried. "Was that a cave-in? What caused it? I felt the ground move. An earthquake?"

Rick stood, embraced Sarina and gently cradled her face in the crook of his neck. He patted her back, alternately caressing her head.

"No Hon that was no earthquake." Rick said softly. Gently he broke the news to her. An explosion had been set off back by the entrance. Possibly, probably, the cammo dudes caught up with them again. Then, regrettably, he told her Beth was dead.

The couple stood, in silence. Dust floating through yellowed beams of light. They embraced each other fiercely, trying to hold back the horrors of their situation.

Sarina's knees gave out on her and Rick tried to lower her to the floor gently. She sat there, knees drawn up against her chin. Her hand gently reached out, patting Beth's back.

"I'm sorry. Oh, I'm sorry Beth," Sarina mumbled the Lord's Prayer, which Rick had only heard once before recently.

Rick looked around, taking stock of the situation. Now there were only two of them. Someone may have sealed them into the mountain, but he was not going to give them the satisfaction of giving up. They would continue to search the cave. Rick wanted to know what was being hidden down here. What could possibly be worth the lives of five people?

Looking around, Rick located two backpacks, but Beth's was missing.

"Sarina, help me find Beth's pack. We're going to need every thing we can get our hands on to survive this."

Sarina ran her hand across Beth's back one more time, then stood, searching the floor with her light. "I don't see it, Rick. Could it be under, you know, ugh Beth."

Rick almost reverently rolled Beth over. He straightened her body as much as possible. The backpack was nowhere. Rick looked up. Flashing the beam of light around, he tried to see over the lip. He couldn't see anything, but if the pack wasn't down with them, it had to still be up there.

"I have to go up there. We will need those supplies while we try to locate another way out of here."

"Don't. Don't leave me here. What if there's another explosion?"

"There won't be. The first one sealed the entrance. Who ever did it expects us to die in here. We're not going to give them that satisfaction. Wait for me," Rick said.

"Let me come with you then. We'll check out the tunnel together. Maybe it hasn't been sealed."

"All right. I'm going to tie the backpacks together and take the other end up with us. Then if we need to, we can haul them up. I don't want to climb with them." Rick tied the pack handles together, looping the other end around his belt.

Rick started back up the near vertical shaft, using the footholds Sarina discovered. When Rick reached the ledge, climbing became a chore. He scrabbled over the loose gravel pulling himself up using precarious handholds.

After pulling himself over the top, Rick laid in the dirt panting. Sarina finally reached the ledge and waited. Rick caught his breath and sat up. He uncoiled a rope and dropped one to Sarina.

"Grab the rope and climb. I'll help pull you up." Rick took a good grip on the rope as Sarina put her weight on it.

## *25*

Beth's backpack was laying against the far wall, covered with dust and small stones. Sarina opened it. Inside, she found a snub nosed .38 revolver, a small wallet and even smaller notebook buried under food packs, water and some clothing.

"Rick, look at this," Sarina said softly. The truth of their situation still sat heavily on her heart. She knew they were cut off from fresh air and sealed within the bowels of the mountain. She would have given up, had it not been for Rick's positive attitude.

"What, babe?" Rick finished hauling their packs up.

"Here, why would Beth carry this?" Sarina handed him the pistol.

"Protection. That's why I have mine. Just in case we meet a cave bear or worse. Anything else."

"Yeah, well what about the wallet and notebook. We left ours locked in the jeep."

"Whoa. Look at this." Rick flipped the thin wallet open. Inside was a military style ID card with security stamped across the front in bold red letters. There was no mention of a specific service, just the glaring red letters. Inside the notebook, they discovered a record of their travels and date by date entrances recording findings, people and places.

Rick was shocked by an entry labeling the L. A. mission a failure. The next notation mentioned

Lawrence's help with the video tapes. Much to Rick's surprise, her kidnapping and drugging was not part of her plan. Beth must not have been aware that Layne worked for another government agency.

"My God, we had, and maybe still have, two separate agencies after us. According to this, they knew nothing about each other," Rick said.

"How could Beth be with them? Didn't you work with her before? Wouldn't you know?"

"Yes, we worked on four or five other articles before this one. Just like now, she acted a little bitchy, but otherwise pretty normal."

"Did she try to stop you from getting information or were you followed by anyone?" Sarina asked.

"No, both articles involved supposed crashes, but we never found enough information to give credence to either one."

"Could this explain why you were dead-ended on the Randell case? You know she fed information to her people and they told the magazine to shut down the article?" Sarina asked.

"That would explain a lot, especially on the Randell story, but also other small things. You know just small aggravating problems."

"How did you get hooked up with Beth?"

"Let me think about that." Rick paused for a minute. "In all cases, the magazine paired us off."

"Do you think the magazine is in on this? Could they send her out on articles that could possibly discover the truth?"

"That sounds awfully far-fetched. How could they know what would and would not be found. I think that she was only assigned on certain types of articles. Recently I did two articles on abductions. Both proved to be hoaxes. She didn't work with me on them," Rick said.

"Think about it. Two hoaxes, no Beth. Two crash stories, Beth. Now a story on Roswell and an Alien Autopsy and Beth."

"Wait a minute, this story was to be only about the autopsy film which proved to be another hoax, not a story about the Roswell crash."

"The tie-in is that the autopsy was supposed to be of the Roswell alien," Sarina said.

"That does make sense. The films were stolen to keep us from being able to use them to expose the hoax, then when we found Donald Dyba and his drawings, he was disposed of and the government tried to kill us."

"Well, they finally succeeded in doing that." Sarina sighed.

"Hey, babe, we aren't dead yet. They will only succeed when we give up and roll over for them. I'm not going to give them that satisfaction." Rick hugged Sarina and kissed her forehead, "There has to be a way out of this."

"But the security people killed her too. Do you think she knew about that?"

` "No, remember, she cried out 'no' a couple of times. Something happened to change their plans. She didn't plan on dying down here, that's for sure," Rick said.

"Well, let's move on, we won't find anything here."

Rick checked his watch, shining his flashlight

on its face. He couldn't believe only three hours ago, all of them were outside breathing fresh air.

Rick tied the packs together again, then lowered them down besides Beth's body. The two of them quickly followed, having become familiar with the footholds by now. Stowing the rope away, Rick stuck his head and shoulders through the hole that offered their only hope.

A narrow crawlway extended twenty feet then expanded into another darkness that their flashlights could not penetrate. Rick pulled back. He removed the rope from his pack and measured a couple of four feet sections. After cutting them off, he made a loop in one end and tied the other to his pack. He passed the other piece of rope to Sarina. She followed his directions, mirroring his movements. The looped ends were wrapped around their ankles.

Flat on his stomach, Rick wriggled his way along the narrow passageway. The walls were serrated but smooth. It reminded him of pictures he had seen of an intestine. Dragging the pack behind him, he could not hear or see Sarina.

Minutes later, Rick crawled into a large room. The floor seemed to be littered with a multitude of boulders. There was little sign of stalagmites or stalactites. As Sarina crawled through, Rick realized that hardly any normal cave type formations existed.

"Lord, look at the size of this room," Sarina waved her light beam around, her voice echoing back to her.

"It is pretty big. We need to start around one side and keep going until we come back here."

"What about the center of the room?" Sarina

asked.

Rick swung his light across the chamber. Darkness engulfed the light. Nothing but shadows showed. Both of the powerful beams used together clearly exposed a small portion of the hidden chamber.

"Here, let me help you." Rick untied Sarina's pack for her, helping to settle it on her shoulders, then bent down and made a pile of rocks in front of the crawl space they came through. The couple walked shoulder to shoulder in their exploration of the chamber. Large, almost flat rocks covered the floor. These blocks had fallen from the ceiling many years before the couple arrived on the scene. The ceiling was at least thirty feet above the floor. Shadows cast by every outcropping of rock raised their expectations of an exit tunnel.

Rick judged that they had traveled halfway around the cavern when they came across the first promising tunnel. Sarina dug a candle out of her pack, lit it and placed it in a puddle of its own wax, marking the entrance as they continued their search. The candle should burn for at least twenty-four hours. More than enough time to circle the chamber.

Sarina lit one more marker candle before the couple stumbled across Rick's pile of rock marking their starting point.

"Let's look around and see if we can find anymore footprints showing where the boys explored."

"Wish we'd thought of that earlier, Sarina. We may have walked all over them."

"We haven't been across the room, only

around the side. Maybe we will still be lucky."

Rick and Sarina moved ten feet apart then slowly walked across the room scrutinizing the floor. A thin layer of fine dust covered portions of the large blocks of stone.

"I found something." Sarina called, she dropped to one knee and looked at a small wrinkled object on the floor.

"Hold on, here I come." Rick worked his way around two large stone blocks on the floor before he saw her kneeling over something. "What is it?'

She turned to him, holding up a chewing gum wrapper. "We definitely know those boys have been through here."

"Well, we know somebody was here. It probably was the boys. Look, there're two sets of boot prints leading toward the second candle."

The prints disappeared across solid rock, but reappeared at the entrance to the second tunnel. Just to be sure, Rick checked the other tunnel. There were also scuff marks. Sarina insisted on starting with the first opening. After removing their packs again, and tying the short ropes back on, Rick decided to let her lead the way through a three-foot diameter tunnel.

Sarina and Rick followed the shaft until it dead-ended at a thin chimney that rose past the beam of her light. Rick checked his watch and realized it was mid-afternoon. The couple returned to the big room and took their meal break. At the same time, Rick replaced batteries in half their lights.

Next, the couple moved into the remaining shaft. In places, Rick had to squat down to walk. The shaft twisted back and forth continually while dropping elevation on a gradual downward slope.

"Rick, I, ugh, I'm getting some really strange feelings," Sarina whispered.

"Hey, hon," Rick took her in his arms. "You should. All of this stress is catching up with you. Hell, our only exit was blown closed and Beth was killed. On top of all of that, you're stuck here in total darkness with me."

Sarina found his lips and kissed him deeply. "Um, you're the only good part of all of this. My feelings are similar to those out at the crash site, when I blanked out. It has nothing to do with what has happened."

"You better not pass out on me. I'll have to wrap you up in a blanket and leave you." Rick smiled into the darkness.

"You just try to leave me." Sarina poked him in the ribs. "Just try buster."

Twenty minutes later, they found themselves in a cavern of much larger dimensions than the last one. Rick estimated that they had descended over two hundred feet since they entered the ground and were now close to ground level outside.

A dull gleam bounced off a large rock object in the center of the chamber. The object grew in size as the couple approached it.

"This is it, Rick. My feelings are associated with this. We found it."

"This is it," Rick repeated softly. The object took on the outline of a saucer. One hell of a large flying saucer. "I remember reading about machines thirty feet in diameter, but this one appears much larger than that."

Slowly they circled the object. Now, they could see that the ship was not circular in shape as Rick originally believed, but rectangular or triangular. Closer inspection showed that the other side was heavily damaged. Metal siding was crumpled and crunched on the far side and shoved against the cave wall.

Sarina sobbed. "Oh, no. No." Tears welled in her eyes. She started mumbling words. Many images leapt at her, bombarding her inner mind with images of people about three feet tall scurrying around instruments and smoking equipment. Panic. Hurt. Terror. It was all there. Flashes almost like a slide show left the impression that the mother ship had crashed. Sarina dropped to her knees as her vision blurred.

A dozen or more little gray men survived the crash. Inside the ship were smaller scout ships. None of the crew could release any to escape during the confusion just prior to the crash. More mind pictures showed the crew members that survived the crash trying to make contact with another ship even larger than theirs.

Four bodies were laid out side by side. Lost. Somebody or something was lost. The craft had crashed right in front of a huge opening in the earth. The deep cool darkness was welcomed to the crew. They took shelter from the grueling summer heat of the desert.

Rick sat next to her, holding her close, stroking her hair. "It's okay baby. It's okay."

"I'm tired, Rick. All of a sudden, I'm overwhelmingly tired. All I want to do is rest."

"Is it really you that is tired or are you being influenced by feelings from this place?"

"It's me," Sarina moved off to the side. "It's all that is now inside of me. You know." Her hand swept the area in front of them.

As they walked around the large craft again, they learned more. Cocked at an awkward angle, they could see one whole section was crumpled inward. A large pile of dirt lay against the damaged side holding it up. Rick climbed up until he could stand even with the top of the craft. Sarina stood to his left.

Light appeared to be drawn into the metal, or maybe it was heavily tarnished. Rick didn't believe that only half as much light was being reflected back as should be.

On top, a bubble approximately ten feet long and three feet tall protruded from the surface. A black area stood out against their light beams. Approaching it, Rick realized a hatch was opened to the interior. Looking closer he couldn't find a cover. Casting their beams into the craft, shadows still clung everywhere.

Flooring of open metal grids one inch square greeted them. Inside, they discovered what looked like a control panel with whole series of circular push buttons. Each one was thumb sized and carried a hieroglyphic symbol of some sort. There were three rows of buttons, with as many as twelve individual hieroglyphics in each row.

Sarina gasped, holding her hand in front of her. Rick swung his flashlight up, throwing a glare off the wall in front of the control panel.

"Turn off your light and look at the wall."

Gradually Rick's eyes became accustomed to the dark. Astonished at what his eyes were seeing, he rubbed them time and again. "What the hell?" They were looking through the skin of the ship out across the cavern.

"Yeah, that's what I thought," Sarina said. "I've been flooded with so many images. I wasn't sure if what I was seeing was real."

"It's real all right, hon." Rick shook his head in amazement. He could see everything outside of the spacecraft. Even though it was total darkness, he could make out the cavern walls, crevasses and individual boulders.

"It looks like dusk, just before the sun sets, don't you think?" Sarina asked.

"Or early morning before the sun pops up." Rick nodded. "If I shine my light on the surface of the wall, it appears like any solid wall, but without any light, it's transparent."

"How do you think it appears on the outside?'

"Stay here, Sarina, I'll go out there and see." Rick walked back to the hatch and stepped through. He froze. His eyes were blinded by the sudden darkness of the cavern. Rick grabbed the frame of the hatch to keep his balance; his equilibrium was totally out of whack.

"Sarina, if you come out, do it real slow. Some force throws your eyes and mind out of alignment."

Rick heard a mumbled reply as he worked his way around to the left. The craft was tilted close to twenty degrees. Rick was thankful for the gripping non-skid surface of his hiking boots. Shining his light on the surface of the craft, he noticed that it was not flat as he first imagined.

Dropping to his knees, Rick ran his fingers over the outer surface. He was right. There were shallow grooves about a quarter inch by a sixteenth of an inch running from the front up and around the exposed bubble then beyond, toward the back of the ship. Quickly his mind raced. Possibly they helped in controlling the craft as it flew in the atmosphere of a planet, or underwater or during extreme weather.

Rick reached the front of the bubble and saw that it resembled a teardrop on its side, the narrow end facing the front of the craft. He could not see inside, holding his light at any angle showed a solid metal wall.

"Sarina," he called. "Turn your light on, then off again."

"What?"

"Turn your light on, then off again." Rick heard the cave echo almost drown his command.

"OK, there."

Rick was disappointed. He had hoped that her light would have the reverse effect of darkness and he would be able to see inside the craft. He made his way back inside. Suddenly, he felt tired. Checking his watch, he realized they had been up continually for over twelve hours.

Sarina took out their small paraffin stove, lit it and set a small pot to boil water. Rick helped lay out a small meal of dried fruit and meat with a dehydrated pack of rice. Two granola bars completed the feast. When the water boiled, Sarina threw in a couple of tea bags.

Soon, not only the aroma of herbal tea filled the control room, but also the temperature had risen noticeably. The cold, dark chill was missing. "Mmm. That was pretty good, considering. I think I'll take a quick constitutional, then hit the sack."

Rick agreed, adding, "First one up makes morning tea."

Rick could not believe it. He had slept for eight hours. Rolling over, he noticed Sarina was not on her bedroll and that a faint glimmering of light from the stove lit up the control room.

"Good morning, sleepy head," Sarina called from the hatchway. She hurried over to him and planted a kiss firmly on his lips. "Um, um. That was good."

"I've got something a lot better than that, if you don't think it would be out of place."

"Oh yeah, big boy," Sarina dropped beside him. "How could alien beings think that making love would be out of place?"

Rick fumbled with the buttons on her blouse. "Maybe they would think I'm going to assault you."

"Sure hope so!" Sarina cooed. "If they can read thoughts, they are getting a heavy load right now."

Sarina moved away from him, rose to her knees and started to remove her flannel shirt. Rick levered himself to his elbows and watched. He hadn't remembered Sarina as being braless before. He reached out with his right hand only to have it slapped away.

"Naughty boy. You'll have your chance soon

enough."

In the dim light of the stove, Sarina's breast stood out like two enticing mounds of vanilla ice-cream topped with strawberries. A shallow shadowed navel accented her ever-so-slightly-rounded stomach. She unbuttoned her jeans and slid them down slowly, drawing her panties with them.

At the juncture of her long dancer's legs, a narrow cultivated forest of curly black hair pointed its way to ecstasy. Next, she leaned over and unbuttoned his shirt, spreading it open. Then she bent, kissing him and just touching her nipples to his exposed chest. A deep moan erupted from Rick.

Sarina blocked his hands as he tried to cup her breasts. She leaned back undoing his jeans and dragging them down below his knees. Her hands wrapped around his manhood, gently stroking it as she kissed his lips again.

Rick tried to move, but Sarina pressed against him. His arms went around her, pulling her even closer. One hand dropped, cupping her right buttock.

Their tongues dueled, as they exchanged moans. Slowly, Sarina's hips rose, one leg swinging over his body to straddle him. Her left hand took him and guided him into her.

Sarina arched her back and moaned in ecstasy, settling further onto him. Rick felt her dampness and as her muscles greeted him, groaned loudly, raising his rear from the floor.

A warmth they never knew existed surrounded the two. Naked, they were comfortable although the cavern surrounding the craft was cold. In the control room, on the floor both man and woman felt totally in control, confident.

Side by side, they lay holding onto each other.

"Rick, I love you and always will."

"Me too, Sarina. I never thought I would feel this way about anyone, but I love you too."

"Oh, do you think our feelings have anything to do with being here? You know, influenced by our surroundings?" Sarina pouted.

"We'll just have to try this again under different conditions and see." Rick smiled.

## 26

Together, the couple explored deeper into the spacecraft. They found a narrow, steep spiral staircase dropping to the next deck below the bridge or control room. That was how Sarina and Rick thought of the room where they slept.

Light continued to be absorbed by the surrounding metal walls. A central hallway ran the length of the ship with small doorways evenly spaced on each side. From floor to ceiling, the hall could not have been over four feet tall. Rick and Sarina felt uncomfortable in the hallway, as they had to bend over.

Each of the eight rooms the pair examined looked like crew quarters. A double tiered bunk bed was against the far wall and on either side stood a locker about three feet wide extending from floor to ceiling. All the doors were ajar and Sarina could find no sign of clothing or personal effects.

"Rick, I have been getting more images."

"Tell me about them. Are they alien beings?"

"Yes, I have been seeing short beings about three feet tall. Anorexic by our standards. Disproportionately large head. Small almost non-existent ears, nose, and mouth. Their eyes are sort of oblong, large and slanted slightly."

"That fits the Roswell aliens very close, Sarina."

"That's what I'm seeing, Rick, I'm not making any of this up." Sarina glared at Rick.

"Hold on hon," Rick held his hands defensively in front of him. "That description came from somewhere. I'm saying that it matches what has been reported. This is probably where the description originated. This tells us that the witnesses were telling the truth."

Sarina stood looking across the room, a blank stare plastered on her face. Rick went to her, grabbed her by both shoulders and gently shook her.

"Hey, hon. Hello, don't you dare fade out on me. We can't afford you checking out for any amount of time."

"Huh?" Sarina's eyes flickered. "What? Did I say something?"

"No, all you did was start going comatose on me."

"I had this really deep down feeling that everything was going to be all right. I don't know how, but this is the second time that I have been told we were safe."

"Safe. Safe from what? We're sealed up in a cavern with the single largest and most important UFO discovery in the history of man, and you say we're safe?" Rick laughed, surprising himself at the desperation in his voice.

"When we first saw the ship, I had this feeling of safety and security. You know, like we were given permission to take our time and visit the craft."

"Well, if that's the case, then ask this feeling when the hell it is going to show us the way out." Rick shook his head and threw his hands in the air.

"OK, hon. We'll do it your way."

Smiling, Sarina kissed him deeply on the lips. "Thank you, babe."

An hour later, the couple was finished exploring the level they were on. It appeared to be completely turned over to crew use. Two floor hatches couldn't be opened and there appeared to be no other way to enter a lower level.

Rick and Sarina settled for sharing one of the four remaining bottles of water and a power bar each for lunch. Then they walked back through the ship taking pictures everywhere they went. The experience was eerie. Normally, as a camera flash goes off, there's an almost blinding glare of light. Inside the ship though, the flash was dissipated but seemed to light the subjects adequately.

After shooting their first roll of film on the interior, Rick decided to do a photo survey of the outside of the ship. Sarina noticed a drop in the temperature outside of the spacecraft. It appeared that the metal absorbed or reflected body heat, making the interior comfortable. When they crawled under it, they saw what resembled an open bomb bay door.

Again, flashlights failed to illuminate the interior enough to show detail. Rick took one picture of the hole before they tried to climb into it. Sarina suggested they use some of the pieces of metal and boulders lying across the cavern floor to build a ramp up to the doorway.

Working with the metal was easy. For it's size, it was light as a feather. Between the two of them they could lift and carry a thirty-foot section with no strain. The metal would twist and bend then spring back to its original shape almost instantly.

Rick was afraid that since it was so flexible, it wouldn't support them when combined with the boulders. That idea dissolved as soon as he jumped on a piece. The jarring impact telegraphed all the way to his teeth.

"Damn that hurt," Rick said.

"What was that?"

"Go ahead, jump over here with me. Just be sure your tongue isn't between your teeth."

"Ouch," Sarina called out in surprise. "How did that happen? There must be a rock underneath."

"Nope, just open space between two rocks. It must have something to do with physics, you know, strain applied to an object, or something along that line."

"If that's true, then how did this thing get torn up?"

"It must have been one hell of a crash is all I can say."

Looking inside, they saw only smooth walls. There was one section that had what appeared to be foot holds molded into the metal, but it was about fifteen feet from their position.

Rick spotted a crossbeam above him about the same distance. After retrieving one of their ropes, he tied a fist sized rock to one end then threw it over the beam. Rick was successful on the third try.

Sarina laughed as Rick tried time after time to swing back and forth toward the section with the footholds.

"OK, smarty-pants, you try it." Rick said in

exasperation as he passed the ends of the rope to her.

"I will, mister-know-it-all." Sarina smiled as she tied a large knot at foot level. She climbed onto the knot then just like on a playground swing, she used her body to pump back and forth aiming her feet at her target.

Sarina got closer and closer until she could almost get a handhold. When she reached out to grab one, she upset her symmetry and suddenly she was flying in another direction. With a jolt, she hit the opposite side of the bomb bay.

A piece of metal snagged the sleeve of her shirt, almost jerking her off the rope. The material gave way with a soft ripping sound. Only when the tear caught a seam did it stop.

"Rick, flash your light on me. Hurry. I'm stuck on something." Sarina's voice rang with urgency.

"Okay, hon, hold on. Are you all right? What are you stuck on?"

"Flash that light up here and I'll know. Over to the right. Up a little, yeah, keep it there."

"What is it? What do you see?"

"Nothing, I just like ordering you around." Sarina giggled.

Flick, the light went out.

"OK, OK, just kidding. Hey, turn on the light."

"Rick, turn the light on." She heard him snickering.

"OK, big boy. Please turn on the light."

Flick, Sarina was rewarded with the beam of light.

"Now, can you tell me what you see?" Rick asked.

"There's a jagged beam here that goes up at an angle. It almost meets another ladder on that side. I think I can climb it."

"Swing that rope back to me, then climb up a ways. I'll come over and join you," Rick said.

Sarina led the way up along the edge of the metal. Rick's foot slipped two or three times, almost causing him to loose his balance. They easily crossed to the footholds. After a thirty-foot climb, they reached a narrow walkway that crossed the length of the hanger.

Cables and suction-like appendages hung from the ceiling. They reminded Sarina of an umbilical cord. Rick agreed and figured that if that was true, then up to eight smaller scout type spacecraft could have been hangered here.

Sarina finished shooting their second roll of film and loaded another, noticing that there was only one more fresh roll left. They couldn't find any way to climb further up into the craft. By gauging the depth of the craft, they guessed that there could still be at least one more deck level possibly two between the hanger and the crew quarters.

"Where are all of the scout ships?" Sarina asked. "From my visions, none of them were able to escape. I wonder what happened."

"We'll have to keep looking around, maybe part of the debris scattered around is from the scout ships."

"It doesn't look like there's much more to see around here. Let's head on out."

Back on the cavern floor, they started walking a search pattern. They looked for anything that would help explain how the ship ended up here, locked deep inside a mountain in the middle of nowhere.

"Hey, over here, Rick." Sarina said. "I don't think these footprints are ours."

Rick quickly moved to her side. "Nope, those don't look like the boys or ours either, from what I remember."

The couple followed the prints away from the saucer. They froze, lights shining about five feet ahead of them. "Tire tracks? In here? How?" Sarina asked.

Rick knelt beside them. "Not tire tracks, but bulldozer tracks. Someone used a bulldozer in here."

"How did it get in?"

"I'm not sure, but at least one was used to push the spacecraft around, then shove the dirt under it."

"I bet there was a large natural entrance over that way, then they closed it."

"Yep. Remember that rockslide we passed coming up here. What do you want to bet that's where the entrance was?"

In one portion of the cave, it looked like somebody had cleared off a large smooth rock and possibly used it as a table. Four small rocks sat on top, one in each corner. Cigarette butts were scattered around a small cubbyhole off to one side. Sarina spotted a crushed metal cup from an old army canteen. Evidently, it was overlooked as the owner left.

Rick searched the ground for a three-foot area

in all directions from the rock table. He almost missed the yellowed paper under a crumpled Lucky Strike pack. It had been torn from a pocket notebook and written on. In the poor light, he had a hard time deciphering the cramped print. He stuffed it in his shirt pocket for later.

"Over here Rick," Sarina called. "There's another tunnel here."

"Hold on, I'm still checking out this place."

"Small foot prints. I see small footprints." Rick heard scuffing sounds as if Sarina were jumping up and down.

"Hold on, Sarina, I'll be right there."

"Hurry, Rick, I'm being drawn to the tunnel."

"Hon, you wait right there. I'll be along in a minute." Rick was almost finished with his survey, finding nothing new. Suddenly he stopped. Rick listened. Silence.

"Sarina."

Silence. Rick spun around in a circle. His light stabbing here and there in the darkness.

"Sarina!" Rick called louder.

Silence.

Rick took off in the direction he last remembered seeing her.

"Answer me, Sarina."

The only sound was his stumbling feet.

"Dammit, Sarina. Answer!" Rick shouted.

Against the back wall he stopped and swept the floor with his beam of light. Still, the only sound was his panting and he swore he could hear his heart thumping in his chest.

Cautiously Rick moved forward along the

wall, shining his light across the floor, looking for Sarina's footprints, or worse, a stilled body.

Softly, almost a whisper, he heard, "Oh my God!"

"No!'

Finally, Rick noticed a dark shadow beyond a boulder. Hurrying to it, he stumbled to his knees, ripping a hole in the material of his jeans. Looking down at the cut knee, he noticed a marking on the ground.

Two symbols were etched into solid rock. One resembled an arrow pointing to the tunnel mouth. An Egyptian hieroglyphic was the only comparison Rick could make with the other symbol. A circle with a triangle superimposed.

Close by, two footprints stood out in a narrow passageway layered in fine dirt. One was clearly Sarina's boot waffles, while the other was from a child's soft soled shoe.

"Sarina, hey hon, where are you?"

Again, silence, but it was soon broken by a subdued sobbing, similar to a thin trickle of water across sandstone.

Rick moved carefully down the tunnel, swinging the beam of light ahead of him. Softly, he called her name.

The only response was more sobbing. Rick realized that he must be getting close because the crying was louder and more distinct. He could almost make out words interspersed in the sobbing.

"The bastards." Sobs changed into a faint wailing. "The bastards."

Fifty feet further, Rick spotted Sarina. He

could make out a lighter image that had to be Sarina. She sat on the floor with her legs curled under her. Next to her was another form. It was covered in a material similar to the spacecraft. Shiny, but not shiny, reflective but not mirroring.

Suddenly, it struck him. A being. Rather the body of a being. Here on the floor of the tunnel. Not near the ship, but far off. Hidden, lost. Isolated.

"Sarina, how are you doing?" Rick knelt next to her, favoring his injured knee. "What do you feel?"

"He's peaceful. There was a lot of pain. Pain and anger, Rick." Sarina looked at him, her left hand still resting on the creature's forehead. "But, he's peaceful now."

"Do you know what happened?"

"Only glimpses. Fleeting images. The anger and pain blot out practically everything else. There is a final feeling of calm and serenity."

Rick looked at the creature's face. It did have a peaceful appearance. Its eyes were closed, the lids sunken over the sockets. He could still see that at the eyes had been large and slightly slanted. Nostrils showed along with just a bud of a nose. The mouth was slightly open but no lips or teeth could be seen.

"Why was he angry and in pain?"

"I believe he suffered from internal injuries, that is what killed him. The anger, I'm not sure."

"Why didn't you wait for me?'

"Something, I guess his spirit drew me here, almost as if it were an emergency. Once I discovered the footprints, it was like I was a rainbow trout stuck on a fisherman's line. No matter how much I fought, I was being reeled in."

"Well, what do you want to do now? We can keep on looking around, or if you need rest from this, we can do that to."

"You know what I really want to do? It may sound funny, but."

"Go on, what Sarina?"

"Can we sort of bury him?" Her eyes begged.

"Sure," Rick agreed. "We can cover him with rocks and say some words."

"No, I mean, well, I want to take him back to the ship and put him in one of the bunks. You know. That is the only place he would feel at home, if you know what I mean."

Rick returned half an hour later with a piece of metal they could utilize as a stretcher. Sarina remained with the alien's body, alternately sobbing and whispering to it as if it were a baby in distress.

Silently the couple half dragged, half carried the body back to the ship. They had to stop several times and stretch since the tunnel was only about four feet tall and they had to bend over to get through. Rick wrapped the body in a blanket, tying both ends up. After tying a rope around one end, he lowered the body down the stairwell to Sarina. The alien weighed practically nothing as she held him reverently to her bosom.

Sarina gently placed the nearly mummified body on a bunk bed then again, prayed, and performed a short ritual. Anger glared in her eyes as Rick took more pictures. She understood the reasoning, but emotionally felt that it was a desecration.

"We need to eat something and rest before we leave," Sarina said.

"Are we ready? I want to be sure we have plenty of pictures. What about drawings, do we need any?"

"We have a mess of pictures. Why waste time now drawing? If we get back to town, the photos will be enough to blow the lid off the whole UFO conspiracy. Or, like Donald Dyba, we could be killed just as easy for the photos as drawings."

"True, I see your point. While we eat, we need to rest and inventory our film, notes and equipment. Then, we'll get out of here," Rick said. "Why do you think that tunnel is the way out?

"He told me. Somehow he knew."

While they ate, Sarina told Rick about more of the images she saw while with the alien. There was the crash, caused by repeated lightning strikes that created equipment malfunctions. After the crash, there was total confusion as the survivors tried to help each other. "Finally with the arrival a group of uniformed men, the army I guess, the beings thought they were rescued. But the soldiers pushed and shoved the dazed and injured aliens into groups." Sarina voice was void of emotion. "There was no regard for the wounded. Bodies were roughly thrown into the back of trucks. Our guy was deeply shaken, watching this happen. Then the ship was ransacked from one end to the other. Flat bed trucks appeared with a crane to remove the scout ships.

"The sole survivor hid from the soldiers when he managed to crawl into the cave for safety. That afternoon he watched as his ship was shoved inside.

Early the next morning after a quick survey by the soldiers, the cave mouth was blown closed, sealing them together in a common coffin."

Sarina shook from head to toe. Her cheeks glistened with tears.

"How could they treat those poor little guys that way? How could they?"

Rich shook his head in solemn agreement. "Fear, plain old fear."

After a couple of hours of rest, Rick and Sarina went into the aliens' tunnel. It took them one whole day to find their way out. Twice they had to scale narrow chimneys and in one place, they crawled on their bellies down a hundred foot long passageway.

A twilight of roses and purples greeted them. Their exit was barely large enough to slide through, but they had to wait all night. A sheer cliff dropped away from the hole for at least forty feet. Rick wasn't sure where they were or how far they had actually traveled underground, only that their way out faced south west.

Sarina noticed two faint lights flickering off in the distance as she looked out at freedom. They could not decide from their vantage point if they were campfires or came from an isolated farmhouse.

Early the next morning, Rick poked his head out, looking for a way down. They forgot their ropes down at the spaceship and they weren't in the mood or condition to return for them. Morning sunlight glared off of glass. Rick realized that it was the same type of reflection as they saw at the debris field. Vehicles, at least four.

Ant sized people were milling around. Twenty minutes later, a procession started in their direction. The ants grew in size to become recognizable as individual people. Suddenly, the group shifted direction heading away from them. The mouth of the cave must be off in that direction by a half mile.

One at a time, the people broke off from the line until they were scattered roughly in an even pattern appearing to be approximately twenty feet apart. Then they started to walk a search pattern.

"Help, help us!" Sarina wailed.

"They can't hear you hon. They're too far away."

"They have to!" Sarina screamed. "We have come too far to be stopped now."

Rick searched his mind. Surely they had something to signal with. He was almost positive that there was something they could use. He pulled his backpack to him, and shoved his hand inside. By now, it was nearly empty. They had eaten most of their meager supplies. He remembered that if it weren't for Beth's share of food, they would be starving now.

The gun! It was wrapped in a spare shirt at the bottom of his bag.

"Get back, Sarina, cover your ears." Rick unwrapped the pistol, holding it at arms length. He flicked the safety off, then stuck his arm out of the hole as far as possible.

Bam, Bam. The explosion grated their teeth, and slammed against their eardrums. Bam.

Rick shook his head to clear it then poked his

head outside. He could see the people down there were stopped. They gestured. Finally, one held his hand over his head and Rick heard an answering shot.

## 27

"Boy, we're glad to see you." Rick clapped Walter on the back. The helicopter that pulled them from the side of the cliff had just set down close to the sheriff's cars.

"What the hell are you two doing way up there?" Gomez said over the whine of the rotors. He approached Rick, patting him on the shoulder, his other hand carried Rick's backpack.

Rick turned to Sergeant Gomez, then shot a warning glance at Sarina. Was he as dirty and grimy as she? He decided that it didn't matter; she was still great to look at. Earlier, they decided while waiting for rescue not to divulge any information to anyone until they had a chance to think it all out calmly.

"Nice to see you too, Gomez," Rick smiled.

"Here you two are, seemingly nice folks out to visit our quaint little town. You're here less than a week and have been in my office twice under questionable circumstances, now because of this old coot, we spend two days out here looking for you." Gomez spat in the dust.

"We are deeply appreciative of that too. Aren't we Sarina?"

"Yes we are. Thank you, Sheriff Gomez."

Gomez pulled his white western hat off and slapped it against his thigh. "Hell, I'm gonna run you two in for GP. I can't wait to hear what fantastic story you have to tell this time."

"Nothing to tell, Gomez. We went caving and something happened. There was a cave-in and our original entrance was blocked," Rick said.

"Yes, and we were very lucky to discover another way out," Sarina added. "Otherwise we would still be down there, probably dead by now."

Gomez ushered them to his squad car. Rick held back, looking for Walter. The old man was standing off by himself, observing the scene. Briskly, Rick grabbed his backpack and slipped away from Gomez heading for Walter.

"Hey, Walt, will you drive my Wagoneer back for me?" Rick took out his keys and unlocked the door. As he handed the keys to Walter, he tossed his backpack on the floor of the passenger seat. In a whisper, he told the man to keep the bag safe.

Rick and Sarina had a hard time keeping awake on the way back to town. Even Gomez's constant prattle and questions couldn't hold their attention for long. Thinking back to their experiences of the last few days, it took on a dream-like quality. Did it all happen? It seemed now too far fetched to be reality.

Flying saucers, alien bodies. That was for weirdoes, nut cases. Rick investigated other people and their tales. Now he had his own. Would the photos be enough evidence? He wasn't sure any more.

Possibly, he could contact the New Mexico chapter of the Mutual UFO Network. They would know how to handle the situation. Once MUFON got a hold of the photos and information, our government would have to reveal the story. The whole world would then learn the truth.

People would then know that we're not alone in the universe and once Sarina has a chance to tell her story, people will truly be amazed. How could anyone doubt after this?

"Hey, Prescott. Wake up. We're here. Now, you and your lady friend will be separated until we get to the bottom of this." Gomez turned around in the seat facing them. "By the way, speaking of lady friends, where's your other one? Beth something."

Quickly, Rick thought. If he told Gomez the truth, then he would want to go out to recover the body. If he lied, Gomez might find a witness that saw them drive off together. Any other story would be just as fraught with danger. Sarina made the decision for him.

"Beth had to leave. She went out with us early in the morning of the first day, but the next day we left her at the motel. Something about not being paid enough to crawl around in any more holes," Sarina said.

"No one saw her leave. That's rather suspicious." Gomez frowned. "Around you two, people have a habit of disappearing."

"Isn't that the truth?" Rick said in a disgusted tone. "First that guy at the side of town."

"Donald Dyba," Sarina said.

"Then Layne, and now Beth."

"Yes, sheriff, why don't you stick close to us?" Sarina added. A twinkle in her eye.

"Laugh now you two. We'll get to the bottom of this, one way or another."

The couple was led into the Sheriff's station again. By now, the two knew the routine and appeared to be helpful getting logged in. Once they were checked in, they were assigned the same holding cells they occupied the previous two times.

Twenty minutes later, they heard a ruckus out front. A man was yelling at one of the officers. The voice was almost familiar to Rick.

"You cannot hold them without a charge. Anybody who watches TV knows that, you dimwit. Now, tell me what those two are charged with or do I have to go get my nephew? He's a lawyer and a damned good one too."

Other voices were heard trying to calm down the irate citizen, but to no avail. He continued to harangue the officers in the front.

"Damned fools, dimwitted, half-assed, pea-brained, jackalopes. That's what you people are."

"Okay mister that's enough. Wainwright, throw him in the cell with his friends. See how he likes those apples for a while."

"Yes, sir, Sarge. Will do."

Seconds later, Walter was propelled into the cellblock, escorted by the young deputy Rick had seen earlier at Dyba's house.

"Walt, what are you doing here?"

"What do you think, Mister Prescott? Rescuing you."

"You ain't rescuing nobody, you old coot," The officer said.

"That may be what it looks like to you, but you're young and foolish. So your opinions don't count." Walter threw him a fake smile.

The deputy practically tossed the old man into the cell and into Rick's arms. Both men recoiled against the brick wall breathless.

"Now look what you've gone and done, young man," Walt rasped. "Assaulting two helpless prisoners, and one being a senior citizen." A humorous smile crept up on his face.

"There ain't been no assault, yet, old man."

"Did you hear that, Prescott? Not only do we have assault, but now this ill begotten son-of-a-goat is threatening us."

"Hush, Walt. You're going to make things worse."

"Yeah, hush, ya old fart." The officer slammed the cell door closed and left the room, anger showing openly on his face.

"Damn, Walt. What gives? I asked you to protect my things and you end up in here with me. What kind of protection is that?"

"Not to worry, friend. Everything's under control. We'll be out of here in no time." The old man chuckled.

"Walt," Rick looked around conspiratorially. "What I gave you to hold for me is probably the most important information in the free world."

"Son, I said not to worry. I buried it at the bottom of my trashcan, and covered it with all kinds of trash."

Rick frowned. "Trash cans, my God man. You call that safe?"

"Sure do, I'm the only person to empty the print shop's trash. You see, we recycle a lot of the waste paper, so someone has to decide what to trash and what to keep, that's me." Walter grinned proud of himself, thumbs pointing to his chest.

"God, I hope you're right. I'm not exaggerating about the importance of that bag."

Walt patted Rick on the back, and nodded in agreement.

Fifteen minutes later, Sheriff Gomez entered the cellblock. A look of intense anger flushed his face well beyond his natural Hispanic complexion. Rick noticed both fists were balled tightly.

"Prescott, I don't know who you really are, but I'm sick and tired of you fucking up my community." Gomez stood facing Rick through the steel bars. Slowly, he reached for his key ring, found the one he needed and shoved it into the lock.

"You and your lady friend will be out of town by dark, or I'll personally kick your goddam ass all the way to Belen and turn you over to some other unlucky sheriff."

"Now, now, Gomez, isn't that being a little dramatic?" Walter chuckled. "This town ain't big enough for both of us. Out of town by sundown. That's cowboy bullshit."

"And you, old man. I wish to hell I could throw you out with them." Gomez was livid.

Walt smiled at Gomez, "How about if I keep them with me at my place tonight? I'll be responsible for them."

"No way in hell. Out of my jurisdiction by dark. In fact, after you get your business done, you come back here and I will personally escort you to the county line."

"Thank you, Sheriff Gomez. Sarina and I will

be back just as fast as business allows." Rick smiled, cutting a dark glare at Walt to keep his mouth shut.

Outside, Rick leaned close to Walt, frowning at the tobacco haze surrounding the old man. "Why do you suppose Gomez released us as quickly as he did?"

"I'm sure my son had something to do with it. I bet you he called and chewed on his ear some."

"Your son? How could he get us out of here?" Sarina asked.

"It's this way, he works in Sante Fe, the Attorney General's Office." Walt smiled, crinkling his face. "No, no, he only works there, some kind of clerk or something. I called him and explained what was going on then told him to call Gomez at a certain time."

The trio climbed into Walt's old worn-out Ford pick up, then headed over to the print shop. It was locked when they arrived. Walt led them inside and into his little cubbyhole in the back. An empty trash can greeted them.

"My, my." Walt said, staring into the bottom of the gray metal can.

Rick grabbed Walter by the arm and spun him around. He cocked his arm back, prepared to hit the old man. Sarina grabbed Rick's arm just in time.

"Stop it, Rick. This won't help us find the bag." Turning to Walter, she asked, "What happened? You said no one else emptied the trash but you."

"I don't know. Check the rest of the wastebaskets."

All of them were empty.

"Whose side are you on?" Anger steamed in Rick's gut. All the film and the scrap of paper he found in the cave were in the knapsack. Beth's gun, badge, and two more small pieces of metal were hidden there too.

"Now we have nothing. Absolutely nothing to prove what we found out there." He stopped abruptly. Turning to Walter, faces bare inches apart.

"You're another goddam mole! This whole project has been full of moles. One dammed agency after another on my tail. None of them smart enough to tell anybody else."

"Boy, what the hell you talking about. Agency, mole. You think I'm some kind of government spy or something? Settle down." Walter shook his head in dismay. "Talk some sense into him, Sarina."

"Tell you both something," Sarina said. "Let's find that bag, then we can sit down and discuss conspiracy."

"If you put it here, who could have removed it?"

"I don't know, Rick. Give me a few minutes to think."

"Where does the trash go when it leaves here?" Sarina asked.

"There are two dumpsters out back. The smaller one is for the trash and the larger one is for recycling."

"Let's go. Who ever emptied the wastebaskets may have dumped everything in there."

The trio hurried out back into the chill afternoon air. Behind the print shop stood two tan metal bins. One lid was up on the smaller one while an old carport cover sheltered the larger one.

Walt readily climbed into the trash bin and started rutting through the mess. "Rick you take the other one, it should be cleaner. Sarina, you can wait here."

Fifteen minutes later, Rick kicked the side of the dumpster. "It's not here, Walt. We've been at this a half hour. We should have found the bag by now." Rick slid over the side.

"I reckon you're right. I swear I don't know where it is. You don't know how bad I feel about this." Walt climbed out of the dumpster.

"Sorry doesn't cut it. You cannot believe how important the contents of that bag are." Rick stood in Walt's face, staring Walt down. Walt backed off, raising his hands in front of him.

"It can't be lost. After all we went through. It...it just can't be!" Sarina sobbed, clinching her fist and pounding it into her palm.

Rick wrapped his arms around Sarina, comforting her. "We'll find it."

"I know, let's go back inside," Walt lit another of his cigarettes. The couple followed him back inside as he blatantly ignored the large red NO SMOKING sign under the small window in the door.

"What are we doing back here?" Sarina asked as she sat on the edge of the receptionist's desk.

"I plan to find out who closed up the shop. Whoever had to sign out."

"Maybe that person cleaned up, is that it?"

"Yep, basically. Let's see. The log should be over here on the wall." Walter took the clipboard off its hook, flipping back three or four pages. "Ah ha," Walter nodded. "Just as I thought, Jay closed up. Sometimes he will help me empty the cans. It makes him feel good." Walt stepped on the butt of his cigarette, coughing.

"Walt, those things will kill you one day." Rick said.

Walter lit another, the fifth one in his current chain smoking marathon. "The secret is, one day, I plan on dying of natural causes long before the big C can take me down."

The old man coughed again, uncontrollable for a minute before it subsided. His nicotine stained yellowed fingers walked through the rolodex on the desk. With his other hand, Walt picked up the phone and punched in a series of numbers.

A knock on the door broke the silence. Walt wiggled a finger, indicating that Rick should answer the door. He looked out the window and frowned. "Oh, no. Just what we don't need." He swung the door open.

The familiar Hispanic accented voice brought Sarina and Walt to attention.

"Isn't it rather late in the day for you to be dallying around out here at the school?" Gomez asked.

"Just straightening up some last minute details," Rick said.

"Your last minute details better not take you past sundown, Prescott, or you'll find your ass back in jail. Friends or no friends."

Rick looked at his watch. Rick said, "We still have over an hour-and-a-half."

"I'll be watching. And waiting."

"Thanks for caring, Sheriff Gomez," Sarina said.

"Watch yourself missy, or you'll see how much I care." The sheriff slammed the door behind him.

Rick turned back to Walt. "Well."

"Well, what, Prescott! Well, what do I think about Gomez, or well, have I gotten in touch with Jay?"

Rick shrugged, "Yeah. Well."

Walt hung up the phone and patted Rick on the shoulder. "I'll tell you about Gomez as I drive you back to your motel. As to the missing stuff, I left a message."

In the pickup, Walt told them his plan. Seeing no other alternative, Rick reluctantly agreed. Walt dropped them off, waved good bye and pulled out of the parking lot and headed south.

Thirty minutes later, Rick and Sarina had the Wagoneer loaded and the bill paid. Before driving to the sheriff's office, they filled the tank with gas. Rick pulled into the lot. He grabbed Sarina's arm as she started to get out. With a shake of his head, he said no. Then he leaned on the horn.

"Get off that horn." A deputy yelled, sticking his head out of the door.

"Tell Gomez to hurry his ass up," Rick called back, taking his hand from the horn.

"Don't make him mad," Sarina said. "He may arrest us again."

"He harassed us, now it is our turn. Besides, if he is mad, Walt's plan will work better." Rick waited two minutes then tooted twice more. He kept his eye on the office door.

"Uh, Rick, look behind us." Sarina said softly.

In the rearview mirror, Rick saw Gomez sitting in his car across the street. The man was motioning for him to come over. Rick dropped the gearshift into reverse and backed out next to the patrol car.

"Howdy," Rick said with a smile as he dropped the shifter into drive and moved off.

Gomez stayed one car length behind the Wagoneer as they pulled into Main, heading north. Rick drove slow, trying to catch the traffic lights red. As they neared McDonald's, Rick grinned and tapped Sarina's knee.

"Get this," He said.

At the last minute, the Wagoneer turned into the fast foods parking lot. Gomez followed a noticeable frown on his face. Rick pulled to the drive through and ordered burgers and fries for both of them. He also ordered a coffee, hot for the sheriff.

After picking up his order, he drove just far enough forward for Gomez to stop at the window. When the girl leaned out with the coffee, Rick pulled out, hitting the highway at speed, fishtailing the Wagoneer.

"Hope the asshole spilled his coffee." Rick laughed.

"He's going to pull us over for this."

"Naw, he'll be happy just to have us out of his lair."

As they crossed the overpass to drop onto I-25

North, Gomez caught up with them.

The two cars stayed close together until they neared the rest area north of town. Rick slowed until the two cars were only one length apart. Sarina scanned the rest area and tapped Rick on his shoulder. The Wagoneer started to pick up speed again.

Rick drove the rest of the way to Belen ten miles over the speed limit. Gomez hung back about a quarter mile, then closed back up on them at the off ramp. The Wagoneer pulled into a Day's Inn parking lot. Rick got out and returned minutes later waving a room key at Gomez.

Slowly the patrol car moved onto the street, southbound for the freeway back to Socorro.

## *28*

"I hate to tell you this, but a black Ford followed you up here."

"What!" Sarina said.

"You sure about that, Walt?" Rick smacked a fist into his palm.

"Sure as I am of my name. I don't know where it picked you up at, but it hung back about a quarter mile behind Gomez. Almost gave me trouble getting on the freeway at that rest stop."

"How do you know it just wasn't somebody with business here in Belen?" Sarina asked.

"When you and Gomez pulled in here, they continued to the end of the block before turning around. Then the passenger used a pair of binoculars to keep an eye on you. I held back behind them and followed the car to the next motel down the line, the Belen Inn about two blocks down. The license wasn't normal either."

"Well now, that changes everything. We don't want them to catch on that you're helping us. We'll need to meet someplace else," Rick said.

"I'm one step ahead of you." Walt told them his plans for them to return to Socorro and hunt down the bag. "It has to be lost because otherwise there'd be no need for somebody to follow you. Especially if they know what's in the bag."

Rick figured that once the government found

the photos and metal, then the chase would be completely off. Relief and a sense of dread washed back and forth over Rick at the same time like a rising tide washing over a tide pool.

Seven-thirty by Rick's watch. Darkness was an hour old when the couple walked in and out of the Chicken Shop. Walt waited for them behind a semi-trailer. Walt's pickup sputtered and wheezed all the way back to Socorro.

Little traffic was on the highway and Walt kept an eye on the rear view, but he didn't see any headlights. Of course, he reminded himself that a driver could be following without lights. That would be safe enough unless a big rig decided to high-ball down the road. The moon wouldn't be up until after they pulled into Socorro. Even then, it would be a weak moon, not capable of lighting much of a way.

Walt lived in an old house down by the river, east of the highway. Even in the weak light provided by a corner street lamp, Rick noticed that the yard and house were very well kept. Tall elderly cottonwoods looked tired with their bare branches hanging over the Spanish tile roof and carport.

"This is a nice place," Sarina said.

"The missus used to nag me so much on keepin' the place up, I just sorta still hear her callin'."

"Sorry," Sarina said.

"Not to worry, she's been gone ten years now. Died of heartbreak. She lost her youngest boy. Very mysterious like."

"How did it happen, if I may ask?"

"You remember that article I showed you?"

"You mean, the bodies we found? One of

them was your son?"

"Yes and no. My wife was married before and had a hard time of it. When I met her, she was recovering. I couldn't believe my luck. Hell, she was a good ten years younger than me. The only child still at home was the little one. I only knew him about two years."

"God, I'm sorry," Sarina hugged Walt.

"We never did get too close. The boy wasn't into trusting too many people, especially men. One day he was suppose to have a scholarship back east, then he was gone. We never knew what happened. Amy, my wife, she knew he was dead. For the first couple of years we got reports of him from around the country. Then nothing."

"You received letters from him?"

"Yes, there were letters and post cards, but Amy said it wasn't his writing. It looked okay to me, but what did I know. Anyway, after a couple of years, the cards and letters stopped coming."

"Did you contact the authorities? What about the other boy's family?" Sarina asked.

"Gomez was in charge back in them days. He told us that when he tried to contact the Feds, he was stonewalled."

"So that's why you don't care for him."

"Yeah, I figure that he had a hand in killing Amy. Oh, I know that he didn't do nothing' really, but she just pined away after that. She knew in her bones her boy was gone." Walt's eyes teared over, his cigarette trembled as he tried to put a match to the end.

"All this time, he was in that mine, but

nobody knew. How could they do that?" Sarina said softly.

"You've paid your dues. It's time to tell you the whole story." Rick said. The trio sat around the kitchen table. Rick wasn't surprised to find the interior of the house just as well kept as the exterior. Furnishings reminded him of the early sixty's.

For well over an hour, Rick and Sarina told their story. They left nothing out. Walt was shocked at the violence involved. At the end of the tale, Walt cried openly.

Now he knew why his wife's boy had died, and the secret that had to be kept at all costs. Walt swore his assistance in breaking the story. In the past, he had a reason to dislike Gomez, but at this point, he would get even for his Amy and the son taken before he had a chance to know him.

"Wait a minute. You said that your boy was in Santa Fe working in the Attorney General's office," Sarina said.

"That's Amy's other boy. He was a couple of years older. We got to know each other pretty well over time. That's why he ended up in Santa Fe. To see if there was anything he could do to find his brother."

"Does Gomez know all of this?" Rick asked.

"I don't think so. He could remember parts here and there, but not the whole story," Walt said, a smile slowly building on his face. "He may be in for a surprise."

"It may be late, but I'm gonna go call on Jay. Want to join me?" Walt stood, took coffee cups to the sink, rinsed them and headed out the door.

"Can't miss this," Rick said as the couple joined the old man.

Jay lived in an apartment by the campus. A light was still on in the front window. Walt could have awakened the dead as he pounded on the door. A stereo was playing, competing with Walt's knock. He knocked louder.

The volume dropped about ten decibels and they heard a man's voice telling then to hold their water. Jay opened the door a crack and peered out. "Walt, what are you doing here?"

"You have something of mine." Walt said.

"What are you talking about Walt?" Jay asked.

"Didn't you clean up the shop today?"

"Yeah, I did. Oh, you mean that backpack. It's locked in the cabinet under the coffee maker. You know there's a good camera in it. I don't know how it ended up in the trash." Jay said.

"You sure that's where it is?" Walt asked.

"Yes, Walt, I am sure." Jay frowned. "What's so important about that bag?"

"I'll tell you tomorrow," Walt said. "Thanks."

"But...hey, Walt." Jay called, as Walt stomped off, followed closely by Sarina and Rick.

The trio hurried back to Walt's old pickup. Jay's apartment was only a short drive from the print shop. Hardly worth the drive, but they didn't want the police to see them.

Walt parked away from the front door. A bright light hung over the door with a Chinaman hat shade. If a patrol car came by, Rick and Sarina could drop in the seat. Everyone knew Walt's old truck and wouldn't question it.

A light went on as Walt slipped through the door. A couple of minutes later, he was back, a dark bag over his shoulder. To the best of their knowledge, they weren't seen.

The drive back to Walt's home was quiet. Anticipation clung to the stuffy, cigarette tainted air in the cab of the truck. Sarina, sitting between the men, reached across Rick and rolled down the window, hoping to exchange the stale air inside for the fresh chilled midnight air outside. Lights glared in the side mirror, catching her eye.

"Is somebody following us?"

"I don't think so, them lights just came around that last corner," Walt said.

"There can't be very much traffic this late at night in a town like this."

"You'd be surprised. There is traffic almost all night long. Here, we'll turn at the next block and switch back in the central rotary down town then cut over to Main." Walt spun the wheel, cutting sharply to his right, past an all-night grocery store.

The other vehicle continued on past the intersection. Walt breathed a sigh of relief. "It looks as if it was just somebody on his or her way home."

Walt continued on to the rotary, then circled around and headed back down the same street he originally turned on. "I changed my mind on that route. This will tell us much quicker if we're being followed."

There was no sign of any vehicles headed either direction on Main Street. Walt turned and continued back to his house. Rick had Walt stop two blocks away and Rick jumped out and walked ahead, looking for any suspicious car.

Sarina started hot water for coffee and tea as soon as they got inside. Walt cleared off the kitchen table and Rick emptied the backpack onto its surface. The camera, Beth's pistol, her wallet, and the remains of their food supply along with the pieces of metal were all there. Also, Rick noticed a small metal canister that resembled a film can.

"Sarina, bring me a cup of coffee please," Rick said, waving to her and Walt to be quiet. He pointed to the suspect can and fingered his lips hushing them. Everyone gathered around the table, staring at it. Sarina shook her head and waved a negative finger while Walt gave it the finger.

Walt left the room and returned a minute later with a large yellow tablet and a pen. On it, he wrote, "If this isn't yours, and it ain't mine, where the hell did it come from?'

Rick wrote back, "How well do you know Jay? Could he have put it there?"

Walt wrote, "He's just a kid. I don't think so."

Sarina scribbled, "What is it? It looks like a film canister to me. Why all the secrecy, where's our film?"

"I didn't have any film cans like that. Walt didn't put it here, so, it's suspect." Rick poked through the pile again, and then searched the backpack. Their three rolls of film were missing.

"Our film is definitely missing!" Rick wrote.

"Suspect of what?" Sarina added. "Somehow a roll of film got in there. Maybe it belonged to Beth and when we dumped her pack into ours, it came along accidentally and since it was so damn dark, we never saw the thing."

"That could be, but it could also be a plant by one of them," Rick noted.

Walt said, "Hey, anyone need sugar or cream for their coffee?" Then he wrote, "We better try to keep up a running conversation unless we want to tip them off about this thing."

"What do you guys think it is? Is it just a film can?" Sarina wrote.

Rick sighed, "Maybe it is some sort of listening device. If so, that would explain why the car that pulled out behind us didn't follow any more. They heard our plans and knew that the device worked."

"In that case, won't they be breaking in about now and arresting us and collecting all of our stuff?" Sarina wrote, looking around apprehensively.

The three managed to keep up a running conversation about the quality of the coffee and their plans for the morning. Which was actually only a few hours away. Finally, Walt sighed heavily and shook his head.

"Okay by you folks, I'm going to get some shuteye and will straighten out this mess later."

"Walt, you need to run us back to our motel in Belen before morning. We don't want our watchdogs to discover that we gave them the slip already."

"The hell you say," Walt pointed at the metal canister. "It's over."

Walt stood by the sink, leaning heavily on the centerpiece. Eyes stared dully out the window. Two blocks down, headlights slowed, then stopped. A moment later, the lights snapped off. As the dome light came on, Walt threw his left arm behind him, waving his hand and snapping his fingers.

Sarina and Rick turned in time to see Walt whip out a heavy coffee mug, invert it and drop it over the film can.

"Come on you two. Grab that bag. Let's go. They're coming up the front way."

"Who?" Sarina asked as Rick started trying to stuff the bag's contents back inside.

Walt grabbed the pistol, slapped the bag away from Rick and pushed them to the back door. "This way, now!" Walt hissed, shoving the pistol into Rick's hand.

The couple stumbled down the step into the small backyard. A tool shed stood white against the night along the rear property line. Walt pulled out a ring of keys and fumbled for the correct one as he herded Rick and Sarina into the shed.

The door swung open noiselessly. Against the dark wall stood a darker shadow shrouded in black. Walt whispered for the couple to wait. A moment later, he emerged with a motorcycle. Rick noticed, after a quick glance, that the motorcycle was vintage 1960's.

"Wheel this down that dirt track until you reach the river. You'll find another dirt track following the river. Head north until you reach an open area with picnic benches. Take the road west there back to I-25. Then get back to Belen. I'll contact you there."

Rick shook hands then pushed the bike down

the trail. Sarina hugged Walt, whispered in his ear, then hurried after Rick.

Walt locked the shed, and hurried back to the house. Locking the door behind him, he grabbed the backpack off the table and scooped the contents back inside. He ran to the bathroom and buried the bag under a load of dirty clothes.

A booming came from the front door. It seemed to Walt as if the door was being torn off its hinges.

"This is the police. Open up!" a slight Hispanic accented voice shouted.

Walt hurried to the door, stood to the side, flipped the latch and twisted the knob. If Walt had been behind the door, he would have been knocked down as Sheriff Gomez charged through the door.

Crowding close to Gomez, two more officers poured into the room, weapons were drawn and held at arms length, pointing in every direction. Gomez wheeled toward Walt. His open palm slammed into Walt's chest, shoving him against the wall.

"Paco, open the back door. Armstrong, search the house." Gomez called over his shoulder.

Looking the old man in the eye, Gomez asked, "Where are they, *cabron*? Where are the man and woman?"

Walt shrugged.

Gomcz slammed Walt against the wall again.

"We saw you together earlier today. You brought them back here," Gomez sputtered in Walt's face. "Now, *cabron*, where are they?"

"I don't know. Look around," Walt said barely containing his own anger.

More officers entered through the back door. After wandering from room to room, everyone gathered around Gomez in the living room by the open front door.

Gomez grabbed Walt by the arm and led him to the kitchen forcing him into one of the chairs. "Don't stand around here like a bunch of *pendejos*. Search the grounds. They have to be outside or someplace nearby."

In the middle of the table, Walt eyed the inverted coffee cup.

Two men in dark suits appeared by the kitchen door. One of them cleared his throat drawing Gomez's attention. "Well?"

"They aren't here. We have expanded the search around the area, but don't worry, we will find them."

"Sheriff." A deputy called, out of breath from running. "I heard a motorbike start up down by the river."

Gomez pointed a finger at Walt, "Don't move, *cabron*." He flew out the back door, calling to his officers. "Paco, head down to the river, and find out which way they went. The rest of you, in your cars. Stand by for Paco's report, and then get the bastards."

"Lost them again, Gomez?" A short dumpy man in a dark three-piece suit asked.

"I was not told to arrest them until you two showed up."

"That's why you are a small town cop. After they escaped from the mountain, you should have held them," The taller man said.

"By then, you knew that they had seen too

much."

Walt became alarmed. He was hearing too much. These men were talking as if he was not present. Evidently, Gomez, no matter how important he acted, was just another peon to these men in suits.

"Don't blame me for your fuck up!" Gomez growled. His face took on a flush.

"Not our fuck up, Gomez." Williams pointed a pudgy finger at the sheriff. "Yours."

"When you Feds change your game plan, you have to let the other players know, just like a coach at a football game."

"You're being paid too much to sit on your fat ass and play small town cop. We expect quality work, not this shit," the tall one said.

"What about your boys who tried to kill them at that mine? Huh?" Gomez said proudly. "Or the ones who blew up the mountain. They failed. What about them?"

Williams looked at the other man, "Know about a mountain, Hyram?"

"Not me,. Williams," He turned to Gomez, "What about the mine? The team was killed, supposedly by the clowns we are chasing." He moved into Gomez's space, noses only inches apart. "You want to join them in their failure?" Hyram poked Gomez in the gut with three stiff fingers. "Huh?"

Walt watched Gomez slowly melt. The deep flush on his face turned pale. The sheriff was whiter than any Hispanic he had ever seen before. Gomez breathed in short gasps and his Adam's apple bobbed. For the first time, Walt was seeing the sheriff scared.

What position did that put him in, he wondered? Not only had he been witness to sensitive discussions, but now to a sheriff being threatened. Walt stood silently against the wall, trying to become one with it. He hoped that he would be forgotten, but he realized that his troubles had just began.

Earlier, as the three of them set around the small dining table in his kitchen, Sarina had given him a reason to hate Gomez. Now, it became a double-bladed sword. After the way Gomez was treated by the Feds, he would want to get even with Walt.

Walt watched Williams move to the table and glare at the coffee cup. There was nothing else out of place. All the dishes used earlier were sitting clean on the drain board by the sink. Slowly, Williams bent over the table, eyes focused on the cup.

"What do we have here?" he asked, poking his finger at the lip of the inverted cup. "Your clean table is about to stain. Somebody should have dried this cup first." Williams stuck a finger through the cup's finger loop and lifted it, exposing the metal film can now resting in a small pool of coffee. "Hey Hyram, now we know why the mike suddenly cut out."

Walt was left alone in the front room. The two suits stood around the table looking at the hidden microphone while Gomez, rubbing his gut, moved slowly toward them. The old man weighed his chances of running, figuring that if the two agents noticed him, they would definitely shoot him. He decided he couldn't let that happen. He knew what he would do to Gomez now, if he were given a chance.

Gomez' radio squawked, the message unintelligible. Gomez growled a response then conferred with the two agents. Quickly they decided a plan of action and headed for the front door.

On the way out, Gomez stopped in front of Walt, a fiery glare in his eye. His hand came up quickly and with the same judo punch, jabbed Walt in the gut again. "Don't leave town. We have unfinished business, *cabron*."

"You bet we do," Walt whizzed in a barely audible voice.

## 29

Sarina found the cold night air invigorating after the run through the woods. She tried to keep ahead of Rick, leading the way down to the river from Walt's tool shed. She was doing quite well until she tripped on a protruding rock. She scraped her arms and banged her knee. Now, on the back of the motor bike hanging on for dear life, she could feel an almost painful throb in her left knee.

At first, Rick tried to drive using the meager light provided by a quarter moon, but after a near catastrophe with a tree stump in their path, he slowed down and turned on the headlight.

Off in the distance behind them, Sarina saw a couple of faint flashlight beams shining back and forth. They knew the direction the bike was headed. Not only the taillight but also the peculiar whine of the old bike gave them away. Their only chance now was to hide from the police, as there was no way to outrun their radios.

When they reached the cut-off to the highway, Rick stopped. Behind them, in the distance a pair of headlight bobbed up and down. Above the headlights, a light bar flashed red and blue strobes.

"Hold the bike, Sarina," Rick said as he swung his right leg over the handle bars. With a quick look around on the ground, Rick located a fist-sized rock. "I hope Walt will forgive me." He said, swinging the rock into the small red lens, shattering it and the small bulb inside. Rick tossed the rock off to the side and swung back into the seat.

Over his shoulder, Rick explained, "Sarina, this trail seems to continue along the river. I want to keep to it. If we swing back to the highway, I'm sure the cops will have the road blocked."

"You're in charge. Just get us out of here."

Rick purposely turned down the road to the left leading to the highway. He twisted the handlebars back and forth shining the headlights everywhere. Then he stopped, switched off the light and returned to the intersection. Although the police car was gaining on them, he traveled slowly until they passed beneath the branches of a large mesquite bush.

Hidden by the bush, Rick flipped the lights back on and opened up the throttle. Sarina saw the police car turn partially onto the other road and stop. She hit Rick's shoulder, shouting in his ear.

"Stop. Turn off the engine and light!" She pounded his back.

Rick did as she said then turned to look over his shoulder.

"What was that for?" Then he saw the lights from the squad car. Off to the west, they could hear the sounds of an eighteen wheeler using its engine as a Jake brake on a downhill grade. The highway could not be more than a mile or so away.

As the police car continued its turn, Rick started the bike and drove as quietly as possible for a few minutes. Then he revved up the engine again. About five miles further, they discovered a small cable car hanging on a large steel cable suspended over the Rio Grande. Rick stopped at the base of the pylon supporting the cable on this side.

"What is this?" Sarina asked.

"A cable car. There must be a flood gauge or flood control gate on the opposite side. This may buy us some time. Rick scrambled up the steel beams to the small platform at the top. As he hoped, only a five-foot long piece of rope held the small gondola secure. There was another piece of rope the same size tied at the other end of the car.

Rick untied the two ropes, then re-tied them together as one. Knotting one end, he lodged it between two of the wires making up the floor of the gondola, then he dropped the loose end. He climbed down and stood by Sarina. The loose end of the rope hung about three feet off the ground. Rick tried to lift the bike but after three tries, he realized he couldn't lift it high enough or hold it up that high.

"Sarina, I don't want to leave the bike here. We need to find a piece of wood or tree limb about as thick as your wrist and a foot long."

The two searched for five minutes in the semi-darkness, always aware that time was running out. Finally, Sarina came up with a short twisted piece of metal that looked as if it may have been part of an earlier gondola.

"This will have to do it," Rick said as he tied the rope to the middle of it. "Help me lift the bike and pass the metal bar between the front wheel and the frame. If we jam it in, hopefully it will hold."

Rick lifted the bike to his shoulders. He could not keep it steady and grab the rope at the same time. Sarina pulled the rope with her right hand as she tried to raise the front of the bike. With a creak, the gondola moved away from the pylon, throwing Sarina off balance. With a yelp, she let go of the bike. The full weight of the bike was suddenly passed to Rick whose muscles were already screaming in agony. Rick nearly lost the bike, dropping it back to the ground.

"What happened Sarina? Are you all right?"

"I lost my balance."

"We need to be careful. I don't think I can do this too many more times." Rick slowly pumped his arms drawing circulation back to stressed tissue.

"Help me pull this thing back," Sarina said. "Otherwise, we'll have to lift the bike another foot."

"I have a better idea." Rick laboriously climbed the tower again. Reaching the top, he removed his belt and used it to hold the car against the top pole. On the ground again, he bent over breathing heavily.

"We have to hurry." Rick said.

"I'm tired, and so are you. We need to rest."

"Can't stop yet. I saw a light back down the road. It's probably the cops."

Two agonizing minutes later, the bike swung like a pendulum below the cable car. As the two climbed the tower, they could hear his belt groan as it held the full weight of the car and motor bike. Sarina crawled into the car causing it to sway from side to side. The belt buckle bent and separated. Rick dove for the car as it slowly moved away from the post. He landed with the upper half of his body in the car, kicking and clawing for support and traction. Sarina reached out and grabbed his shirt from behind the neck to steady him.

The car gathered speed as it moved out over the river.  Below the car the bike continued to twist and turn at its own pace, jerking the car along. Normally, the cable would drop very little as one person crossed, pulling himself along hand over hand. The combined weight of Rick, Sarina, and the bike taxed the cable to its limits.

As the cable stretched, the rear wheel of the bike dipped into the water two or three times. Halfway across, the car started to slow down. Momentum was being eaten up by the jerky swaying motion of the undulating bike.  Rick looked up at the cable and saw a short handle protruding below the wheel assembly at each end.

When the car came to a halt, Rick pulled the handle hoping it was a brake.  It worked.  Now they were suspended half way across the Rio Grande. Despite the big name, this time of year the river was low.

About a mile back down the road, headlights bounced through the rutted river road.  No lights flashed angrily from a light bar, although Rick was sure the vehicle had one.  He reached up and grasped the cable firmly in both hands.

"When I say now, release the brake and help pull.  Be sure to use the brake again so we don't loose any cable we manage to pull through."

Sarina nodded in agreement and grabbed the handle with both hands.

"Now."  Rick grunted and pulled with all his might.  They moved.  At first only an inch but then another, followed by two more.  Sarina applied the brake long enough for Rick to get another hand hold.

Painfully, the car moved toward the far side of the river. As the car reached the far bank, Rick noticed this side was higher. He dug his scout knife from his pocket.

"Sarina cut the rope holding the bike when we get a little further on."

"Won't the drop hurt the bike?" Sarina frowned. All this work and now they were dumping the bike. "What will Walt say?"

"We have to, Sarina. Otherwise we won't make it. Look." He said pointing across the river. "Here comes that car."

Moments later, the gondola bounced into the air as the cable was freed from the weight of the bike. Below them, they watched as the rear of the bike struck the ground and rebounded at least three feet into the air. The second time it hit the ground, it landed on both tires but at an angle. As the bike bounced again, it headed toward the river but only covered half the distance before falling on its side.

Without the extra weight, Rick could pull the cable car faster. They were only five feet from the end when the police car pulled up next to the opposite pylon.

Setting the hand brake, Rick whispered, "Hide your face and hands and don't move." The car still swung gently as if a breeze were blowing.

"Will they see us?"

"I hope not. It depends on how careful they look and how powerful their lights are."

One of the lights mounted on the police car swung up to the pylon illuminating it. Slowly the beam moved in their direction, following the cables.

"Hide your face." Rick whispered again as the light slowly passed over them then down their pylon and swept across the riverbank away from the sluggish brown water.

Suddenly, the light snapped off. Rick could only see the officer leave his car only because the dome light came on. After standing at the rear of the car for a moment, he got in and drove off slowly, flashing his spotlight back and forth.

Rick climbed down the metal tower after Sarina. Together they inspected the bike. Miraculously, it survived with only minor damage. The mirror on the handlebar was broken and its frame was twisted into the dirt.

Rick and Sarina separated and searched up and down the riverbank for a path away from the river. Sarina found one. A narrow animal trail led away from the river but to the south.

Although Rick's arms and back cried out for a rest, there was no time. They had no way of telling when the police would pick up their trail again. Rick didn't want to contemplate what lay ahead of them at their motel. Walt described two men who were keeping surveillance on their room. By now, they may have entered the room and searched it.

Rick was glad they followed Sarina's suggestion to leave all belongings in the car, hidden as much as possible. It would make moving faster after they recovered the backpack. They would somehow have to contact Walt again for the bag.

Dawn was fast approaching, and they were still on the road. They pulled into the small town of

Bernardo, parked the motorbike behind the gas station, and waited. A highway patrol car cruised through town at no more than five miles an hour. The officer inside examined each building, alleyway and the few parked cars. The couple remained hidden behind the gas station.

After the patrol car crossed the river and drove out of sight, Rick looked around. Two old buildings sat off by themselves. Neither one was in very good condition. A large slated barn was leaning down wind with its door hanging by one set of hinges. The smaller building may have been a shelter for animals as Rick could find no indication that a fourth side ever existed.

"Stay here. I'll be back in a couple of minutes."

"Where are you going?" a worried frown crossed Sarina's face. "Over there to the barn. I want to find a place to hide the bike."

"How do you plan on getting to Belen if we hide the bike?"

"We'll hitch a ride or something, but the police are definitely looking for a bike with a man and woman on it."

"I don't want to stay back here alone, I'm going with you." Sarina held out her hand. Rick helped her to her feet. Hand in hand, they walked to the barn.

Rick realized the interior was in just as bad shape as the exterior. A loft at the far end was probably the only thing keeping the structure from collapsing. At that, the floor of the loft was drastically off center. Bales of hay that had been stored up there slid to the ground a while ago, bursting the wiring and scattering hay in mounds across the floor.

Sarina bent over, pulling a corner of cloth sticking out from a hay pile. Together, they tugged on the corner until an old ratty horse blanket emerged.

"Get the bike," Sarina said. "I'll look for more. Maybe we can cover it with this."

"Find a comfortable place for us to take a nap that would be out of sight."

Rick returned with the bike. He didn't see anyone on the streets yet, although it was nearly six in the morning. Sounds carried on the dry cold air verifying that people were awake. So far they were lucky.

Once inside, Rick looked around. No Sarina. Softly, he called her name. No response. Rick leaned the bike against an upright post. He pulled the pistol from his pocket. Cautiously, he searched the ground level. Way in the back, there was an open area surrounded by waist high bales of hay.

Sarina was rolled into a fetal position with her hands together tucked under her head. Her long lustrous black hair looked beautiful, even though it was full of hay. Rick knelt beside her and gently brushed stray hair from her face. Then he got up and went back to the bike to hide it in a corner, under the blanket and hay.

An hour later, Rick was still awake, fatigue overwhelmed him, but he could not sleep. Images careened through his head like the little silver ball in a silent pinball machine. He watched Sarina sleeping soundly. An occasional soft moan escaped her lips, although she hardly moved.

A gunshot startled Rick either awake or brought him back from a daydream, he wasn't sure. Only the heart stopping pop of a gun close by was foremost in his mind. Rick grabbed the pistol beside him and on hands and knees crept around the corner of their hiding place.

At the second shot, Sarina came awake with a scream. Rick turned and lunged at her, his hand outstretched to cover her mouth.

Her eyes still trying to focus, as her mind tried to assimilate the unfamiliar surroundings. Sarina saw only a figure attacking her. She rolled onto her back, drawing her knees to her chest. As the figure fell toward her, she kicked.

The blow caught Rick in the ribs. With the air knocked out of him, he fell inert beside Sarina. She reached out, grabbing a handful of hair just as her eyes swam into focus.

"Oh, my god. Rick!" Sarina sobbed as she bent over him. She took his head in both hands. Her mouth closed over his in a kiss.

Rick gasped for breath, sputtering in Sarina's face. "God woman, can't you find a better way to end a relationship?"

Giggling, Sarina smothered him with kisses, apologizing as she went.

Tires crunched outside brought the couple back to reality. A car door slammed followed by a voice whistling "*La Macarena*." Rick looked around the edge of the bales watching a shadow approach.

A large floppy western hat covered the man's head, keeping his features in the shadows. All Rick could tell was the man was dressed in western work clothes with a black and white checkered vest. He stood up slowly while motioning Sarina to remain low and silent. The whistling came to an abrupt halt.

"Hey, man, what you doing here?" the man asked.

"I was tired and needed a place to rest. Hope you don't mind. I didn't disturb anything."

"Yeah, okay," the man said. Cautiously he backed up, looking all around the barn. "Yeah."

"Excuse me, but I mean you no harm." Rick held up both arms, showing he didn't have a weapon.

"You in some kind of trouble?" He asked.

"No, I'm just traveling through and got tired, that's all." Rick said.

"You sure you ain't in trouble, you know with the law and stuff."

"We're only in trouble with my family," Sarina said as she stood. Her hands were adjusting her blouse. "My daddy and brother caught the two of us, uh, shall we say, compromised. Those two cannot believe that I'm old enough to think for myself." Her award-winning smile took over.

"What the!" He backed again. "How many of you are there?"

"Only the two of us. Promise," Sarina smiled, "We are on the run from my family."

"Where's your car?" The man asked as Rick and Sarina made their way to the middle of the barn, they saw his Hispanic features. He was probably in his late twenties, around Sarina's age although she looked ten years younger than she was.

"My daddy shot it full of holes up by Scholle.

That was where he caught us."

"Is he still on your trail?" The man asked. "I don't want to get mixed up in any family squabble."

"We're not sure. We tried to make them believe we were headed for Mountain Aire, then Santa Rosa." Rick tried to piece together his mental map of New Mexico.

"I guess it's all right." He kept looking at Sarina, eyes covering her body.

"Could we impose on you?" Her hand held the top button of her blouse.

"Depends. What do you want?"

"We need a place to clean up a little, then a ride to Belen." Rick let Sarina do the talking, having seen her magic at work before. He would swear that she was not only psychic but clairvoyant as well.

"We can pay some."

"Sure, hop in the truck; it's only a short way to my trailer."

## *30*

Walt waited until morning, not wanting to bother Jay again. Gomez was going to pay. That much Walt knew. All of his past guilt and agony over his wife's death and the missing boy surfaced. Like magma boiling out of an old lava tube, his feelings turned to heated anger ready to consume anything in its path.

Danger. Walt screamed to himself. Danger. During his life, he had seen too many people's lives destroyed by unbridled anger. He needed a way to channel it. Moving back to the kitchen, he started a fresh pot of coffee. Then he dug his way through a lifetime of memories buried in the back of the hall closet.

Walt discovered what he was looking for just as the aroma of fresh coffee drifted down the hall. With a pleased look on his face, he grabbed the double-barreled shotgun in his left hand and after kicking a pile of junk on the floor back into the closet, he returned to the kitchen. He set the weapon on the table and poured himself a large mug of steaming coffee.

Out in the tool shed, he found a couple of hand saws, files and sandpaper. He returned a few minutes later for a mid-sized table clamp. As an after thought, Walt pocketed some string and a small oil can.

By sunrise, he was done. For the last two

hours, he focused on Sarina and Rick. In his heart, he knew they were safe somewhere. He wished he could help them, but right now he would run down the film and keep the knapsack safe. They would return for them and he wanted to be ready. Gomez would not interfere with them again. Walt knew that now.

Back in the closet, Walt located a box of shotgun shells. He broke open what was left of the double-barreled twelve gauge and dropped two faded shells in the chambers. With a flick of his wrist he closed the gun. An old pair of boots supplied a leather thong, which he tied through the finger guard. Now he had a wrist strap for a weapon that was very deadly for about ten feet, but not too good beyond that range.

Walt grabbed a coat with deep pockets. He dropped the gun in one and a dozen shells in the other. Before going to the printing office, he treated himself to a nice breakfast. After all, he deserved it.

Jay was already at the office when Walt arrived. He sat on the edge of the desk and looked at Jay. Walt pulled out a cigarette and lit it. After taking a deep drag, he blew the smoke in the young man's face.

"Why'd you do that, Walt? You still pissed because of the knap sack?" Jay coughed, waving his hands to clear the smoke.

"It's not the backpack," Walt exhaled all over Jay again. "You know what I want."

"You want to give me cancer, that's what."

"I may give you something kid, but is sure as hell won't be cancer." Walt flicked the ashes on the desk. In a harsh voice, "You still have something of mine and I need it."

The young man sat at the desk, a frown on his face. Between trying to clear the air and coughing he was having a hard time thinking. With a grunt, he placed both hands flat on the desk and tried to rise.

"I don't think so," Walt firmly shoved him back down. "Not until we get something straight."

"Walt, stop acting crazy. I know what you want and I'm going to get them for you. Let me up."

"Yeah, well tell me where they're at."

"Damn. What's got into you? You smoke some weird shit or something? I don't ever remember you being like this."

"Just help me along." Walt sighed. "Where are they?"

"Geez, here I thought I would do you a favor, old man. But I guess I figured wrong."

"Wait, wait a minute. You mean you took all that film to some photo service to be developed? Without asking?"

"What did I just say? Damn, are you dense or something?"

"When will it be ready? Where did you take it?"

"It's back that was what I was going to get. That little shop down by Denny's did it for me."

"Oh, my God. Has anyone seen the photos?" Walt paled.

"Not that I know of," Jay said. "I only picked them up this morning. I was hoping to surprise you."

"Well, you sure as hell did that, young man." Walt tried to chuckle as he patted Jay on the shoulder.

Noticing the mood swing, Jay tried to get up.

Walt didn't stop him. He went to the file cabinet and unlocked it. Opening the third drawer, he dug under a pile of papers and pulled out a bunch of envelopes. "Here they are."

Walt took them and shoved them into the pocket with the shotgun shells. He dug his wallet out of his back pocket and thumbed through a bunch of bills. He pulled out two twenties and dropped them on the desk in front of Jay.

"Hey, thanks, and sorry for the hassle. I've been under a lot of pressure lately." Walt playfully punched him lightly in the shoulder then headed for the front door.

Outside, Walt tried to look around without being conspicuous. He hoped that no one was following him. The photos weighed on him. From his discussions with Rick and Sarina, he had a good idea what was in his pocket. He felt as if everyone was watching him.

Walt drove around town aimlessly, hitting a fast food joint for a soda. After thirty minutes, he was sure no one was behind him. An old adobe dwelling that had been abandoned for years sat on the corner two blocks from his house. The roof fell in last year and now the walls were slowly melting back into the earth they had originally come from. A large unkempt willow still grew in the yard. Its limbs hung low as though mourning its loss of purpose.

Parking next to the deserted house, Walt could see the front of his house while remaining hidden from casual view. He shook the warm cup of soda rattling the little ice remaining, slurping noisily on the straw. Finally he had no more excuses, and he reached into the coat pocket to retrieve the three photo packets.

Nervously, he opened the first envelope and withdrew the pictures. His breath caught in his throat. The photos clearly showed a tired and dirty Sarina standing in front of a large silver gray metallic object. The object was so large that it occupied the entire background.

Walt knew what the thing was, although many people would argue that it could possibly be any number of different objects, such as a large oil tank or even the side of a large trailer.

The next three shots were similar, showing the woman, Sarina, pointing to various parts of the object. In some of the photos, a curve could be easily distinguished while in others severe damage to the outer skin was noticeable.

The entire first roll was taken outside of the spaceship, in the huge dark hanger area or in and around the control room. Lighting was sketchy in many of the pictures and a person would have to use their imagination to fill in many details necessary to agree that these were photos of a space ship. The bridge of the Star Ship Enterprise looked more authentic then the collection held in his hand.

Crew quarters started the second roll of film, but still Walt couldn't see any sign that announced the authenticity of the photos. He shuffled through half the roll before he was overwhelmed.

"Oh, my God. Look at that, will you?" Walt said in a stage whisper. No one heard him, but the words expressed his shock. "Oh my. Poor, poor, Sarina."

One shot showed what at first looked like a child in a Halloween costume. On closer inspection the detail was too good. No body could apply makeup that well. In the next photo, Sarina still tired and dirty but now also sad. Her eyes looked dead but wet at the same time.

Knowing her, Walt could almost feel Sarina's sorrow. In his mind, she must have undergone an extremely stressful emotional experience. Tears welled in Walt's eyes at the next two photos. These showed the alien's body at rest on one of the beds in the crew quarters. In one photo, Sarina knelt beside the body as if in prayer. Rick must have taken it as a candid, because Sarina would not be capable of staging a shot like that.

After looking through the rest of the pictures, Walt went back to what he called the funeral photo. That was how he thought of it. Sarina knelt by the alien's small frail body. For some reason, Walt slid the picture into a separate envelope then into his shirt pocket, stuffing the rest of them back into their envelopes.

Wiping the tears from his eyes, he jammed the packets into his jacket. Looking around outside, Walt could not find any sign of surveillance. He pulled the truck into his driveway as if everything was normal and entered the house. Inside, he could find no evidence of a search.

Walt dug the backpack out of the hamper and put the pictures in it. For the next hour, he looked for a safer place for the bag. High in the back of the bedroom closet he found his wife's old suitcase. He stuffed the backpack in it and returned it to its original location.

As he settled down with a fresh cup of coffee, the phone rang. A stranger with a Hispanic accent asked for him.

"Yep, this is me all right, what can I do for you?" Walt said as ideas ran through his mind.

"The pretty lady with the eyes said that I should tell you where to find your *motorcycleta*."

"Who are you? What are you referring to?" Walt asked, fearing Gomez had set up a trap.

"My name *es no importante, senor*," the man said, "Your *amigos* are safely where they wan' to be. They fear *pellagro*-ah, danger for you-but to tell you the *motorcycleta* is safe in my barn."

"I'm still not sure what you mean."

"*Senor*, I only tell you what the *senorita* say. My ol' barn is in Bernardo on the main road. It is falling down, you come and get your machine *por favor*."

"Well, thank you for the information. I'll see what I can do," Walt said before he hung up.

Walt wanted to believe the man that Rick and Sarina were safe, but after last night, he wouldn't put anything past Gomez. The man may be trying to trap him. He couldn't figure out why Gomez would want to, unless the officer thought Walt knew where Rick and Sarina were hiding.

That would mean that the couple succeeded in escaping from the police. After another cup of coffee, Walt checked the loads in his cut-off shotgun and the extra shells. He had nothing to loose by the trip to Bernardo. On the other hand, if Gomez were setting him up, Walt would make sure it was the last thing Gomez would ever do.

Forty-five minutes later, Walt turned his old pickup off Interstate 25 and dropped down the ramp to downtown Bernardo. A few adobe buildings on the verge of decay dotted the poorly maintained county road. To his right, he saw an old gasoline station that he assumed to be open since the front door and one of the bay doors was raised. Otherwise, not only the station, but the town seemed devoid of life.

At the intersection of the county road and an unnamed dirt and gravel road, Walt noticed that a slatted barn leaned way over to one side. With a lot of imagination, he could tell that at one time it had been painted red. The door hanging from one hinge stood ajar. Walt got out of the truck and reached into his right coat pocket wrapping his hand around the butt of his make shift gun.

Cautiously, Walt stepped inside. He half-expected to see Gomez with a stupid grin on his face, and half expected Rick and Sarina. He was disappointed on both counts. The barn looked empty. Walking around, he saw the front tire of his motorbike poking out from a pile of hay.

Walt removed the hay. Finally finding the old horse blanket across the seat and handle bars. A noise was barely audible above the rustling of the hay. Walt reached into his coat pocket. He spun to his right and dropped to one knee.

Sighting down the short barrel, Walt saw a young Hispanic male.

"*Ola, senor* Walt," he shouted, falling backwards trying to raise his hands.

"Who the hell are you?  You almost got yourself shot."  Walt also fell back against a bale of hay.

"Don' shoot man," the man said, "*Senorita* Sarina say you are good man.  Don' shoot."

"Who the hell are you?"  Walt growled.

"I call you, 'member?  I helped *senor* Rick and the beautiful *senorita* Sarina to get to Belen.  An' they ask me to tell you about the *motorcycleta*."  The young man said.

"Well, then *caballero*, just settle yourself down on that bale and tell me exactly what the hell you know about all of this."  With the barrel of the sawed-off, Walt motioned him to a seat.

Ten minutes later, Walt knew all about Rick and Sarina's escape.  He was pretty sure that they were safe in Belen.  Hopefully, he thought, they have managed to recover their vehicle and lost the two men who were following them.

With the assistance of the young man, Walt secured his bike in the back of his pick up.  The two men then parted ways.  The Hispanic returned home while Walt drove back to the interstate.  After some thought, Walt realized his best bet was to return home and wait.

At home a blinking red light on his answering machine greeted him.  There were two messages.  The first was from Jay asking Walt to come back to work while the second one was a very short message from Rick.

"Hey, we'll talk later."

## *31*

Rick approached their motel on foot from the side and rear, remembering what Walt told them about two men following them up from Socorro. Sarina was just far enough back to make it difficult for the two to be captured together.

They collected the few belongings that were in the room and were out in Rick's Wagoneer in less than five minutes. Because the jeep sat for more than a day, the engine coughed several times before it finally caught. Through the rear window, Rick saw a dark sedan pull into the lot. The passenger pointed toward them.

Rick threw the gear shift into reverse and screeched the tires pulling away from the curb. Dropping the gear lever into drive, Rick pulled away from the slowing sedan. As they neared the end of the motel, Rick whipped the steering wheel around in a vicious right turn, barely missing an ornamental corner column.

The sedan sped up, trying to catch them. On the turn, the late model black car fishtailed to the left then back to the right. The Wagoneer passed between a large metal trash container and the rear corner to the building.

As the driver of the sedan tried to follow Rick, sparks flew as the left side of his car scraped the metal trash bin. Directly behind the motel, about twenty feet from the back wall was a stand of mesquite bushes. A narrow track led through them at an angle. The Wagoneer disappeared down the track.

Rick slowed the Wagoneer as they shoved their way through the mesquite line. Remembering a drop off just beyond the tree line, he whipped the wheel to the left and jammed the gearshift into second. He didn't want to alert the driver behind him to any possible danger, so he kept his foot away from the brake.

The transmission managed to slow their forward motion just enough to allow the vehicle to roll over the edge and down. Rick then hit the gas pedal and reached the bottom of the drop off at full speed. Behind them, the black sedan tore through the gap. As it came to the drop off, the car tilted on its left side and finally rolled. The sedan managed to complete three rolls before ending up on its side. Rick saw the car come to a rest at the bottom of the steep hill as they crashed their way past a low hedge of brush and onto the parking lot of a new housing addition.

The Wagoneer bounced its way onto the interstate heading north to Albuquerque. Ten miles up the road, Rick took the Los Lunas exit and pulled into a Quik Pik. He got change from the Indian woman behind the counter before heading for the pay phone.

Three minutes later, they were back on the road, following Highway Six. This was a shortcut for people heading west and wanting to skip the rigors of heavy traffic and perpetual construction in Albuquerque.

Sarina sat quietly through the chase and all the way to Los Lunas. While Rick made his phone call, she bought two soft drinks, some chips, and two sandwiches. Back in the car, she asked, "Where are we going?"

"After we join I-40, we'll turn east and go until we reach the Lagunas Pueblo Casino. There will be enough old beat up cars there to hide this thing. That's also where we'll meet Lawrence. He's currently running a check on Major Hogue."

"Major who?" Sarina thought. "Oh, him. The guy who wrote that note we found in the cave."

"And the earlier note. Remember the one you found in the tin at the cairn? The names are the same. Hopefully when Lawrence gets there, we will have an address." Rick ate while cruising well within the speed limit, always keeping an eye on the rear view mirror.

"When do we see Lawrence?"

"When he gets there. We have a fairly safe place to wait, so we wait. Who knows, maybe we'll hit the jackpot while we wait."

"Yeah, sure. I want a place to clean up. I feel all grimy."

"You're still beautiful. Maybe you can touch each of the machines and feel which one will pay. We could use some cash about now."

Sarina poked him in the ribs. "Just like a man, you only want to use me."

"True, true," Rick said, "but most people just want to use your talent. I want your body and mind."

She poked him again, but giggled.

Thirty minutes later, Rick exited the interstate

and slowly drove though the casino's parking lot. Rick pulled the Wagoneer in front of an old Ford truck with a homemade camper jutting out over the end of the tailgate. Hand in hand, the couple entered the casino.

Inside, the couple passed an elevated security booth. Beyond the doorway, they were struck by the clanking of coins, flashing of lights, warm stuffy air and a greasy cooking odor. The Indians, who remained quiet even when they hit a jackpot, occupied many of the slot machines. Travelers and many people from the surrounding towns made up the other customers.

Off to the right was an area with live poker tables and behind that was a small grill with tall stools and a countertop. The restrooms were all the way to the rear of the building, next to an other elevated security booth. The couple made their way in that direction.

Five minutes later, Sarina found Rick sitting calmly at a nickel video poker machine. He fished around in his shirt pocket withdrawing a ten dollar bill.

"Enjoy yourself, but don't spend it all in one place." Rick chuckled.

"You just keep an eye out for Lawrence. Are you sure we can afford the money?"

"We need a change of pace, and we won't spend very much. I don't expect Lawrence for a couple of hours yet."

"Rick," Sarina sighed. A deep frown scored her forehead. She reached out and touched his cheek with the back of her right hand.

Rick's hand caught hers. He squeezed reassuringly. "I know. I love you. Please try to relax. We need a break and this was all I could think of."

Rick watched Sarina's back in admiration and with a little lust as she moved down the isle to some nickel slot machines. He realized that in many ways, he was a very lucky man. He hoped his luck would hold. They had come so close to uncovering the truth, an unbelievable truth that many people would still not recognize. His thoughts wandered to the rolls of film that were missing, along with the mysterious film canister that seemed to have appeared out of nowhere.

From someplace in Sarina's direction, Rick heard a squeal. Rick asked a nearby change girl what had happened. A barely audible voice came over the change girls radio announcing a jackpot on the nickel slots.

Way to go, Rick thought. Sarina used her talent or powers or whatever. Not having any luck on his poker machine, Rick cashed out, pulling t money chit from the collection slot. Moving around to the other side of the bank of slot machines, Rick was surprised to see a squat woman with unruly dishwater blonde hair bouncing in her seat, going 'woohoo' over and over. A floor person stood behind her writing in a small notebook.

"Surprise," Sarina whispered in his ear. Rick jumped, startled by her voice..

"You scared the hell out of me." Rick twisted around in the narrow aisle to face her.

"I thought you would come over to see who

won." Sarina's eyes sparkled even in the dim room. She wave several chits in his face. "That was my machine. That woman was sitting next to me and was complaining about always loosing. I felt something and gave her the machine."

"Wow! All this time, I was kidding, but you really did feel something?"

Sarina grabbed Rick's collar and dragged him to the snack bar. Although the greasy smell was almost overwhelming, it was still a relatively quiet place.

"Listen here, buddy," Sarina scowled, poking Rick in the chest. "I feel bad about what I did, okay!"

'"Bad, why do you feel bad?" Rick was stunned. "You gave that lady a jackpot. What you did was good, no, great."

"But, I know we need money also. Then, I feel guilty because I used my talent."

"Whew, did you actually hocus-pocus the machine, or did it sort of nudge you? If it nudged you, then you only responded, you didn't use anything. What you did was still very good. Anyway, we aren't hard up enough for money that we need to skimp."

Sarina tried to look Rick in the eyes, but she hung her head.

Rick wrapped his arms around her, pulling her body next to his. He whispered into her ear, then nibbled it.

Rick steered Sarina outside. They slowly walked back and forth in front of the casino.

Lawrence found them that way when he arrived. "Hey kids, buy me a beer and I'll tell you anything."

After brief greetings, they went back inside. Sarina collected their pay chits then headed for a change booth. Rick bought Lawrence a Coke, since alcoholic beverages were prohibited on the reservation.

"What the hell are you two up to now?" Lawrence shook his head. "My phone is tapped and for the last two days, I've been shadowed."

"Do they know where we are? Or is it possible that the FBI finally caught on to your piracy?"

"No way." Lawrence shook his head again. "I'd know if they were on to me. This has to be related to you and Sarina." He nodded toward the casino.

The two men watched Sarina approach, folding bills and stuffing them into her small purse. Rick patted the stool beside next to him and ran his hand lightly across her back as she sat down.

"Okay, here it is. I'm almost positive that I was not followed. There was a tail on me, but I shook him before crossing the Rio Grande on the west side of town. Even so, I'll leave first and head on toward Grants. Then you two can get out of here," Lawrence handed Rick a piece of yellowed paper. "Here is what you requested. Good hunting."

"Thanks. I owe you big time for this." Rick unfolded the note.

Lawrence stood, clapped Rick on the back then hugged Sarina. Rick noticed that Lawrence palmed something off to her before leaving. "Call me if you can. There's a number that should be safe."

"What's in the note?" Sarina asked.

""What did Lawrence give you?" Rick countered.

"Show me yours first."

"But it's more interesting looking at yours." Rick smiled.

"Don't change the subject, big boy."

Rick grinned ear to ear as he handed the yellow paper to her.

"It's the address and phone number of our mysterious Major Hogue."

"It also says that Lawrence isn't sure if he's alive or dead. The information is eight years old." Sarina waved the note in his face.

"Well, we'll find out in a couple of days. The address is just outside of Dayton, Ohio. We'll leave in a few more minutes."

"I wish we could contact Walt and let him know what's going on."

"Oh, I called him from Los Lunas. Sorry, I forgot to tell you. He knows we will be away for a while. Now, what did Lawrence give you?"

She held up a roll of hundred dollar bills. Lawrence's note was wrapped inside the bills.

"Love, I want the whole story from you as soon as you're safe. Take care. Lawrence."

They left, heading east to Albuquerque. Rick took the Coors Road exit, dropped down to Central Avenue. The route across town was a lot longer, but they hoped that there was less chance of being spotted. Rick's caution was partially justified, as reports came over his CB radio warning drivers of an unusual number of radar traps on both the north-south and east-west lanes of the freeway.

To be on the safe side, Rick crossed over the freeway to Menaul Boulevard and traveled all the way out to Juan Tabo before sliding back on to the freeway close to the town of Moriarty.

It took them two more days to reach Dayton, Ohio. Rick followed the map through town on Ohio 4, pulling off on the shoulder. In front of them was a large white sign set in tan concrete proudly announcing "Welcome to Wright Patterson Air Force Base." It went on telling about the different aircraft squadrons stationed there, displayng each one's shield.

"Why are we here?" Sarina asked.

"Major Hogue," Rick muttered, not taking his eyes off the gate.

"I know that, but why here at the gate."

"Atmosphere, I guess. Somewhere on this base is supposed to be Hanger 18, where Donald Dyba made the alien body for that autopsy. According to him they have real bodies here."

"Why don't we drive slowly around the base to see what we can see, then we'll get out of here. I feel as if somebody is watching us."

At dinner, they spread the local map across the table, searching for Hogue's street. After locating the address, they found their motel and plotted their route. Sarina called and talked to Hogue's daughter.

"The major is not doing too well," Sarina said after the phone conversation.

"Oh, no. What's wrong?"

"The guy is eighty-seven and suffering from lung cancer. It seems that he smoked a couple of packs of cigarettes a day for sixty some years."

"Ouch, will it be possible for us to see him?" Rick asked.

"The daughter said he would probably be happy to talk to us. It seems that he doesn't have many friends. Now that he's bedridden, she's the only one visiting him."

# *31*

Sarina knew her first thoughts were cruel. Major Hogue looked like death was staring him in the face. His skin resembled yellowed parchment. The few hairs he had remaining made her think of old steel wool. Only his eyes told Sarina of his strong spirit.

Battleship gray eyes looked her over, inspecting each and every curve and bump. Gray eyes rested on her modest bosom and caressed her hips.

"Well Major, do I measure up?" she asked, sweetly broadcasting a wickedly friendly grin.

"Yes, you do, my dear," the Major croaked, trying to laugh.

"In that case, maybe we could ask you some questions?"

"Honey, you can ask me anything." Hogue wiggled his eyebrows.

"Dad, now you be nice. You know you ran off the last nurse by being too familiar with her."

"Diedra, you stay out of this. Damn, can't an old man have some fun? Especially one who is going to croak at any moment."

Diedra patted him on the shoulder looking at Sarina and Rick sheepishly. "Don't we both wish, Dad." Tears welled in her eyes.

"Okay seriously, what do you two youngins want with an old warhorse like me? Diedra said something about my army days."

"Yes, well..." Sarina looked at Rick and was rewarded with an indifferent shrug. His eyes turned to the daughter, Diedra. She nodded.

"Actually, we would like to talk about the years just after World War II. Nineteen-forty-six and forty-seven."

A frown dug deep crevasses across the major's forehead. Eyes darted from Rick to Sarina. "Mmm. Let me think." The room grew quiet. Only the deep raspy sound of Hogue's labored breathing disturbed the silence.

"As I remember," he said slowly, "not much happened. Right after the war, everyone feared they would be dropped. You know, cut backs."

Sarina nodded. "According to some information we received, you were out in New Mexico at the time."

"New Mexico? No, I don't believe so." Hogue paused and gasped for breath. "No, I believe that I was stationed out on the west coast."

"I thought sure you were down in Roswell, New Mexico, in July of nineteen-forty-seven."

Hogue's eyes fluttered. His left hand had started a little dance of its own. Rick knew they struck a nerve. He reached into his pocket and took something out.

"Uh, Diedra, maybe we could get the Major something to drink?" He motioned for her to follow him, leaving Hogue and Sarina alone. As Rick passed her, he placed a folded yellow paper in Sarina's hand.

Sarina waited until Diedra was down the hall.

"Major Hogue, I have evidence that you were in charge of a special project in or around Roswell. Also, you helped hide something special in a cave. I know what it was you hid, because Rick and I have seen it."

"Anything that happened back there was, and as far as I know, still is, Top Secret." Hogue wheezed, fisting and opening his hands.

Sarina smiled and sat on the edge of his bed. Slowly, she opened the paper Rick passed her as he left the room. "You know what this is, Major Hogue? I found this next to a pile of crumpled Lucky Strike cigarette packs and about a thousand butts. Now, that alone should be enough, but this note also has your name on it. It mentions bodies and four saucers as being transported out of the area and the rest being buried in Bat Cave."

The old man grunted, trying to wave her accusations away like a troublesome insect. "Preposterous."

"Many of the remaining pieces had chalked numbers and letters on them. We have photographic evidence."

"Show me your photos, then maybe you have something."

"Major, I'm tired of this. We need to know your involvement in this. My life has been threatened twice, I have been shot at a couple of times and Rick, my partner, has even been wounded. Once, we were forced to kill in self defense. Now, we need to know what the hell is going on."

"I can't believe that anyone would try to kill you over this. It's even higher then Top Secret, but we only detain those people who are at risk, maybe jail them, but not kill anyone."

"I'm sorry to be the one to burst your bubble, but one of my friends has been killed and about six military or secret service types have also died."

"Let me see that paper, and tell me more about what you saw in that cave of yours."

Sarina was filling him in on the mother ship when Diedra and Rick returned. Hogue's daughter held a serving tray with four glasses of iced tea. The narration stopped when they entered the room.

Diedra passed the glasses around and looked questioningly from Sarina to her father. "Is everything all right?"

"Yes, daughter it is. Everything is fine. I think it's about time to get something off my chest. It has been my albatross for way too long. I can't see how the other people involved could contain themselves this long." Hogue wheezed more, taking a sip of his tea through a hospital straw.

"Right after the war, the Army formed a special unit to check into flying saucers. For over a year, we had very little to go on until that guy Arnold saw some flying disks over Washington state. Later, they called them flying saucers. Then things started hopping.

"I found myself commanding the southwest detachment of Moon Dust, only at that time we were called Starlite . Our job was to recover anything coming from space.

"My detachment came up with an idea to confuse the issue. It was suppose to make a horses ass out of people talking about saucers and little green men. Only, it got out of control."

"You're talking about the crash at Roswell, New Mexico, right?" Sarina asked.

Major Hogue tried to laugh but fought down a coughing spell. "Roswell. You hear so much about it. That one backfired on us!" More coughing followed.

"Ouch." Hogue gasped, clinching a hand over his chest. His eyes squinted in agony. After a few minutes, the major continued.

"Roswell never happened." He smiled, eyes glowed through the agony. With a shake of his head, he continued. "Ain't that a crock? The most famous flying saucer crash of recorded history never took place."

Rick looked at Sarina. Shock, then confusion, filled his face. "What the hell are you talking about? Too many people have first hand accounts of the crash. There's no way that many people could be lying."

"That is the hidden beauty of it. They aren't lying. They are and always have been telling the truth. They are telling everyone exactly what they saw."

"Then I don't get it?" Sarina said.

"What happened? That night in July there were two separate reported crashes. One near Corona and the other one out past Socorro," Rick said.

"There were two separate crashes, but not at or near Corona. The big crash was near Bat Cave. You found the left overs from that. The other site was what people have been calling the debris field. That was the second one. There were no witnesses to that one, only the cowboy who came along after it happened and he was easily delt with."

Hogue worked through another coughing spell.

"You mean that the crash at Corn Ranch actually happened?" Rick was surprised.

"Hell no! We faked that one to cover the real one. When that cowboy got involved, we made him collaborate our story. It sure helped confuse things for years."

"How did you fake the Roswell crash?" Sarina asked.

"What about the flying saucer and bodies that were found there?" Rick frowned.

"Hee, hee, now this is really rich. Let me back up and tell you the whole thing, then you decide."

Major Hogue, then a brand new captain, was stationed at Roswell Army Air Field, one of the most secure Army Air Fields in the United States. The detachment had two A-26 Intruder bombers at their disposal. Earlier in the year, an experimental aircraft, the V-173, which was also known as the YP-49, had crashed on its second flight killing its crew of two. Because of its unique shape, it was referred to as the flying flapjack.

The experimental aircraft was approximately thirty feet in diameter and saucer shaped with two skinny engine nacelles sticking out. A bubble just forward of the center held the pilot and copilot. The wreckage was shipped to Roswell Army Air Field and slung under one of the A-26s along with some debris. A lot of the debris was balsa wood sandwiched between two thin sheets of aluminum. A second aircraft was fitted for aerial photography and would chase any UFO in the area. Then they waited.

On the evening of July the third, radar picked up a large unidentified object flying a triangular pattern that included White Sands Proving Ground, Roswell Army Air Field and way to the north, Los Alamos.

Radar operations were startled when another smaller object seemed to disconnect from the larger one and fly its own pattern. An hour later the two flew directly toward one another.

By this time, Hogue's second plane, outfitted for day or night aerial photography, was ordered up into the air to chase down the two unidentified objects. A tremendous electrical storm was moving into the area. The chase plane caught up with the two craft near Albuquerque. They were headed in a generally southern course.

The combat photographer on board captured the whole episode on film. For five minutes, they filmed the mother ship with the smaller craft darting around it like an anxious puppy. Then a bolt of lightning streaked across the sky, striking the large spacecraft.

Smaller fingers of light reached out from an intense ball of light that now encircled the mother ship. One of the fingers bounced off the smaller craft, while another one licked the A-26 bomber. All electrical equipment was affected. Needles pegged on meters, fuses popped, circuit breakers snapped. The engines sputtered then went silent.

The combat trained crew now fought for their lives. Quickly the pilot turned on a heading that would take them to Roswell Airfield. He dragged back the control yoke, trying to give them a long glide path. The photographer caught the two alien ships just as the smaller one glanced off the large craft. It was evident to the photographer that after the collision, both space craft were in serious trouble. The radio man started replacing fuses and closing the circuit breakers as his aircraft glided on a straight course. The pilot managed to restart one engine and regain control of the aircraft. Close by, the damaged saucer was losing altitude. They followed it, taking pictures until it belly flopped into the desert near a rancher's windmill.

The high speed caused the saucer to slide across the ground then bounce back into the air. The aircraft crossed a small valley before crashing into the crest of a small hill, then it slid down sixty feet to the bottom of an arroyo.

As Captain Hogue became aware of the damaged saucers he ordered more ground units dispersed to search them out. Shortly before dawn, one saucer was located. A few bodies were discovered. Then, more news. Apparently the mother ship also crashed west of Socorro, New Mexico. While awaiting more detailed information, he set into motion operation Kenneth Arnold, in which a false crash would be created, allowing the military to later debunk the entire event.

From Socorro, he received a disturbing report. The crash site involved multiple ships and beings. The first unit on the scene announced they had found a large spacecraft. They also discovered some people from a university. While containing the archaeology professors and students, the sergeant in charge requested Hogue's presence as soon as possible.

All of the fourth of July, Captain Hogue planned. The meteorologist had good news. Another storm was brewing; this one should hit Roswell around ten at night. His remaining aircraft was put on alert.

Five o'clock in the afternoon, Hogue held a mission briefing. The A-26 ground attack aircraft was to immediately fly into White Sands Proving Ground where there was a small secret airstrip waiting them. The two crews had flown into and out of the secret field many times before on training missions. The crew would then wait for further instructions.

Captain Hogue made arrangements and went over the cover-up procedure they would follow. Hopefully, someone would find some of the soon-to-be planted wreckage. Later, after aiding the civilians in starting the flying saucer story, they would clamp down with their own version of the weather balloon or unveil the unusual aircraft. Then the captain left for Socorro.

By this time, Project Starlite was in full swing. Recovery crews were at both crash sites. Hogue wasn't prepared for what they found by Bat Cave. A large mother ship had crashed. Bodies were everywhere. Two soldiers had acted in a cowardly way by clubbing some of the surviving aliens to death.

Luckily, an officer arrived on the scene and managed to capture two more aliens alive. These were later sent to Wright Patterson, along with one of the two intact scout craft found inside the mother ship. The smaller saucers were quickly loaded onto a flatbed trailer and hauled across back roads to Carrizzo where they were loaded onto a train and moved to White Sands awaiting orders from Socorro. One of the saucers was moved to a new secret base being established somewhere in southern Nevada.

About dark, Arnold was activated. The A-26 was to fly north, then turn on a south easterly course. The plane would carry the remains of the crashed V-173 or flying flapjack. As it passed the actual crash site, it would start the bomb run in which the wreckage would be dropped closer to the town of Roswell.

After successfully dropping its load, the aircraft was to fly to San Antonio to await the rest of the Starlite detachment.

All materials and bodies recovered were to be shipped out on back roads through Capitan and down to the railhead in Carrizozo. Somehow, during the confusion of the recovery operation, some soldiers took a truck load of debris from the real crash site into Roswell. In addition, a medic moved two bodies and an injured alien to the Roswell Army Airfield hospital. Towns' people slowly became aware of the events, thus reversing the faked crash, turning it into a real event which necessitated a much more detailed and messy effort to hide from the population.

In this way, while the Corn site was a fake crash, an actual crash was reported accidentally in the area. Luckily, the Socorro event was much easier to bury and keep hidden. Major Hogue also explained the cairns as being markers delineating the search area for the soldiers at the debris field, validating Rick's earlier thoughts.

## *33*

Sarina stood with her eyes wide open. "You mean the whole story was a put on? Everything that happened in the desert by Roswell is fake?"

"Yes, it was an elaborate show. We could've proved any time we wanted to that it wasn't a spaceship."

"Then why try to kill us?" Sarina wrapped her arms around her body.

"You uncovered the real crash site, and according to your story, recovered some bonified flying saucer metal. I guess that even today, the military doesn't want the real story to come out. It would make them look very bad."

"Why allow your story to continue? What happened?" Rick asked.

"I was supposed to orchestrate the entire story. There was going to be an announcement officially ending the testing of the YP-173 project, but I was stuck at Bat Cave, trying to clean up the mess there. We were going to claim a test flight crash of a secret project aircraft that resembled flying saucers.

"We had some rancher or farmer see the crashed saucer, then a group of damned bone diggers showed up. We thought they might have seen our soldiers assaulting the beings.

"That's when things went crazy at Roswell. Too many people said too many things and all hell broke loose. By the time we got the situation under control, too much damage had been done. That was when big brass got scared and sent Army Intelligence people around in enlisted uniforms threatening people." Hogue paused for breath and emptied his glass of tea. "And somebody switched stories to a damned weather balloon."

"All the stories say that the crash happened on the night of the fourth. How did you arrange that when it happened on the third?" Rick asked.

"Easy. When people are threatened with endless incarceration or jogging their memory a day and a bunch of miles, you'd be surprised how easy it is to change their memory."

"What about the archaeologists? How did they disappear?"

"They didn't. For the professors, there was unlimited funding for future enterprises. The students suddenly found themselves recipients of multiple scholarships." Hogue waved the piece of paper at them. "Now, you tell me about this."

Rick told the Major their whole story. Twice coughing spells interrupted him. The Major couldn't believe that they missed one of the creatures.

"We'll try to return so you can see the pictures," Sarina said.

"Yes, and I would like to video tape your story, just the way you told it to us. This is what the people of the United States and the UFO community need," Rick said.

"I don't think so, Sarina. I'll have to take your word for it. I'm too sick. As for your idea, Rick, no. Even if I wanted to, I wouldn't betray my oath or country."

"But you told us, what's the difference?" Sarina asked.

"A dying old man has to confess. Confess to somebody who would believe him. Now, go. Please go. Leave me in peace."

Sarina thanked Diedra for allowing them the visit. Rick handed her a card with a phone number. "We'll be in touch. If anything comes up, please call."

That evening, they headed back to Socorro.

## *34*

The Wagoneer's tires crunched gravel as they pulled into Walt's driveway. The old man met them at the door. He looked older and more worn-out than they remembered.

Walt stepped out on the stoop, taking his hand out of the pocket of his trench coat. He looked up and down the street, then motioned Rick to park the Wagoneer around back and hurry inside.

"Welcome back, strangers. I got a message for you two."

Rick patted Walt on the back and shook hands warmly, while Sarina hugged him and pecked him on the cheek.

"You got your motorcycle back?" Rick asked.

"Yup. It was curious, but it worked out okay."

"Sorry for the damage we did to it," Rick said.

"Don't worry. It served a great purpose. That's all that's needed." Walt smiled as he poured coffee. Then he put some water on for tea. Everyone settled around the kitchen table. Walt quickly told them about finding the pictures, then he dropped his bad news.

"I got a phone call from a woman named Diedra. She said to tell you the major died peacefully in his sleep the night you left. He told her he finally felt good. She also said thank you." Walt had a question mark stamped on his face.

Sarina and Rick alternated in telling Major Hogue's story. When they finished, Walt shook his head in disbelief, then left the table. When he returned, he placed three packets of photographs in front of Rick.

"Even now, after all has been said, seeing is believing." Walt refilled the two coffee mugs and set out Sarina's tea.

Rick and Sarina took turns thumbing through the pictures, stopping every once in a while to remember an event. Walt asked many questions about them.

"Do you think we could get back in there?" Walt asked.

"We may have to climb down that opening we escaped from. I don't know if I could find it though."

"Yeah, let's try it," Sarina said, eyes sparkling. Tears formed when she saw the picture alien's body. "Please."

"I could find the place. Hell, I spent enough time looking for you two, I remember the whole area," Walt said.

They discussed supplies and planned the climb, then settled back for the rest of the day. Walt finally got around to telling them about what happened between him and Gomez. Then he showed them his sawed-off shotgun.

"Next time I have a run in with that bastard, I'm gonna be tried for murder."

Knowing the old man's mind was set, the couple nodded in solemn agreement.

Early the next morning, Rick pulled the Wagoneer onto Highway 60. Soon they were past

Magdalena, viewing the huge radio telescope dishes of VLA from ten miles away. With the sun rays just touching them, they resembled a huge field of giant mushrooms. Glaring sunlight greeted them.

Half an hour later, the Wagoneer wheeled into Datil, a small village at the intersection of a state and county road. As they turned south, Walt caught his breath.

"Okay?" Rick called over his shoulder

"Yeah, but maybe not for long."

"Why, what's the problem?" Sarina turned in the passenger seat.

"There was a hummer beside that little cafe back there."

"What's that?"

"A military jeep," Walt said. "They drive through here often enough, with that Army Reserve unit in Socorro, but this one had desert paint, not that god-awful green."

"Why would that make a difference?" Rick asked.

"Regular Army, not reserve. There may be more out here."

"Keep your eyes peeled then." Rick scanned the area.

Soon, they found their cut-off. Rick slowed down.

"Go, go, Rick. Keep going. Don't even act like you're going to turn." Walt's voice rang out with urgency. "Eleven o'clock." He directed their attention to their left front.

Rick kicked the Wagoneer back up to speed and tried to be casual as he looked out his left window.

"Damn, I see them now."

"Wow, I barely saw them with that desert netting covering them." Sarina said.

"We'd be in deep shit if we turned off back there."

"We're probably pretty high on their wanted list right now."

"Now what? I want to get back there more than ever."

Walt pulled out an area map and started searching. "Go on down for two turn-offs. The second one to the left will help us get closer."

After locating the turn off, Rick tried to drive slow enough to keep their dust trail down, but it could not be eliminated. Slowly, making turns at water tanks and corrals, the Wagoneer worked it's way closer to Bat Cave.

"Whoa. Stop. Look ahead. Over by the mountain. That's where Bat Cave is. See that dust cloud? Something big is going down."

"There's a rise over to our left. Get my binoculars out. I want to take a closer look." Rick grabbed the glasses and jumped out, heading for the hilltop.

Five minutes later, he returned, out of breath.

"Damned if they don't have a couple of those big helicopters over there. It looks as if they're getting ready to lift something. Also, they have a gunship on the ground. It's rotors are barely turning. There's also some earth moving equipment."

"We're too late," Sarina cried.

"Maybe so, but we can still get pictures of

376

them moving the stuff," Walt said.

Rick turned the Wagoneer and headed back south. Soon they were climbing. Two switchbacks later and they were again moving north, this time near the top of the mountain.

Rick pulled into a stand of tall mesquite trees. They offered some cover from the air. The cliff was less than about sixty feet away. A huge dust cloud practically enveloped the two heavy-duty helicopters. Rick dropped the envelopes of photos into the hidden compartment. Everything they had accumulated was safely locked inside.

Walt led the way to the edge, paying little attention to the dust cloud. Below, they saw four large flatbed trailers, the kind the military uses to haul armored vehicles around on. Two large front-end loaders were still bulldozing dirt out of the way, re-opening the original entrance to Bat Cave.

Rick viewed the scene through the viewfinder of Beth's camera, zooming the lens back and forth framing his pictures. He just finished moving to a closer position when Sarina tapped his shoulder.

"Oh, no. We have company," Sarina pointed to a brown pickup truck.

"What?" Rick looked around, startled. His mind still focused on the action below.

"Gomez. He just showed up."

"Damn! How the hell did he know?"

Gomez pulled his beat up brown pickup under the trees next to Rick's Wagoneer. He settled his cowboy hat squarely on his head and adjusted his gun belt. Slowly, he moved toward Walt.

Sarina turned to Walt. He was reaching into

his coat pocket. "No," she shouted. "Not yet."

Walt turned slowly, facing Gomez. "Well, well, asshole. We meet again."

"Thought you had more sense than this, especially after our last little talk. Raise your hands." Gomez accented his speech by drawing his pistol and waving it back and forth.

"Over here, all of you." He shouted above the heavy whooping of the helicopter, motioning them toward his pickup.

Rick and Sarina took their time approaching the sheriff. Rick raised his hands. His right one stopped at the camera strung around his neck and snapped took a picture.

"What do you plan to do with us?" Walt asked.

"I should kill you right now, old man," Gomez smirked, "but there are too many witnesses. Instead, I'll have to turn you over to them." His chin pointed toward the valley floor.

Rick edged Sarina to Gomez' right, forcing him to look back and forth across a widening field of view. Walt kept closing the distance between him and the sheriff, forcing his attention.

"Stop right there. I swear I'll shoot, witnesses or not."

"Come on, sheriff, you can't shoot him," Rick said. He lowered his arms, and took the camera in hand. "Smile." He raised the viewfinder to his eye.

Gomez looked back at Rick. "Put that damned thing down."

"You're going to shoot me for taking your picture?" Rick moved closer. "Smile again. The last one you had your mouth open."

Gomez raised his service revolver, "Stop, damn it."

Walt's hand flashed into his pocket, whipping his sawed-off shotgun out, firing in one swift motion. His practice paid off.

Gomez' hand dissolved as the 00 buckshot hit it. Howling in pain, he doubled over cradling the stub to his chest. Walt moved closer. He ripped Gomez sleeve off and applied it as a tourniquet to the wound.

Slapping Gomez in the face, he said, "I might let you live, asshole." Then he shoved the man into Rick's Wagoneer. He slammed the gun barrel against the sheriff's head, stunning him.

Quickly, Walt reloaded the shotgun. "You two kids, hide so they can't see you from the air."

"Walt, what are you doing?" Rick asked.

"My God, Walt. It's all over now."

Walt ran to Sarina, held her face for a moment and said, "Live long." He handed her an envelope, and scampered back to the Jeep. Walt grabbed the sheriff's radio from his belt. Figuring Gomez's radio was tuned to the military frequency, he spoke into the microphone. "Officer needs assistance." Leaving the mike open, he pointed the barrel skyward and fired the gun twice, throwing the radio away afterwards.

Running to the edge of the cliff, Walt loaded the gun again. Standing there, he fired down at the two helicopters. He reloaded and fired again. Finally, he saw the black gunship rise and move toward the top of the cliff.

Walt ran to the Wagoneer. "Keep down you two. Hide."

Climbing into the driver's seat, Walt started the jeep and drove away slowly. As the gunship rose over the lip of the cliff, he floored the jeep.

The gunship closed the distance, hovering above the jeep. Walt slowed, stuck his head out of the window, aimed, and fired at the helicopter again.

The gunship dropped back and climbed, gaining altitude as the jeep pulled away. Smoke erupted from a rocket pod slung under a stubby arm of the aircraft.

Sarina cried out, "No," She tried to rise from her hiding place in the center of a group of mesquite bushes. Rick pulled her back down covering her head, as the Wagoneer exploded, throwing hot metal in every direction.

Rick hushed Sarina telling her to be quiet. He wrapped his arm around her protectively. The gunship weaved back and forth in a half hearted search pattern. Then it moved back, dropping over the edge of the cliff.

There was nothing left of the Wagoneer but smoldering wreckage.

Rick led Sarina over to the sheriff's pickup shortly after the helicopter disappeared. Luckily, the keys were still in the ignition. He drove slowly to keep from raising a dust trail. Minutes later, they headed further south down a dirt track they had not seen before. In the rear view mirror, Rick saw the black gunship rise again, swing over the cliff and land beside the wreckage of his Wagoneer. Cammo dudes leapt to the ground, moving in every direction.

The couple took other roads, trying to cut east and south away from the military helicopters.

Finally, they reached the gravel road that led north to VLA. Sarina motioned Rick to turn following the signs to VLA.

Rick pulled into the graveled parking lot at the visitor center. They entered the building and cleaned up in the bathrooms then walked to a small gazebo near one of the large white radio telescope dishes. They needed to rest.

Silently, they hugged each other, watching the sun drop below the horizon to the west. In the reds of the sunset, a thin plume of smoke rose from the area of Bat Cave.

Sarina snuggled against Rick, burying her head against his neck. The high desert night air was calm and clear, but cold.

"It's over, isn't it?"

"Yes, it is. We lost everything when they blew up my jeep."

"What do we do now?"

"I'll keep on writing articles, telling what we know, but without any evidence, it is all conjecture."

"What about the pictures in the camera? The ones showing Gomez and Walt?"

"They may help keep us out of jail, but that's about all."

Sarina reached deep inside her pockets, stretching against the cold. Her hand touched an envelope. She remembered Walt handing it to her.

"Wait, Walt passed this to me before he..." Sobs choked off the rest of her comment. She handed Rick the envelope.

Inside, he found a photograph and what looked like a letter. In the dim light, he could barely make out Sarina's form and something else.

"Sarina, here's your gift from Walt." He pulled some matches from his pocket and struck one.

In the flickering flame, Sarina was kneeling beside a cot like bed, her hands held in front of her as if in prayer. A small alien being lay in repose on the cot.

## END

29154017R00222

Made in the USA
Charleston, SC
03 May 2014